The Real History of Tom Jones

THE REAL HISTORY OF TOM JONES

JOHN ALLEN STEVENSON

THE REAL HISTORY OF TOM JONES
© John Allen Stevenson, 2005.

All rights reserved. No part of this book may be used or reproduced in any manner whatsoever without written permission except in the case of brief quotations embodied in critical articles or reviews.

First published in 2005 by
PALGRAVE MACMILLAN™
175 Fifth Avenue, New York, N.Y. 10010 and
Houndmills, Basingstoke, Hampshire, England RG21 6XS
Companies and representatives throughout the world.

PALGRAVE MACMILLAN is the global academic imprint of the Palgrave Macmillan division of St. Martin's Press, LLC and of Palgrave Macmillan Ltd. Macmillan® is a registered trademark in the United States, United Kingdom and other countries. Palgrave is a registered trademark in the European Union and other countries.

ISBN 1–4039–6643–5

Library of Congress Cataloging-in-Publication Data

Stevenson, John Allen.
   The real history of Tom Jones / John Allen Stevenson.
     p. cm.
   Includes bibliographical references and index.
   ISBN 1–4039–6643–5 (alk. paper)
   1. Fielding, Henry, 1707–1754. History of Tom Jones. 2. Identity (Psychology) in literature. 3. Foundlings in literature. I. Title.
PR3454.H7S75 2005
823'.5—dc22   2004053371

A catalogue record for this book is available from the British Library.

Design by Newgen Imaging Systems (P) Ltd., Chennai, India.

First edition: February 2005

10 9 8 7 6 5 4 3 2 1

Printed in the United States of America.

for Jilli

Contents

Acknowledgments — ix

Introduction: Missing Pictures — 1

1. Stuart Ghosts — 17
2. Savage Matters — 47
3. Black Acts — 77
4. Hanging Judges — 103
5. Gypsy Kings — 125
6. Mirror Plots — 159

Afterword: Sleepless Nights — 181

Notes — 187

Index — 219

Acknowledgments

I have accumulated considerable intellectual indebtedness in writing this book, and I am not at all sure that the act of acknowledging those debts will repay or even consolidate them, as I would like. Still, it is a pleasure to recollect the generosity of others, gifts of time and learning that have made this a better work than would otherwise have been possible.

Versions of much of this study were first presented at various meetings of the American Society for Eighteenth-Century Studies, and I am grateful to those audiences for their attentive and helpful responses. Earlier and (as I now see) incomplete versions of chapters 1, 3, and 6 appeared as essays in, respectively, *ELH, Eighteenth-Century Fiction*, and *SEL*; that material is reprinted here with the permission of these journals, all of whose editorial suggestions and interventions improved my thinking about the ideas I discuss here. I have turned, time and again, to that electronic trove of collective wisdom known as the Eighteenth-Century Interdisciplinary Discussion Group, so ably moderated by Kevin Berland. The C18-L is a rare resource, with an unsurpassed capacity to provide information that is both rapid and reliable.

Colleagues in the field have helped in innumerable ways, and I hope that the list that follows is complete: Marshall Brown, Alison Conway, Simon Dickie, Frans DeBruyn, Robert Folkenflick, Timothy Erwin, Gary Gautier, Thomas Krise, Thomas Lockwood, Roger Lund, Albert J. Rivero, Jim Rosenheim, Laura Rosenthal, John Sitter, Simon Stern, and Howard Weinbrot. Closer to home, colleagues here at the University of Colorado, Boulder have read portions of this study or provided crucial information: Fred Anderson, Katherine Eggert, Peter Knox, Warren Motte, and Will West, as well as a number of scholars now resident elsewhere: Margaret Ferguson, Richard Halpern, and David Simpson. For help with some questions of law, I want to thank Sue Chetlin and Michael Heydt. I was fortunate to be a Faculty Fellow in the University of Colorado, Boulder's Center for Humanities and the Arts in 2000–1, and this study benefitted substantially from that happy and stimulating time. I was helped by the staffs at Norlin Library on the Boulder campus, especially the Inter-Library Loan Office, and at the British Library.

A few must be singled out for especially signal contributions. Several Deans and Associate Deans of the College of Arts and Sciences lent needed support: Peter Spear, Merrill Lessley, Todd Gleeson, and Graham Oddie; the latter two made a late and indispensable intervention. Marilyn Gaull provided the aid of her unmatched editorial eye, and a crucial boost at precisely the right time. Kenneth Johnston, as a visitor to Boulder in 2003, read most of a late draft with great and helpful care and supplied in addition that most precious commodity, a title. My friends and colleagues, Christopher Braider, Steven Epstein, and Charlotte Sussman read the entire manuscript, supplying both the fuel of encouragement and a number of improvements. Jeffrey Cox has not only read this book with his characteristic trenchancy, he kept me on track when I was tempted to wander or to sink in one slough or another.

My deepest debts are the most personal. My parents, John and Russell Stevenson, provided the gift of an upbringing in which books and reading were a central and nourishing joy. Their exuberant response to Tony Richardson's film version of *Tom Jones*, moreover, indelibly impressed my ten-year-old mind and in some fundamental way planted the seed that produced this book. Their unflagging interest in this project and their unquestioning faith in its author mean more than I can ever say.

Jill Heydt-Stevenson sustains me daily, as she has sustained me for fifteen years now. In a quite literal sense, her rare combination of intellect and heart have made it possible for me to think the thoughts and to write the words that have become this study. The effort to discover words of gratitude that will ever suffice baffles my best skill, so the book itself, as an offering of thanks, will have to do.

Introduction: Missing Pictures

An Unheard of Case

In February 1749, the greatest comic novel of the eighteenth century, Henry Fielding's *The History of Tom Jones, A Foundling*, was published. Such was the demand that all 2,500 copies in print had already been sold by the date announced for its official publication, a phenomenon that one observer believed to be "an unheard-of case." *Tom Jones* quickly sold 10,000 copies, making it one of the great best-sellers of its time; it has never since been out of print.[1]

Less than three years before the novel appeared, on 16 April 1746, a British army led by King George II's own son, the Duke of Cumberland, crushed the rebel forces of Charles Edward Stuart, the romantic figure best known as Bonnie Prince Charlie, on soggy Culloden Moor, near Inverness. In a battle that lasted less than an hour, one thousand Jacobite loyalists were killed, a double decimation in a force of five thousand. Thus ended the hopes of many Britons for a Stuart restoration to the throne they had lost almost sixty years back. Though no one knew it at the time, Culloden was a remarkable watershed: after centuries of intestine strife, it not only marked the last occasion on which two native armies faced each other, it was also the final land battle fought on British soil.

More than piquant contiguity connects these events, for a great deal of the plot of *Tom Jones* unfolds against the background of the Jacobite Rebellion of 1745–6, typically known by its short-hand name: "the Forty-Five." That rebellion constituted the greatest domestic crisis that Britain faced in the eighteenth century, and the slaughter at Culloden, while decisive for one side, only highlighted the long, bitter rivalry for the throne between the houses of Stuart and Hanover. The roots of that conflict stretched back to the Glorious, or "Bloodless" Revolution of 1688 when the Stuart Catholic James II fled his throne under unrelenting Protestant pressure; the blood not spilled then was saved, it seems, for another day.

Coleridge famously celebrated the experience of reading *Tom Jones* as akin to stepping into the sunshine: "And how charming, how wholesome Fielding is! To take him up after Richardson is like emerging from a sick-room heated by stoves into an open lawn on a breezy day in May."[2] So it is. But Fielding's unsurpassed conjuration of a comic universe also recalls and considers some of the darkest and most difficult issues in the world of the mid-eighteenth century, very much including the sanguinary realities of 1745–6. Critics have typically been uncomfortable with that disparate conjunction of harsh history and pasture-fresh comedy, and such discomfort may explain why many critics have ultimately dismissed the presence of the Forty-Five in the novel as unimportant, a lightly sketched backdrop essentially irrelevant to the real action upstage. Wilbur Cross, in his important older biography of Fielding, typifies this line of thought, when he says that *Tom Jones* is "but loosely connected to the Jacobite rebellion."[3] Such a dismissal ignores, however, how important and traumatic the Forty-Five had been to those who lived (and did not live) through it; to wave off its presence in the novel accepts uncritically the position of later historians who, complacently armed with a knowledge of the outcome, have said that the Stuarts were not really much of a threat.[4] I believe that *Tom Jones* provides an opportunity both to see how Fielding engages these issues, but also to recover more clearly how momentous they were. I emphasize the deep peculiarity of the juxtaposition that I have just drawn. Imagine a novel, largely set in New York City in September 2001, published less than three years later; imagine, moreover, that this novel uses the terrorist attacks as an integral part of its setting. Finally, think of a novel with such a setting and published in such a time frame that turns out to be a comic masterpiece, and one might begin to sense the singularity of the relation between *Tom Jones* and the historical context in which it appeared.

The Real History of Tom Jones discovers for modern readers a new Henry Fielding, and a fresh way to look at his relation to the British eighteenth century. He was an artist who embraced a distinctive perspective on his time, an ironically playful balance between the polarized positions that dominated so many contemporary debates. That balance implies a detachment that he rarely found in his life or other writing. In the 1730s, he had been London's most successful playwright, but his comedies and farces carried a polemical edge, often directed at Prime Minister Robert Walpole. The Theatrical Licensing Act of 1737, which required that all plays be submitted for the Lord Chancellor's approval, succeeded in its intent to end Fielding's theatrical career, and so, like many at loose ends about employment, he turned to the study of the law. Ultimately, he took his place as perhaps the last of that distinguished line of English writers—figures such as Chaucer, Spenser, Milton—who were also important public men. As magistrate for Middlesex and Westminster, he earned a position as one of London's most prominent legal figures, and his writing about crime and the innovations he brought to the Bow Street magistrate's office have guaranteed him a place in every history of English law enforcement.[5]

As he struggled to establish himself in the law, Fielding supported himself by a variety of ephemeral and usually political writing: partisan vehemence ran high, he had a talent for invective, and, always debt-ridden, he needed the money. At the time, such writing earned him loyal patrons and terrible enemies alike, but, for later readers, his strong identification with certain political and legal positions has worked to create what seems to me to be a false context for his novels, and clouded a modern audience's ability to see what Fielding the *artist* thought. In *Tom Jones*, in particular, Fielding—freed from political hack-work—created for himself a perspective on politics and history which is far more expansive, more subtle, and in particular more complexly ironic than anything else in his prolific career as a writer. The intellectual pleasures of that perspective cannot be fully recognized, however, without a thorough knowledge of Fielding's time, and in this book I have set about recovering that necessary history. What I see as the novelist's detachment from his moment—his balance—represents no rejection of history. History is not a nightmare from which he is trying to awake. Rather, he wants to stand apart so he can more truly understand the realities of the times in which he found himself.

Any reader of the novel immediately recognizes that it bristles with an extraordinary number of references to contemporary persons, places, and events, well beyond the fact that it sets two thirds of the narrative during the last weeks of 1745. The names alone constitute an almanac of mid-eighteenth-century England: the famed boxer, John Broughton, quack doctors like Misaubin or Joshua Ward, actors such as Kitty Clive and Fielding's good friend, David Garrick; the "celebrated mantua-maker" Mrs. Amey Hussey, the hanging judge Francis Page, and the man who made Bath into England's resort of choice, Richard (Beau) Nash all make cameo appearances. Contemporary political figures pop up: Fielding's patron, John Russell, Duke of Bedford, as well as William Pitt the elder, to whom Fielding reputedly read the novel while it was still in manuscript.[6] The passage of 250 years has effaced some of the places that *Tom Jones*'s landscape makes vivid: London's notorious hanging tree at Tyburn, and the establishments where Mr. White purveyed chocolate, and Mr. Will provided coffee are all gone. But many of the sites that the novel names do survive: the Bell remains a thriving inn in Gloucester, visitors continue to taste the waters in the Pump Room at Bath, and an enthusiast can still trace the route that Tom follows on his adventurous journey from Somerset to London; most editions of the novel include a map of England's West Country, showing the exact route that the hero took.

My purpose in this book, however, surpasses the recovery of oddments of information about the eighteenth century. Rather, I aim to show how a detailed knowledge of certain central contemporary matters—matters such as the Forty-Five and the dynastic politics at its heart, questions of class and inheritance, and the problem of crime and its proper punishment—reveal a new image of Fielding and his achievement in his greatest novel, where he engages with eighteenth-century history on almost every page. That history manifests itself in the kind of trivial allusions cataloged above, but it emerges more importantly in the deep structures of the novel, and my procedure here is to show how references to contemporary people and events, often quite small or subtle, work together to constitute a powerful consideration of the era's most pressing historical problems. *Tom Jones*, for me, is both an object of study in its own right, and a remarkable path into the heart of Georgian England.

A Word which Our Posterity will not Understand

In an aside late in the novel Fielding affords us a small commentary on the problem of historical reading. In the middle of the Sophia-Fellamar plot, as the besotted Lord trails his beloved about her social rounds, the narrator interrupts the action to say:

> Having in this Chapter twice mentioned a Drum, a Word which our Posterity, it is hoped, will not understand in the Sense it is here applied, we shall, notwithstanding our present Haste, stop a Moment to describe the Entertainment here meant, and the rather as we can in a Moment describe it.
>
> A Drum then is an Assembly of well-dressed Persons of both Sexes, most of whom play at Cards, and the rest do nothing at all; while the Mistress of the House performs the Part of the Landlady at an Inn, and like the Landlady of an Inn prides herself on the Number of her Guests, though she does not always, like her, get any Thing by it. (898)

Fielding here highlights not so much a historical detail about eighteenth-century entertainment as the importance of historically informed reading. Long before Walter Scott wrote *Waverly* and so officially launched what has come to be known as the historical novel,[7] he understood in a profound sense that *all* novels are "historical novels," that the very attention to the quiddity of life that made the new genre first popular, and then dominant carries the danger of an expiration date. To change metaphors, the half-life of historically infused fiction means that the radiant glow of the real always becomes dimmer and dimmer over time. Fielding's little gloss on the word "Drum" functions thus as an internalized footnote for an audience not yet born, but, by highlighting not only the obscure detail, but also the act of defining that detail, he insists that such information has a crucial value. The paradox thus is that the Drum as a "real" event may be the very acme of superficiality, but an understanding of what a Drum looked like is far from trivial, is in fact necessary knowledge for the reader of *Tom Jones*. The passage points to the presence of time's winged chariot, but also holds out hope that later readers might nonetheless be able to catch a ride.

The difficulty, of course, is that most such references in the novel remain unglossed. Fielding speaks with an almost breathtaking confidence here that he will have readers ages and ages hence, but he also toys with that audience by the ironic question that this passage uncomfortably raises but does not answer: what else don't we know? But the epistemological uncertainty Fielding thus creates is accompanied, I think, by a kind of friendly challenge. If generations yet unborn do find themselves reading *Tom Jones*, then they must find a way to recover the history that Fielding could not always be bothered to explain.

A modern audience cannot possibly get back all the history that *Tom Jones* so capaciously contains, and the title of this study is inevitably tinged with the irony of its own bravado. But however much the goal of recovery recedes from the present moment, it remains my intent in *The Real History of Tom Jones* to provide a renewed sense of the novel's historical vibrancy by a close examination of six different issues where the matter of history is especially rich; these are also all matters of the first importance to Fielding himself. The first of those issues is the 1745 Rebellion, which is the focus of the first chapter, but which (like the Stuarts themselves) reappears throughout the study. As noted above, the Forty-Five has not always been taken seriously by critics of *Tom Jones*: Fielding's apparently wavering interest in the matter (the Rebellion arrives without warning one-third of the way into the narrative and departs almost as abruptly three hundred pages later) seems to suggest that it is mere window dressing, providing Tom with a good excuse to move in one direction, at least for a while, after his exile from Paradise

Hall. But I believe that questions of dynastic politics are central here, if often subtle. Modern readers can recognize or be taught the overt references: who the Duke of Cumberland is, or why the soldiers Tom meets are headed north, or why his servant mumbles prophecies about horses up to their stirrups in blood. What has been lost, and what I have tried to recover, are the ways that Stuart history is sunk deep in the design and texture of *Tom Jones*, in such apparently small touches as the gamekeeper's name or Partridge's cowardice, as well as in the largest matters of plot: this is, after all, a novel about the disputed inheritance of a considerable property.

A Master of Composition

It is important to recognize that Fielding often places what seem to me to be his most searching historical thinking in odd corners of his long novel, in episodes that are frankly digressive, like the gypsies or the trip to Drury Lane to watch *Hamlet*, or in shadowy parallel plots, like the plight of Bonnie Prince Charlie or the way the life of Richard Savage echoes that of Fielding's hero. *Tom Jones* is perhaps best known as a masterpiece of plotting, and no critical judgment on the novel has been so often repeated as Coleridge's encomium (which I now invoke once more): "What a master of composition Fielding was! Upon my word, I think the *Oedipus Tyrannus*, *The Alchemist*, and *Tom Jones*, the three most perfect plots ever planned."[8] That emphasis on the perfection of the plot has led some critics to see similar polish in the design, and a few have even discovered in it the kind of perfect balance and order that marked the graceful Palladian architecture that Fielding's contemporaries so admired.[9] Most readers, I dare say, do not experience the novel in that way: it is a tale made up of many interruptions, asides, and embedded commentaries. Fielding himself knew that his "history" would not appear in an orderly way to his readers and memorably warned his audience against dismissing any part of it simply because it seemed to be irrelevant:

> ... we warn thee not too hastily to condemn any of the Incidents in this our History, as impertinent and foreign to our main Design because thou dost not immediately conceive in what Manner such Incident may conduce to that Design. This work may, indeed, be considered as a great Creation of our own; and for a little Reptile of a Critic to presume to find fault with any of its Parts, without knowing the Manner in which the Whole is connected, and before he comes to the final Catastrophe, is a most presumptuous Absurdity. (524–5)

Dilation and divagation, not symmetry and graceful design, seem the book's dominant modes. And it is in those moments of apparent wandering by the way that the novel's history appears.

The main plot—the story of an identity lost and found—does, as I note above, have a powerful historical resonance, and I am concerned throughout this study to make those connections clear. But I believe the apparently extraneous matter in the book is just as, and perhaps more, important for the reader who wants to find the real history in *Tom Jones*, and so I focus on episodes or material that in no way advance the story. Partly, these scenes function so well as sites of historical investigation because of a kind of pictorial quality, and several of the episodes that concern me here have a strong ecphrastic flavor. Digression and ecphrasis go naturally hand in hand. To break from the main action of a narrative, as occurs in *Tom Jones* when Fielding presents us with a night at *Hamlet* or a gypsy king's description of his people or in a detailed description of a trial for stealing a horse, means immediately that a frame has been established, with the digression nested inside. Such strongly framed material, by the intricacy of design involved, should serve to focus attention on what is inside, which are miniature history paintings—if the reader knows how to look, already grasps (to use the earlier example) what a Drum really was.

The six chapters of "The Real History of Tom Jones" thus each tackle a different section of the novel in which the matter of history is especially rich. Chapter 1, "Stuart Ghosts," focuses on the 1745 Rebellion. Here, I look at the specific references to the Jacobite invasion, focusing on the way in which the exiled royal family haunts the novel, a ghostly presence that points to the way that they also haunted Britain for many years after they lost the throne. The Stuart presence in *Tom Jones* provides, in fact, a great deal of both structure and plot for the novel. As a family, they had long identified with the traditional literary genre of romance, and Fielding subtly uses romance form to sculpt the character of his titular hero and to shape the birth mystery at the heart of his plot. Tom looks a lot like Bonnie Prince Charlie, and the secret of his parentage is a plot device with uncanny echoes of the disputed birth of Charles Stuart's father, the event that precipitated the Glorious Revolution. In his reshaping of the artistic clay that the Stuarts provided, Fielding suggests reasons for their appeal to the English populace, a stance diametrically opposed to the unilateral pro-Hanoverian position that he took in his partisan journalism. In this novel, Fielding clearly understands the arguments in favor of both dynasties, and underlines that equipoise by creating characters and situations that blend together ideas and actions associated with both royal families. For example, the Man of the Hill projects a persona that while overtly anti-Stuart in his politics, also embodies a number of Stuart traits, including exile and a Catholic theology. Such reversibility—from one angle, he looks Hanoverian, but from another, Stuart—suffuses the novel, and marks Fielding's remarkable ability in *Tom Jones* to transcend unilateral partisan alliances.

Chapter 2, "Savage Matters," focuses on a figure I interpret as a Bonnie Prince Charlie figure writ small, the poet Richard Savage. Like the Stuart prince, Savage thought of himself as someone who was deprived of his rightful inheritance, and he set about trying to recover his name—or at least to make a living out of cashing in on what losing his name had cost him. He understood quite well that there was money and celebrity in a well-marketed victimhood. Fielding nowhere names Savage in *Tom Jones*, yet his story, well-known in London for several decades (in part because of a sensational murder trial, but also because he was the subject of Samuel Johnson's first biography), parallels not only Charles Stuart's vicissitudes, but Tom Jones's somewhat more humble troubles as well. By thinking in detail about Savage and his relation to the novel's hero, especially *Tom Jones*'s representation of maternity and its frank depiction of family hatred, I show again (as in chapter 1) how Fielding uses contemporary materials to shape his plot, and also how his first readers might recognize that original material in its recast shape. Fielding emerges here in competition with one of his most prominent adversaries, Samuel Johnson, as rivals for narrative control of a certain kind of story, "the history of a foundling," that Savage and Tom have in common; that story, in turn, has much to say about how the class structure of eighteenth-century England felt to those—like Savage, like Tom Jones, like Fielding himself—whose status was ill-defined. In exposing this connection, I help explain why Johnson hated Fielding so much and (to many) so mysteriously.

A very minor character, the gamekeeper Black George, takes center stage in chapter 3, "Black Acts." He comes and goes in the plot, like an apparently insignificant instrument in a long symphony, and his one memorable act, pocketing Tom's entire fortune of five hundred pounds at the hero's moment of greatest need, seems to mark him as a villain, however small. But Fielding drapes the gamekeeper with an impressive array of historical connections, through his name (which he shares with the king), his profession (hedged round with bizarre and contradictory legal restrictions, including the notorious Black Act), his literacy (necessary for him to be able to recognize eighteenth-century banknotes as in fact money), and his crime (not, strictly speaking, a theft at all, since Tom had already lost the money anyway). Fielding manages through these connections to embody in him a complex consideration of property law, of social status, as well as of the day's dynastic controversies. Not least, Black George emerges as a muddied but still recognizable mirror image of Fielding himself, since the strange position of gamekeepers (working like a servant, looking like a gentleman) mimics in a subtle way the status problems in the novelist's own life. Finally, I reveal how Black George is a different kind of fictional character, not the simulacrum of a person that we expect to find in a novel, but instead an entity who functions as a site of historical association, one who can thereby provoke a complex consideration of questions that Fielding's era found most troubling.

Theft pure and simple is the subject of chapter 4, "Hanging Judges." Tom's servant, Partridge, interrupts the Man of the Hill's long tale and recounts the trial of a horse thief he had witnessed some years earlier. Some critics and biographers have taken his description to allude to an actual trial that took place in 1737; certainly, a few of the names that Partridge drops are real, especially that of Sir Francis Page, one of the age's most famous jurists, and one notorious for harshness. This brief episode demands attention: in a novel filled with crimes or near-crimes of all kinds, this is in fact the only courtroom proper that *Tom Jones* depicts. Fielding loads this small vein with legal ore, and it provides a surprisingly rich occasion for him to explore the justice system in which he was already working at the time he wrote *Tom Jones*, and affords a glimpse into problems that he would face even more insistently after the novel's publication, when he began his work as magistrate in Bow Street. In particular, the scene in Page's courtroom allows Fielding to explore the most outlandish aspects of eighteenth-century criminal law, especially the brutality of an almost single-sanction system of punishment that mandated death by hanging for even small property crimes. Outside the novel, in his legal writing, Fielding's position on the punishment of thieves was as severe as Page's; in *Tom Jones*, however, he again finds a way to locate himself outside competing alternatives, as he identifies with Page even while revealing the utter corruption of his judicial practice.

Chapter 5, "Gypsy Kings," continues to explore the theme of theft, now in relation to that immigrant group most notorious for their reputation as thieves, the gypsies whom Tom and Partridge encounter shortly before their arrival in London. No attention has been paid by critics of *Tom Jones* to the realities of gypsy life in eighteenth-century England, but knowledge of their position and especially of the folklore that surrounded them (a context I recover by means of the fraudulent autobiography of that notorious eighteenth-century rogue, Bampfylde-Moore Carew) turns out to be crucial for a full understanding of a remarkably subtle episode. By introducing them into his near-encyclopedic narrative, Fielding can further explore the novel's theme of theft, as he exposes a pervasive pattern of robbery at the heart of English society. At the same time, the gypsy system of government—a remarkable combination of autocracy and democracy, and a system about which the Gypsy King tells Tom a good deal—allows the novelist to return again to the question of Stuarts and Hanoverians, and to connect the problem of robbery even more closely to arguments about who should be sitting on the throne. The gypsies come to represent another of Fielding's reversible signifiers, embodying a meaning that oscillates between Stuart and Hanover without ever coming to rest on one side.

Chapter 6, "Mirror Plots," turns to another occurrence that many people in Georgian London actually experienced: an evening at Drury Lane, watching David Garrick play Hamlet. The scene, another digression from the main action, takes a surprising turn, however, in that Fielding does not focus his attention on Garrick, the age's greatest actor, but on Partridge, and his reaction to the performance. The effect is comic, since Tom's naïve servant takes the ghost of old Hamlet to be real, but Fielding's design here is not only to make us laugh. Partridge reveals himself as an important witness to historical problems that the others in the theater wish to forget, and Fielding signals the importance of his testimony by a small reference to a Prayer Book illustration. That image, one that depicts the foiling of the Gunpowder Plot of 1603, has never before been analyzed in relation to *Tom Jones*, but I show how it provides a kind of mirror, not only for the action of this scene, but for the sense of history that Fielding has developed throughout. The juxtaposition of a real performance, a real play, and a real date (the novel's time line places this scene in December 1745, the height of the Jacobite invasion), creates a powerful tableau, one that allows Fielding to consider the Stuart claim to the British throne, not merely in relation to the politics of that moment, but in the light of British history for centuries past, with its repeated pattern of rebellion and civil war. Partridge, in his palpable reactions to the action before him, becomes a stand-in for the English nation, responding with fear, but also with some sense of heart, to a spectacle of history both dreadful and ironic. The servant, an unlikely vehicle for the sophisticated Fielding, nonetheless serves to suggest his creator's profound understanding of history as an unfolding of pragmatic choice rather than as the triumph of ideological truth.

Habitual Double Irony

Irony is one of the central concerns of *The Real History of Tom Jones*, and my particular interest is the relation between the way Fielding writes history and the way he uses irony. That is, irony is not just a literary technique for him but a mode specifically for historical understanding. Fielding's irony, however, is of a very particular kind, one best described many years ago by William Empson. Empson's reading of *Tom Jones* still represents as trenchant an understanding of the novel as we have, and what he memorably calls "double irony" remains perhaps the best way to understand how Fielding works both as an artist and as a student of history. It is worth recalling his intricate description in detail:

> ... the style of Fielding is a habitual double irony; ... Single irony presumes a censor; the ironist (A) is fooling a tyrant (B) while appealing to the judgement of a person addressed (C). For double irony A shows both B and C that he understands both their positions; B can no longer forbid direct utterance, but I think can always be picked out as holding the more official or straight-faced belief. ... Presumably A hopes that each of B and C will think "He is secretly on my side and only pretends to sympathize with the other"; but A may hold some wise balanced position between them, or contrariwise may be feeling "a plague on both your houses."[10]

Empson, it seems to me, could very well have had in mind the Janus-faced poise between apparently irreconcilable positions that, this study argues, is Fielding's most characteristic stance with regard to historical questions. The effect is not a plague on both Hanover and Stuart, for instance, but something more like the "wise balance" that Empson describes. If Fielding wishes a "plague" on anything in this novel, that curse is reserved for any perspective that refuses to see how history always turns the flat demands of the contingent moment into something that requires double vision, and which tends to produce, in the wise historian, the perspective of double irony.

To see Fielding as a historian who practices double irony reveals a very different picture of the man than the one who emerges from, say, his political journalism, where he so stoutly defended the interests of the Whigs, and it is equally at odds with the image one could gather from his later legal writings, such as the *Enquiry into the Causes of the Late*

Increase in Robbers, where he positions himself as a particularly severe and inflexible theoretician of the criminal law. Double irony requires both playfulness and detachment, an ability to see, for example, how Whig and Jacobite rhetoric is marked by a stubborn reversibility, as when each side appropriates the property metaphor for the throne they both want, so they can claim that the other camp are just so many thieves. From such a position, Fielding can condemn Judge Page and the English legal system as a cruel travesty of justice, and at the same time make fun of those, like Partridge, who refuse to honor its mechanisms, just as he can simultaneously idealize and laugh at the gypsies. Throughout *Tom Jones*, whenever the matter is history, Fielding generally chooses not to take sides, but rather to stand aside, to adopt a perspective that allows him both to judge and to sympathize.

A passage in the middle of the novel has often troubled readers of *Tom Jones* because it promises a kind of doctrinal clarity that it also refuses to provide. The context is important. The parallel journeys of Tom and Sophia have taken them through the perilous passage that is the inn at Upton; the two lovers have almost, but not quite reunited, and they are on separate roads again. Sophia has learned of Tom's dalliance with Mrs. Waters, and she has left behind, as warning and as lure, her totemic muff. The narrator pauses at length to tell his readers that her lingering resentment of Tom is grounded less in his infidelity (unbeknownst to him) than in some liberties that she believes he has publicly taken with her name. He then moves to what promises to be a grand pronouncement:

> But so Matters fell out, and so I must relate them; and if any Reader is shocked at their appearing unnatural, I cannot help it. I must remind such Persons, that I am not writing a System, but a History, and I am not obliged to reconcile every Matter to the received Notions concerning Truth and Nature. But if this was never so easy to do, perhaps it might be more prudent in me to avoid it. For instance, as the Fact at present before us now stands [that is, the true source of Sophia's resentment], without any Comment of mine upon it, tho' it may at first Sight offend some Readers, yet upon more mature Consideration, it must please all; for wise and good Men may consider what happened to *Jones* at *Upton* [that is, missing Sophia] as a just Punishment for his Wickedness, with regard to Women, of which it was indeed the immediate Consequence; and silly and bad Persons may comfort themselves in their Vices, by flattering their own Hearts that the Characters of Men are rather owing to Accident than to Virtue. Now perhaps the Reflections which we should here be inclined to draw, would alike contradict both these Conclusions, and would shew that these Incidents contribute only to confirm the

great, useful and uncommon Doctrine, which it is the Purpose of this whole Work to inculcate, and which we must not fill up our Pages by frequently repeating, as an ordinary Parson fills his Sermon by repeating his Text at the End of every Paragraph. (651–2)

And so, tantalizingly, ends this paragraph, without reiteration—or even iteration—of whatever "Doctrine" it is that Fielding, a most uncommon parson indeed, wants to "inculcate." The whole passage feels like a testy admonition to his audience to, in essence, read better. But if we do succeed in reading better, what great and uncommon doctrine do we glean?

It seems to me that what we can gather here is not a doctrine so much as a position, a place from which the narrator and, if we are smart enough, his readers can look upon two opposed doctrines, including of course historical ideologies, and see what is true and what is foolish about each. The "wise and good" see in Tom's missed opportunity with Sophia a providential punishment for his "wickedness" in fornicating with Mrs. Waters; the "silly and bad" console themselves that, while something bad did happen to him, it was specifically *not* for the reason that the wise and good think—to wit, said fornication—but rather due to an "Accident" that Tom does not even suspect. Fielding's "Reflections," he makes clear (it is almost the only thing he does make clear) would "alike contradict both these Conclusions." The good, that is, should not be smug about the wickedness of others, nor should the bad be complacent that they will escape blame for their sins. But what, beyond such a double ironical mutual critique, would his conclusion be? And would he even come to a final judgment of some kind? He does, after all, oppose the "conclusions" of these two sides to his own "reflections." Those reflections do not, in this case anyway, appear to produce Empson's "plague on both your houses," but can we discern "some wise balanced position" here?[11]

Fielding's reticence in this passage is a bit like a frame without a picture: one has the sense of a label saying "great, useful, and uncommon Doctrine," but the tag points to nothing. It would be all too easy to draw an ungenerous conclusion. Double irony, one might say, is another name for evasion, for a detachment that is simply Fielding's refusal to choose—or, if he has chosen, to play some kind of withholding game in which he declines to reveal what his choice really was, a robe for to go invisible such as shows up on prop lists for the Elizabethan stage. I see it differently. Fielding's concern may not be to sort out good and bad, wise and silly (the careful reader will have noted that the words "right" and "wrong" do not appear in his peroration). Rather, he may be more intent upon critiquing the very notion of "sides," of our habit of turning divisions of human experience into categories of judgment. "Received Notions concerning Truth and Nature" are the enemy here, precisely because such ideas produce what amounts to a useless opposition, in which the only question is who is right, who is wrong. One effect of his reticence is that Fielding disables the reader's ability to agree or disagree with his "Reflections," whatever they are. All we know is that he finds something lacking with regard to "Truth and Nature" in the conclusions about Tom drawn by both the wise and the silly. The position of double irony, then, is a place in an almost literal sense: it is a vantage point, a perspective, an angle of vision; it is a way of looking, not an object that the looker sees. What that means in terms of the way Fielding looks at the historical issues of his time, or for that matter, at himself, will be the work of this book to demonstrate.

Missing Pictures

What Fielding saw when he looked at himself is another one of this study's central concerns. His image is notoriously elusive. London's National Portrait Gallery is justly famous for displaying a comprehensive set of images of almost everyone British, living and dead, who ever accomplished anything, or who simply achieved fame or notoriety. But in the galleries devoted to the eighteenth century, along the walls lined with figures in wigs or turbans, knee britches, and long coats, one picture seems prominently absent. The author of *Joseph Andrews* and *Tom Jones* is nowhere to be found. Fielding's literary rivals and detractors, Samuel Richardson, Tobias Smollett, Samuel Johnson, all return the viewer's gaze, as do his friends, David Garrick and William Hogarth, and so also do his political patrons and enemies, men like the Duke of Bedford and the Great Man himself, Sir Robert Walpole. His own brother and successor in his magistrate's job, Sir John Fielding, commands a large space from which, blind as he was, he can create no illusion of looking at the passers by, and can only awkwardly lift a dark shade to expose his shriveled and unseeing eyes. But Fielding has no place in these rooms, no face to display among his contemporaries, gathered again and forever in this space given to the immortality of the human image.

That absence is not a matter of deliberate exclusion, one more insult inflicted by the legions of Fielding's political, legal, and literary opponents. The problem is that the portrait that should be there—large, in oils of course and impressive, like the one of John Fielding—does not exist and never did. We do know a little about what Fielding looked like from scattered comments by himself and others: he was a tall man, strongly built, with a substantial nose and chin. There is a posthumous drawing that Hogarth did for the 1762 edition of *The Collected Works* (one where the facial promontories are quite large), but it is little more than a caricature, and the artist, so the story goes, could not call up his old friend's face when asked to contribute this picture eight years after Fielding's death, and was able to produce it only when a helpful lady produced a silhouette of the novelist's profile. I suspect that such a picture provides no very definitive guide to his appearance, and yet it is the only image we have that is at all reliable.[12] The fact is, the picture of Henry Fielding does not exist. He never took the time—or more likely, had the ready cash—to sit for a portrait, and the face and character we might hope to discover—sharp-eyed and amused, perhaps, or sternly laying down the law—is buried forever in his unlikely final resting place, Lisbon, where he sought to recover his health, but found only a grave. Fielding, it is clear, was a man who covered his tracks remarkably well. Even the chameleon Shakespeare left a few portraits.

He is not invisible however, and it is part of my argument in *The Real History of Tom Jones* that he is everywhere present in what I, like most readers, believe to be his unassailable masterpiece. But that presence is a subtle one. My point here is not to elaborate the sneering judgment pronounced by his old rival, Samuel Richardson, "Tom Jones is Fielding himself, hardened in some places, softened in others. . . . His brawls, his jarrs, his gaols, his spunging houses, are all drawn from what he has seen and known. As I said . . . he has little or no invention" (197). My aim, rather, is to show how, in the interstices of *Tom Jones*, in the digressive episodes, minor characters, and vaguely sketched backgrounds that are my primary interest, Fielding has seeded his novel with surprisingly complex self-portraits, meditations on his birth and family, his class status, his work in the law, and his politics. But Fielding's art is not merely autobiographical, interesting as that might be. The places in his novel where he hints at how he sees himself turn out to be the moments where he is most engaged with his own historical moment; his self-portraits, that is, are also small histories of eighteenth-century England. This should not be surprising: Fielding, like other great artists, saw himself as the measure of his world. Joyce, through his own alter ego, Stephen Daedulus, put it better: "His own image to a man with that queer thing genius is the standard of all experience, material and moral."[13] What I hope to discover and clarify in the pages that follow is something more about what Henry Fielding thought "his own image" to be; in doing so, the image of his world—mid-Georgian England—will emerges with greater—and sometimes surprising—clarity as well. We are on the cusp of several important Fielding anniversaries as I write these words: October 8, 2004 marks the two hundred and fiftieth anniversary of his all-too-early death, and April 22, 2007 will be his three hundredth birthday. The time is never wrong to try to know more about great art and great artists, but a fuller, richer picture of Fielding's astounding novel seems like a worthy tribute to attempt for the beginning of his fourth century.

Chapter 1
Stuart Ghosts

His Favorite Things

In his old age, in by-then permanent exile in Italy, the land of his birth, Charles Edward Stuart, once known as the Young Pretender, forever romanticized as Bonnie Prince Charlie, spent much of his time reading; among his "particular favourites," one title stands out: *Tom Jones*.[1] His choice of reading material is striking, both because Charles Stuart and the 1745 Jacobite Rebellion, which he led, actually figure in Fielding's novel and because the weight of available evidence outside the novel suggests that Fielding despised the Stuarts and their Jacobite followers. What, then, did the no-longer Young Pretender find to like about *Tom Jones*? It is quite possible that the mere fact that his greatest adventure was featured in a widely read and admired novel was gratifying to the Prince's vanity—bad publicity, even then, being better than no publicity at all, especially to a lonely exile. But was Fielding's novel only bad publicity? It will be one of the central contentions of this study that, in *Tom Jones*, Fielding's politics almost always resist unilateral definition, and the ways in which he incorporated Charles Edward Stuart and his Rebellion into the novel, the focus of this chapter, powerfully demonstrate how he frustrates simple ideological labels. The fact of Charles' affection for the work of an old adversary like Fielding is certainly a tantalizing site of speculation, but it is also provides a good opportunity to begin rethinking what we believe we know about Henry Fielding and the Stuarts.

The traditional view of that issue has been shaped, understandably enough, by the novelist's numerous pronouncements on the subject in the extensive political journalism he published in the 1740s. In particular, scholars and critics can point to the anti-Jacobite pamphlets of 1745 and *The True Patriot* of 1745–6; both the pamphlets and the newspaper (largely written by Fielding) are responses to the rebellion, and indicate his alarm at the uprising, his contempt for the Stuart claim to the throne, and his ridicule of the Jacobites. Indeed, after the rebels were safely defeated, he insisted that he would have been among "the first in the String of Loyalists, who would have had the Honour of being hanged had the Rebellion succeeded" (*True Patriot* 277–8). Later, in 1747–8, he weighed in with *The Jacobite's Journal*, where he adopted a transparently ironic pose as an ardent Jacobite, John Trott-plaid, Esq.[2] The ostensible inspiration for this new journal was a renewal of Jacobite activity, but the paper primarily served as a general propaganda organ of the Pelham administration then in power.[3] In 1749, in his "A Charge Delivered to the Grand Jury," he asserts: "There is but one Method to maintain the Liberties of the Country and that is, to maintain the Crown on the Heads of that Family which now happily enjoys it."[4] Summarizing these sentiments in his biography of the novelist, Martin Battestin speaks confidently of "Fielding's abhorrence, so often expressed in his writings, of the entire family of Stuarts" (427).

Tom Jones was written more or less simultaneously with this polemical material, and those who have looked at dynastic politics in the novel have tended to view it through the lens thus provided. Not surprisingly, perhaps, most critics have seen the novel as confirming and extending the loyalties expressed in these more ephemeral forms.[5] Fielding was no Jacobite in his heart—that's certain. However, Fielding's use of Stuart materials is more central to his design than has been acknowledged, and the way he has incorporated such matter is both more playful and more ambiguous than we had suspected. In particular, I think that this playfulness and ambiguity suggest a way of looking of history, ironic yet complexly sympathetic, that is profoundly at odds with the kind of intellectual straightjacket that political partisanship demands. I am guided here by the assumption that there is no necessary connection between an imaginative work like *Tom Jones* and the kind of polemical writing Fielding turned his hand to in the 1740s. Such connections are certainly worth exploring, but they do not provide a privileged perspective, and I begin by setting them aside so that we might examine the politics of the novel itself in a fresh way.

On the Road

The first question to ask about the Stuarts and their role in *Tom Jones* is both simple and crucial, and it concerns the matter of placement. Where are the references to Charles Stuart and the Rebellion? The first mention of the Forty-Five in the novel occurs rather late, in Book VII, chapter 11. Tom, dismissed from Paradise Hall and on the road, meets a company of soldiers, who, it turns out, are on their way north to fight the rebels. The narrator notes, "By which the Reader may perceive (a Circumstance which we have not thought necessary to communicate before) that this was the very Time when the late Rebellion was at the highest; and indeed the Banditti were now marched into *England*, intending, it was thought, to fight the King's Forces, and to attempt pushing forward to the Metropolis" (368). While Fielding does not give an exact date, the information given here places this encounter rather precisely as sometime in the last week of November 1745. We know the timing of the action here so precisely because of information given earlier in the paragraph: the troops that Tom encounters "expected to be commanded by the glorious Duke of Cumberland" (367), and the Duke was not named commander until November 23. Fielding's coy parenthetical comment attracts our attention at least as much as the information conveyed and raises the central question: *why* has he not thought fit to mention it before? Why has Fielding decided to introduce the fact of the Forty-Five just *here*? Charles Stuart, after all, had landed in Scotland the previous summer and had enjoyed various military and political successes throughout the autumn; he had crossed the Tweed and entered England on November 6. Why has Fielding waited so long to introduce the subject?[6]

And if the sudden appearance of the soldiers in the novel's seventh book makes us wonder about Fielding's earlier silence, the abrupt disappearance of all explicit Jacobite and Stuart references in Book XII, after Tom and Partridge encounter the gypsies, is equally strange.[7] While we do not have to follow those who have mapped the plot of *Tom Jones* onto a calendar, with exact dates assigned to all events from the day that Tom leaves Allworthy's house,[8] it is clear enough that if Tom meets the soldiers in late November, then the action in London takes place in December. In other words, the last third of the novel begins to unfold at precisely the same time as the high-water mark of Charles Stuart's invasion: he reached Derby, about 100 miles from London, on December 4, and began his long retreat back to Scotland two days later. Fielding himself spoke in *The True Patriot* of the rebels' effect on London that month as being "a Terror scarce to be credited" (154). Yet, in the novel not one word passes anyone's lips about (depending on one's point of view) these dire or hopeful occurrences. As I argue in chapter 6, the Rebellion and its effects, in fact, have not disappeared from the novel at all, but their persistence in the London section of the novel is indirect, and the question remains: why are the explicit references confined to these middle six books?

The apparently casual way in which references to the Forty-Five appear and disappear from the novel is, no doubt, one large reason why most critics have tended to downplay its importance in *Tom Jones*. As noted earlier, Wilbur Cross said that the novel was "but loosely connected to the Jacobite rebellion" (III, 283–4), and that judgment has proved accurate to most, though not quite all of Fielding's critics. Ronald Paulson, in his recent biography, seems closer to the truth when he states, "the central paradigm of *Tom Jones* is the historical event of the Forty-Five."[9] What seems apparent to me is that, far from being loosely connected to the novel or a matter that comes and goes in Fielding's field of attention, the Forty-Five is an intrinsic part of the novel's *design*. And that importance comes into clearer focus when we notice how precisely Fielding has placed his first and last references to the Stuart invasion. That is, we first hear of the crisis almost as soon as Tom is forced from Paradise Hall, and our awareness of it ceases with the gypsies, almost Tom's last encounter before he reaches London. In other words, Fielding's attention to the rebellion coincides almost exactly with the so-called "road" section of this famously symmetrical novel. Fielding's silence about the Forty-Five in the first six books is balanced by an equal reticence in the last six. It is only in the middle of the narrative's three-part architecture—country\road\city—that the Forty-Five is explicitly visible. But why the road, and what political significance does it have?

The answers to those questions are complex, but we can begin with a relatively straightforward point: the road creates a parallel between Fielding's hero, Tom Jones, and the central figure in the rebellion (and future novel-reader), Charles Edward Stuart. This parallel is not at all a matter of personality or character. Charles Stuart was a depressive paranoid, one whose personality bore little or no factual resemblance to his fictional counterpart. Rather, Tom and the Young Pretender become interesting as doubles or analogues when we consider what it was that the Stuart prince represented. The Young Pretender comes to us, as he came to most of his contemporaries, champions and detractors alike, not as a historical figure with clear biographical contours, but as a fiction, indeed as nothing less than a legend in his own time. He was not just someone who hoped to become Charles III, he was Bonnie Prince Charlie, a youth both reckless and charming, and, at least for the Jacobites, a figure nobly and courageously seeking to redress an old injustice, an exile sadly separated from the home and the throne of this ancestors.

Some of the ways in which Tom Jones partakes of this Jacobite matter are immediately clear. He may not be consciously seeking an inheritance on the road, but he has certainly lost one, and lost his home besides.

Even more importantly, as we have seen, he is first figured as an exile at the same moment that Charles Stuart first appears in the novel, thus enforcing the sense of their parallel fate. Here are not one, but two handsome, dispossessed, and reckless young men traveling through the frost of late November 1745.

This parallel has been noted by other critics, although there has been little sustained analysis. Michael McKeon, for example, almost as an aside remarks, "If the plot of Tom the bastard bears a subtle relation to the conservative career of the Young Pretender, wandering in search of his patrimony, it is less an imitation than a parody fueled by Fielding's anti-Jacobite contempt for the hereditary claims of the Stuarts" (418). McKeon speaks here as if the purpose of such a parody is self-evidently Hanoverian in its loyalties. But while parodies do generally work to degrade their object, they do not often achieve as a by-product any particular elevation of the parodic vehicle. Rope-dancing in Lilliput certainly lampoons the competition for office in early Georgian England, but Swift does nothing thereby to make rope-dancing itself look more noble. In the same way, if Tom's wandering is a parody of Charles Stuart's (for the Pretender could hardly be parodying Tom), what do we do with the fact of our continuing affection—even admiration—for Fielding's foundling? McKeon asserts, but nowhere demonstrates, that the parallel works as an attack on the Pretender; why shouldn't it work to create a contagious sympathy for Charles, as our hearts open to the plight of all the dispossessed?[10]

Ronald Paulson also suggestively describes some of the analogies between the Prince and Fielding's pauper, but seems to be finally uncertain about the significance of the parallel:

> I would like to know more about Fielding's response to the undeniably romantic boy who landed in a remote corner of the kingdom with only a few men to win back his father's crown. Whether Tom or Prince Charles Edward came first is, I suppose, an academic question. . . . Either Fielding is turning the myth upside down, or he finds that, in an ironic way, the myth of the gallant young prince is closer to the one he had already sketched in *Joseph Andrews*. . . . That is not to suggest that he is in any way more sympathetic with the prince's career than he was in *The Jacobite's Journal*, but only that a common myth of alienation from one's true home and wandering as an exile or fugitive tie these two heroes together. (206)

While Paulson in the end backs away from questioning Fielding's sympathies, his tentativeness here is refreshing and worth pausing over.

For one thing, he does not assume that Fielding's political journalism tells us all we need to know about what the novelist thought of Charles Stuart. And the irony he identifies here, contra McKeon, seems to be at Fielding's own expense; the story he likes to tell, the redemption of the lost, turns out to be one the Stuarts like, too. But the hesitations in Paulson's analysis invite further thought.[11] Why is Fielding attracted to this story? Further, once one has acknowledged the parallel between Tom and Charles Stuart, what does one do with it? I like to approach that question in two ways: first, through genre; second, through the potent political problem of legitimacy.

The question of genre arises because of the way that Fielding has limited the overt Jacobite allusions and references to one part of his narrative design. The road section of the novel, Books VII–XII, encompasses virtually all of them. What we might call such geographical confinement of the Stuart material has no necessary generic implication, but if we look more closely at these books we can see how, far more than either the country section that precedes them or the London books that follow, in this part of *Tom Jones*, we come closest to the world of romance. "Romance" may seem like an odd word to invoke in a study devoted to examining this novel historically, for romance-based analysis has tended to be a tool favored by critics who were trying to take this novel out of history and to link it to a rather stable universe of romance conventions.[12] As J. Paul Hunter has put it, "The attempt . . . to claim *Tom Jones* for romance seems almost to deny any history at all, for it attempts to blend all literary and cultural study into an examination of eternal themes and variations."[13] Hunter's point is undeniably true about what romance-oriented critics have traditionally made of the novel, but what intrigues me is the possibility that the concentration on the road of both the material related to the Forty-Five and romance conventions is an issue with a specifically historical importance.

Paulson calls Charles Stuart an "undeniably romantic boy" but his romance-character goes beyond the vaguely romantic air we tend to assign all lost causes. McKeon has argued that there was a particular embrace of romance by the Stuart family; it was, so to speak, their narrative form of choice for self-description (213–14). The signal instance of this connection is Charles II's narrative of his escape from Cromwell's troops after his disastrous defeat at Worcester in 1651. This was a story he loved to tell, and finally, thirty years after the event, he dictated an account to Samuel Pepys. Whatever actually transpired in those frantic weeks of flight, the combined efforts of time and the king's own imagination reshaped them into a masterly romance, complete with disguise in peasant garb, miraculous escapes, and even (as McKeon wittily puts it) "arboreal metamorphosis" (213), as Charles takes refuge in a tree. Though Pepys's transcription was not published until 1766, knowledge of the king's account of his adventures was widespread, and there is an uncanny resemblance between his narrative and the one that would later be constructed by his great-nephew to recount his own months of desperate flight in the aftermath of his disaster at Culloden, a period immortalized and glamorized with its own romance-title as "the Prince in the heather."[14] Charles Edward Stuart, too, has a tale of disguise and transformation, of hairsbreadth escapes.

At least on the road, Tom Jones is another undeniably romantic boy and again, he is romantic not just because his own cause seems impossibly lost, but in quite specific ways. There is, first of all, the fact of his wandering, so reminiscent of both the typical quest-structure of romance, and also of the way that the quest in such narratives is rendered—that is, loosely, episodically. Whether he knows it or not, Tom is seeking Sophia and the recovery of his good name (in all senses), but that *telos* comes to us in the partially concealed form of apparently disjointed or digressive encounters, with landlords and soldiers, with amorous damsels and angry husbands, with beggars and gypsies, and scary old men. Like the knights of old, Tom fights, he loves, he pauses to hear an instructive story, but he always keeps moving on. These close resemblances of Tom's story to romance conventions can appear either as an anachronism or as the "timeless" power of romance-structure to inform all narrative. But the parallel to Charles Stuart makes a possible here an interpretation of Fielding's use of romance elements that is not archetypal but historical. For he has invoked romance-structure, not just anywhere, but precisely in the context of the Forty-Five, in the context, that is, of a moment in history that itself had taken on the form (or at least the flavor) of romance.

Fielding signals us that he has something like this in mind early in the road section, in the introductory chapter to Book VIII: "A wonderful long Chapter concerning the Marvellous; being much the longest of all our introductory Chapters." This is one of the key chapters in the entire novel. In it, his discussion (among much else) disparages the cheap superstitious thrills of romance, though it also and crucially gives the historian the license to include the marvelous (402). Book VIII, which follows this introduction, seems intent on using that license and is especially dense with both Stuart matter and marvelous occurrences, including Tom's reunion with Partridge, himself a Jacobite loyalist, as well as his meeting with the Man of the Hill, the ghostly remnant of the events of 1685–8. The conventions of romance—remarkably coincidental meetings while wandering the road, encounters with ghosts—apparently are unavoidable when discussing Stuart history, and the eruption of the Forty-Five has, it seems, turned all England into the territory of romance. Thus, Tom looks most like a romance-hero, and Fielding's "History" looks most like a romance, in the same section of the novel where the action most directly invokes the materials of Stuart history, and where Tom most explicitly resembles Charles Stuart. In this way, Fielding uses the conventions of romance not only to structure Tom's character, but also to show how those same conventions shape the image of Bonnie Prince Charlie as it appeared in the public eye.

It seems inadequate to analyze the relationship between these two romances—Tom's and Charles'—as a merely parodic one. Given Tom's appeal to most readers, one strong effect of this parallel is to concede the appeal of Charles Stuart as well. Such a concession by Fielding can be variously interpreted, but one possibility is quite simply that, in *Tom Jones* at least, he refuses to demonize the Stuarts or their followers. In this context, we recall Johnson's angry words in *Rambler* # 4 about writers who fail to separate vice and virtue in the character of a hero.[15] By universal assent, and as I examine in detail in the next chapter, he has *Tom Jones* and its hero in mind, but Tom's mixed nature seems to parallel Fielding's apparent sense of the Young Pretender's mixed character—dangerous, wrong, champion of a bad cause, but appealing nonetheless. Indeed, Fielding's appropriation of Charles's romance for Tom suggests some kind of compliment, however subtle, from the fierce Whig polemicist for his old antagonists. In particular, there is here the sense of one artist paying tribute to another. Fielding, it seems likely to me, understood that the Stuarts' stories were better than the tales Hanoverians told. Such an understanding does not remake Fielding into a Jacobite sympathizer; it does, however, reveal him as a shrewd (and perhaps amused) observer of one powerful source of the Stuart's continuing appeal. To admire the Stuart's story, to appropriate it for his own uses, is not without political implications, to be sure. Romance is not only an old form of story-telling, it is a kind of tale with particular ideological implications. McKeon is certainly persuasive in arguing that romance is an aristocratic form,[16] and Fielding's willingness to appropriate the conventions, to embed them in what he claims is a new species of writing, suggests that his admiration for the new world of England in the mid-eighteenth century, complete with foreign kings and an increasingly mercantile economy, may have been more pragmatic than deeply felt.[17]

Warming-Pan Babies

But the Stuarts, however canny they were about wrapping themselves in the glittering tinsel of romance, had at the base of their claim for restoration the ancient and powerful argument of hereditary right (though this is, of course, an issue central to a thousand romances; the distinction, however, is heuristically useful). And that brings us to the second deep parallel between Fielding's novel and the career of Charles Stuart—the question of legitimacy.

At the heart of the Jacobite question, to review briefly, is the fact that in 1688 the Roman Catholic convert James II was forced to leave his throne (abdicated it, according to the Whigs) because he had allegedly abused his power in various ways, promoting his religion and insisting on his absolute prerogative. The result of this "Glorious Revolution," as it came to be called, was that the Stuart monarch was replaced, first by his Protestant daughter Mary and her husband, William of Orange, and then by her Protestant sister, Anne, the last Stuart to rule England. But Anne, despite pregnancies so numerous (seventeen) as to suggest some measure of desperation, produced no surviving heir, and so long before her death in 1714, the Revolution Settlement of 1701 had determined, first, that no Catholic could be king (though this had also been written into the Bill of Rights of 1689), and then, as a necessary consequence, that the monarchy would next pass to the heirs of Sophia of Hanover, a granddaughter of James I, and the Protestant closest in blood to the throne. Thus it was that her son, George, came to inherit the monarchy in 1714.[18]

What we sometimes call the Jacobite century—from the Revolution of 1688 to the death of Charles Edward Stuart in 1788—would never have occurred had there been no argument about the monarchy and legitimacy. From the Jacobite point of view, the Stuarts were the legitimate monarchs on the basis of the ancient principle of hereditary right; it was by that right that the throne belonged to James II, then to his son, called James III by his loyalists, and then to his son, Charles Stuart. The Whigs, on the other hand, who had engineered the changes of 1688, thought hereditary right was ultimately subordinate to both religion and English liberty (which they claimed James II had violated); therefore, Catholicism and tyranny were overriding illegitimacies. The argument thus came down to one about the nature of legitimacy, and the principles that define or establish it: is it birth? is it religion? is it political belief?

Quite obviously questions of legitimacy and inheritance dominate the plot of *Tom Jones*, and those questions, in turn, connect with political issues in the British state. Fielding slyly invites such a comparison at the very outset of the action. After describing Allworthy's virtues, he concedes that such virtues alone do not provide interesting enough material out of which to construct a novel and that "Matters of a much more extraordinary kind are to be the subject of this history . . ." (38). Fielding then moves immediately to a description of Allworthy's discovery of Tom in his bed. The foundling motif, of course, is as much a staple of romance as a wandering knight, but again, Fielding's use of a romance convention has a specific *historical* resonance and a connection to matters that really were extraordinary. Early readers of the novel must have been struck by the parallels between Tom's mysterious appearance and the controversies surrounding the birth of James Edward Stuart (Bonnie Prince Charlie's father) on June 10, 1688. In order to make the significance of the parallel clear, that event needs to be recalled in some detail.

The birth of a son to James II and Mary of Modena, his second and much younger wife, helped bring about the downfall of James. It is thus one of the defining moments in Jacobite history, and became, for all sides, an extraordinarily dense site of debate about legitimacy. James might well have lost his crown anyway, but there is little doubt that the appearance of a child both male and Catholic to a couple whose previous efforts at childbearing had proved futile was an event of decisive importance. So important, in fact, that many of those who found the king's religion and style of rule intolerable immediately denied the reality of the birth. The queen had never been pregnant, they said, or she had miscarried, or her baby had died, either immediately or within a few weeks. The accounts were various and often comically contradictory, but one assertion dominated: the child presented as Prince of Wales was no legitimate offspring of the king and queen. Rather, he was someone else's child: the son of a miller, many thought, or of a wet-nurse in St. James's Palace, or of an Irishwoman secretly brought over for this dark and devious purpose. This changling was then smuggled into the queen's bed and passed off as the new Stuart heir. The most popular argument was the insistence that this interloper had been surreptitiously introduced into the birthroom in a warming pan, and the warming pan (itself an image of a surrogate womb) became the material object that gave the controversy its name: James Edward Stuart was "the warming-pan baby."

The weight of historical evidence is firmly on the side of the Stuarts here. Royal childbirths were court theater of a high order, and Mary gave birth before a roomful of witnesses, Protestants and Catholics alike; no less than 42 of them ultimately gave depositions testifying that the queen gave birth that June morning. But the warming pan was a convenient story for those opposed to James: William of Orange exploited it to the full, and Anne (who had rather conveniently been in Bath that day) remained publicly forever dubious that the child was her half-brother. Nor did the story die out as the years passed. It was revived throughout the Jacobite period—over fifty significant printed references between 1688 and 1745, according to one historian of the incident—and Bishop Burnet's version, from the *History of His Own Time*, was reprinted in *The Gentleman's Magazine* in the middle of Charles Stuart's invasion, in January 1746.[19]

It is unimportant whether the story was genuinely believed or was a cynical fabrication of the Whigs. Whatever its exact origin (and such rumors are always overdetermined), the tale of the warming pan is deeply revealing about the mind of the Whig opposition to the Stuarts. First, the story of the warming pan tacitly acknowledges the importance of hereditary right. It is one thing to say that religion is more important than birth; it is quite different to say that, well, religion is probably more important than birth, but remember, James II never had a legitimate son. Second, as an image, the warming-pan baby seems to represent, even literalize, Whig fears that a Catholic had been brought into a place where he did not belong—the misplaced infant, in other words, functions as an image of a misplaced king. The tale thus marks both the newborn heir and, in time, his son, Charles Stuart, as interlopers, illegitimate heirs who have somehow been insinuated (or who would insinuate themselves) into a place where they did not belong, to which they had no legitimate right.

That right, of course, is supposed to pass by the law of primogeniture, from father to son, in a line of patrilineal succession. But this brings us to a striking oddity at the heart of this matter: the controversy here is not about paternity, but about maternity. The decisive question in this affair asked whether Mary of Modena gave birth to the child presented to the nation as the Prince of Wales. For an age whose reproductive anxieties typically centered on questions of fatherhood, the warming-pan story curiously deflects attention away from what we might expect—the inherently speculative act of conception—and onto what should have a sure evidential status, childbirth.

The tale of a baby in a warming-pan has immediate resonance for a reader of *Tom Jones*—and we should keep in mind that such resonance would have been particularly clear to contemporary readers, many of whom would have recently reread or heard the old story not long before they took up the new novel. Again, what we might assume to be a timeless motif drawn from the reservoirs of romance—the discovery of a foundling—turns out to have a particular historical connection. To be sure, the scene in Allworthy's bedroom looks quite different from the crowded tableau at St. James: Fielding's worthy man discovers Tom by himself. But while no warming pan or other agent of conveyance is mentioned, Tom's appearance in Paradise Hall is inseparable from an act of smuggling. In both the warming pan rumor and in the novel, a baby of mysterious parentage is born in an unknown place and then secretly positioned in a bed where it does not belong. Continuing the parallel, both birth-narratives have the effect of producing controversy, with debate between those who see the child as misplaced and so deserving of dismissal or exile (Mrs. Wilkins thus standing in for the Whigs in 1688), and those who see it as there by right, either (as in the Stuart case) because the rumor is a lie, or because (as with Tom) report has it he is Allworthy's secret son: a bastard, yes, but the Squire's own, one he can neither acknowledge nor send away. Allworthy himself presents an interesting *tertium quid*, acknowledging illegitimacy but refusing dismissal. He makes the best of circumstances and "breed him up as his own" (44).

Tom Jones also parallels the odd emphasis on maternity we saw in the warming-pan myth. The scene of Tom's discovery seems to mock patriarchal anxiety by comically envisioning what looks like a patriarchal fantasy: the novel opens on a miraculous scene of apparent male parthenogenesis. Women, the source of all that male anxiety about spurious issue, aren't even necessary. But from the moment Deborah Wilkins arrives in the room to add an uncharitable third to this image of dyadic patrilineal bliss, the question becomes who was the mother, a question Mrs. Wilkins investigates with "all imaginable Diligence" (45)—further aligning her with the 1688 Whigs. While she (and we) end up on the trail of the wrong woman, her impulse is confirmed by the novel's denouement. In the end, it is the identity of Tom's mother, not Bridget's partner in a secret summer romance, that matters.[20] Allworthy, far from being the patriarchal fantasy he first appears to be (a landed bachelor with a male baby in his bed), turns out to be only an uncle, a slant and celibate relation who provides no seed for sons, only the estate that one of his dueling nephews will inherit.

It was, of course, the Old Pretender, not his son, who figured in the warming-pan controversy, but the parallel of the two stories nonetheless works to enforce the sense of an analogous connection between Tom Jones and Bonnie Prince Charlie. The warming-pan as a mark of illegitimacy is itself inheritable, as Fielding makes clear in *The Jacobite's Journal* for 9 January 1748. Expounding satirically on the mysteries of Jacobitism, he imagines an "ancient Deity" at the source of the Stuart faith, among whose names are "*Satus iterum, Solusque Bimater* [twice-born, child of two mothers]; i. e., that had two Mothers; which . . . clearly allude[s] to the famous Story of the Warming-Pan" (125). The warming-pan is thus both historical and typological; it is, Fielding implies, the place where all Stuarts are found.

It would be easy enough to pass this over as another unremarkable instance of Fielding's anti-Jacobite polemic, but for the fact that he seems to have appropriated elements of the warming-pan story for the birth of his own hero. Tom, after all, carries the name of his "other" mother, Jenny Jones, right to the end of the novel—he, too, is a child "that had two Mothers." And if we ask the natural question—what is the old Whig Fielding up to?—we can see again how the parallel here fits in with the general pattern I describe: the difficulty we face if we try to make Fielding's use of Stuart materials in *Tom Jones* fit into a preconceived scheme about his political allegiances. In British politics, the warming-pan may be a ticket to exile, to delegitimation; in the novel, however, it is the apparent interloper, the smuggled baby, who finally inherits.

Fielding here appears to be well aware, with a playful irony that deserves consideration, of a profound truth about British politics after 1688: that with the Glorious Revolution, Britain had committed itself to what I would describe as a choice of illegitimacies. David Hume, in his 1748 essay "Of the Protestant Succession," puts it in a similar way. Weighing the two sides' arguments as dispassionately as he can, he offers this conclusion:

> Thus, upon the whole, the advantages of the settlement in the family of STUART, which frees us from a disputed title, seem to bear some proportion with those of the settlement in the family of HANOVER, which frees us from the claim of prerogative: But at the same time, its disadvantages, by placing on the throne a Roman Catholic, are greater than those of the other establishment, in settling the crown on a foreign prince. What party an impartial patriot, in the reign of K. WILLIAM or Q. ANNE, would have chosen amidst these opposite views, may, perhaps, appear to some hard to determine.[21]

In other words, Hume points out, there are advantages and liabilities on both sides, liabilities I call irremovable illegitimacies that, whatever the outcome, had to be managed, rhetorically, ideologically, above all, politically.

The 1701 Act of Settlement only made permanent the problematic outcome of James II's removal: from then on, the throne would be held by someone outside the direct line of succession, or (if the Stuarts were ever restored) it would be held by a Catholic. The terms of the debate suggested an ideal solution—a Protestant Stuart—that Monmouth tried to embody and which died with Queen Anne.[22] It goes without saying that neither the Whigs nor the Jacobites conceded the compromised position they each found themselves in (Hume sets up his argument as that of an "impartial patriot"; 216). They could not concede because neither would admit for obvious political reasons that a double-principle of legitimacy—that is, birth *and* religion—was in fact at work. From the viewpoint of the Stuart champions, birth determined legitimacy, period. Similarly, the Hanoverian party insisted that religion overrode the claims of birth. But there is a pattern of defensiveness on both sides. As we see, the very existence of the warming-pan rumor betrays a Whig anxiety that hereditary right *does* mean something and thus the birth of a son to James II must be denied. The Jacobites, in turn, insisted (as Fielding formulates this article of faith in *The Jacobite's Journal*) "*that a Popish Prince may be the Defender of a Protestant Church*" (106; Fielding's italics). In other words, by insisting in this way that the monarch's religion doesn't matter, the Jacobites implicitly concede that it very well may. Thus, both parties tacitly admit the force of the opposition's primary argument.

If I am right about Britain in the post-1688 era—that it faced a choice between illegitimacies—we readily see how that difficulty helps structure Fielding's novel. For the important event toward which the plot inexorably moves is Allworthy's choice of heir, a choice we also see as poised between two illegitimacies. The good choice turns out to be Tom, not as Blifil calls him "a beggarly Bastard" (130), but a well-born bastard, a nephew to the Squire and a good and generous man besides. Having at the last moment pulled a father for Tom out of his conjurer's hat, Fielding could obviously have revealed as well a secret marriage or imagined some other legitimating device. But he doesn't, and Tom remains a bastard.[23] The bad choice, of course, is Blifil, Tom's half-brother, a man with perhaps a better technical claim (since his parents were married) but who was conceived out of wedlock (Bridget, we learn, was delivered of her second son "Eight months after the Celebration of [her] Nuptials" (78), thus casting a shadow on Blifil's perfect legitimacy),[24] and who reveals himself in the end as morally illegitimate, for he is not only a schemer and a hypocrite, but an heir of Cain, someone who quite deliberately connives at capital accusations against Tom, whom he knows (even if we don't) to be his own brother. Allworthy, like Britain, has no perfect choice, and while Blifil's crimes appear to make it an easy decision, the whole force of the novel suggests how very difficult those crimes are to perceive.

It is tempting and would be perhaps not inaccurate to associate Tom with the Hanoverians, Blifil with the Stuarts. Tom's birth legitimacy is less sound than Blifil's, just as George I's was less than James III's. Blifil's moral legitimacy is less than Tom's, just as the Stuarts (from the Whig standpoint) were done in by the crimes of James II. But that kind of simple alignment would do no justice to the subtlety and complexity with which Fielding has established his parallels. For such an interpretation would have to ignore what we have seen, that is, the way in which Fielding has also allied Tom with the Stuarts and the way his attractions partake of the appeal of that other reckless young man, Charles Edward Stuart. It would thus be both impossible and false to hammer all this out into some consistent political position. That impossibility suggests what should not surprise us, though it is a suggestion no one writing on Fielding's politics has made, that Fielding is being not only balanced but also playful with those fraught issues that so divided Britain and which left so many scars. Tom is redeemed, he inherits, but he remains illegitimate, a compromised choice who inherits on the slant, a man who borrows the strength of his final claim from both the pragmatism of the Hanoverian claim and the mythos of the Stuarts.[25] Whatever Fielding may have said about the Stuarts or the Jacobites elsewhere, in *Tom Jones* he appears to mock the black and white world of partisan debate by allowing for a more mixed vision, one that both concedes and appropriates what is appealing about the Stuart cause.

Falling into the Marvelous

The parallels Fielding has created between Tom Jones and Charles Edward Stuart tend to dissolve our old certitudes about Fielding's politics, at least the politics of this novel. This new perspective is reinforced if we look at another character in the novel, one who has very specific connections to the Stuarts and their cause: the Man of the Hill. Fielding devotes almost seven chapters of *Tom Jones* to his hero's encounter with that eccentric figure, much the longest digression in the novel. Readers have frequently asked a simple question as a result: why? Even when we concede that this is a novel whose pace is often leisurely, and one which is threaded throughout with digressions and baroque filigree of all kinds, this is an exceptional bit of retardation. Why do we spend so much time with a character who makes no later appearance, and who tells neither Tom nor us anything that we really need to know?

I think that the Man of the Hill has some important historical work to do in the novel, but to understand that role, we must first look briefly at the way he has traditionally been viewed. The only defense of Fielding's inclusion of this character and his long story that has ever made much sense is the contention that the old man offers a kind of tacit cautionary tale. At a point in the novel when Tom—uncharacteristically glum due to his apparently futile love for Sophia and his disgraced banishment from Paradise Hall—wishes to indulge his "melancholy Ideas" (443), he finds himself hearing the life story of a man who has done nothing *but* nurture his depression for half a century. By the end of the episode that looks like a bad idea, and while Tom never explicitly rejects the model that the Man of the Hill embodies, he also more or less immediately resumes the kind of resolute good cheer and good nature that have marked him from the start. Indeed we find him indulging, not his melancholy, but his life-affirming gluttony and lust with Mrs. Waters the very next day.

Such an explanation, that the Man of the Hill embodies an alternative path to be avoided, is essentially allegorical. Just as, say, Spenser's Red Cross Knight falls into doubt about Una, and then immediately meets a character named Fradubio, so Tom, feeling melancholy, finds himself hearing the story of the monumentally depressed Man of the Hill, as a nascent mental state finds embodiment in a coincidence made possible by the happy allegorical logic of the road.[26] Lending weight to this understanding of the old man's function is his name, or rather, the absence of a name. A name, along with age and gender, are two of the categories we normally use to classify the people we meet, but the Man of the Hill, while he tells us exactly how old he is—since he was born in 1657, we know he is 88—never mentions his name. He provides names such as Gresham or Watson for others in his story, but he never names himself, leaving the narrator to call him "the stranger" or "the old man" or "the Gentleman." We do learn, however, that the locals refer to him by that most emblematic-sounding designation, "*The Man of the Hill*" (446). This seems particularly striking in a novel where Fielding otherwise is perfectly content to resort to descriptive designations like Thwackum and Square. Why not give such a name to the stranger: Hillman or Olds or the like?[27]

The singularity of the old man's designation suggests, I think, that an allegorical reading of the Man of the Hill might be fruitful, but the Spenserian model invoked above may not be the best one to use. Allegory like Spenser's is rooted in theological certainty, and Spenser weaves his "dark conceit" in *The Faerie Queene* in order to point to a transcendent, unified truth. If we want to confine the old man's significance to a moral one (The Road Not to Travel), then such a model is useful, but to me the real interest of the episode lies in its relation to history, and the way Fielding here employs something like allegory as a means of examining history and historical process. For the allegories in *Tom Jones* are concerned, not with God, but with the contingent and conflicted world of mid-Georgian Britain, and Fielding uses his dark conceits, not as a parabolic means of leading us to the right doctrine, but rather as a way precisely to confound any easy or straightforward understanding of history.[28] His allegorical point, we might say, is not unity, but multiplicity and contradiction—as we saw earlier in the way that Tom's story could be said ambiguously to allegorize the life of Charles Edward Stuart. If we understand how the Man of the Hill episode works as historical allegory, I think we also have a clearer sense of the overall meaning of the Stuart materials that have been the focus of this chapter.

We must begin where the episode itself begins, with Partridge's fear of ghosts. Afraid of being left alone while Tom climbs a hill so that he can indulge his *penseroso* mood, Partridge persuades his companion instead to seek shelter at a dwelling where he has spotted a light. His relief is almost immediately overwhelmed, however, by what we come to know as his reflexive response to virtually every outside stimulus: superstitious fear. As Tom and his friend await a response to their knock on the Man's cottage, "*Partridge*, whose head was full of nothing but of Ghosts, Devils, Witches, and such like, began to tremble, crying, 'Lord have Mercy upon us, sure the People must be all dead' " (444).

There are no real ghosts in book VIII of *Tom Jones*, or anywhere else in the novel, yet this section is full of entities that function like ghosts. Just two nights before they meet the old man, Tom himself had been mistaken for a spirit. After he is attacked by Northerton, Tom is "concluded to be dead" (378), and then, after he regains consciousness, is bandaged, and sent to bed, he gives a sentry the fright of his life:

> The Clock had now struck Twelve, and every one in the House were in their Beds, except the Centinel, . . . when *Jones* . . . issued forth. . . . It is not easy to imagine a more tremendous Figure than he now exhibited. He had on . . . a light-coloured Coat, covered with streams of Blood. His face, which missed that very Blood . . . was pallid. Round his head was a Quantity of Bandage. . . . In the right Hand he carried a Sword, and in the left a Candle. So that the bloody *Banquo* was not worthy to be compared to him. In fact, I believe a more dreadful Apparition was never raised in a Church-yard, nor in the Imagination of any good People met in a Winter Evening over a Christmas Fire in *Somersetshire*. (387–8)

Needless to say, the tone here is facetious, but the elaborate description of Tom as a ghost points to the ways in which his condition does mimic death—cut off from the life he has always known, with no prospect of return. He is, in fact, seeking death by joining the company of soldiers, and he tells Partridge soon after that he desires only to die in battle: "my chief End and Desire is a glorious Death in the Service of my King and Country" (439). He reiterates this to the old man after he fights off the thieves that have attacked him: "there can be no Merit in having hazarded that in your Service on which I set no value. And nothing is so contemptible in my Eyes as Life" (449). Partridge, too, resembles a being returned from another world: Tom's new companion had departed the novel in disgrace back in Book II, chapter vi, and his serendipitous return in Book VIII, as Tom's barber and surgeon, gives him a distinct air of the revenant. Indeed, when he meets Allworthy again (a few weeks later in the plot), his former judge will say, "I thought you had been long since dead" (935–6).

So, the two characters who enter the old man's ominous cottage on that cold November night are themselves rather ghostly, and what they discover there is a nexus of further spectral references. After the old man is rescued by Tom, he asks his deliverer, "You are a human Creature, then?" (448)—his doubt here thus mirroring the reaction of the soldier two nights before. The Man himself, it turns out, is the terror of the neighborhood ("the Country People are not, I believe, more afraid of the Devil himself" (446), we learn from his housekeeper), and he is often mistaken precisely for a ghost: "Some few Persons I have met by Chance, and have sent them Home heartily frighted, as from the Oddness of my Dress and Figure they took me for a Ghost or a Hobgoblin" (483). Later in Book VIII, Partridge interprets the Man's story with a tale of his own, in which his friend Frank wrestles with, and is soundly beaten by, a being he takes to be the ghost of a horse thief against whom he had testified.

Partridge is the only one present in the old man's cottage who actually believes in ghosts, and it is important to pause for a moment over that fact. His superstition is, on the most basic level, meant to be comic, a stock response by an apparently stock character: word of the decline of magic has not yet reached the lower classes nor has the Gothic novel arrived to make superstition again respectable for a better class of reader.[29] Servants such as Partridge, or farmers like his friend Frank, or lowly enlisted men like the sentinel—a trio that suggests something like the vast majority of the English population—are, it seems, controlled by an antiquated set of beliefs that are then retailed for our amusement.

But Fielding has already given Partridge's superstition a specific and historical context. In their last conversation before encountering the old man, Partridge has revealed his Jacobite loyalties to Tom in a way that simultaneously establishes both his politics and his superstitiousness: "all the Prophecies I have ever read, speak of a great deal of Blood to be spilt in the Quarrel, and the Miller with three Thumbs, who is now alive, is to hold the horses of three Kings, up to his Knees in Blood" (440). Thus, Partridge is not just any pre-Enlightenment ignoramus; he carries a particular and charged identity as a Jacobite, and Fielding apparently wants his conviction of the reality of ghosts and witches to represent a belief system continuous with his loyalty to the house of Stuart. A fool will not, we might conclude, confine himself to only one idiotic idea, but will embrace a variety; the effect is to equate belief in ghosts with a belief in Stuarts.

But the point is more subtle: Fielding does not link Partridge's supernatural credulity to his Jacobite loyalty willy-nilly; rather, he does so because the Stuarts were already connected—self-connected, we might say—to superstition. There were, for instance, the demonological interests and publications of King James I, and the laws which that first Stuart monarch had written against witches are explicitly invoked at the beginning of the episode: the old man's housekeeper looks so frightening, Fielding tells us, that "if [she] had lived in the reign of *James* the First, her Appearance alone would have hanged her" (445). There was also the Stuart monarchs' regular practice of the magical ceremony of the royal touch as a cure for scrofula, and their insistence that they ruled through divine right, an ideology presented as a political theology, one that linked the power to govern to a supernatural origin. In this context, Partridge's superstition seems less like a conventional point of class mockery than a way to suggest an entire world-view, one that encompasses not only servants but kings.

With the Man of the Hill episode, then, we encounter again the intersection of history with material that we normally associate with romance, in this case, the supernatural. And like the romance motifs—foundlings, wandering heroes—discussed earlier, the supernatural reveals itself in this novel specifically *as* a historical issue. Fielding has prepared us for this connection in the introductory chapter to Book VIII, the book dominated by the Man of the Hill, and we now need to return to the ideas advanced there in more detail. By itself, this chapter reads like a rather conventional critique of the absurdities and improbabilities typical of romance, and Fielding's arguments center on traditional discussions, old as Aristotle, about the relationship between fiction and probability. He advises "Historians" (such as himself) to avoid ghosts, elves, and fairies, and he directly disparages the genre of romance: "It is by falling into Fiction therefore, that we generally offend against this Rule, of deserting Probability, which the Historian seldom if ever quits, till he forsakes his Character, and commences a Writer of Romance" (402). The distinction he draws here, however, between history and romance is, as we have seen, a problematic one when the subject is Stuart history, and Fielding, whatever he may say about romance, allows himself that crucial latitude already noted, to recount the marvelous: "if the Historian will confine himself to what really happened . . . he will sometimes fall into the Marvellous but never into the incredible. He will often raise the Wonder and Surprise of his Reader, but never the Incredulous Hatred" (401–2). The argument here creates a context for Partridge's superstition more complex and perhaps more appealing than either transparent foolishness or political anachronism. Fielding has recommended a kind of openness by the historian to the marvelous in the everyday, to people and events that, perhaps, are as extraordinary as ghosts but which are nonetheless real. We recall here that Partridge reappears after his long absence from the novel almost immediately after these introductory remarks, and they serve, in some sense, as a preparation for what he brings to the narrative, as well as subtly indicating the possibility of a deeper alliances between Fielding himself, the historian who "sometimes fall[s] into Marvels," and Partridge, the servant in the thrall of the supernatural. Moreover, Partridge's Jacobitism clearly enables his sympathetic aid to Tom—long before he meets his putative son, the barber has believed in the triumphant return of an exile, and the extension of his allegiance from one dispossessed heir to another seems almost automatic. Whatever his mistakes, whatever his ignorance, Partridge's superstition also demands our close attention.

The Stuarts, with their trappings of superstition and the distant clamor of their invasion, provide more than a background for Book VIII, and the Man of the Hill episode provides one of the novel's most important instances of direct discussion of the Rebellion and its long attendant history. Near the end of his story, we learn that the old man's life had once intersected with Stuart history, as his long tale of degradations and suffering is, rather suddenly, interrupted by a political note: "I had been for some Time very seriously affected with the Danger to which the Protestant Religion was so visibly exposed under a Popish Prince" (477). The Catholic King he refers to is, of course, James II, and his sense of the dangers that monarch represented leads the Man of the

Hill to join the Rebellion mounted by Charles II's son, the illegitimate but safely Protestant Duke of Monmouth. The Man barely escapes with his life after Monmouth's decisive defeat at Sedgemoor, goes into hiding, and quits that concealment only when word reaches him of the Glorious Revolution. But his emergence is temporary, and somewhat curiously, what we think would be a happy political outcome leads him to a now-permanent retirement from the world. When Tom meets him, almost sixty years later, it turns out that he believed that 1688 marked a permanent end to the Stuarts, and he is profoundly shocked when his young guest breaks the news of the new rebellion. Tom's comment bears attention because it highlights what he thinks is the particularly marvelous quality of the Forty-Five: "it has often struck me, as the most wonderful thing I ever read of in History, that so soon after this convincing Experience, which brought our whole Nation to join so unanimously in expelling King *James*, for the Preservation of our Religion and Liberties, there should be a Party among us mad enough to desire the placing his Family again on the Throne" (477). The Man of the Hill reacts with something like that "incredulous Hatred" Fielding had mentioned, as if Tom has brought tidings of a gigantic hand in armor or a portrait that walked: "You are not in Earnest! . . . there can be no such Party . . . I cannot be imposed on to credit so foolish a Tale" (477–8). From the Man's point of view, the 1745 Rebellion is literally unbelievable. Nonetheless, as we know with Tom, however improbable, it is historically true. It may not be so foolish to believe in ghosts after all.

All the specters we have heard about in this section of the novel—Tom, Partridge, the hanged horse thief, the old man's housekeeper, the Man of the Hill himself—thus point to the unreal, yet true phantom lurking in the countryside, the ghostly figure of Charles Edward Stuart, elusively slipping southward at just this moment in the story, the dead hand of the past reaching out to recover a throne and nation wrested from his grandfather almost sixty years before. Tom calls the Jacobite rebellion "the most wonderful thing" he knows of in history, and the Forty-Five, the latest evidence of the Stuarts' remarkable posthumous existence is, in the terms established by Book VIII's introductory chapter, "marvellous," as if the past itself, dead and gone, had come to life again.

If the Stuarts and Fielding's cast of characters at this point in *Tom Jones* all partake of a certain ghostly identity, they also share another quality, one that works to reinforce their spectral flavor. They all are exiles. In looking at the question of exile here, we begin to see more clearly a surprising likeness between the Stuart hater, the Man of the Hill, and his Stuart antagonists. Exile is, to be sure, a rather haunted condition, and those who return from long exile are always ghostly—think of Pip's Magwitch. The Man of the Hill episode seems especially rich in these ghosts of exile. The Man himself, as we have seen, removes himself from the world after the 1688 Revolution, and if he still lives in his natal land, his isolation is as great as if—like the Robinson Crusoe figure that he so strongly resembles—he were marooned on a desert island. His servant notes, "I have lived with him these thirty Years, and in all that Time he hath hardly spoke to six living people" (447). He is a classic exilic type, the self-exile, the person who finds the time and place in which he lives insupportable and who sets himself deliberately apart from it.

It is important, I think, that we see the old man as an exile rather than as a hermit, which he also resembles. The vogue for hermits was high in the eighteenth century, and many gardens and parks came to be decorated with grottos and other rough dwellings, often complete with a resident hermit. This retired life of contemplation was simultaneously celebrated by the widespread popularity of poems about hermits, and there was a strong renewal of interest in Milton's "Il Penseroso": it was often imitated, and in 1755 the poet William Shenstone caustically remarked that "I cannot help remarking that Milton's Il Penseroso has drove half our Poets crazy."[30] Fielding seems to have this fashion in mind when, with gentle satire, he gives Tom the impulse to climb Mazard Hill to indulge his melancholy; our hero has, in fact, just alluded to Milton (436), and the Man himself, with his night walks, bears a superficial resemblance to the speaker in Milton's poem. As he tells Tom, "Day and Night were indifferent Seasons to him, and that he commonly made use of the former for the Time of his Repose, and of the latter for his Walks and Lucubrations" (486). But Milton, we remember, is seeking the "pleasures" of Melancholy, and the old man, whatever else he has found in his retirement, has found no pleasure, none of that "calm Peace, and Quiet" that Milton sought, and which was doubtless the genuine impulse behind what became merely fashionable. The Man of the Hill lives not in a garden, but in a wild and wilderness spot, and his overriding personality trait is cynicism and bitterness. As Talleyrand said of the Bourbons (when, their own exile over, they returned to the throne), he has learned nothing and forgotten nothing. He embodies, that is, not the hermit's peace in retirement but the long and well-nourished resentment of the exile.

Our travelers, Tom and Partridge, are themselves absent from home, and absent precisely because they have been sent away—Tom just days before and Partridge long ago, but both of them forced to depart, and both for sins they did not commit. As such, they represent that most characteristic form of the exile in the eighteenth century, the outlaw. Tom's supposed crimes against Allworthy are not prosecutable under the penal code, but they were certainly judged to be egregious violations of the household order of Paradise Hall; his fate, after his trial and conviction by his benefactor, is the same as that of countless real criminals of his time, exile—or as they called it, "transportation."[31] Allworthy "banish[es] him from his sight forever" (310). He may not have been sent to the colonies or forced to work a term as an indentured servant, but he has been sent away for his crimes just the same. Partridge, innocent of the crime of which he was accused, sees in Tom's return his own path to restoration: "if he could by any Means, therefore, persuade the young Gentleman to return Home, he doubted not but that he should again be received into the Favour of *Allworthy* . . . and should again be restored to his native Country; a Restoration which *Ulysses* himself never wished more heartily than poor *Partridge*" (427).

These different characters all point specifically back to the Stuarts, resident since the Revolution in 1688 in France or Italy. As such, they represent another prominent type of the exile, the political exile, for they are a family forced from their native land because they insist on or represent political beliefs at odds with those maintained by those in power. All these exiles are akin, and not only because they share a state of banishment and all resemble ghosts. The similarities between Tom Jones and Charles Edward Stuart are not the only Stuart parallel that Fielding incorporates into his novel, for the Man of the Hill himself can be seen as a type of the Stuarts.

On the face of it, he seems a most unlikely candidate for such a role: he is a strong supporter of the Protestant succession, first through his role in Monmouth's revolt, and then by his vehemently stated opposition to the Stuarts and their advocates. His opposition to the Stuarts seems grounded largely in matters of religion. As we saw above, he takes up Monmouth's crusade because he was "seriously affected with Danger to which the Protestant Religion was so visibly exposed" under a Catholic monarch. He refuses at first to credit Tom's report that a new rebellion is afoot, a denial that is grounded in his conviction that no Protestant Englishman could possibly be a Jacobite: "There may be some hot-headed Papists led by their Priests to engage in this desperate Cause, and think it a Holy War; but that Protestants, that Members of the Church of *England*, should be such Apostates, such *Felos de se*, I cannot believe it" (477–8).[32]

The Man of the Hill thus looks like a true-blooded Protestant in his politics, but—and here we began to see his own crypto-Stuart identity emerge—he is a rather odd Protestant in his religious practice, for his life since 1688 has been strikingly Roman Catholic and monastic in its withdrawal, its claims to contemplativeness, and its *contemptus mundi*. His response to the Glorious Revolution is not, as we might expect, a celebration of the triumph of his cause, but is rather this self-imposed exile on the fictitious Mazard-Hill, and he tells us his life from the date of the Protestant triumph until his encounter with Tom, as noted above, "is little better than a Blank" (480). The extinction of the Stuart claim, it seems, is the death of history, or the death of his history, anyway. As he tells Tom at the end of his story, "Thus, Sir, I have ended the History of my Life; for as to all that Series of Years, in which I have retired here, they afford no Variety to entertain you, and may almost be considered as one Day. The Retirement has been so compleat, that I could hardly have enjoyed a more absolute Solitude in the Deserts of the *Thebais*, than here in the midst of this populous Kingdom" (483). And like a monk in the desert that he invokes—Thebes, in fact, was the birthplace of Christian monasticism—he spends his solitary days, he says, in contemplation of God, "the Worship of that glorious, immortal, and eternal Being" (484), and in contempt of his fellow humans, "puzzling . . . to account how a benevolent Being should form so imperfect, and so vile an Animal" (484).

The fact that his "History" ends in 1688, and that his life since then is little better than a blank, however, aligns him through his own terminology with the Jacobites he so despises. He describes them as *Felos de se*, that is, as suicides. Yet his own fate after the Glorious Revolution seems very close to self-extinction. Suicide has threaded its way throughout this section of the novel: there is Tom's longing for a glorious death in battle, the old man's own suicidal thoughts at the nadir of his youthful fortunes, and the bad friend he saves from an attempt to drown himself. Self-destruction, indeed, seems to have been a Stuart trait, whether in the folly of Monmouth (who was beheaded after his rebellion came to grief), the political ineptitude of James II, or the military recklessness of Bonnie Prince Charlie, culminating in the disaster at Culloden.

For someone who claims to despise the Stuarts, the old man seems deliberately to mimic their fate, either symbolically through his self-destructiveness and covert Catholicism, or more literally in the fact that his exile begins at precisely the same moment as theirs. His pronouncements may be in perfect accord with the Revolution Settlement, but his behavior suggests instead Catholicism and the deposed dynasty. All those who mistook the Man of the Hill for a ghost seem to have had it right after all: the spectral figure that Tom and Partridge encounter seems like a ghostly stand-in for the Stuart family itself.

But to take this as the final word about the significance of the Man of the Hill ignores all the ways that he stands for just the opposite set of values and beliefs. What he represents is contradictory, a feature of this character that is nicely epitomized by the peculiar information Fielding gives us about the old man's age. It is peculiar because it is an unusually precise bit of knowledge in a novel where such concrete particularity is often missing, but it seems to have a paradoxical valance: does it emblematize his loyalty to the Protestant cause, or does it suggest the way his history mimics that of the Stuarts? He is, as we have seen, 88 years old in 1745, and for an eighteenth-century audience that number would immediately call to mind the events of 1688. The Man of the Hill's politics seem, on their face, to be the politics that were victorious in that Revolution year: Protestant, Whig, anti-absolutist. But there was also a losing side in 1688, and a set of supposedly discredited politics and values, and the Man of the Hill appears simultaneously to embody those; it is certainly the year when both he and the Stuarts began their exile, and despite the fact that his politics triumphed, he behaves precisely like someone who lost. What I suggest is that his age serves cleverly to align him with *both* sides and that such doubleness is the trademark characteristic of Fielding's historical allegory. Such allegory is marked, as with Tom and Charles Edward Stuart, by what I call allegorical reversibility—that is, Fielding's creation of characters and situations whose emblematic possibilities seem obvious, but whose emblematic significance points simultaneously in opposite ways.

The Man of the Hill cannot be consigned to any straightforward ground of signification. He is at once immured in history, yet not reducible to any unilateral historical meaning. This contradictory pattern of significance points, I believe, not to a deconstructive vanishing point of undecidability (as II. O. Brown seems to believe about the novel's parallels to real events), but rather to the duplicities and paradoxes that emerge in any considered historical understanding. The old man *is* a marvel, inspiring on close inspection both our "wonder" and "surprise," as Fielding said real history could do; he embodies the irreconcilable poles of British history in 1745—Protestant and Catholic, Stuart and Hanover. Such doubleness is not, I hasten to add, meant to suggest some happy vision of a harmony that the nation could find if only it could put aside or reconcile its differences. The Man of the Hill figures forth the fact that difference, opposition, conflict are themselves the very ground of historical meaning. The implication is that any historian who tries to paper over such contradictions, to say that any event or person means one thing, is in fact writing the kind of bad history Fielding warned against in the introduction to Book VIII: a simple meaning would indeed be "improbable" and so worthy, as he tells us in strong language indeed, of our "incredulous Hatred" (402).

Revising History

To conclude this chapter, I make two points: first, about Fielding's politics and his relation to the history of his time; second, about Fielding the man, that elusive and fascinating figure. Much of the commentary on Fielding's politics in the last few decades has been devoted to the attempt to understand his positions and loyalties within a fairly broad, somewhat factionalized spectrum of interests that have come down to us under the umbrella term "Whig."[33] Initially, this was a labor of correction, trying to pry Fielding loose from an older scholarly tradition that had labeled him "Tory," often on no better evidence than that he seemed like the heir to the Scriblerians, and since Swift and Pope were Tories, so too must have been Fielding.[34] Over time, the Whig view of Fielding has grown more detailed and subtle, in part under the influence of the historical studies of the school of Namier. Namier had seen English politics of the mid-eighteenth century as ultimately resistant to understanding by any bi-partisan model; rather, there was a single broad ideological consensus (Whig) within which individuals and groups competed to protect their interests. Thus, interest—not ideology—became the key. What Namier described for the 1760s gradually took hold as a model of interpretation for all British politics from the time of Queen Anne's death in 1714 when the Tories fell, and what we might call such expanded Namierism has dominated studies of Fielding's politics for a long time.[35] For critics working within that historical model the only problem for the student of Fielding's politics is his position within this broad Whig consensus.

The historical consensus that proclaimed a Namierite political structure for the decades before the 1760s, however, has been challenged over the last two decades, with the attack led by a diverse group of revisionists. There is a good deal of variety in this more recent work, but a couple of assumptions are shared by most of the scholars working in this vein. One, ideological differences (in the form of an active Tory party) did not disappear at the time that George I took the throne. Two, the Jacobite threat, far from being marginal or derisory, remained a central alternative for many to the Hanoverian regime, at least until the failure of the

Forty-Five Rebellion. The degree to which these points are related is a matter of much dispute, with some arguing for considerable Jacobite fellow-traveling among the Tories, while others insist that there was little connection.[36] That argument is unimportant here. What is significant, I think, is the way that the revisionist perspective can help us make more sense of Fielding's handling of the Stuart materials in *Tom Jones*, especially the matters under consideration in this chapter, the parallels between Tom and Charles Edward Stuart, and what I call the allegorical reversibility of the Man of the Hill.

The general tendency to downplay the importance of the Forty-Five in *Tom Jones* may have been a mirror of the similar tendency among historians to minimize the role of the Jacobites in the political life of England in the first half of the eighteenth century. Literary critics who are trying to work historically are inevitably dependent on the historiographical traditions of their time, and for those who have worked on Fielding's politics, the traditions that came to hand for much of the last century offered little reason to take Jacobitism in the novel very seriously. Let me hasten to reiterate that the revisionist perspective does not mean that we have to stand Fielding on his head. What the new eighteenth-century history does do, however, is take the 1745 Rebellion as seriously as it seems to me that Fielding did, and thus it allows us to appreciate more fully the manifold and subtle ways in which he has worked the issues it raised into his intricately-designed work.

Revisionism also allows us to construct a somewhat different context for Fielding's Hanoverian Whiggism. In the old Namierite tradition, Fielding's statement in his "Charge to the Grand Jury," quoted at the beginning of this chapter ("to maintain the Crown on the Heads of that Family which now happily enjoys it") would be evidence for that school of thought's insistence on a broad ideological consensus underlying the partisan debates and divisions of daily political life. A radical (and, to be sure, controversial) revisionist like J. C. D. Clark also insists on an underlying consensus, but of a rather different kind.[37] For Clark, that shared belief is not the commitment to limited monarchy and growing enlightenment at the heart of the old Whig history; rather, it is the persistence of a deeply-rooted attachment to doctrines like a strong monarch and a powerful Church. We do not have to accept Clark's fundamental premise, that England remained what he calls an *ancien regime* state until the Reform Bill of 1832, to appreciate how his vision of the persistence of old ideologies enables us to see afresh Fielding's political sympathies, at least in *Tom Jones*. Brean Hammond, among others, has argued for the conservative nature of what he calls Fielding's "cultural politics"—"cultural" here as distinct from "partisan."[38] What Clark in particular has done is to make distinctions between the cultural and the political (in a partisan sense) more problematic and to show how quite conservative assumptions (about the monarchy, as well as about property and religion) were shared by both Hanoverians and Jacobites, both Whigs and Tories. It is that conservative consensus that lies beneath the apparent divisions of partisan debate. In that sense, it seems to me that Clark's work is very much in the spirit of Namier—there *was* a shared ideology. But the consensus that he describes is rather different than the one at the heart of the old Whig history, and indeed, the ideological charge that the label "Whig" now carries is something a bit different than it was in the older historiographical traditions. Fielding's recognition that the Stuart family romance had a powerful appeal (like his conflicted treatment of the gypsies' absolutist form of government, as we see in chapter 4) tends to confirm this revisionist perspective: with Fielding, we have a strong Whig partisan showing surprising sympathy for—or at least obviously compromised opposition to—ideas we would, on the basis of his purely partisan comments, expect him to despise. We do not have to turn Fielding into a Tory to appreciate that strain in his thought—and in the thought of many Whigs—which regarded traditional ideas, not as an old order to be viewed either with scorn or affectionate nostalgia, but as a persisting source of social and political belief.[39] The way in which Fielding has incorporated the Stuart romance into his own, and his method of conflating Jacobite and Hanoverian threads in the same narrative matter, suggest a powerful understanding that his nation and his historical moment cannot possibly be one simple thing, even though the partisan positions he expressed elsewhere required that such ambiguities—inherent in the very sediment of history, which inevitably layers past and present—be ignored or eliminated.

It is thus possible to see how the strands of political material I discuss in *Tom Jones* are consistent with and illustrative of some of the perspectives of these revisionist historians. But Fielding is not only interesting as an illustration of how certain beliefs were shared by a party or class, he is also a subjective intelligence of great power, and it is at least as important to think about the implications of these questions for Fielding the man. Anyone who has studied Fielding's biography, even so massive a sifting of all the available evidence as we see in the Battestins' biography, cannot help but be struck by how much we don't know. Fielding comes to us as a collection of plays, as a succession of pamphlets and journalism, as a name frequently and bitterly attacked in the papers, as the author of a several substantial fictions, as a magistrate presiding over a sordid world of London crime. But the inner man is almost completely missing. There is no journal, precious few letters (those mostly about money), a dearth of direct recollection. In that vacuum, biographers and critics alike have struggled to discover or hew out some image of the subjective space that Fielding occupied—an enterprise whose peril is obvious. One large problem with many of these heroic attempts is the assumption that the resulting image should be whole and consistent—Cross's "good" man, Battestin's crusading reformed rake, Cleary's happily committed Broad-Bottom Whig, and so on. But perhaps such an image of an organically unified self is the wrong model to bring to our study of Fielding. We know, and will probably always know, too little about the interior of Fielding's life, about what he thought inside himself when he watched the world of events both great and small unfold about him. We know instead a series of highly mediated, often contradictory texts, texts that span a bewildering variety of occasions, speeds of composition, genres, intentions. That is, of course, true of many writers, but it seems to be especially true in the case of Fielding. What we know for sure is that he wrote most often under the pressure of enormous financial exigency.[40]

Political writing often meant economic survival for Fielding and his family and it is at least plausible to suspect that this descendant of aristocrats and son of a spendthrift general should have felt some anger at finding himself in a world where he had quite often to make his way by exploiting partisan debate, by constructing out of political rancor the most ephemeral kinds of instruction and delight. One response (and I by no means argue that this was the only one) is just the kind of playfulness with opposition and division I have tried to describe in this chapter. When writing for himself—I am tempted to say, having hired himself, for Fielding made considerable money off *Tom Jones*—Fielding transforms the materials of his hackney drudgery into play.

Fielding had shown that kind of irony in a very self-conscious way earlier in his career. One of his last plays, *Eurydice Hiss'd*, was built on a doubling between himself and Robert Walpole, a parallel that Battestin calls "demeaning" to Fielding and that he is virtually helpless to explain (*A Life* 221). To me, the equation of playwright and prime minister (and a prime minister who would very soon put the playwright out of business with the Licensing Act) looks ahead to something like the equally odd brotherhood of Tom Jones and Bonnie Prince Charlie, or the peculiar mixture of Whig and Jacobite in the Man of the Hill—or as we see in chapter 4, the ironic kinship Fielding acknowledges with the age's brutal hanging judge, Francis Page. The novelist is certainly, in Empson's terms, showing understanding for each of two opposed positions. Analysis in strict partisan terms is mute in the face of such apparent anomalies, but they begin to make sense if we imagine a Fielding who may always have chafed at the demands of partisanship. Fielding's political doubleness in *Tom Jones* can thus be seen, at the very least, as a bit of revenge on the intellectual straightjacket offered him by his patrons in the political world. I think that there is more here than mere revenge, however, for I also believe that, whatever resentments Fielding may have felt, his art is most deeply concerned to try to understand the times in which he found himself in ways that his journalism and pamphlet work simply would not allow. And so, he imagined fictional worlds where he could transform the all too human demand for absolute choice in the face of oppositions into an elaborate imaginative structure where he could find his own position, truer to his own judgment, truer to his sense of history.

I do not argue here that, in *Tom Jones*, Fielding somehow escaped or eluded the political issues or pressures of his time in some final or absolute way. The very fact that he incorporated or appropriated or reflected those concerns in his novel is sufficient proof of the influence "the history of his own time" (to borrow Bishop Burnet's title) continued to exercise on him even at the highest reach of his artistic power. But what Fielding does with politics and history in *Tom Jones* is neither predictable nor simple, and any reader who enters the novel looking for the man who had to write so often in the service of some political master will miss much of the complexity—and entertainment—that the novel has stored. To return to the beginning of this chapter, it is impossible to know why the old and bitter Young Pretender liked Fielding's novel, but it is tempting to think he saw with more clarity than many of Fielding's readers the surprisingly broad-minded vision of history beating at the heart of *Tom Jones*.

Chapter 2
Savage Matters

Gossip at Prior Park

Charles Edward Stuart was not the only famous pretender of Fielding's time. There was also Richard Savage, and if Tom's story bears more than a passing resemblance to that of the Young Pretender, it also—with its illegitimacy, its class uncertainty, and its murderous relative—looks a lot like the life of this once well-known poet, conspicuous in the London literary scene until his death in 1743 as the self-proclaimed natural son of the Earl Rivers and as the author of works—their titles so resonant for readers of *Tom Jones*—such as "The Bastard" and "The Wanderer."[1] He is mostly remembered today as the subject of the first substantial biography written by that most notorious of Fielding's literary adversaries, Samuel Johnson. *The Life of Savage* appeared just at the time when Fielding was about to begin *Tom Jones*, and it is the argument of this chapter that Johnson's biography of Savage, or perhaps the details of Savage's life, like the image of Bonnie Prince Charlie, provided a likely source for Fielding's novel and its at times disreputable hero. That possible indebtedness of novelist to biographer, in turn, may illuminate an old question: why did Johnson hate Fielding so much?

Even so loyal an acolyte as James Boswell sensed that there was something peculiar in the intensity of Johnson's feelings toward Fielding, something a later age might call overdetermined, but which the pre-Freudian Boswell had to label "unaccountable": "I cannot refrain from repeating . . . my wonder at Johnson's excessive and unaccountable depreciation of one of the best writers that England has produced."[2] It was clearly still nagging him as he wrote his great biography near the end of the century, and he attempts a touching effort there to make it up between the two, years after both men were dead. He launches this frail bark, notably, by invoking *The Life of Savage*. In the first edition of the *Life of Johnson*, noting the generous praise showered on that earlier biography in *The Champion*, Boswell comments, "This paper is well known to have been written by the celebrated Henry Fielding. But, I suppose, Johnson was not informed of his being indebted to him for this civility; for if he had been apprized of that circumstance, as he was very sensible of praise, he probably would not have spoken with so little respect of Fielding."[3] Alas, even this kind attempt at posthumous diplomacy was futile: an early reader of the biography wrote Boswell letting him know that the review of *Savage* had been written by James Ralph, not Fielding, and subsequent editions corrected the error.

While Fielding may not literally have reviewed *The Life of Savage*, there can be no doubt that he knew Savage's life, and in this chapter, I again focus on the ways in which Fielding incorporates in his novel narrative possibilities inherent in the atmosphere of his time. Savage's life, especially perhaps as formulated by Johnson, had a shaping influence on Fielding's narrative. There is an additional layer here, however. I think that there is a strong possibility that Fielding was not only working with a story whose features he found narratively attractive, but one he found personally potent as well. No one has ever thought of *Tom Jones* as an autobiographical work, but from the time the novel appeared and Samuel Richardson huffily insisted that Fielding had "little or no invention,"[4] many readers have had the strong sense that the central energies of the work reflect the dominant concerns of the novelist's life.[5] The secondary question—Johnson's reaction to Fielding—may seem tangential, but if I am right in judging the sources of his anger, particularly about *Tom Jones*, his dismay provides a rich case study for how a contemporary reader responded to the novel, not just as a work of fiction, good or bad, but as a text that reimagines source material that others knew or had worked with themselves.

Since the life of Savage is the starting point of this argument, it is useful to summarize very briefly some of the salient features of that extraordinary existence. In 1715, a young man facing a magistrate on a charge of seditious writing (Jacobite, as it happened—pretenders tending to stick together) identified himself as Richard Savage, the illegitimate son of the late Earl Rivers; the Earl, whose name had been Richard Savage, died in 1712. Savage claimed this identity based on papers that he said he had found; these stated that he was the offspring of an adulterous relationship between Rivers and the former Countess Macclesfield, now remarried and named Anne Brett. Her first marriage had ended amidst wide public interest, by a 1698 Act of Parliament, the first parliamentary divorce since 1552.[6] Mrs. Brett stoutly denied the connection, stating that the two children she had borne Rivers were dead, and she never subsequently wavered in those denials. Savage, in turn, never modified his claim to high birth, but lacking the inheritance he believed should have been his, he entered upon a sporadically successful literary career as a poet and playwright. His life took a turn towards real disaster in 1727, when he killed a man in a tavern fight, was convicted of murder, and was saved from hanging only by a royal pardon. Savage lived always in a hand-to-mouth way, with periods of desperate poverty alternating with high living when a patron or friend (and there were many) supplied him with funds. He died in Bristol jail in 1743, imprisoned for debt.[7]

Fielding knew about Savage, of course, even if direct evidence is small. One "Richard Savage" is listed as a subscriber to Fielding's *Miscellanies* (1743), but it is impossible to know if this was the poet; it certainly would have been typical of his profligate nature, however, to subscribe to a book he probably could not afford. Fielding does directly refer to Savage in the 27 June 1752 number of the *Covent-Garden Journal*, where, in a facetious essay on the publishing trade, he tells a possibly apocryphal story about the way in which Savage's trial for murder improved the sales of his poetry.[8] Even without this reference, one can still be sure that Fielding knew about the sensational murder trial and its outcome since they coincided with his first entry into the world of London letters in 1727 and early 1728. The volumes of poetry that Savage published, however, are not listed in the catalog of Fielding's library, though most of the poems had initially appeared in the prominent London periodicals of the time.[9]

Other evidence is more conjectural but quite suggestive. In September 1742, for very different reasons, both Fielding and Savage found themselves in Bristol. The novelist was doubtless still enjoying the success of *Joseph Andrews*, published earlier that year, but he continued his work as a lawyer because of his perpetual financial necessity, and thus he was in Bristol, as he was each fall during this period of his life, riding the Western judicial circuit. Savage was there as well, having recently abandoned his more or less forced rustication in Wales; he had been sent there with a small annuity in 1739 by a group of friends who hoped that a removal from the temptations of London would be good for him and his work. He was on his way back to London, ostensibly to supervise the publication of his revised tragedy about Sir Thomas Overbury. There is no evidence that the writers met, but they must at least have heard of each other's presence in Bristol, a small town by London standards, with no extensive literary community. More tellingly, they both shared a patron who lived nearby, Ralph Allen.[10]

Allen was Fielding's new and generous friend, and the novelist visited and stayed with him at his estate at Prior Park during that month.

Moreover, Allen was also one of that group, led by Pope, who had put together the annuity for Savage, which was to support him in Wales. That same September, just at the time that he was hosting Fielding, Allen received a letter from Pope, with an enclosed letter for Savage, and careful instructions on its delivery: "Savage plagues me with his Misunderstandings & Miseries together . . . and I must send him an answer. You see it inclosed [sic], & I beg you to add and put into it an order for five guineas. . . . I must further desire you to inquire whether he be in any particular misfortune, or in Prison?"[11] It would be very likely that Allen shared gossip about Savage with Fielding, and the novelist might have been especially interested in news of a fellow writer as impecunious and financially unstable in his own way as he was, and who would soon (as Pope feared) be confined for debt to the Bristol jail.

The name "Jones" also provides a strikingly literal link between Savage and the novel. In 1741, while still in Wales, Savage met and courted an attractive widow whose heart, in the end, he did not win. But during his courtship he wrote her several love poems, and being Savage and in need of money, he saw to it that they were not for her eyes alone but were also published in *The Gentleman's Magazine*. Her name (which the published poems announce) was "Bridget Jones," a neat combination of the names of Tom Jones's real and assumed mothers. More tantalizingly—since it would be hard to know how Fielding might know this, except perhaps through Ralph Allen—the name of her deceased first husband was "Thomas Jones."[12]

The coincidence of names becomes most suggestive in the overall context of connections between the poet and the novelist. Savage and Fielding shared prominence on the London literary stage throughout the late 1720s and 1730s, and ultimately they did find themselves at the same moment in the provincial town of Bristol. While they came there for different reasons, they also had a patron in common, the kind of subterranean bond that serves as a reminder of how disparate lives can nonetheless be linked. Any or all of these connections make more probable what would have been likely in any event, that Fielding read Johnson's *Life of Savage* when it was published on February 11, 1744.

If Fielding knew, or knew of Savage, did he know Johnson? The Battestins have found evidence that the two men did meet one time. During Fielding's tenure on the magistrate's bench, while Johnson was still struggling to bring the long labor of his *Dictionary* to a close, the wife of one of Johnson's copyists was arrested for disturbing the peace and the great lexicographer appeared in Fielding's court to post her bond (*A Life* 504). This meeting has come to light only because of the

Battestins' indefatigable work in the legal records; neither writer mentions it in any surviving document. Nor is there any indication anywhere of Fielding's opinion of Johnson. What has endured is Johnson's opinion of Fielding, though the source of most of that knowledge is—not surprisingly—Boswell, either reporting comments he heard himself or remarks that were passed on to him by others. The number of such pronouncements is actually quite small, and of course date from long after Fielding's death in 1754, since Boswell did not meet and begin recording Johnson's opinions until 1763. Most of the famous jibes occur in just two conversations, one in the spring of 1768, the other four years later in April 1772 (II, 48–50, 173–5). Here is where Johnson calls Fielding a "blockhead" and a "barren rascal," as well as where he makes the memorable comparisons with Richardson, unfavorably contrasting what Johnson called Fielding's characters of manners to Richardson's characters of nature, or claiming that, as artists, Fielding was a man who could merely tell time while Richardson could tell how the watch was made.

What is most striking about Johnson's opinions regarding Fielding as Boswell reports them is not his well-known unilateral preference for Richardson, but the personal animosity that appears to motivate his comments.[13] "Blockhead" is not a term of dispassionate judgment. Nor was such animosity merely a peculiar feature of his conversation with Boswell, it also appears with equal vociferation in the anecdote Hannah More recounts in her *Memoirs* (1780): "I never saw Johnson really angry but once. I alluded . . . to some witty passage in *Tom Jones*; he replied, 'I am shocked to hear you quote from so vicious a book. . . . I scarcely know a more corrupt work' "(qtd., Boswell, II, 174 n. 2). It is important to note here that the animus seems directed toward *Tom Jones* alone. Johnson acknowledges that he never read *Joseph Andrews* (II, 174), and that he admired *Amelia*, which he claimed to have read through without stopping (III, 43). Boswell insists that these beliefs represent "an unreasonable prejudice against Fielding" (II, 49), but he offers no explanation for their origin. He nowhere mentions the more measured dissection of Fielding's art offered by Johnson many years before, in *Rambler # 4* (31 March 1750). This essay does not actually mention Fielding or *Tom Jones* by name. By general assent, however, Fielding is understood to be the target of Johnson's insistence that characters in what he calls the "modern form of romance" must be not only morally good, but unambiguously so.[14]

To summarize, Fielding certainly knew of Savage, and probably knew a good bit about the life of someone who was a prominent and scandalous figure in the world of English letters from the time the budding writer arrived in London until Savage's death in 1743. There are striking parallels between elements of this life, turned into a memorable narrative in Johnson's *Life of Savage*, and the plot of *Tom Jones*—bastardy and concealed birth, a vicious relative, and a hero imprisoned for murder. Johnson, in turn, had a deep dislike of Fielding and his greatest novel, a dislike that first emerges in *Rambler # 4*, published about a year after *Tom Jones*. To this point, I merely asserted a similarity between what we might call the "matter" of Savage and *Tom Jones*, but what does that mean for the novel? why might Fielding have been attracted to this material and what did he do with it?

The Discovery of his Real Mother

Fielding, I think, was attracted to Savage for reasons far beyond the intriguing fact that they shared a patron and possibly crossed paths near the end of Savage's life. Looking at the poet, either in Johnson's version or from the viewpoint of what he had heard over a fifteen-year period, Fielding must have been struck by a number of parallels to his own life. I think he then filtered these parts of his experience through Savage, creating a layered composite named Tom Jones, who—here, as elsewhere—mingles the autobiographical, the historical, and the fictional. Tom thus is a character who provides a mirror in whose complex image both Fielding and Savage are visible. In turn, and just as importantly, that connection between Fielding and Savage opens a new and illuminating perspective on the genesis and significance of the character, Tom Jones.

Both Fielding and Savage looked at themselves as natural aristocrats fallen into financial difficulty. In Fielding's case, the perception was quite true: he was related to the Earls of Denbigh and Desmond. Unfortunately, his father, Edmund Fielding—a military man who ultimately reached the rank of Lieutenant General—was the younger son of a younger son, and he was a person who was in no way nor at any time responsible with what money he did have.[15] When the twenty-year old aspiring writer first met his cousin, Lady Mary Wortley Montagu, he told her that he would be forced to make his living "as a Hackney Writer or a Hackney Coachman."[16] Fielding's wit here is characteristic, as is his honesty. He had no illusions about his financial prospects, though he doubtless harbored bitterness over his father's improvidence and the very real consequences of that irresponsibility for himself. The very first words of *Tom Jones* take on a certain self-directed irony in this light: "An author ought to consider himself, not as a Gentleman . . ." (31).

With Savage, it is important to distinguish between who he really was (which may never be finally established) and who he said he was, the natural son of the Earl Rivers. He never shrank from this illegitimacy; rather, he proclaimed it because it was the source of his invincible conviction that his blood was noble. But having been (he thought) cheated out of the inheritance that the Earl would have provided, he, too, was forced to live by his pen.[17] As Johnson dryly puts it, "[Savage] was therefore obliged to seek some other Means of Support and, having no Profession, became, by Necessity, an Author."[18] The irony here parallels Fielding's comment to Lady Mary, and both statements serve as reminders that authorship—rather like the time-honored paths of the army and the church—had now become an option for gentlemen without funds. Doubtless Tom Jones himself would have become a writer if the true facts of his parentage had not fortuitously been uncovered. But if writing in the Eighteenth century had become a "Profession," it was only rarely financially sufficient, and both men consistently were forced to cultivate what turned out to be substantial talents for inveigling money out of many of the people who crossed their paths. The fact that, in Ralph Allen, the two writers shared a patron only underlines their kinship in the always economically shaky world of eighteenth-century letters.[19] Neither Savage nor Fielding was always able to cover his obligations, and both, in fact, were arrested for debt. Indeed, when Fielding heard of Savage's death in Bristol jail, he might have thought, not only of his own time in a sponging house, but of his improvident father, who had died just two years before, confined by his debts to the Rules of the Fleet Prison.[20]

Maternity was a fraught issue for both men. Johnson's *Life of Savage* uncritically recounts Savage's conviction—probably both sincere and inaccurate—that Anne Brett was his mother, and that she not only abandoned him, but was the artful Fury who saw to it that he was first denied a £6,000 inheritance from Earl Rivers, and who later almost managed to thwart a royal pardon after he was convicted of murder. Her implacable rejection of someone who insisted that he was her son and who persisted in seeking her love, is probably the most indelible image that a reader takes from Johnson's biography. Fielding himself was a partial orphan, having lost his mother days before his eleventh birthday. His father quickly remarried, and Fielding's relations with his stepmother (that is, his *first* step-mother, since his father would be widowed and remarried several more times) appear to have been very bad, including a nasty custody battle between Fielding's father and the novelist's maternal grandparents who thought the new mother unfit.[21]

Thus, with the issues of birth, maternity, and the lifelong struggle for money, there are, if not duplication, then elements in the narrative of Savage's life that would strike a resonant chord for Fielding: the young man supremely confident of his birth, forced to make a difficult financial way by his talent for literature; a child in search of maternal love denied or lost. Richardson, in the comment alluded to earlier (meant as a nasty crack, of course), said that Fielding's heroes were versions of himself, and the statement is worth fuller quotation: "Tom Jones is Fielding himself, hardened in some places, softened in others.... His brawls, his jarrs, his gaols, his spunging houses, are all drawn from what he has seen and known. As I said . . . he has little or no invention" (197). Richardson, as so often, is indulging in self-justification here: he is the novelist of the brothel who had somewhat defensively to insist to an interlocutor that he "never, to my Knowledge, was in a vile House, or in Company with a lewd Woman, in my Life" (233). Invention, as he calls it, was his stock in trade. Less self-interested critics, however, may find it both understandable and instructive to believe that Fielding was attracted to narrative material close to his own experience, and that he might well find inspiration in what he could see as a slightly askew version of himself. If Fielding used Savage to reimagine himself, a new answer then follows to another of Richardson's complaints about his rival: "What Reason ha[d] he to make his Tom illegitimate . . . ?" (127). Fielding made Tom illegitimate because in the dark mirror of Savage's life, he found a way to tap his experience while also transforming it. How, then, does Fielding's knowledge of Savage, and his recognition of some kinship with the poet, translate into the plot of *Tom Jones*? How does he make a new story out of these existing materials?

Again, there is much we do not know. Fielding kept no journals where he might have charted his progress on the book, nor is there any correspondence discussing the novel's composition. Such writing was not remunerative and Fielding wrote little for which he was not paid. The manuscript of *Tom Jones* was destroyed in the Gordon Riots, and as I discussed in chapter 1, there is an open question about when he began writing the book.[22] The novel must have been started after the publication of *Joseph Andrews* in 1742, and almost certainly also after the appearance of the *Miscellanies* the following year. Savage's death, then, and the subsequent appearance of Johnson's *Life* occur at just the moment when Fielding was mulling a second project in that new species of writing that he thought he had invented. Beyond this, the evidence for influence will have to be internal to the two texts.

In one of the rare critical comments that connects the *Life of Savage* to Fielding, Frank Brady says that the *Life* "reads like a tragic version of *Tom Jones*."[23] He thus points to the similarity, but does little more than note the connection, and rather oddly assigns narrative priority to Fielding. Savage's life, he says, looks like Fielding's work made into tragedy, when in fact, of course, it would have to be the other way round, given that Savage was dead and his biography written by the time Fielding began his novel. But Brady does point to the profound generic gulf between the works, and if Savage or Johnson's *Life of Savage* was a source or inspiration for Fielding, it would be because the novelist saw a way to turn the matter of Savage into comedy. That in itself is rather strange and surprising. For the most prominent parallels between Savage's life and the story of *Tom Jones* are not very promising comic material, consisting as they do of illegitimate birth, maternal abandonment, murder, and the threat of the gallows, not to mention the ugly presence of the notorious hanging judge, Francis Page. Yet that generic transformation—tragedy into comedy—is crucial, both for understanding what Fielding wanted to do, and what it was about *Tom Jones* that might have provoked Johnson so much. Johnson insisted on seeing Savage's life as a kind of Greek tragedy, and told his story as such. But if Fielding, as I think, was engaged in an imaginative act of self-recreation, he could hardly wish such a fate for himself, and so he took the elements in Savage's life that he found personally powerful and transformed them into comedy, though comedy that often bears traces of its darker origin.

Early in the *Life*, Johnson summarizes the quick succession of blows that Fortune delivered to the infant Savage in his unmistakably dense and vigorous way: "Such was the Beginning of the Life of *Richard Savage*: Born with a legal Claim to Honor and to Riches, he was in two Months illegitimated by the Parliament, and disowned by his Mother, doomed to Poverty and Obscurity, and launched upon the Ocean of Life, only that he might be swallowed by its Quicksands, or dashed upon its Rocks" (6). By "illegitimated" here, Johnson does not mean that Savage's bastardy was a parliamentary fiction; rather that, because he was supposedly born to the Countess Macclesfield while she was still married to her first husband, he would legally be considered the son of her husband, even if he actually was the offspring of the affair between the Countess and Rivers. Whatever the truth of Savage's birth and parentage (and the most recent study of the question is persuasive that however dubious the poet's full claims, they are not definitively dismissable[24]), the first facts of the narrative of Savage's life as Johnson presents it are these: his parentage is noble but illegitimate, he is disowned by his mother, and he subsequently loses to death both a benevolent godmother and a nurse who treats him as her own son. In *Tom Jones*, the hero begins life in a similar way: he also is the illegitimate but well-born offspring of an adulterous liaison. Moreover, he, too, is denied by his mother, and denied in a way, as with Savage, that serves to create a multiple maternal abandonment: Bridget bribes Jenny Jones into accepting responsibility for the child, but Jenny is then immediately sent away. Tom is thus abandoned by both his real and putative mothers. The difference between his lot and Savage's, of course, is that Bridget's actual plan for Tom is not a false or foster mother, but adoption by her rich bachelor brother.

Savage was never shy about proclaiming his equivocal birth: his lament/celebration of his condition, "The Bastard," was one of his best known works, and his frequent and very public pleas for recognition from Anne Brett invariably also served to remind the world of his status. It is much the same with Tom Jones. As I mentioned in chapter 1, there could easily have been some further ruse in the plot to render Tom legitimate in the end, but there is not, and throughout the novel, Fielding employs the label frequently, as if he wants to underline his hero's status, with no attempt to hide or soften his stigma of illegitimacy. While Tom is an infant, Captain Blifil smugly proclaims "the Legality of punishing the Crime of the Parent on the Bastard" (79). Young Blifil will later echo his father, flinging in Tom's face the reminder that he is "a Beggarly Bastard" (130). Nor does Tom escape when he takes to the road; a landlord at an inn says of him, "for all his laced Waistcoat there, he is no more a Gentleman than myself; but a poor Parish Bastard bred up at a great Squire's about 30 Miles off" (365).[25]

Fielding seems slyly to play with the parallel of Bridget and Anne Brett. In a passage that begins as a discussion of Bridget's hatred of her late husband, the narrator considers her feelings toward her two sons, Blifil and Tom: since "she absolutely hated [Captain Blifil], . . . [i]t will not be greatly wondered at, if she had not the most violent Regard to the Offspring she had by him. And, in fact, she had so little of this Regard, that in his Infancy she seldom saw her Son, or took any Notice of him; and hence she acquiesced, after a little Reluctance, in all the Favours which Mr. *Allworthy* showered on the Foundling" (139). She has, in a sense, abandoned both sons here, but her passivity works to show her distaste for her legitimate child and to work in favor of her bastard. Those motives, of course, remain opaque, both to those around her and to the novel's readers. Thwackum and Square, for instance, cannot conceive that she does not actually hate the interloper: "she was imagined to hate the Foundling in her Heart; nay, the more Civility she showed him, the more they conceived she detested him, and the surer Schemes she was laying for his Ruin" (139). Fielding then partially clarifies what her housemates remain blind to: "she certainly hated her own Son; of which, however monstrous it appears, I am assured she is not a singular Instance" (139). Hatred for the offspring, hatching plots for his ruin—the language here closely parallels that of Johnson in his portrait of Anne Brett, but Fielding embeds such material in a complexly ironic discussion of two sons, one overtly acknowledged but covertly detested, the other denied but secretly favored. It is as if Brett's relationship to Savage, with its disavowals and secrets, its hatred and cruelty, has been divided between these two boys. The sad concession about maternal hatred—"however monstrous . . . I am assured is not a singular Instance"—could be a direct allusion to Savage's story, with the authoritative "assurance" coming from Johnson himself.

Johnson's condensed catalog of maternal monstrosity is worth recalling:

> The Punishment which our Laws inflict upon those Parents who murder their Infants, is well known, nor has its Justice ever been contested; but if they deserve Death who destroy a Child in its Birth, what Pains can be severe enough for her who forebears to destroy him only to inflict sharper Miseries upon him; who prolongs his Life only to make it miserable; and who exposes him without Care and without Pity, to the Malice of Oppression, the Caprices of Chance, and the Temptations of Poverty; who rejoices to see him overwhelmed with Calamities; and when his own Industry, or the Charity of others, has enabled him for a short Time to rise above his Miseries, plunges him again into his former Distress? (20)

Such an implacable spirit of persecution does not describe the rather passive Bridget, but it does fit another of Tom's relations, Blifil, quite nicely. Fielding has turned a monstrous mother into an equally monstrous brother, for Blifil resembles Mrs. Brett even more than Bridget does. If Tom's mother is not secretly laying schemes for the hero's ruin, his half-brother certainly is, and his schemes exactly parallel those that Johnson claims were hatched by the woman Savage thought to be his mother.

Beyond denying her maternity, Brett tried to hurt Savage in three primary ways: by preventing an inheritance from the Earl Rivers, by seeing to it that he was transported to the colonies, and by conniving to thwart his pardon after his trial and conviction, which is to say, to see to it that Savage died on the gallows. Blifil precisely duplicates these measures: he hides his knowledge that Tom is his brother, he manages to deny Tom the money promised him when Allworthy seems to be dying and sees to it that he is exiled from Paradise Hall, and finally he attempts to suborn witnesses so that Tom's duel with Fitzpatrick can be prosecuted as a murder. Both the poet and the fictional character face the gallows, and the legal peril that both face is intensified by the manipulations of their close kin.

The idea of legal peril leads, finally, to Francis Page, one of the age's longest serving and most notorious judges (and a figure I return to in detail in chapter 4). Notorious, in fact, for brutality.[26] In presiding over Savage's trial, Page acted, Johnson says, "with his usual Insolence and Severity" (34) and Savage himself lampooned the judge (though only after he was safely dead) in a satiric poem that Johnson quotes at length in the *Life* (41n.). Fielding knew of Page from his time on the Western circuit, and the judge might have made his cameo appearance in *Tom Jones* without any prompting from Savage's life. Nonetheless, in light of the other parallels, it is significant to see Fielding dragging Page onto the stage of his novel just a few years after his memorable appearance in the biography of Savage, and appearing in much the same light. Both Johnson and Fielding seem intent on showing how a harsh criminal code can fuel the brutal arrogance of a man like Page. In Johnson's account, he refuses to let Savage speak after sarcastically commenting on his dress, and in Page's appearance in the novel, he jokes in a similarly sarcastic manner at the prisoner's expense, and then refuses to let the accused's counsel speak, "though he desired only to be heard one very short Word" (459). Sarcasm and tyrannical silencing are the hallmarks of his portrait in both narratives.

These parallels could be elaborated at much greater length, but I believe my point is clear: a reader, picking up *Tom Jones* in the winter of 1749, might find him or herself thinking, haven't I read something like this recently? Such a reader might be thinking of the Young Pretender, but she could also have in mind this other great pretender of the age. Of course any reader then or now would recognize that the works are fundamentally different: Johnson's narrative works from its very beginning as a reminder that Savage really was, in the biographer's image of destruction, dashed upon the rocks of life, while Tom, a lucky bastard if ever there was one, is vindicated and wins the girl and the estate. But both the parallels and the overarching generic difference are interconnected and meaningful. The similarities between *The Life of Savage* and *Tom Jones* help clarify two central themes in the novel, maternity and legitimacy. Moreover, the startling difference in what Johnson and Fielding make of those parallel materials provides a key to understanding Johnson's reaction to *Tom Jones*.

Johnson's *Life of Savage* is almost unimaginable without the demonically star performance provided by Anne Brett; her abandonment of her child and her merciless pursuit of his destruction provide the tragic undercurrent for the whole biography, even after Savage has gone on to misadventures—utterly irresponsible extravagance, tavern brawling, offensive behavior to his friends—which can only be seen as self-inflicted wounds.[27] Fielding's own maternal traumas—losing his mother as a child and then the protracted bitter struggle between his father and stepmother and his mother's mother over custody—guarantee that this story would rivet his imagination. As he then reworks these materials for the plot of *Tom Jones*, he creates a most singular image of maternity, at once emptied out and eroticized. Tom, like Savage, is multiply mothered and yet not mothered at all: Bridget gives him life, but Jenny Jones takes credit—or blame—for his existence, and as Fielding recounts his upbringing there is almost no sense of a mother's presence, except for the equivocal and passive presence of the one person left in the house who knows who he really is. As he reaches maturity, however, Fielding recounts that the neighborhood gossip links Bridget and Tom romantically: "at last she so evidently demonstrated her Affection to [Tom] to be so much stronger than what she bore her own Son, that it was impossible to mistake her any longer; . . . and what is worse, the whole Country began to talk . . . of her Inclination to *Tom*" (139–40). This, of course, foreshadows his sexual involvements with Mrs. Waters and Lady Bellaston, both much his senior, and that culminating moment of the counter-plot of the novel (the plot that holds out the possibility of a tragic conclusion) where Tom, in prison and *de profundis*, thinks he has literally slept with his mother: " 'O good Heavens! Incest—with a Mother! To what am I reserved?' " (916).

All these relationships, with their mingling of the maternal and the sexual, point both to the mother's absence and to the way in which such an absence ensures the eruption of the maternal in other relationships, even where it most especially does not belong. But that recalls Savage, who (like Tom) thinks he has discovered the secret of his birth as an adult and whose pursuit of the love of the woman he believes is his mother reveals a devotion in which the filial and the erotic are not easily separated: "*Savage* was . . . so touched with the Discovery of his real Mother, that it was his frequent Practice to walk in the dark Evenings for several Hours before her Door, in Hopes of seeing her as she might come by Accident to the Window or cross her Apartment with a Candle in her Hand" (12). There is an uncomfortable reminder here, not so much of a forlorn son as of Romeo as a stalker—what light through yonder window breaks indeed—and one wonders just what it was that Savage wanted. In *The Life of Savage*, Johnson almost completely effaces Savage's sexuality, and he presents a scene such as this one as a straightforward instance of pathetic filial longing. Fielding, however, has seized upon the complexity of the relationship, and he highlights, in Tom's various amorous entanglements, the particular mingling of maternal and erotic energies more evident, it seems, to the attentive reader of *The Life of Savage* than they were to its author.

At the end of the novel, Tom bears the name of neither his adoptive father nor his real mother, but of the woman who claimed to have borne him, and with whom, much later and when she bears the amniotic name of Waters, he goes to bed. Fielding underscores this by naming him one last time in the very last words of the book: "... when Mr. *Jones* was married to his Sophia" (982). The missing patronymic—and in a nation so devoted to the patrilineal idea as Britain was—is certainly bizarre. As one of the innkeepers on the road puts it, "Why doth not he go by the Name of his Father?" (417).[28] This emphasis on the maternal is consistent, however, with the spirit of the *Life of Savage*, where, as Toni Bowers notes, "Johnson thus dispenses in a single sentence with the issue of Savage's *paternity* and concentrates instead on the greater difficulty (and primary importance) of his *maternity*."[29] The persistence of the name *Jones* points both to the absence of the real mother and to the need for someone in the maternal role, even a notional or fictional mother, present only, as it were, in name. This particular representation of maternity—one that is neither fully present nor finally effaced, one that threatens constantly to slip into something more purely erotic—may be the largest debt that *Tom Jones* owes to *The Life of Savage*, and it is instructive to recall that the fantasy of recuperation that is the end of the novel includes the discovery of the mother's identity but no recovery of her presence. Whatever else he gains, and he gains a great deal, Tom remains a misnamed and motherless orphan.

Tom Jones is also indebted to the matter of Savage in its treatment of what is perhaps the most important issue in the novel, legitimacy. In both the narrative that Savage claims for himself (the one picked up by Johnson), and in the tale that Fielding imagines for his hero, the son is a bastard, and must find his way despite that stigma. But there is something ironic about their illegitimacy: while both Savage's and Tom Jones's social status is legally *filius nullius*, the son of no one, that dispossession is, in fact, the source of what hopes they have. Savage may be a natural son but he is also, he is convinced, naturally an aristocrat, a role he claimed and played his entire adult life. If he hadn't been a bastard, he would have been a real nobody, and perhaps it was Fielding's insight to understand, in a way that Johnson's insistence on the tragic nature of the poet's life made invisible, that illegitimacy was the secret of Savage's success, which (however bad his end) was not inconsiderable. He was a man whom Robert Walpole at one point called "a Friend," and a poet to whom the Queen herself regularly gave money as her "Volunteer Laureate." Similarly, Tom remains a bastard. As I note in chapter 1, a convenient secret marriage could have been unveiled amidst the rest of the good news that cascades through the last pages of the novel, but Fielding refuses to alter Tom's status, and his hero at the end is what he was at the outset, illegitimate, only in a position now, because of the particular facts of his birth, to inherit and to marry. It is not difficult to see Tom's fulfillment as, again, a refracted version of Fielding's own hopes. He was no bastard, but one can only wonder how he registered the ambiguities of his birthright, with its tantalizing proximity to a social position that was neither quite within reach nor wholly out of sight. Fielding, Savage, Tom Jones—all three, in a sense, have to legitimize themselves, and particularly in the case of the two writers, the line between self-creation and artistic expression looks very faint.

Men Splendidly Wicked

What about the mystery invoked at the beginning of this chapter, Johnson's virulent reaction to Fielding and to *Tom Jones*? The earliest document in the feud is *Rambler # 4*, which appeared later in that same month when Johnson made his appearance in Fielding's courtroom. Johnson begins his essay by defining the new literary form that is now known as the novel but which he calls "the comedy of romance" as a "kind of writing . . . [whose] province is to bring about natural events by easy means, and to keep up curiosity without the help of wonder" (19). He then goes on to outline who is qualified to write this kind of work (also the subject of Fielding's introductory chapter to Book IX of *Tom Jones*): "The task of our present writers . . . requires, together with that learning which is to be gained from books, that experience which can never be attained by solitary diligence, but must arise from general converse, and accurate observation of the living world. . . . They are engaged in portraits of which every one knows the original, and can detect any deviation from exactness of resemblance" (20). The essay then takes a turn from this rather Aristotelian beginning, with its definitions and commitment to mimesis, to a more Platonic perspective: "But the fear of not being approved as just copiers of human manners, is not the most important concern that an author of this sort ought to have before him" (20–1). That admonitory "ought" stands out here and Johnson quickly proposes what these authors should have in mind: "These books are written chiefly to the young, the ignorant, and the idle, to whom they serve as lectures of conduct, and introductions into life" (21). His gaze then sharpens on the young: "That the highest degree of reverence should be paid to youth, and that nothing indecent should be suffered to approach their eyes or ears, are precepts extorted by sense and virtue" (21).

The "indecency" he fears turns out to be not so much verisimilar representation as a certain kind of mimetic character, and here is the crux of his argument where Fielding and *Tom Jones* are concerned:

> Many writers, for the sake of following nature, so mingle good and bad qualities in their principal personages, that they are both equally conspicuous; and as we accompany them through their adventures with delight, and are led by degrees to interest ourselves in their favour, we lose the abhorrence of their faults, because they do not hinder our pleasure, or, perhaps, regard with them some kindness for being united with so much merit. (23)

Such mixed characters are Johnson's real subject in this essay, and in the concluding paragraphs he abandons his allegiance to verisimilitude for arguments about the moral urgency of presenting youthful readers with characters who are unambiguously evil or good: "In narratives, where historical veracity has no place, I cannot discover why there should not be exhibited the most perfect idea of virtue. . . . Vice, for vice is necessary to be shewn, should always disgust; nor should the graces of gaiety, or the dignity of courage, be so united with it so as to reconcile it to the mind" (24).[30]

Through long critical assent, Fielding has been designated as the unnamed target of this essay. The Battestins speculate that there might have been something about Johnson's encounter with Fielding in his courtroom earlier that March that produced Johnson's hatred ("Could it be, however, that this brief encounter between these two proud men contributed to the forming of Johnson's famous opinion of Fielding . . . ?"—504). Certainly, the fact that *Tom Jones* had appeared just over a year before—the same February, in fact, that Johnson's tragedy *Irene* had its disappointing run on the London stage—has contributed to the identification of Fielding as the target, as has perhaps his explicit defense of mixed characters in the novel in words that almost seem like a preemptive strike against Johnson: "we must admonish thee . . . not to condemn a Character as a bad one, because it is not a perfectly good one. If thou dost delight in these Models of Perfection, there are Books enow written to gratify thy taste" (526). One has to wonder, however, if the ease with which later readers have identified Johnson's remarks as directed at Fielding is not in part the product of a retrospective reading of the essay, one colored by a knowledge of what he would go on to say about Fielding and Richardson years later. A reader who knew the work of these two novelists, but not Johnson's later diatribes, might well be confused about the target of this *Rambler*. After all, *Clarissa* appeared only very shortly before *Tom Jones*, and its villainous hero, Lovelace, was described by Richardson's friend Lady Bradshaigh as "so wicked and yet so agreeable"[31] Johnson himself would later say of Clarissa: "you may observe there is always something which she prefers to truth"[32] As McKeon has shrewdly remarked of the two rivals, "often enough the two men seem to be praised and blamed for the same thing."[33] Yet, the identification of Fielding as Johnson's subject in the essay is irresistible precisely because, in the light of what Boswell says, it seems like Johnson's real opinion of the man, sanitized and made properly intellectual for the public sphere in which his periodical appeared.

Moreover, the very contradictions in the argument suggest, like his later remarks to Boswell, some emotional struggle about Fielding.[34] From this perspective, it is worth recalling another comment of Boswell's in the *Life of Johnson* (the modern editors significantly cite it as a footnote to the beginning of the discussion of Savage): "Dr. Johnson . . . was willing to take men as they are, imperfect and with a mixture of good and bad qualities" (III: 282, I:161n. 2). To be sure, "men" are not the same as fictional characters, and Johnson had said in *Rambler* #4 that he was speaking of "narratives in which historical veracity has no place." Still, it is worth considering the possibility that the mixed character of Tom Jones might call to Johnson's mind the mixture of talents and flaws that coexisted in his good friend and his biographical subject, Richard Savage, for the portrait in that *Life* is nothing if not the picture of man in whom good and bad qualities are equally conspicuous. That mixture also animates what Johnson in the *Life* insists would have been Savage's greatness, had he (in Johnson's dry phrase) "afterwards applied to Dramatic Poetry": "he had treasured in his Mind . . . the innumerable Mixtures of Vice and Virtue, which distinguish one Character from another" (45). In fact, when Johnson turns to the subject of biography in *Rambler* # 60, later that same year, he will take as his epigraph some lines from Horace that suggest, in fact, the necessity and the moral usefulness of such mixed portraits in the biographer's art: "Whose works the beautiful and base contain;/ Of vice and virtue more instructive rules,/ Than all the sober sages of the schools."[35]

But what if Johnson's reasons were substantive and not merely rationalizations? Such an argument would say simply that he sincerely thought that Fielding's aesthetic principles were morally dangerous, and that the apparent contradiction between his celebration of mixed portraits in biography and his refusal to accept them in novels is based on a difference he perceived between the audiences for these genres. Russell Hunt has made a strong case for the moral argument, pointing out that Fielding's embrace of the doctrine of "good nature," which is the quality in Tom that ultimately overbalances his sins, was at the root of Johnson's dismissal of Fielding, and that this was a critical and intellectual judgment, consistent with Johnson's repeated commitment to reason over emotion as the only sure haven in a perilous world.[36] In this regard, it is notable that Boswell's own defense of Fielding against Johnson's strictures is grounded in emotional terms: "the moral tendency of Fielding's writings, though it does not encourage a strained and rarely possible virtue, is ever favourable to honour and honesty, and cherishes the benevolent and generous affections" (II: 49)—a not surprising point, perhaps, from someone whose own moral record is closer to that of Tom Jones than of Sir Charles Grandison.

What is finally unsatisfactory about allowing the question to rest on purely intellectual grounds is the way such a position sets aside as a distraction or irrelevance the point that bothered Boswell so much: the vehemence of Johnson's dislike. That vehemence, moreover, becomes even odder in the light of Johnson's praise of mixed characters in other venues—such a mixture is what he hoped biography would show, people in all their lights.[37] There seem to be, on Johnson's own terms, ample grounds to praise Fielding, not damn him. When Boswell defends the novelist by saying that Fielding's morality "does not encourage a strained and rarely possible virtue," he echoes Johnson's demand that biography should not present pictures of perfection; bad biography for him was what he called in *Rambler* # 60 "uniform panegyric," based on "an act of piety to hide ... faults and failings" (185). The generic issue—novels versus history/biography—also seems misleading. Johnson knew that the novels of Richardson and Fielding were being read by many who were neither young, nor ignorant, nor idle, including his own conspicuous self, and the fact, noted above, that the aesthetic principles articulated in *Rambler # 4* could as easily be turned on Richardson as on Fielding must give pause. If an educated and serious audience existed for novels—and by the middle of the Eighteenth century, it manifestly did exist—why should it not benefit from the same morally bracing realism Johnson praises in honest biography?

Suppose, then, that there was a personal element in Johnson's reaction to *Tom Jones*, one grounded in some way in his recognition of Fielding's appropriation and transformation of the matter of Savage? If Johnson recognized in the novel the same parallels I have tried to point out here, and I think he did, his reaction would have two primary determinants: his personal relationship with Savage, and his own literary rendering of Savage's life. That distinction is necessary, because *The Life of Savage* is important both as a remarkable piece of writing and as an unconsciously revealing document about the emotional life of its author.

Boswell was not only mystified by Johnson's opinion of Fielding, he also found it hard to comprehend his friendship with Savage. He calls Savage, "a man, of whom it is difficult to speak impartially, without wondering that he was for some time the intimate companion of Johnson; for his character was marked by profligacy, insolence, and ingratitude" (I, 161). Savage was Johnson's "intimate companion" for several years after the latter's first appearance in London, years when the men were sometimes both "in such extreme indigence, that they could not pay for a lodging; so that they have wandered together whole nights in the streets" (I, 163). Johnson's biography of Savage generally conceals this friendship and this shared history, but there is one moment when the screen of the historian falls and the interested witness is revealed. Describing Savage's departure for Wales and alluding to the poet's plans for a productive retirement, Johnson says, "Full of these salutary Resolutions, he left *London* in *July* 1739, having taken Leave with great Tenderness of his Friends, and parted from the Author of this Narrative with Tears in his Eyes" (114). Johnson's third-person reference manages to keep the moment from being fully revealing: whose eyes were filled with tears? Most biographers make Savage the lachrymose one, but Richard Holmes' study of the friendship makes a strong case that the ambiguity may be "the author's" way of hiding the depth of his feelings. If the tears were not Johnson's, why, Holmes argues, would he make the marginal comment, "I had then a slight fever," beside the passage when he corrected the second edition in 1748?[38] Whoever was crying, the emotion of the two men is undeniable, and it is Johnson's devotion to this particular real and very mixed character that Boswell finds a matter of "wonder."

At one point in *Rambler* # 4, Johnson's discussion of mixed characters takes a peculiar turn. He insists that there are certain men whose portraits should never be drawn: "There have been men indeed splendidly wicked, whose endowments threw a brightness on their crimes, and whom scarce any villainy made perfectly detestable, because they could never be wholly divested of their excellencies; but such have been in all ages the great corrupters of the world, and their resemblance ought no more to be preserved, than the art of murdering without pain" (23). Even though the context for this remark is the discussion of the mixed hero in the new comedies of romance, Johnson here seems to forget the generic issue as he alludes directly to history—"there have been indeed," "in all ages." The appeal to history is a troubled one, implying that some biographies should not be undertaken, in flat contradiction to the catholic defense of unvarnished biography which he will mount six months later in *Rambler* # 60. In attacking *Tom Jones*, is Johnson also revealing his own unresolved feelings about the *Life* he wrote not long before? Savage could easily be seen as splendidly wicked, combining on the one hand poetic talent, charismatic charm, and wide knowledge with, on the other, extraordinary venom, irresponsibility, and the impulsive capacity actually to kill a man—and one cannot help but notice that Johnson's remarks here move to murder as the ultimate crime. The peculiarity and self-contradictions of this paragraph at least allow and perhaps encourage the speculation that Johnson may have felt some guilt for immortalizing that mixed character and friend of his youth, Richard Savage—or perhaps the guilt was not for the book but for the friendship itself. Johnson's attack on mixed characters might be connected to his own mixed emotions where Savage was concerned, and the demand that the modern romance eliminate ambiguity could be an attempt to efface such ambiguity from his own inner life.

Johnson's inability to come to terms, either morally or emotionally, with Savage is nowhere clearer than in the concluding paragraphs of his biography, where as most readers notice, Johnson offers two summaries, one that seems like a judgment, and one that seems closer to the pole of sympathy.[39] Sympathy comes first, and in perhaps more rhetorically potent form: "Those are no proper Judges of [Savage's] Conduct who have slumber'd away their Time on the Down of Plenty, nor will a wise Man easily presume to say, 'Had I been in *Savage's* condition, I should have lived, or written, better than *Savage*' " (140). Apparently, this was the original conclusion for, in another marginal comment Johnson made in a copy of the work, he noted that the printed last paragraph was "Added":[40]

> This Relation will not be wholly without its Use, if those, who languish under any Part of his Sufferings, shall be enabled to fortify their Patience by reflecting that they feel only those Afflictions from which the Abilities of *Savage* did not exempt him; or if those, who in Confidence of superior Capacities or Attainments disregard the common Maxims of Life, shall be reminded that nothing will supply the Want of Prudence, and that Negligence and Irregularity long continued will make Knowledge useless, Wit ridiculous, and Genius contemptible. (140)

Which is it? Does Savage's *Life* teach the unexceptionable lesson of prudence, or does it conclude that any such judgment is merely a reminder of privilege, resting on its down of plenty?

Whatever he might have said elsewhere about the usefulness of biography, Johnson obviously is deeply unsure at the end of his first substantial piece of life writing about what use a reader might make of the *Life of Savage*. What he does seem certain about is that Savage's was a life of suffering, as he had made clear at the very beginning of the work, where he describes his subject as "a Man whose Writings entitle him to an eminent Rank in the Classes of Learning, and whose Misfortunes claim a Degree of Compassion, not always due to the unhappy, as they were often the Consequences of the Crimes of others, rather than his own" (4).

Was this what was unforgivable in *Tom Jones*, that it raised the spectre of suffering in many of the guises endured by Savage, and then sweeps them away as if they were only ultimately illusory obstacles to the hero's final happiness? Perhaps. As if anticipating the way in which the matter of Savage lent itself to fictional appropriation, Johnson had himself said, in the advertisement and prospectus for his *Life* that he published in *The Gentleman's Magazine* soon after Savage's death:

> It may be reasonably imagined, that others may have the same design, but as it is not credible that they can obtain the same materials, it must be expected they will supply from invention the want of Intelligence; and that under the title of "The Life of Savage," they will publish only a novel filled with romantick adventures, and imaginary amours. You may therefore, perhaps, gratify the lovers of truth and wit, by giving me leave to inform them . . . that my account will be published in 8vo, by Mr. Roberts, in Warwick Lane. (Boswell, I, 165)[41]

In *Rambler # 4*, Johnson had said of novelists: "They are engaged in portraits of which everyone knows the original, and can detect any deviation from exactness of resemblance." The advertisement, then, suggests Johnson's fear of rival uses of the "materials" of Savage's life, and when he writes *Rambler* # 4 seven years later, as if comparing Fielding's narrative to his own, he insists that "deviations" from a well-known "original" are much on his mind. The problems of deviation also turn up in *The Life of Savage* itself. Speaking of Savage's choice of the Thomas Overbury story for his dramatic magnum opus, Johnson remarks that it is "a Story well adapted to the Stage, though perhaps not far enough removed from the present Age, to admit properly the Fictions necessary to complete the Plan; for the Mind which naturally loves Truth is always most offended with the Violation of those Truths of which we are most certain, and we of course conceive those Facts most certain which approach nearest our own Time" (21). Johnson thought he knew the "Truths" about Savage, and that may explain why he found *Tom Jones*, as a reimagining of that material, so very offensive.

Amorous Inclinations

There may be another issue for Johnson, however, in an area of human experience where *Tom Jones* represents not a "deviation" from the original nor a "Violation of those Truths," but an uncomfortable likeness to Savage, one suggested by Johnson's obviously nervous reference in his self-advertisement to "imaginary amours." There was something sexual lurking about Savage, a louche quality that also affects the friendship. The Johnson who appears in Boswell's *Life* is an almost completely asexual subject. Along with other more recent scholarship, Richard Holmes' study of Johnson and Savage's friendship has attempted to bring the subject of sex back into the discussion of Johnson's life. As Holmes says, "Just as it is difficult to imagine Johnson young, so it seems impossible to imagine Johnson in love. Thanks largely to Boswell, the very phrase sounds faintly ludicrous. But Boswell . . . could never really bear to envisage his sage in . . . lust or passion" (20).[42]

Johnson's *Life of Savage* is as chaste as Boswell's *Life of Johnson*. But the repressed leaks backs in to the narrative in places, as in the image of Savage pacing in front of his supposed mother's window. Equally telling is Johnson's attempt to defend his friend against suggestions that there was any moral impropriety in his relationship with the actress and courtesan, Mrs. Oldfield. Savage claimed that she gave him an annuity of fifty pounds for some time, and Johnson was anxious that this not be interpreted as payment to a gigolo: "That this Act of Generosity may receive its due Praise, and that the good Actions of Mrs. *Oldfield* may not be sullied by her general Character, it is proper to mention what Mr. *Savage* often declared in the strongest Terms, that he never saw her alone, or in any other Place than behind the Scenes" (19). Johnson emphasizes Mrs. Oldfield's own mixed character, with his insistence that her "good actions . . . not be sullied by her general character." Even more to the point, Johnson uncharacteristically demonstrates a tin ear here, failing to note the erotic innuendo implicit in what are announced as back-stage meetings. He had himself reportedly told Garrick, "I'll come no more behind your scenes, David; for the silk stockings and white bosoms of your actresses excite my amorous propensities" (I, 201).[43] Backstage, in the Eighteenth century, seems to have been an especially eroticized piece of geography. The sum Savage receives, fifty pounds, recurs in his *Life* in an almost totemic way. It is the amount given him, not only by Mrs. Oldfield, but also by the Queen as his annuity for serving as "volunteer laureate," and it is also what Anne Brett gives him the one time he is able to extract some money from her. Fifty pounds, that is, synechdotally suggests that mingling of the maternal and the erotic discussed above: it is what an older woman in an ambiguous relation to Savage finds herself able to give. If one imagines Fielding as an attentive reader of all this, certain details stand out. There is, for instance, money given a young man by an older woman, this time explicitly for sexual services; the sum that Lady Bellaston gives her gigolo, Tom Jones, is also "fifty Pounds" (718).[44] Moreover, when Tom hides his aristocratic lover from Mrs. Honour, he places her "behind the Curtain" (747). Such concealments and sexual intrigues, to be sure, are a staple of farce, but that is my point. Johnson's obtuseness about the suggestiveness of his description of the poet and his actress patron indicates strongly some blindness or discomfort when the subject was Savage and sex. And again, the juxtaposition of *The Life of Savage* with *Tom Jones* indicates how Fielding might have seized upon the sexual content of Savage's narrative that Johnson tried to suppress.

Sex, it turns out, was one of the things that specifically bothered Boswell about Johnson's friendship with Savage, and two of the rare sexual notes in all his long biography are struck when the subject of Savage comes up. In describing the friendship early in the *Life*, he conducts a rather porous defense against the imputation that his night-walks with Savage had corrupted Johnson:

> I am afraid, however, that by associating with Savage, who was habituated to the dissipation and licentiousness of the Town, Johnson, though his good principles remained steady, did not entirely preserve that

conduct, for which, in days of greater simplicity, he was remarked by his friend Mr. Hector; but was imperceptibly led into some indulgences which occasioned much distress to his virtuous mind. (I, 164)

The passage is replete with hesitation and uncertainty. Johnson's good principles remained steady, but he was left with a guilty conscience about some "indulgences" in his "conduct." The details of what that bad behavior might be are left tantalizingly unspecified, and one can only wonder how much of Johnson's guilt was produced by his own conduct and how much was the fruit of association, a vicarious taint from close contact with someone who was not averse to tasting London's innumerable opportunities for "licentiousness and dissipation." Recall Johnson's own words in *Rambler* # 4 about splendidly wicked men: "such have been in all ages the great corrupters of the world."

At the end of his biography, Boswell is slightly—but only slightly—more forthcoming as he struggles to explain Johnson's guilt and fear of death:

> His great fear of death, and . . . the uneasiness which he expressed on account of offences with which he charged himself, may give occasions to injurious suspicions. . . . On that account, therefore, . . . I am to mention, (with all possible respect and delicacy, however,) that his conduct, after he came to London, and had associated with Savage and others, was not so strictly virtuous, in one respect, as when he was a younger man. It is well known that his amorous inclinations were uncommonly strong and impetuous. He owned to many of his friends, that he used to take women of the town to taverns, and hear them relate their history.—In short, it must not be concealed, that, like many other good and pious men, . . . Johnson was not free from propensities which were "ever warring against the law of his mind,"—and that in his combats with them, he was sometimes overcome. (IV, 395–6)

This is surely one of the most remarkable passages in *The Life of Johnson*. The passive voice ("I am to mention"), the tangled syntax, the abrupt breaks and shifts (—"In short"), all point to the extraordinary nature of the assertion here, an assertion for which Boswell offers not one shred of evidence, except for Johnson's propensity to listen to whores' stories (apparently a matter of no particular shame since he uses such a narrative himself in the *Rambler*) and his unaccountable association with Savage. Likely, there is projection here, given Boswell's own notorious amorous inclinations, but that does not alter his inability to disentangle the issues of Johnson's guilt, Johnson's sexuality, and Johnson's friendship with Savage. It should be no wonder, then, that

Johnson's relationship to the "materials" of Savage's life was so complex and so emotional.

Nor should it be a wonder that Johnson reacted so strongly to a "novel," crafted in part out of similar "materials," but with, as it were, the sex put back in. For Tom is a mixed character for no other reason than his sexual behavior; he is portrayed as a young man whose amorous inclinations are uncommonly strong, and who—in his lapses with Molly, and with Mrs. Waters, and with Lady Bellaston—shows himself time and again "overcome" in his struggle to remain faithful to Sophia. Yet it is precisely this aspect of Tom's character that Johnson objects to— both in the measured tones of the *Rambler*, and in the more heated terms Boswell or Hannah More recount. Tom is not a mixed character because he betrays a friend or takes a bribe; his sins are those of the flesh. On some very deep and personal level, perhaps, Johnson may have felt exposed by Fielding, and exposed in his most secret and vulnerable place. Again, what that sense of exposure was is a matter that lies beyond definitive conclusion. There is only Boswell's uncomfortable insistence that, where Savage was concerned, Johnson felt some sexual guilt. What does register clearly is the vehement anger of his response to Fielding, and the fact that such a response was called up by a fictional character whose sins were sexual. It would not be easy for any reader to see subjects he was anxious to repress and forget turned into the materials of comedy, and joyful comedy at that.

Johnson's need to repress his disquieting memories of Savage, moreover, might have been especially intense in 1749 and 1750. For if Johnson did visit prostitutes while wandering about London with Savage, or perhaps only was strongly tempted to do so, those "actions" in violation of his "principles" (to use Boswell's distinction) would have been not merely abstractly immoral, they would have represented a specific betrayal of his wife, Elizabeth Porter. She was twenty years older than Johnson and a widow when they married in 1735, and the marriage, though Johnson later insisted on its deep mutual affection, seems to have been difficult: her grown sons refused to speak to her because of her remarriage, Johnson lost most of the dowry she brought when the school he started failed (more money given to a young lover by an older woman), and much of their time together was marked by intense financial struggle. After Johnson came to London, they were often apart. She did not like the city, and took suburban lodgings, while work kept him (or gave him an excuse for staying) mostly in town. It was during this time that Johnson met Savage, and fell under the spell of his tarnished glamor, and it was then, Boswell insists, that his "conduct . . . was not so strictly virtuous." Whenever Johnson read *Tom Jones*, in 1749 or 1750, his wife was already a near invalid, and she died in 1752.[45] In material not included in the *Life*, Boswell found evidence that for some time before her death, she had refused sexual relations with Johnson, using her illness as an excuse. He records a report from a friend of the Johnsons: "They did not sleep together for many years. But that was her fault. She drank shockingly, and said she was not well and could not bear a bedfellow."[46] Whether the Johnson's literally had a sexless marriage or not is beside the point: the larger truth lies in the picture of a union with manifold difficulties. More to the point for this discussion, the nature of Johnson's marriage adds yet one more layer of personal history to think about when imagining his frame of mind in responding to *Tom Jones*. If his sexual guilt involved not only Savage but his wife as well, and a wife now at the end of her life, it would indeed be difficult for him to read a novel in which there is not only abundant sexual activity, but also substantial attention to sexual—and financial— relationships between Tom and much older women. In other words, that mingling of the maternal and the erotic so crucial to the central energies of *Tom Jones* may have been precisely the issue that Johnson was most intent on forgetting.

Finally, the character named Tom Jones might not have been the only problem. Fielding's reputation among his contemporaries was that of a man with an irregular sexual history himself. Although he married for love a woman to whom he was faithful, he still had enjoyed considerable other company in youth.[47] The way that personal image, and the image of Tom Jones, the rollicking but reformable rake, might have merged is exemplified in a remark made by Dr. Burney (the novelist's father), which Boswell—desperate to the last to explain Johnson's feelings about Fielding—added as a note to the third edition of the *Life*:

> Dr. Johnson's severity against Fielding did not arise from any viciousness in his style, but from his loose life, and the profligacy of almost all his male characters. Who would venture to read one of his novels aloud to modest women? His novels are *male* amusements, and very amusing they certainly are. Fielding's conversation was coarse, and so tinctured with the rank weeds of the *Garden*, that it would now be thought fit only for a brothel. (II, 495)

Was Johnson's sexual guilt—and compensatory anger—evoked by *Tom Jones*, by Henry Fielding, or by some stereoscopic image, wherein both converged in Johnson's mind? That he was angry, and that his response was rooted in what Fielding represented (in both senses, as a man and as an artist) about sex is all I assert with any confidence. When we add the figure of Savage, however, and explore the ways in which Savage is bound up with Johnson's probable sexual guilt and frustration, then a clearer path opens to an understanding of why his reaction to *Tom Jones* seems so deeply personal. Boswell was mystified both by Johnson's affection for Savage, and by his hatred for Fielding; perhaps what he did not consider was the possibility that Johnson had an "unaccountable" hatred of Fielding specifically *because* of his equally unaccountable affection for Savage.

Others with the Same Design

There is one more issue to take into account and that is the matter of narrative or literary authority. Savage, in his own day, was a poet of considerable repute and he had the authority of that work, but more importantly, for those under his spell, he had the power of his story, especially the story of his abandonment and persecution. This was a tale that Savage himself seems to have sincerely believed, however improbable it may appear. It was also, and this is the important point, one that Johnson believed, believed in strongly enough to retell in his biography with no cautionary note, and which he left intact when he republished the life he had written as a young man many years later in *The Lives of the Poets*. Johnson represents himself, in his own work as well as in Boswell, as a mind cleared of cant, yet he appears to have accepted Savage's tale uncritically and with what looks like naive faith.[48] If he had reservations, he kept them well-buried. When Boswell speaks of the younger Johnson, walking London's night streets with Savage, as being "imperceptibly led into some indulgences which occasioned much distress to his virtuous mind," he believes that he is talking about sex, and may well be pointing to actual sexual misconduct of some kind. But the phrase also suggests the power that Savage exerted over Johnson, a power that included the authority of his story, of his self-representation as a victim at once heroic and tragic.

But not everyone, even in Savage's admittedly unstable circle, believed that story. Anne Brett was only the most conspicuous of the skeptics in Savage's lifetime, and Boswell, who took the trouble to check birth records, was a notable voice against the veracity of this story at century's end. More important here, perhaps, is the fact that these alternative versions of the life of Savage make their way into Johnson's *Life* of the poet. He may not believe Anne Brett himself, but no reader of the biography can escape the knowledge that her "life of Savage" would have had a very different shape. Other versions exist as well. There is Judge Page's address to the jury, a portrait of the defendant in strong and ironic counterpoint to Johnson's insistence on Savage's marginality: "Gentlemen of the Jury, you are to consider, that Mr. *Savage* is a very great Man, a much greater Man than you or I, Gentlemen of the Jury; that he wears very fine Clothes, much finer than you or I, Gentlemen of the Jury; that he has abundance of Money in his Pocket. . . . " (34) and so on. Note, too, this description of the fate of Savage's story after his break with Lord Tyrconnell, "It cannot but be imagined, that such Representations of his Faults [by Tyrconnell and his friends] must make great Numbers less sensible of his Distress; many who had only an Opportunity to hear one Part, made no Scruple to propagate the Account which they received; many assisted their Circulation from Malice or Revenge. . . . " (68–9). Such promiscuous and uncontrolled circulation of the poet's story suggests something crucial about the matter of Savage: that its proliferation in various guises and with various meanings was somehow inherent, that even more than other lives, it was material to be retold and reshaped in myriad ways.

Fielding in his reimagining of the matter of Savage, seems instinctively to understand the narrative freedom implied by the instability apparent in even so insistently authoritative an account as Johnson's. Certainly, he pretends no obedience to the authority of Johnson, as he cheerfully resculpts tragic business into comic bounty. He has made the material his own, in part, as I argue, because in many ways the material literally *is* his own—his maternal woes, his class uncertainty, his financial difficulties. The effect is that of a palimpsest: the bastard's triumph written over the earlier tale of the bastard swallowed by the quicksands of life. Johnson, one can readily imagine, could not abide with patience such overwriting when the one being overwritten was himself. His original acquiescence to Savage's narrative had become, by and in the act of writing the biography, his own authority. The tale of woe told by Richard Savage to anybody who would listen had become *The Life of Savage*, by Samuel Johnson. Fielding's appropriation and revision of material on which Johnson had thus placed his seal of judgment would represent a challenge, and Johnson's response to any challenge was always thunder. Sex was certainly one reason why Johnson hated *Tom Jones*, but the way in which it represented a rejection of his narrative authority might be another.

The concatenation of the real and the fictional is an exceedingly complex one when considering the triangle formed by Richard Savage, Samuel Johnson, and Henry Fielding. There is Savage's life and *The Life of Savage*; there is Henry Fielding and his idealized self-projection, Tom Jones; there is Samuel Johnson the biographer and Samuel Johnson, the subject of what is still the most memorable biography ever written. There is life writing thought to be truth, a novel proclaimed as a "History," and the lives these three men actually lived. They knew, or knew about, each other, and they knew each other's work. To bring together both the facts about these lives as we know (and do not know) them and the narratives made out of those facts serves again as a reminder of how very slippery are the distinctions between categories like "biography," "novel," and "history"—especially perhaps in the eighteenth century when all these modes were emerging in their modern forms.[49] Out of all these narratives, Fielding created *Tom Jones*, a work of fiction whose connections to the real, to actual people and events in the Eighteenth century, are persistent and pervasive. In turn, in this chapter, I attempt to construct another narrative, a tribute in part to the way that stories, in whatever generic guise they arrive, always beget more stories.

Chapter 3
Black Acts

The Movement of Property

I have been to this point largely concerned with issues of legitimacy, especially in matters of inheritance. But questions of legitimacy are inseparable from issues of property, for what is being inherited is not merely a title or a name, but very tangible material possessions: a kingdom, an estate, cash. That recollection is important for the next stage of this study, which concerns what at first seems to be a very different subject, theft.[1] But theft is not only armed robbery or breaking and entering, and conflicts over property—be the property in question a throne or wealth in some less grandiose form—can quickly seem controlled by the legal and emotional context evoked by more direct and violent encounters. As we have seen, Fielding's narrator refers to the Jacobite invaders of England as "banditti"; Anne Brett's resistance to the filial overtures of Richard Savage were very likely rooted in the well-founded fear that his desire for love would soon turn into an insistent demand for money. At stake in both inheritance and robbery is the movement of property. Legitimacy is a most ambiguous matter in *Tom Jones*, and much the same is true about stealing; property in this novel tends to move in ambiguous ways, and is insistently shadowed by the possibility of theft. A prime example of this phenomenon, and the most troubling property transaction in the novel, is Black George's decision to pocket the substantial sum that Allworthy granted Tom at the time he exiled him from Paradise Hall. It is far from simple robbery.

The Advice of Counsel

In the flood of reversals and recognitions that marks the closing chapters of *Tom Jones*, one act of restoration can easily be lost sight of. Given that Tom, in a matter of hours, goes from prison and the prospect of the gallows to a triumphant place as Allworthy's heir and Sophia's husband, the recovery of the £500 in banknotes he lost on the day he was banished from Paradise Hall seems like a small matter, no more than a precise balancing of the books in this most symmetrical of novels. But among the few brush-strokes that Fielding employs to conclude this business, there is one odd comment—odd, at least, for anyone with a knowledge of eighteenth-century criminal law. Allworthy, having discovered the money and identified Black George as the culprit, asks Lawyer Dowling what legal recourse he has. The question is a tricky one, and Dowling is cautious. George did not, after all, directly steal the money; he found it on the ground and kept it. The lawyer answers that George "might be indicted on the Black Act; but said, as it was a Matter of some Nicety, it would be proper to go to Counsel" (922). A few chapters later, he reports that no criminal charges are possible; the banknotes could, however, be recovered as lost property by an action of "trover": that is, "a remedy to recover the value of personal chattels wrongfully converted by another to his own use" (947).[2]

Why does Fielding bring up the Black Act? It was probably the most notorious of all statutes in the infamous Bloody Code of eighteenth-century English jurisprudence, but, as Dowling is forced to admit, it has no legal relevance to George's action. But Fielding's gamekeeper and the Black Act do share a common world, a world of the game laws, of the hunt, of a changing and sometimes embattled English countryside. Considered together, they provide a new perspective on Fielding's thinking about questions of class and the law, on the peculiar inconsistencies and striking liminality of George's character, and on the way Fielding may be commenting on aspects of his own ill-defined social status. Above all, Black George makes us think again about the ambiguities surrounding what constitutes both theft and legitimacy in Georgian Britain. To see this, we need a rather thick description of the character of the gamekeeper. He is apparently a quite minor character in a very long novel, and it is easy to miss the complex variety of associations that Fielding puts in play around him.[3]

Poachers and Keepers

George Seagrim is first introduced to us, neither by his name nor by his nickname, but by his occupation, "the gamekeeper." What sort of work did an eighteenth-century gamekeeper actually do?[4] That question is not only practical but legal, and to understand the law regulating the work of gamekeepers, we must go back to 1671 and the Game Law of that year. That legislation significantly modified the ancient Norman legal principle that all the game in England was owned by the king and that the hunt was therefore the particular privilege of the monarch, a privilege he could in turn grant to others as moved by his generosity and prerogative. The law of 1671 removed hunting from the monarch's mostly symbolic control and made it the privilege of all gentleman whose freehold property was valued at £100 or more a year (or whose leasehold totaled £150). The Game Law seems thus to have enshrined the value of private property; in a curious way, however, it also compromised it, both because those landowners, and they were numerous, who did not meet this standard could not hunt, even on their own property, and because anyone who *did* meet the qualification could freely enter another's land if his purpose was sport.[5] All game belonged to all gentlemen. The £100 freehold did not, as one might expect, mark off a gentleman's property as a kind of playing field within which hunting might be privately pursued; rather, that magic threshold of ownership passed, one entered a sportsman's paradise where, theoretically, all land and all game were open and available. This law—modified in its details, but essentially intact—survived until 1831.

As one historian of these laws has put it, " 'the king's game' had become 'the gentry's game.' "[6] But in taking possession of that right, gentlemen also took up the monarch's traditional responsibility as well, that of preserving the game. The job of gamekeeper was not an invention of the 1671 law, but in its wake, the rights and duties—and limitations—of the profession were carefully described and circumscribed by further legislation in the decades that followed. Thus, initially, gamekeepers were themselves forbidden to hunt, except in the very rare event that they met the property qualification in their own right. Later, they were allowed to take game on their master's property; this led, in turn, to the practice among some qualified gentlemen of appointing their non-qualified friends as gamekeepers. To counter this ruse, Parliament decided that only one gamekeeper be allowed on each estate, and that, moreover, that gamekeeper had to be a servant of the lord of the manor.[7]

These legal details have their own interest, but they are much more important symbolically than as anything that actually governed social practice. The fact is, where hunting was concerned, England was a nation of scofflaws. Just as there had been an ineradicable Saxon distaste for the Norman idea of a royal hunting prerogative (a distaste still strong some 650 years after the Conquest, as Pope's "Windsor Forest" makes quite clear[8]), so, in the face of the new game laws, there persisted a widespread belief that the ancient rights and liberties of the English included the right to hunt, whether for sport or for food. In the countryside, that meant poaching, even among the prosperous middling classes who might normally have united with the larger landowners in defense of property; in the city, where a taste for game was more a matter of the palate than the field, it meant a thriving trade in illegal meat (since an act of 1707 banned the sale of game[9]). These conflicts between the law and social practice raise fundamental questions: is poaching theft? Is the purchase of poached game the receipt of stolen goods? We think of theft as a violation of exclusive property rights; what does it mean to take something—a rabbit, a game fowl—from a whole *class* of people? What is really at stake here?

Gamekeepers were the often-reluctant foot soldiers in this war between the aspiration to exclusive privilege of those with landed wealth and the stubborn denial of those aspirations by almost everyone else. Their reluctance probably reflected the fact that, both practically and symbolically, they had a foot in both camps. The remarkable liminality of their position must be emphasized, for they had real authority, not only over those below them in status, but also over those above. For instance, they were delegated to confiscate the guns and other "engines" (including dogs) of the poachers they caught, and to use force if their authority was resisted. Such power to at least humiliate and possibly harm or kill meant one thing when the poacher was a poor man, quite another when he was a small landowner. Indeed, the "impertinence" of keepers was a common complaint among the latter.[10] But their ambiguous status went even further. The gamekeepers enjoyed the right to take game for their masters, meaning that, unlike many of their social betters, they could hunt quite legally. They thus enjoyed emblematic as well as tangible rights denied to many rural men, through a wide range of status. Yet, the gamekeepers—because of poverty or because they were tempted by the profits—themselves often engaged in those very practices it was their job to prevent. They enforced laws against poaching, but they also broke them, and they were obliged to harass those who must have looked at times like their doubles, men who poached for food or for cash in exchange for contraband meat.[11] As Charles Kingsley put it in 1862, "a keeper is only a poacher turned outside in, and a poacher a keeper turned inside out."[12] They represent, that is, a kind of paradox of legitimacy, embodying rights granted them by law, but often unable fully to sustain that position by reason of social practice or sheer necessity. Over time, then, they took up positions both inside that great legal edifice that said that the pursuit of game was the pleasure and pastime of the great, and also in the shadow world below and behind that structure—a world where, whatever the law said, most rural men hunted, hunted because they needed to or because they believed that it was their right.

 The novel itself pays little attention to the day-to-day details of Black George's labor—though we can interpret the fact that his fellow-servants "universally dislike" (133) him to be a small commentary on the unpopularity faced even by a quasi-constable in a community where the law is resented or flouted. What Fielding puts in much sharper focus is George's poaching. He is first introduced as a man "thought not to entertain . . . [strict] Notions concerning the difference between *meum* and *tuum*" (119)—significantly, in mock-legal language that suggests, not theft *per se*, but something less easily definable. Over the next thirty pages, we see two specific instances of George's apparently undeveloped sense of property. Later, at the very time in fact that Tom loses his £500, we learn a bit more about the gamekeeper's dealings in illegal game. This evidence rewards careful attention.

 In the first instance, at Tom's urging but against Allworthy's strict command not to trespass, George and Tom wander a few hundred yards onto Western's estate in pursuit of some partridges they had raised on the land of Paradise Hall. George shoots one bird, hides in the bushes, and Tom—for the first, but not the last time—is nabbed *in flagrante delicto*. Western reports the crime to his neighbor with his characteristic heat and demands satisfaction. Tom, serving as the gamekeeper's screenmaster, earns a beating from Thwackum for concealing evidence since everyone suspects that he has an accomplice. Though he never confesses, the truth ultimately comes out thanks to Blifil, and Tom, as a consequence of his loyalty, rises in Allworthy's estimation, while George is fired, less for disobeying the initial command than for allowing Tom to suffer a beating on his behalf. In the second instance, George is convicted of "wir[ing] Hares" (148) on the evidence of a "Higler" who, caught with illegal meat, saves his own skin by "becoming Evidence against some Poacher" (147). Fielding makes it clear that there was only one hare and that George killed it to feed his family. Finally, much later, after Tom has finally engineered a change in George's fortunes and obtained for him a gamekeeper's position with Western, we discover that George is now a thriving poacher. While the keeper is hypocritically helping Tom look for the £500 safely hidden in his own pocket, Fielding mentions two things. One, that George was in the vicinity "in order to lay Wires for Hares, with which he was to supply a Poulterer at Bath the next Morning"; and two, that "he had, by selling Game, amassed a pretty good Sum of Money in Mr. *Western's* service" (314)—service that has lasted something over a year at that point. In other words, the same man who was once a helpless victim of the game laws, now seems to be turning their prohibitions to his own profitable advantage.

In Black George, Fielding presents us with a complex dialectic of mitigating and aggravating circumstances, a kind of dance in which he never quite allows us legal rest, as we see if we look to the game laws to specify just which crimes he has committed. First of all, we need to note that Tom himself has no legal right to hunt—though it was common, if not strictly legal, for any squire to allow whom he pleased to hunt on his own property.[13] George, for his part, can take game only on Allworthy's estate. By invading Western's land and shooting a bird there, they violate both the game laws and the laws of trespass.[14] The normal penalty for such non-aggravated poaching was a £5 fine or three months' imprisonment. £5 was the typical annual wage of a gamekeeper,[15] and that fact—along with his reasonable fear of the wrath of Allworthy—may help explain George's willingness to let Tom cover for him. Fielding further mitigates George's behavior, both for hiding behind Tom and for killing the bird in the first place, by emphasizing that the birds had been raised on Allworthy's estate and by the narrator's insistence that the young man had "over-persuaded" him (120).

A similar air of mitigation surrounds what we know of George's second game law violation: "The Gamekeeper, about a Year after he was dismissed from Mr. *Allworthy's* Service . . . being in want of Bread, either to fill his own Mouth, or those of his Family, as he passed through a Field belonging to Mr. *Western*, espied a Hare sitting in her Form. This Hare he had basely and barbarously knocked on the Head, against the Laws of the Land, and no less against the Laws of Sportsmen" (147). George has certainly again broken the game laws—jobless wretch that he is, he cannot kill a hare on Western's property or on anyone else's for that matter, including, if he had any, his own. The description of George's prosecution would seem to be an apparently unambiguous instance of Fielding's direct critique of the oppressive nature of these laws: "by this Means [that is, testifying against the gamekeeper] the [Higler] had an Opportunity of screening his better Customers: For the Squire [Western], being charmed with the Power of punishing *Black George*, whom a single Transgression was sufficient to ruin, made no further Enquiry" (148). A poor man is not merely punished but ruined, and a Squire who is "charmed"—Fielding puts the knife in pretty deep—with his own arbitrary power to effect this ruin makes no proper investigation to see if others are involved. The load of oppression heaped on George's back as we read these two incidents is great: he loses his job for one partridge and he is prosecuted for a single hare. He is victimized by Western's zealous prosecution, by Allworthy's "inflexible Severity" (133), and by a legal system that ignores his famished necessity and rewards the self-interested testimony of a greater criminal than himself.

Throughout these chapters, which first introduce us to Tom, to Blifil, to Western, and to (in Empson's great phrase) the lethal hatreds of Paradise Hall,[16] Fielding seems simultaneously and unambiguously to create sympathy for George and contempt for those forces which conspire to injure him. The gamekeeper is hungry and powerless and the law crushes him like a fly. The satiric targets throughout this section of *Tom Jones* are not George but his enemies: Western, whose fervor in defense of the game is revealed as a mere hypocritical excuse for his own bloodthirst (see, esp., 120); Allworthy, a good man we are repeatedly told, but clearly also a blind and dogmatic justice of the peace; and the game laws themselves, founded not so much on the possessions as the presumptions of the propertied, and targeted at the weak.

Nonetheless, Fielding proceeds to cut the ground from beneath the moral and legal certitudes he has apparently so firmly established. For when George returns to the novel in the sixth book after an absence of over a hundred pages, no longer hungry and no longer unemployed, master of a large sum of money and a confirmed poacher for profit, he appears as the traitor to friendship who—practiced close observer of the ground that he must be—spots and keeps Tom's £500. The effect is to cast a retrospective pall over our early sympathy for him, as the victim of the concerted folly and cruelty of his masters is revealed as someone who richly deserved everything he got.

The Names and Faces of Servants

George's other names, like his occupation, mark him as ambiguous, and we learn those early in our reading of the novel. Blifil first speaks the name that will prove to be the most commonly used, "Black George," at the very moment that he betrays the secret of the gamekeeper's role in the partridge hunt (131). A bit later, we learn his full name, George Seagrim (174). "Seagrim," however, is the least used and least interesting of George's three names,[17] and it is not in any event the name we most readily associate with this character. He is most often "the Game-keeper" or "George" or "Black George," mostly the latter. Tom, at least while in Somerset, is a bit different from everyone else in that he never calls his friend "Black George," preferring to call him by his Christian name or by his occupation, but the other characters, and the narrator himself, do not hesitate to call him by the compound. But at this point in the novel neither the narrator nor the characters give us any indication how or why George is "Black."

There are a number of oddities here, one being that he is called by his first name at all. The other servants and quasi-servants in the novel—Mrs. Wilkins, Honour, Partridge—are called by their last names. The peculiarity of Fielding's decision to emphasize his gamekeeper's Christian name is compounded when we recall the particular name that he has chosen. "George" should strike us as a very odd name indeed for Fielding, so vocal a supporter of the Hanoverian establishment in his journalism, to bestow upon even a minor villain. (Indeed, he doubles the gesture, and at the other end of the social register: the only other "George" in the novel is Sir George Gresham, the profligate Oxford classmate who corrupts the Man of the Hill.) George I had ascended the throne in 1714, and his son, George II inherited it thirteen years later; he would rule until 1760. So, at the time of the publication of *Tom Jones* in 1749, one George or another had occupied the throne of Great Britain for 35 years (and indeed, two more would keep George as the king's name until 1830). Thus, it is at the very least curious that the monarch's name should appear in Fielding's novel almost exclusively connected to a character we associate with poverty, victimization, greed, and the betrayal of friendship (and the brief appearance of George Gresham connects the name to yet another false friend).[18] The link between Black George and the monarch is made even firmer when we remember that "George" was an extremely rare name until the Eighteenth century. Despite the status of St. George as the nation's patron saint, "George" did not become a common name until the Act of Settlement (1701) placed the royal succession in the House of Hanover.[19] Thus, most real Georges in the mid-eighteenth century were probably named for the king.

But we are hardly done with the oddities of the gamekeeper's naming. Why "*Black* George?"[20] There are almost no nicknames in *Tom Jones*, perhaps as noted in chapter 1, because Fielding has given so many characters allegorical or descriptive names, many of which sound like nicknames already.[21] If nicknames imply a desire to be more affectionate or more singular in the specification of identity than the normal and mostly generic range of given names allows, what nickname could improve on "Thwackum"? Black George's name, then, is unique in the world of this novel, being a nickname that appears to have arisen (for reasons that remain unknown a long time) from the community of which he is part. But if Fielding leaves us to wonder through most of *Tom Jones* exactly why George is called "Black," he finally does satisfy our curiosity. Toward the end of the novel, Partridge, long absent from the Somerset world of the narrative's beginning, runs into George in the streets of London. He tells Tom, "I knew him presently, though I have not seen him these several Years; but you know, Sir, he is a very remarkable Man, or to use a Purer Phrase, he hath a most remarkable Beard, the largest and blackest I ever saw" (829). On the next page, speaking of the fine livery that George wears in Western's service, Partridge reiterates this new (to us) information: "if it was not for his black Beard, you would hardly know him" (830). Like other nicknames, then—"Lefty" or "Red"—the specification here is metonymic: George is in some way uniquely recognizable by one physical trait remarkable enough to seem inseparable from who he is: a big, black beard.[22] Yet his name is not merely this physical trait: he is not "Blackbeard," but "Black George."

The apparently innocuous fact that George is bearded should, in fact, give us pause, for, in the eighteenth century, in England, it was remarkable when anyone at all was bearded. The simple fact is, as near as historians can recover it, that throughout the century, almost without exception (sailors and Jews were often bearded) every man in the kingdom shaved. As one scholar of these matters has put it, "After the end of the seventeenth century, for a hundred and fifty years, faces were to remain smooth."[23] The question arises, naturally enough, whether such matters of fashion had anything to do with the laboring or serving classes to which George belongs. Lacking a photographic record, we have to turn to other visual sources. If we look at the work of Hogarth or Rowlandson, both of whom frequently took subjects from the lower classes, the faces they depict are almost universally clean-shaven. Even a sequence like *The Rake's Progress* or *The Harlot's Progress*, crowded as they are with the dregs of eighteenth-century society, shows no beards. Plate eight of the former, for example, the well-known image of Bedlam, shows even the madmen, who might reasonably be expected to ignore fashionable norms of hygiene, perfectly smooth-faced.[24] Now, certainly artistic representations may be idealized or made to conform to conventions of appearance, and we should not necessarily conclude, based on the evidence of Hogarth, that the keepers at Bedlam roused their charges each morning with basins of hot water and straight razors at the ready. But that is the point. Whatever the reality—irrecoverable in any absolute way—the representational convention was that everyone shaved, and Black George, to be sure, is just that, a representation. Fielding, against the fashion, against the standards of convention, has given his gamekeeper what Hogarth never gave his madmen or prisoners and what Rowlandson never gave his hedgers or ditchers, a beard; further, he made that beard George's defining feature. No wonder then that Partridge—who, after all, works as a barber among his other professions and who first converses at length with Tom while shaving him—calls it "remarkable."[25]

The Legibility of Lost Property

The character who picks up Tom's banknotes, then, comes to that action already strongly but ambiguously marked—by his work, by his name, by his appearance. And his ambiguity extends to his crime. For as we noted above, he does not steal the cash (though critics often refer to it as a "theft"[26]), he simply picks up what has fallen out of Tom's pocket and keeps quiet about what he has found. Few readers would defend this action, especially in light of the wealth of aggravating circumstances Fielding heaps on George's behavior here (aggravations in direct contrast to the many mitigations with which he surrounds George's earlier crimes). He helps Tom look for the money, he commiserates with him on its loss, and the hypocrisy of it all is compounded when we recall what we can hardly forget, the manifold acts of kindness and generosity Tom has shown him in the past. It is the sort of behavior for which we say, "There oughta be a law." But as we learn at the end of *Tom Jones*, there's not one, at least not a law that is able to *punish* George, only the law of trover that allows lost property to be recovered. George has done wrong, no doubt about it, but it is not a wrong that the law is prepared to punish. England is not Lilliput, and ingratitude is not, as there, a capital crime, not even a misdemeanor.[27]

The distinction between what is stolen and what is lost seems straightforward enough—one is a matter of design, the other a matter of accident. But is it? The question was of particular concern for those who thought about crime in eighteenth-century England. In 1725, the notorious Jonathan Wild, the self-styled "Thief-taker General" of Great Britain, was hung at Tyburn. Before his fall, he had been something of a criminal genius, a man who had worked, masterfully, both sides of the law, profiting from the thefts of those he controlled, from the rewards of those whose property he returned, and from a (for a time) grateful government through the bounties he collected on those thieves he chose to betray. He had also been the eponymous "hero" of Fielding's first extended piece of prose fiction, *Jonathan Wild*. At the heart of his system was a "Lost Property Office," where—for a price, of course—victims of theft could recover the stolen goods that Wild had received from his thieves. The system did little to discourage theft; it only discouraged theft by those independent-minded souls who wanted no part of Wild's control and so left themselves open to his betrayal. But the system, however cynical, did serve to return property to those who wanted it back, and who were willing to participate in the fiction that their goods were merely "lost."[28]

Were Tom's banknotes lost or stolen? The money moves from Tom to George as neatly as if the gamekeeper had picked his friend's pocket or held one of the guns he could legally carry up to the young man's head. But that is not how it did move. The transfer of funds is a murky compound of Tom's hysterical fit of grief after his exile (as he rolls about, the money falls out), his ignorance (both about the fact of the loss, which he does not discover until later, and the amount, which he learns about only at the end of the novel), and George's professionally sharpened eyes. The scene is not one of violence or even of subterfuge but of accidental discovery and strategic silence. Fielding may here be casting a typically ironic eye at Locke's discussion of property in the *Two Treatises of Government* (a book we know the novelist owned). There, Locke developed his famous "labour-mixing" theory of property, that is, the idea that something becomes owned when an individual invests his labor in putting it to use. The discussion centers on issues of land and improvement, but it begins with an example that recalls Black George:

> The *Labour* of his Body, and the *Work* of his Hands, we may say, are properly his. Whatsoever then he removes out of the State that Nature hath provided, and left it in, he hath mixed his *Labour* with, and joyned to it something that is his own, and thereby makes it his *Property*. . . . He that is nourished by the Acorns he pickt up under an Oak, or the Apples he gathered from the Trees in the wood, has certainly appropriated them to himself. No Body can deny but the nourishment is his. I ask then, When did they begin to be his? When he digested? Or when he eat? Or when he boiled? Or when he brought them home? Or when he pickt them up? And 'tis plain, if the first gathering made them not his, nothing else could. That *labour* put a distinction between them and common.[29]

We might call this the "pickt up" theory of property. While Tom's banknotes are not acorns or apples, they are lying on the ground, and George certainly exercises the labor necessary to find them and put them in his pocket. The game laws themselves seem to be an attempt to deny the validity of the labor-mixing inherent in hunting (though of course they predate the *Two Treatises*). George "espies a Hare sitting in her Form," and knocks it on the head, a fine piece of work, no doubt about it, but still a crime in the eyes of the law. A "keeper" like Black George (this shorthand usage goes back to the fifteenth century) may often be a finder, but he was often unable to keep what he found. Tom seems to understand the ambiguities here, and later characterizes and extenuates George's action to Allworthy as a "Temptation" (969)—as George had once been "over-persuaded" by Tom himself to pursue the partridges onto Western's land. Temptation suggests impulse, itself a mitigation in the eyes of the law.

What is it exactly that George picks up and thereby takes from Tom? He pockets £500 in *bank-notes*, a form of currency that is somewhat different from the kind of money we are accustomed to. Our own bills are covered with mysterious letters, numbers, arcane symbols, and the signatures of various government officials, but unless we have specially marked them ourselves, they appear to us as essentially anonymous—mass-produced, apparently identical, freely circulating, a currency that needs no authority beyond itself. Not so in the Eighteenth century. When George tries to invest his windfall with old Nightingale, Allworthy recognizes the notes: "The Bank Bills were no sooner produced at *Allworthy's* Desire, than he blessed himself at the Strangeness of the Discovery. He presently told *Nightingale* that these Bank Bills were formerly his . . ." (920). As James Thompson explained in a pioneering essay on Fielding and money, eighteenth-century "paper money is not government issued, neither anonymous nor impersonal in this period."[30] More like a modern check, though the analogy is not at all exact, it typically bore the names of those whose hands it had passed through—drawers, bearers, assorted endorsers along the way. So, the notes that George finds and hopes to "lay out either in a Mortgage, or in some Purchase in the North of England" (920), are not cash as we normally think of cash. Rather, they resemble personal possessions, marked probably with both Tom's and Allworthy's names, and in some ways more like a necklace or a watch than a simple sum of money. But the bills *are* negotiable; Nightingale takes them and is looking into the possibilities for investment that George has suggested. The bills are thus another point of ambiguity among the many ambiguities that surround Black George. Not exactly stolen, but not simply found like acorns under the oak; not anonymous cash but not precisely a signet ring either.

These bank-notes thus are not only ambiguous as property, they are also texts, in a way that is foreign to us. The personal markings on the bank-notes—names, signatures—imply, not merely that the notes can be read, but that they *must* be read. In a very real sense, they are without value outside an act of reading. Fielding makes this point very clear by presenting us with two occasions in the novel where money is lost. Besides Tom's loss, there is also that of Sophia Western: a "little gilt Pocket-Book," containing a £100 bank note (631). Tom discovers the pocketbook on the road, in the hands of the beggar who found it, and the discussion that ensues clarifies the fact that these bills are not uniform or even immediately recognizable as what they are: when Tom opens the book, "a Piece of Paper fell from its leaves . . . which *Partridge* . . . delivered to *Jones*, who presently perceived it to be a Bankbill" (632). The bill, that is, has to be read to be recognized, not only as a simple possession (Tom's, Sophia's, whoever) but specifically as an item of value. The beggar, who "could not read" (632) literally does not know what he has. Coins, the usual form money took in the Eighteenth century, would not present such a problem of recognition to a nonreader, just as an illiterate person today would presumably recognize bills as money.

Fielding's doubling of the scenes of bank-bills lost and found obviously functions to point a contrast between the loyal Tom and the disloyal George, but it also raises a question: how does George know what he has found? Can he read? Such an ability would by no means be assured for one of his status,[31] but (again, toward the end of the novel) Fielding settles the issue. Speaking of George, Partridge tells Tom that "we are both of an Age, and were at the same charity School. *George* was a great dunce, but no Matter . . ." (829). The gamekeeper may have been a bad student, but he did go to school and his immediate understanding of the treasure he's found (in contrast to the beggar on the road, who bemoans the fact that his parents did not send him to charity school, for then "I should have known the Value of these Matters as well as other People"—635) is now clear. In whatever minimal way, Black George can read and his literacy—as the parallel scenes make clear—is inseparable from his act of appropriation. If he fell, as Tom says, because of the strength of "Temptation," that temptation is grounded in the fact that he can read.

There is one other possible association here. The history of the idea of "benefit of clergy" is far too complicated to outline here in anything like the kind of detail it needs.[32] Suffice it say, then, that this institution, which began as a way for those in the Church who had been charged with a crime to be placed under the jurisdiction of the ecclesiastical courts, came to be a legal fiction whereby those who demonstrated their literacy (if in a wholly factitious way: the test passage was always the same and so could be memorized) were not, on a first conviction, subject to a capital sanction for a whole range of crimes. Practically speaking, it was a way to institute a principle of mercy in a code where death was mandated for all felonies; but symbolically, it suggested some inherent connection between literacy and innocence or at least between literacy and access to mercy. Fielding's construction of George's ambiguous crime becomes even more curious in its light. The assumption here seems to invert the symbolism of the old tradition; with George, literacy is not equivalent to a presumption of innocence but rather is a cause of guilt.

Faces Blacked or Otherwise Disguised

Lawyer Dowling suggests at first that George might be indicted under the Black Act. What *was* the Black Act?[33] At least ostensibly, it was meant to address a specific problem, an increase in certain kinds of violence and vandalism in some forested areas, mostly in the south of England: Waltham, Windsor, Hampshire. Groups of men blackened their faces and killed deer or stole rabbits or cut down trees or fired off their guns or wrote anonymous and threatening letters. The Act, legally known as 9 George I, cap. 22, but popularly known as the Waltham Black Act or simply as the Black Act, was rushed through Parliament with little debate in the spring of 1723 and was intended to suppress this kind of activity, especially the killing of deer. But the sanctions here were much more severe than the fines characteristic of the game laws (though we need to keep in mind that deer were *not* classified as game—wild animals—but as private property). For a modern student, the Black Act provides a ferocious reading experience, damning all kinds of rural mischief as capital villainy. However, a key aggravation had to be present to trigger the full wrath of the law: the deer had to be killed or the head of the fishpond broken or the tree cut down while the perpetrators were "armed with swords, fire-arms, or other offensive weapons, *and* [with] . . . their faces blacked, or . . . otherwise disguised"[34] (my emphasis). All told, the Act added at least 50 capital crimes to a criminal code already swollen with opportunities to hang people.[35]

The gap between the crimes addressed and the sanctions proposed is more shocking to a modern observer than it would have been to many in the eighteenth century. There was no philosophy of proportional punishment, that is, the idea that punishments should be graduated according to the severity of the crime.[36] What Pollock and Maitland dryly said of the ancient English law in their magisterial *The History of the English Law Before the Time of Edward I* remained quite true in the era of the Georges: "The one punishment that can easily be inflicted by a state which has no apparatus of prisons and penitentiaries is death."[37]

While various legal commentators and would-be reformers pointed out the absurdity of a system that had few options beyond a fine or a noose, real reforms—such as a workable system of imprisonment or a police force—were far away in the nineteenth century, the work of Sir Robert Peel. We should also keep in mind that Parliament was much more willing to write capital legislation than the courts were to enforce it, and the image that a reading of the Black Act conjures up in the modern mind—rural vandals hanging from every gibbet in the land—is far too grim for the reality. Few people actually were hanged because of the Black Act. At the same time, the Act cries out for interpretation. Why even threaten to hang somebody for cutting down a tree, whether his face was blacked or scrubbed?

Three primary explanations exist.[38] The first says that the "Blacks" actually were thugs and a quite scary lot, and that in a system with few options for the punishment of criminals, the path of greatest fearfulness seemed safest. They looked, to the eighteenth-century eye, like what we would call terrorists, and the threat of terror, as we know, does not always bring forth a measured response. Second, some have insisted that there were real connections between the Blacks and the Jacobites (1722 had been the year of the Atterbury plot), and nothing was more likely to stir up a passion for severity in the Hanoverian establishment than sympathy for the Stuarts. Finally, there is the theory of the Black Act's most comprehensive historian, E. P. Thompson. He insists that the law reflected what he calls "the Whig state of mind" (197), in particular, its insistence on exclusive property rights in the face of resentment from those in rural areas who depended on patterns of customary appropriation. The old forest economy had paternalistically allowed many in its midst to live by a kind of gleaning—scavenging, cutting turf, collecting fallen wood, and the like. The newly rich landowners under the Georges, mostly Whig, wanted an end to such customs and when conflict broke out, they turned for relief to a Parliament all too ready to serve "the interest of the government's own closest supporters" (206). For Thompson, the Blacks and the Act written to suppress them were an instance of "something close to class warfare" (191), with a "predatory elite" (245) arrayed against an infuriated underclass motivated quite often by "malice against the gentry" (256).

Thompson is very convincing when he argues that the Black Act originated in a conflict that must be understood in terms of both status and of shifting conceptions of the meaning of property (though he does not mention Locke). He probably understates the element of anti-Jacobitism in the passage of the legislation (in the terms he himself uses, a group of people anxious to preserve their customary rights might very well also be attached to a customary dynasty). He possibly overstates the importance of a specifically *Whig* state of mind in establishing the law (since the Act passed with broad bipartisan support[39]). From the perspective I develop here, he may be guilty of another distortion. What Thompson wants to describe as class conflict in the history of the Blacks might be better or additionally understood as class confusion.

As I noted earlier, one legacy of the game laws was to create a sense of a common grievance, and hence a surprising alliance among the poor and the small landowners. Douglas Hay remarks that the "game statutes . . . antagonized a great many men who usually were the first to support the defense of property and the conviction of thieves. . . . [The laws] created something of an alliance between farmers and labourers, who poached together and supported one another. . . ."[40] If we look more specifically at the Black Act itself, it is Thompson who admits that "persons of estate and quality" were involved in Blacking in some areas (140)—an alliance consistent with the old poaching brotherhood of foresters and small landowning farmers. So, one useful way to look at the tangled history of the Blacks and the laws they inspired is not to think of the conflicts in the countryside as the fruit of firmly established positions and clearly marked sides, but rather as the anxious product of a real ambiguity about property and rights—who hunts? who owns? who uses?[41] The Black Act, like the Game Law of 1671, can be seen as an attempt, however clumsy or draconian, to bring some kind of clarity to a world where matters of both property and status seem to have struck many among the privileged as all too murky. We can also usefully think of this is as a conflict between the legitimacy of the law and the legitimacy of tradition, and the problems that arose from it can be seen as a commentary on the resistance of tradition to the innovations that the law desires to impose.

Such status uncertainty was nowhere more acute than with the gamekeepers. As we have seen, that confusion grew out of the 1671 law, and the Black Act did nothing to dissipate it. Thompson tells us that the battles in the forest of the 1720s involved "Blacks and keepers" (63). As we might expect, the gamekeepers could be in the first line of either defense or attack against the Blacks, those men who had added a new measure of terror to the old and (to many) honorable pursuit of poaching. But, as we would also expect, the reality was not a simple opposition of rebels and enforcers, and in this regard Thompson states the ambiguity of roles nicely: "Gamekeepers were at the vortex of [the] conflict; sometimes they were terrorized into aiding the poachers; sometimes they were agents of terror and freebooters on their own account" (225). This instability in their position is exemplified by the contrasting fates of two keepers caught up in these struggles. One, Baptist Nunn, a zealous enforcer of the law and doer of his master's bidding, makes "that most difficult of eighteenth-century transitions" (220), from servant to gentleman. Another gamekeeper, however, Lewis Gunner, despised by all sides, resorted to the kind of terrorism favored by some Blacks (he fired a pistol at a man in a public house) and was himself prosecuted and condemned (though not hung) under 9 George I, cap. 22 (225–6).

Thompson's general scorn for the forest authorities means that, despite his use of such examples, he is not fully sensitive to the liminality of the gamekeepers' position, isolated as they were by their authority and their (sometime) criminality from those both above and below them. They were at the same time tools of the rich and potential rebels against the law. Where they could, they profited off old poaching traditions, yet they sometimes prospered as well from this new and harsh law aimed in part at the very customs some of them relied on. Thompson does not really acknowledge the difficult ambiguities of such a liminal position, but he does mention at one point what could be another, more material plight. Speaking of those unlucky gamekeepers who had not succeeded in achieving that potentially lucrative mix of salary, perquisites, and poaching that some of their fellows enjoyed, he quotes the Duke of Kent as saying in 1716 that the underkeepers of Windsor had not been paid for years and that "some of these poor men who subsist chiefly by that salary do at this time want bread" (34n.).

The Two Georges

If Thompson tends to neglect the ambiguity inherent in the status of gamekeepers, Fielding wants to highlight it. The character of Black George, like any real gamekeeper in the world in which Fielding created him, is everywhere marked by ambiguity, liminality, and instability. And this instability shows up most powerfully in the way that Fielding has contrived to give us, not one, but two Georges. For George Seagrim's function in *Tom Jones* tends to fall into two, not easily reconcilable roles.[42] On the one hand, we have a George rather like those underkeepers whom the Duke of Kent pitied. A hapless victim, he is a poor man unable to support his family, and a rather dimwitted pawn in the hands of those men more wealthy or more clever than he. He poaches, but he does so for meat, and on a very small scale, and not at all successfully. This is the George we see in Allworthy's employ and just after he is dismissed, and he appears to us as the object of Tom's benevolence and as a vehicle by which Fielding can satirize certain kinds of rural injustice, the game laws in particular. But there is another George, the gamekeeper who works for Western. This character wears fine livery (is, in fact, such a trusted servant that the squire brings him to London), he has actually accumulated a significant sum from a suddenly more lucrative poaching career (he offers to help the imprisoned Tom with money), and he aspires to pull himself up even further by becoming a member of the investing classes, an absentee landlord in fact. As Partridge says to Tom, "you would hardly know him."

We could explain this marked doubleness in Fielding's minor character in various ways. First of all, this reversal—the subject of satiric sympathy becomes the object of moral judgment—is characteristic of Fielding's slipperiness, of the way in which his art tends to thwart our desire to rest easy with the various opinions we form as we read. In that sense, he is another example of that double-irony I discuss throughout this study. Moreover, we might trace the sketchy outline of some kind of character "development" in George, whereby the wretch of the early chapters becomes (under the influence of oppression, perhaps, or due to the turning of *Fortuna*'s ancient wheel) the canny or lucky exploiter of circumstance that we see later.

These interpretations have the virtue of suggesting a completed narrative, either of a reader's complacency overturned or of an individual character's development. But I do not think that they really have much to do with Black George, who seems not to *be* a character as we often think of characters in novels, not the "round" ones associated with the school of Richardson, nor the "flatter" characters often attributed to Fielding either. In *Joseph Andrews*, Fielding had described his fictional practice in traditional neo-classical terms as the description, not of "an Individual but a Species," but I do not believe that we should view the instability so apparent in George's character as the novelist's attempt to suggest a range of behaviors possible under the generic label, "gamekeeper."[43] Black George is a much more interesting example of the novelist's art than that, precisely because he seems to me to be an example of a completely different kind of representation. He is not a novelistic version of a person, even a generic person, so much as he is a particularly dense site of association. As a site of association, his various behaviors and traits do not have to cohere as a character, because they—which is also to say "he," George—can work quite well as commentary.

That commentary is centrally concerned with the question at the heart of this chapter, the way in which the ambiguous position of gamekeepers in eighteenth-century England, figures in and highlights much larger issues of property and legitimacy in that culture. As we have seen, keepers were police and criminals, preservers and killers, comfortably off and poverty-stricken. They enforced the game laws and the Black Act, yet, like George, they were sometimes threatened by these same laws that they were empowered to uphold. Above all, they were men of a most uncertain class status, privileged (to hunt, to enforce the law) like their betters, but, like their inferiors, sometimes operating outside the law, either by choice or by pressure of necessity.[44] I am not concerned here with individual differences, with the fact that some keepers flourished while others struggled and failed. Rather, whatever the success or failure of individuals, there was a certain ambiguity written into the position itself, an ambiguity that Black George, through his doubleness, and through the density of the associations that Fielding has put in play around his character, represents.

The primary associations that Fielding has attached to Black George concern his criminality and his class status, but other moral and political issues emerge as well. We best see how those associations function by returning to what is, in many ways, the gamekeeper's defining act in the novel, his decision to pocket his friend's banknotes. As we have seen, that moment is itself remarkably ambiguous. George has not broken the law; he is not, strictly speaking, a criminal in this matter. However morally reprehensible, his selective silence about a few items lost and found is not something that the criminal code chose to punish. Allworthy, always on the lookout for ways to put the law to moral uses, is predictably outraged at what he sees as the inadequacy of the system in this regard: "I think a Highwayman," he tells Tom, "compared to him, is an innocent Person" (969). A highwayman, however, is not innocent, only less ambiguous, and Fielding, with Black George, insists on maintaining to the end the legal ambiguity of George's action—it remains an appropriation of another's property that stubbornly refuses classification as theft. The action itself thus functions as a marker of ambiguity, of a gamekeeper's legally liminal position. Surely, too, there is implicit in this narrative another ironic glance back at the career of Jonathan Wild, a cleverer man than George but another exemplary figure for anyone concerned with the limits of the criminal law, perhaps particularly where property is concerned, and the tendency of its categories to resist either stability or comprehensiveness.[45] Wild was no gamekeeper, but his career raises the same troubling question, how well does the law define what is criminal? How sharp is the line between property that has been stolen and property which is merely lost?

But if George has violated no statute in the criminal law, he may be guilty of transgressing some unwritten law of class, and Fielding, I think, invites us to think about George as someone who is sinning above his station in life. We think immediately of George's literacy. By doubling the acts of trover in *Tom Jones*, Fielding goes out of his way to emphasize the idea that an illiterate Black George would, in a quite direct way, have discovered nothing when he spotted Tom's banknotes. The other sharp-eyed character in the novel, the beggar, does not know what he has. From a moral point of view, it is because the gamekeeper can read what he has found that he does wrong. But from an economic perspective, George's literacy becomes the potential fulcrum for his transformation. Legible paper becomes negotiable currency, and George, though a dunce at school, reads just well enough to find himself closeted with old Nightingale, seeking a mortgage to buy, hoping to make a new identity. We remember Baptist Nunn, the gamekeeper turned gentleman, who Thompson tells us, was also able to read (65). So, we could say that George's is a status crime because it requires what remained, in the eighteenth century, the largely status-bound ability to read in order to commit—an early instance of a kind of white-collar crime.

But the possibility that George represents a class criminal runs deeper than this. Shortly after writing *Tom Jones*, after his ascension to the magistrate's bench, Fielding published a different kind of consideration of crime, *An Enquiry into the Causes of the Late Increase of Robbers*. There he argues that what was perceived to be a burgeoning crime rate in mid-century is a result of poor people trying to follow the taste for luxury that they see among the wealthy. Fielding insists that such imitation, what we might call social mimesis, is destructive, leading to idleness and worse among the classes whose lot it should be to know much work and little pleasure. (Magistrate Fielding tolerates such displays among the rich, with some irony, as good for the economy.)[46] But George's ambition is not at all the same thing as the behavior of the criminal classes that Fielding discusses in the *Enquiry*. His aim is not, after all, an indulgence in the immediate pleasures of gambling or strong drink, but a good return on a sober investment. This is social mimesis of a different order, for what George mirrors here is not the frivolous, but the prudent, side of wealth. He takes his windfall, not to the tavern or brothel, but like a good capitalist, to an investment banker. Who knows, in time and with a good return, he might very well achieve his own property qualification and so hunt in his own right. There indeed would be an end, once and for all, to the liminality of his peculiar position.

But that question of mimesis brings us back to hunting. It is apparent to me that the game laws and, in its own much fiercer way, the Black Act were centrally concerned with the regulation of particular forms of *imitation*. Something less tangible than property, but no less precious, was at stake. It is not that the apples on the ground, or even the hare in her form, are someone's property, but that a certain activity—the hunt—somehow *belongs* to a particular kind of person. Such privileges, these laws seemed to say, therefore should be inimitable. In this light, we see that something more was at stake than the mere loss of deer. Poaching becomes a kind of hunting under false pretenses, and thus a dangerous imitation; to kill deer, as the Blacks did, was to mimic the sport, *par excellence*, that embodied the privilege of the great. And yet, those laws also created an anomalous group licensed, as it were, to imitate—the gamekeepers. The law wants to clarify status, and by clarifying it, to reinforce its legitimacy; Black George reminds us that status is somehow beyond regulation, or at least beyond the dream of unambiguous clarity. By virtue of their office, George and his fellow gamekeepers could carry guns and take game, and thus, in this symbolically powerful way, mimic their betters. Little wonder, then, that George should look above his own station for a model of what to do with his money.

But what about George's beard: how does that anomalous growth fit into this frame? I think that we are now in a position to see the way in which it functions as a reflection of that fear of the hidden face inscribed in the Black Act's prohibition of men going about "with their faces blacked or otherwise disguised." George is disguised in several ways, of course, most obviously perhaps by his hypocrisy. The face of loyalty that he offers to Jones is only a mask for his readiness, given the right temptation, to betray him.[47] But his black beard is also, in this context, reminiscent of the blackface worn by the vandals of the 1720s. For those men, figures of such terror for the gentry, a blackened face was a badge of anonymity, an announcement that, in a social order sometimes called face-to-face, their faces were unreadable. If the troubles in the countryside were linked to status confusion, a face in disguise seems, at least symbolically, to be an attempt to promote that confusion by erasing familiarity. A known face, we hope, is a badge of stable identity; a hidden face can be anything.[48] "I thought there was not an honester Fellow in the World," says Tom, learning what George has done (969). "I thought I knew him," he might have said, but that was his mistake. Tom's old friend has been, in a real sense, faceless to him. What a bearded George presented was, it turns out, a blank or blackened surface on which a warmhearted young man could project his charity and his paternalistic assumptions. The gamekeeper—both this fictional character and his real-life counterparts walking through the English landscape—is never quite fixed, never quite who he seems to be.

Finally, why is Fielding's gamekeeper not merely "Black" but also "George"? Why is all this weight of contextual evidence pressing on not just any name but on the name of the monarch? In his journalism of the 1740s, as we have seen, Fielding expressed quite strongly his support for the Hanoverian succession, but again, I do not think that there is any reason to assume that those pronouncements are necessarily an unproblematic expression of his political sentiments. Not that we should assume, on the other hand, that Fielding was constructing here a seditious or overtly Jacobite allegory. There is allegory here but it is much like the one we saw in chapter 1, which is to say an allegory that does a double ironic take on history, one that looks at both sides without finally resolving itself into either. What is "George" in *Tom Jones*? George is a kind of thief, and yet a thief whose crime is untouchable. There were certainly men in Fielding's time who would have associated that statement not with George Seagrim but with all those Georges in the House of Hanover. The fact that such a "Jacobite" reading is possible does not mean that Fielding endorses it, but it does suggest that he is both aware of its force and complex enough in his thinking to incorporate it in his novel. What seems to me to be at work here, as in his appropriation of the mythos of Bonnie Prince Charlie, is neither simpleminded loyalty nor subtle sedition. Fielding has constructed, through his choice of a name for his gamekeeper, a small and deeply ironic commentary on legitimacy in a novel where issues of legitimacy face us at every turn. That commentary can raise questions about the claims to power advanced by the Hanoverians without necessarily rejecting them.

Black George, as we see him, can never be fully legitimate in the eyes of the world he inhabits, either as a hunter, or as an agent of the law, or as a property owner. His illegitimacy rests in his moral insufficiency, but even more so it rests in the radical ambiguity of his position. That ambiguity is not only a creation of the law, but an ironic by-product precisely of the law's desire to regulate ambiguity. A similar problem attaches to the House of Hanover, determined not by birth but by Act of Parliament to be England's ruling dynasty. Fielding, an ironist of a capacious scope, would not have to wish for a restoration of the Stuarts to be able to see the ways in which the legitimacy of the Georges was a matter of legal construction and the public's acceptance—a product, that is, of law and consensus, not of nature or God. To remind us that the House of Hanover might never be quite right in the eyes of a public who remembered that the Stuarts were forced off the throne is not the same as the wish that the new dynasty be removed. To suggest, with the greatest subtlety, that King George is a poacher of thrones—even, to push the analogy of Hanover and Seagrim a bit further, to suggest that the king is in questionable if not criminal possession of an object "lost" by its original owner—may have been a necessary ironic counterbalance to Fielding's other, publicly expressed belief that having gained that throne, the monarchs imported from Germany should be allowed to keep it.

The Gamekeeper and the Magistrate

Fielding, then, has created a character who is most difficult to stabilize in our minds: George is a victim, a traitor, and a social climber; he is the object of our sympathy and the target of our scorn; and he subtly suggests certain difficulties in the political position of the monarch. I argue that he is best understood as a site of historical associations, a recurring figure in the narrative whose various appearances allow Fielding to construct a kind of commentary on issues of status, the law, and dynastic politics, but even that commentary is hard to summarize or make consistent and whole. Certainly, Fielding does seem suspicious of George's ambition, and he may well have believed that the kind of social mimesis that his gamekeeper represents is more insidious even than the art of luxurious imitation practiced by the underclass of London. The rigors of the Black Act, Fielding seems to say, may be more appropriate for George than Dowling's narrow construction of it could ever have imagined.[49]

Yet the ambiguity with which Fielding has so carefully surrounded Black George means that such a judgment can never be definitive. In fact, on two occasions, Fielding explicitly signals us to withhold any final condemnation. In the introductory chapter to Book VII ("A Comparison between the World and the Stage"), immediately after the gamekeeper pockets the bills, Fielding imagines George's action on the stage and speculates about how different elements of the audience might judge it. His conclusion, rather like Johnson's at the end of *The Life of Savage*, is that "the Man of . . . true Understanding is never hasty to condemn" (328). And he seconds this idea later, for when George visits Tom in prison at the hero's own blackest hour, we are told that "*George* was of a compassionate Disposition, . . . notwithstanding a small breach of Friendship which he had been over-tempted to commit . . ." (917).

The breach hardly seems small, yet by this point in the novel we perhaps can understand that the over-temptation which mitigates his betrayal may be a matter, not of George's character, but of his place in a social structure not of his own making.

Such reminders of the virtue of withholding judgment take on a new urgency when we open one final angle of vision on this discussion. The status ambiguity that George and his profession embody so well should remind us of the plight of Richard Savage, with his claims to be a noble bastard, both well and ill-born. As we have seen, Fielding found in that life a mirror for contemplating the problematic nature of his own position, and I believe that there is something similar at work with George. The novelist, that is, may have felt some personal identification, if not with Black George himself, then with all the issues of status confusion and illegitimacy that he seems to suggest. In the last months of 1748, Fielding was rushing to finish *Tom Jones*, despite a debilitating attack of his gout, and in addition to his new labors as Justice of the Peace for Westminster (he had taken office on 25 October). After only a few weeks in his new job, Fielding recognized, as Battestin puts it, "that he could neither prosper himself in that capacity [as Westminster JP] nor serve the public adequately unless he also became eligible to act in the commission of the peace for Middlesex County" (488). Unfortunately, for Fielding to attain this additional office, he needed to meet a property qualification: to become magistrate for Middlesex, he had to possess "property worth £100 a year clear value" (488). The lifelong spendthrift and debtor did not meet that standard, and for help he turned to his patron, the Duke of Bedford. Thus it was that on December 13, Fielding requested that the Duke assign him enough property to produce the income required. Bedford agreed, and on January 9, "he conveyed to Fielding for a period of twenty-one years and at an annual rent of 30l. certain properties" in central London (449). Fielding took the oath for this second magistracy on January 12 and was securely ensconced in both his new positions by the time that his publisher entered *Tom Jones* in the Stationer's Register on February 3 (451).

The first two volumes of the novel, encompassing the Somersetshire books and including the accounts of George's poachings and his discovery of Tom's money, had been issued the previous November, but the final scenes of the novel—the chapters where we learn of George's beard and education and his planned investment and of Dowling's advice—were still (as far as we know) in the process of completion as Fielding struggled to meet the qualification and so consolidate his new professional status. Even if the problem of the property qualification had not been a concern at precisely the same time as he was finishing his novel, Fielding's interest in a magistracy like Middlesex was longstanding (Chesterfield had recommended Fielding for the position as far back as 1747—*A Life* 448). He had, in other words a quite personal interest in the idea of the meaning of property worth £100 *per annum*. The magistracy of Middlesex and the ability to hunt are not, to be sure, the same thing, and the qualification itself was somewhat different, since the right to hunt required either a £100 freehold or a £150 leasehold, while £100 from rented property was sufficient to make a magistrate. But the similarity in the qualifications is also striking, and the idea of a £100 threshold, and his own insufficiency in the face of it must have struck the novelist forcibly in thinking about creating for his novel the character of a gamekeeper, a job itself in large part defined by the idea of a property qualification.

The point of the parallel I draw here is to emphasize the complexity of the pattern of both distance and identification that appears to exist when we look at Fielding and Black George together, as it had with the novelist and Savage or Bonnie Prince Charlie. It would be easy to take his portrait of the gamekeeper as simply critical and socially conservative: class ambiguity (and the mobility such ambiguity may allow) is dangerous, the cash nexus will erode or destroy the bonds of community, the literacy of servants puts dangerous ideas in their heads, and so forth. But then we are brought up short, for Fielding also has some striking things in common with Black George. Both author and character are excluded by the absence of property from the worlds they aspire to join. After all, what property qualifications were intended to do was to limit certain activities (like hunting) and certain occupations (like magistrate) to those who could unambiguously claim to be landed gentlemen. Fielding, however, was both a gentleman and unqualified, and he could not help but be struck by the fact of the ambiguity in his own situation. In this light, we should remember that the full extent of George's aspiration is made clear only at the end of *Tom Jones*, composed at just the time when Fielding himself is attempting to vault over the obstacle placed in his path by the very social order he seems so fervently to embrace. The complex pattern of distancing and identification implicit at all levels in the character of Black George finally works to overturn, once more, our sense of certitude. In this glass of his own creation, Fielding has figured—darkly, humorously—an image of some part of himself.

Chapter 4
Hanging Judges

Private Prosecution

The Man of the Hill's long story may seem digressive enough, but in its early stages, Fielding interrupts it with another tale. Partridge, ever ready further to dilate this dilatory novel, insists on telling "a very short Story" (458) about a trial for horse theft that he had witnessed years before. The interruption occurs at just the moment when we learn that the Man's own trial, for the theft of forty guineas from his Oxford friend, has been dismissed because the victim did not show up to testify. That testimony would have meant, the old eccentric tells us, certain conviction and—given the law—a death sentence. Partridge intends his story as a kind of complement to the Man of the Hill's tale of failed prosecution: he recounts a trial where such testimony was given, with dire consequences, not only as we might expect for the accused, but also for the witness. These two instances—the indictment and near-trial of the Man of the Hill, and Partridge's account of the court where the horse thief is tried and condemned—are, in fact, almost the only two formal legal proceedings in *Tom Jones*.

It is surprising, perhaps, to realize how few real trials there are in the novel, although it is punctuated by any number of the kind of informal judgments we have already seen, such as the hearings conducted by Allworthy or Western, in their roles as country Justices of the Peace, sitting in judgment of Black George, or Jenny Jones, or Tom, or Partridge himself. But almost none of the novel's possible candidates for indictment by the criminal justice system actually face formal legal consequences, not Black George, not the murderous Northerton, not the highwayman Tom will later encounter, not the gypsies, not the cagey Blifil. In fact, in all the often encyclopedically detailed world of *Tom Jones*, with its great feast of human nature, the nameless horse thief in Partridge's story is the only person whom Fielding actually shows in a full-fledged and complete legal proceeding—and if we believe Partridge, even this trial should never have taken place. Equally significant, in a very long narrative whose hero was "born to be hanged," the horse thief is the only character in the novel who actually ends up on the gallows.[1] *Tom Jones* may be replete with robbery of all kinds, but it is strangely empty of the complementary presence of that system of justice in which Fielding himself was already so active and would be, soon after the novel's appearance, more active still. Given the general invisibility of the legal system in the novel, it becomes important then to look closely at Partridge's story.

The trial that Partridge describes, in its surface particulars (an accused, lawyers, witnesses, a courtroom, a judge, a jury, mechanisms for punishment), looks so familiar to modern readers that we can miss the many ways in which it was very different, and this scene cannot be fully understood without some grasp both of how the criminal law was written, and how it actually worked.[2] As we saw in chapter 3, the written law and legal practice could be very different, and such discrepancies between legislation and reality, while inevitably a part of any legal system, are especially striking in the eighteenth century, and they are prominent among the peculiarities that need discussion here. The key word for understanding the period's criminal law is probably "discretion," and the legal historian Peter King emphasizes how important and singular the place of discretion was in the eighteenth-century: "Although discretionary decisions form a central strand in many criminal justice systems, and most certainly in those of early modern and Victorian England, a strong case can be made for nominating the long eighteenth century as the golden age of discretionary justice—particularly if property crime is the primary focus."[3] Other words for discretion include "unpredictable," and (less neutrally) "arbitrary," and the enforcement of the law was certainly an unpredictable business, one that could appear quite arbitrary, as all the players—victims, judges, juries—had great latitude in determining the outcome of any criminal proceeding.

The starting point for understanding eighteenth-century criminal law is the institution of "private prosecution," and the crucial role played by the person called the "prosecutor." Immediately, we are forced to confront difference, because an eighteenth-century prosecutor was not a lawyer representing the state, but was, in fact, the victim; as Beattie puts it, this is "a system of justice that puts the burden of prosecution entirely on the victim of the crime."[4] The law expected, indeed demanded, that victims report the crime, identify the criminal, gather witnesses, and make a case before judge and jury. To be sure, when the crime is theft (and overwhelmingly, that was the crime on trial in eighteenth-century

Britain), there is always a need for the victim to come forward: even today, if my house is broken into and my goods taken, nothing happens unless I call the police. But here is the signal contrast. There were no police as we know them to call in England in the eighteenth century, nor indeed until the Peel Act of 1829 established the first real police force. Much law, and much legal practice, flowed from this reluctance to institute a police force—an institution that was common elsewhere in Europe (France, for instance, had both national and local police forces by the early eighteenth century), but which came very late to Britain. Many believed that a police force on the continental model would infringe the vaunted liberty of the British subject, and so the nation accepted the resulting vulnerabilities in security as preferable to any abridgement of that freedom.

Without a police force to investigate crime, to apprehend criminals, and to gather evidence in a systematic way, responsibility for prosecution thus fell by default on the victim, the "private" citizen rather than the public official, and considerable peculiarity grew in the law. The greatest oddity was a phenomenon that we encountered with the Black Act: a code of criminal jurisprudence which mandated death by hanging for most offenses, including almost all thefts. The general absence of any infrastructure for the administration of secondary punishments, such as penitentiaries, as we saw in chapter 3, forced death upon the justice system as a kind of inevitable option, but there was a rationale. The logic seems to have been this: drastic sanctions would increase the deterrent power of laws that are intrinsically difficult to enforce. Most crimes will go unpunished, but the criminals who are caught, convicted, and punished will, through the horrible example of their end, so terrify the great bulk of the population that crime will stay in check. Hence, the need for public executions since the example needs the most dramatic possible illustration to work its effect.

How, then, would a theft be prosecuted, assuming the victim wanted to do so? The willingness to prosecute was the first place where discretion might be exercised, and while it is always hard to assign precise weights to actions not taken, the evidence suggests that only a small fraction of thefts were pursued. But if the victim did decide to prosecute, he or she needed first to apprehend the criminal, perhaps through the help of the various rather loose kinds of quasi-police that existed, such as the nightwatch or (in urban areas) a constabulary or even one's fellow citizens through the ancient practice of Hue and Cry, whereby those in the area of a crime had an obligation to help a victim in pursuit of a thief. A magistrate such as Fielding would then hear the charge, and if the evidence was plausible, the accused would be confined in a place like Newgate or another jail, while the accuser/prosecutor would be bound over to appear and make his or her charges in a court. As King sums up the responsibilities of the prosecutor, the process was an "expensive, time-consuming, and often complex task," which involved "organizing the detection, arrest, and possible committal of the offender."[5]

What happened in court also did not follow a fixed path in the eighteenth century, in part because procedures for the conduct of trials were evolving into something more modern and familiar. As a result, generalization is difficult. Over the course of the century, Britain gradually abandoned a system where, in essence, the accused defended him or herself, while the judge played an extremely active role as an examiner and shaper of the trial. Such judicial activity was not merely on behalf of the prosecution: one striking feature of English justice to foreigners was the way the judge was supposed to protect the interests of the accused. According to Beattie, "the judge was thought to have a special responsibility to see that [the accused] were given every opportunity to prove their innocence. This was one of the aspects of criminal procedure that gave rise to the frequently repeated view that English law and the English courts were exceptionally humane and tender with regard to the prisoner's rights."[6] Over the course of the eighteenth century and into the next, this structure gave way to a new kind of trial, one where the lawyers (both a defense counsel and a prosecutor) dominated the proceedings, while the accused and the judge both stepped back. These changes took the better part of the century to work themselves out, and during the transitional phase, there seems to have been enormous variability—from place to place, trial to trial, judge to judge—in how a proceeding might unfold. The business itself was quick, with the whole matter, including jury deliberation, averaging half an hour or less.

A guilty verdict said little about what might happen to a convicted felon, and it is in the area of sentencing that the discretion built into eighteenth-century legal practice is most obvious. Murderers, traitors, and counterfeiters were usually hanged, though even here, as Richard Savage reminds us, the hand of mercy could intervene; the fate of a thief was much more uncertain, and rates of hanging for the various kinds of property offenses varied widely. There was also variability in response to immediate circumstances: someone might hang one year because the need for deterrence seemed high, while the same crime might earn a pardon when the threat was felt to be lower. In general, the more violent the theft (as, say, in highway robbery), the more likely the hanging.

Quite common as an instance of the discretion in the system was a form of jury nullification (sometimes called "pious perjury") whereby the value of the goods stolen was undervalued so as to take the theft below the minimum level required for the death penalty. Occasionally, prosecutors themselves would undervalue the goods they had lost so as to ensure that the criminal would not face the noose.

The institution of benefit of clergy, examined briefly in connection with Black George, was gradually being removed over the eighteenth century, but that institution's attempt to ensure a certain amount of mercy in the administration of the law did not disappear. Mercy came more and more now to take the form of transportation, sentencing the guilty to a term of indentured servitude in the colonies. It is worth remembering that every sentence of transportation was officially termed a "pardon"—a way to remind those who were forced into this kind of exile that their fate, by law, could have been much worse. What was not an option, at least in the modern sense, was prison. Prison was almost always for those awaiting trial, or for debtors, and they were (as Fielding himself would vividly describe a few years later in *Amelia*) places of great corruption. As King makes clear, there was a kind of covert use of imprisonment as a punishment that sometimes took place. A prosecutor, for instance, might decide that the accused had suffered enough during his pre-trial time in jail, and not show up to give witness; the prisoner would be dismissed, but some punishment would have been inflicted, not least the anticipatory horror of awaiting trial. King calls it "a species of summary imprisonment at [the prosecutor's] own discretion."[7] We think of the Man of the Hill, and later in the century, Caleb Williams. But this tactic, like so much else, was an improvisation, and modern prisons as penitentiaries, that is, as places of punishment and rehabilitation rather than as warehouses for the accused, also awaited the Peel reforms. A system of sanctions based, not on exemplary punishment, but on a rational scale of proportionality—a certain crime results in a certain period of incarceration, with capital crimes and punishments made rare—required the efficiency of a police force, so as actually to capture the criminals and gather the evidence. All the calls for prison reform that were made in the eighteenth century by people like Jeremy Bentham were essentially fruitless until the dam of resistance to a police force finally gave way.

Any description of the criminal justice system in eighteenth-century England inevitably precipitates us into the midst of an old and contentious historical debate. An account such as my summary here raises the question, what did this system *mean*? Its peculiarity, indeed its patent irrationality and apparently arbitrary nature, has long required interpretation, and a number of historians have attempted to offer answers to a question that Douglas Hay has put quite well: "We have yet to explain the coexistence of bloodier laws and increased convictions with a declining proportion of death sentences that were actually carried out."[8] In other words, why did the criminal code itself lack the discretion that actual practice embraced? Hay, along with the other Warwick school historians, developed an answer, grounded in Marxist theory, that suggests that the paradox—an increasingly harsh code, but a more merciful practice—was an ideological construct meant to protect the interests of the propertied class (at one point, he uses the phrase "ruling class conspiracy"). For these historians, this system "based on terror," had a deep structure: on the one hand and obviously, it worked to protect property by the ever-present threat of the gallows; simultaneously, however, the frequent use of pardons allowed the authors of this bloody code to disguise their naked self-interest, and give the law the mystified power of ideology. The law could be presented, not as a blunt instrument of oppression, but as a grand and disinterested conception, marked by majesty, justice, and mercy.[9] One remembers the keys to effective leadership offered by that early management expert, Dostoyevsky's Grand Inquisitor: miracle, mystery, and authority.

Opposing this view, we might look to the work of legal historians like John Langbein, Beattie, and King. Langbein in particular has been at pains explicitly to refute Hay's arguments. Using a detailed examination of certain court records, he argues both that the use of capital sanctions shows great continuity with earlier practice (that is, there was not a startling increase in the number of hanging offenses) and that the record demonstrates that most trials for property theft involved people—victims, criminals, and jurymen alike—below the ruling class. The law thus operated "to serve and protect the interests of the people who suffered as victims of crime, people who were overwhelmingly non-elite."[10] Beattie is less concerned to take on Hay directly, but it is clear that the underlying premises of his work do not accept an account of the law as an elite conspiracy; rather he is concerned in a quite empirical way to understand the implications of the growth of transportation as an alternative sanction to hanging, and as a way to institutionalize some form of mercy as the use of benefit of clergy declined. Beattie, too, sees broad support for the law: "if the criminal law had served only the interests of the propertied classes it would hardly have attracted the widespread approval that was clearly bestowed upon it."[11] King, whose work in the field is the most recent, has it seems to me the most judicious understanding of this complex reality. The concluding words of his study merit close attention:

> Although the criminal justice system was mainly aimed at controlling the labouring poor, the poor were able to utilize a wide a range of legal arenas to protect their property, resolve their disputes, or appeal for wages or relief. Although the landed elite enacted the criminal law and sometimes made strategic use of it to strengthen their authority, it was a very much broader grouping—the heterogeneous middling sort—who dominated its everyday workings, who most needed it to protect their property, and who therefore had the most opportunity to make it their own. The criminal law was not only an arena of terror, of exploitation, and of bloody sanction but also of struggle, of negotiation, of accommodation, and almost every group in eighteenth-century society helped to shape it, just as their behavior was partly shaped by it.[12]

King's summary statement seems properly to acknowledge the quiddity and messiness of the criminal law in this period. Of course, there was a desire by the ruling classes to project their authority, but that did not preclude the middle classes and the poor from finding ways to use laws they did not make for their own protection and advantage. Any human enterprise with this many players and this much at stake will develop mechanisms for negotiation, and that drive for flexibility will, in turn, create room for all manner of discretionary action. Here, as so often, the kind of deep structures so beloved of conspiracy theorists give way to the force of contingency and circumstance.[13]

This, then, in brief, is the world in which Page's work as a judge unfolded and in which Partridge acts as our witness. Because there was so much variability, and because courtroom practices were evolving throughout the century, it is important to keep in mind that the trial that Fielding describes is, as it were, a single moment in a very complex and dynamic history. While this scene cannot, perhaps needless to say, tell us everything about the practice of the criminal law in the eighteenth century, it is a significant site for understanding Fielding's perception of that system at work.

There is a tantalizing possibility that the trial in the novel is based on a real one that occurred in 1737. Certainly, Partridge mentions not one, but two historical figures, Justice Willoughby of Noyle as well as Sir Francis Page. Willoughby, who appears in the tale only very briefly as the one who first hears the evidence and binds the accused over for trial, was a magistrate and good friend of Fielding's, and Partridge lets us know he was "a worthy good Gentleman"—apparently a little private puff for an old colleague and, perhaps, a small reminder of the value of the job Fielding himself would soon take on. Page presides over the trial: a one-time Whig MP, and a man whom his own time called *the* "hanging judge," he has a starring role in Partridge's story, and was, in fact, a prominent national figure in the decades before *Tom Jones* appeared. He was the judge at one of the sensational early trials in Berkshire of those accused under the Black Act, and it was he, as we saw in chapter 2, who pronounced sentence of death on Richard Savage at his trial for murder. A target for Pope's satire on several occasions, he earned the dubious immortality of a place in the *Dunciad*. J. Paul de Castro, who advanced the argument for the historical actuality of the trial many years ago, claimed that "the prisoner [that is, the horse thief in the novel] was tried, in fact, at the Salisbury Assizes by Sir Francis Page, . . . who presided over the Western Circuit during the Summer Assizes of 1737, and for the last time in 1739."[14] Frustratingly, despite the confidence of that "in fact," de Castro cites no source for his belief that Fielding bases the scene on an actual trial, though a number of other biographers and editors of the novel have taken his word for it.[15] Its factuality is, in a sense, irrelevant. It is easy to imagine the novelist constructing the scene out of some fragments of experience and hearsay. Fielding knew Willoughby, and he certainly must have heard a great deal about the legendary Page in his own travels on the Western circuit. The wit Page displays is undoubtedly something for which the judge was notorious, and Page's actuality connects the scene to the historically literal without necessarily relying on the specifics of any one trial. Such links to the real, however, should not overshadow the fact that the trial as Partridge recounts it— a quite perfect dramatic monologue—is far too intricately plotted and tonally complex to consider as in some way documentary in the rather narrow sense that de Castro implies. Fielding crafted this little episode with the greatest care.

Charming Sport

Partridge's story is brief but dense with detail. The father of a friend named Frank, "lost a Mare," and it is the son's luck to spot a man riding that horse at a local fair; crying out, "Stop, Thief,"[16] and thus invoking the law of Hue and Cry, he is able to apprehend the man on the horse, and eventually, on the basis of his evidence, the thief is convicted and hanged. But Frank "could never be easy about it. He never was in the dark alone, but he fancied he saw the Fellow's Spirit." One drunken night, Frank encounters what he thinks is the thief's ghost in a dark lane, tussles with it and emerges, Partridge insists, barely alive. The story reaches its comic conclusion when we learn that "a Calf with a white Face [was] found dead in the same Lane the next Morning," but Partridge, ever the true believer in supernatural intervention, maintains the veracity of the encounter in the face of Tom's laughter, and concludes with a vivid image of what he takes to be the reality of testimony at a capital trial: "Lud have Mercy upon us, and keep us all from dipping our Hands in Blood."

The battle with the white-faced calf may provide the episode's comic climax, but that is only half the story that Partridge has to tell, and the scene also gives us a great deal of detail about the trial itself. Frank has been bound over for testimony by a writ of Recognizance that stipulates his appearance. The institution of the "prosecutor," as we saw above, required that a victim come forward as a witness, and there were penalties in law for failure to do so. The Man of the Hill was thus saved by an illegal act when his friend failed to appear, and Partridge is advocating unlawful behavior in this episode; the fact is, however, that failure to prosecute was extremely common. As King puts it, "it is clear that only a very small proportion of indictable property offenders were ever brought to [trial]."[17] The servant begins his tale by establishing a kind of equivalence or kinship between the witness and the accused: "Well, at last came my Lord Justice *Page* to hold the Assizes, and the Fellow was had up, and *Frank* was had up as a Witness." Not only are both victim and thief "had up," Page turns out to be as intimidating to Frank as he will be to the accused, perhaps because he senses some reluctance to offer damning testimony: "He made poor *Frank* tremble and shake in his Shoes. 'Well, you Fellow,' says my Lord, 'what have you to say? Don't stand humming and hawing but speak out." Page then turns his attention to the thief, who, employing what must be the oldest excuse in the annals of theft, claims to have "found the Horse." Page's biting reply (we can only call it gallows humor) is one it is credible to believe he may actually have uttered and which could well have passed into the folklore of the Western circuit: "Ay! . . . thou art a lucky Fellow; I have traveled the Circuit here these forty Years, and never found a Horse in my Life; but I'll tell thee what, Friend, thou wast more lucky than thou didst know of: For thou didst not only find a Horse; but a Halter too, I promise thee." "Upon which," Partridge tells us "every Body fell a laughing, as how could they help it." The trial is hardly a comic occasion, but there is plenty of laughter.

The judge, it seems, has his courtroom audience in the palm of his hand. We must wonder, who makes up the audience? Who would have attended the Salisbury Assizes at a time like the summer of 1737? A typical assizes had a full docket, there would have been numerous proceedings in the course of the day, and other witnesses and concerned parties would be waiting their turn. Partridge's presence, though, is suggestive. He is Frank's friend (though he does not use that word), but he may be there for the same reason that throngs turned out to watch public hangings, for the entertainment value of it all. Or he may be there on legal business of his own: when we much later hear of Partridge's life after he left the neighborhood of Paradise Hall, we find out that he not only worked for lawyers, but faced considerable legal trouble of his own. It is specifically in Winchester jail, we learn, that he spent seven years for debt, and he may be waiting his own trial.

Page, however, does not limit himself to verbal cruelty. Partridge tells us, "One thing I own I thought a little hard, that the Prisoner's Counsel was not suffered to speak for him, though he desired only to be heard one very short Word; but my Lord would not hearken to him, though he suffered a Counsellor to talk against him for above half an Hour. I thought it hard, I own, that there should be so many of them; my Lord, and the Court, and the Jury, and the Counsellors and Witnesses all upon one poor Man, and he too in Chains." In the terms provided by the historical context sketched above, the scene Partridge evokes here is not quite as corrupt as it might otherwise appear since eighteenth-century judges were more invasive than present practice allows, and as we saw earlier, the idea of what we call prosecuting or defense attorneys was only in its nascence, with no consistent procedures for their behavior in place.[18] Granting all that, however, Partridge's portrait of Page's court evokes what would probably be a hard morsel to swallow even for an eighteenth-century audience. Page's decision to allow prosecution to speak (and at such length; this would have been an unusually long proceeding) but to deny the defense would certainly violate emerging standards of fair practice. Moreover, he shows no interest in that bally-hooed habit of the English judiciary to look out for the rights of the accused—quite the opposite, in fact. It is as if Fielding has constructed the scene so as to maximize the contrast between the powerlessness of the accused and the maximum potential for brutality in a system of justice— terrible on its surface, often merciful in practice—here embodied in Page and poised to crush this poor, chained, solitary man to atoms.

The tale is thus remarkably complex. Our narrator, Partridge, is a credulous fool telling a tale about Frank, another credulous fool, for our detached and ironic amusement; but he is also a minor but sensitive tragedian able to expose the criminal justice system's cruelty in one evocative scene. The effects are volatile and surprising. The two narratives that we see—that of Frank and the cow, and that of Page and the horse thief—are not really separable, but, in fact, form a masterful double-plot. The climax of each story is an explicit moment of dramatized laughter: when he hears of the discovery of the dead calf, Tom "burst[s] into a loud Fit of Laughter," and, of course, everyone in the court laughs when Page jokes that the thief has found a halter. One disturbing effect of the parallel is to align Tom with those in the court who laugh at a man about to be sentenced to death. Can Fielding really see the horse thief's fate as something which is just as funny as Frank's encounter with the calf? Further, those in court laugh, Partridge says, because they cannot "help it," raising the equally disturbing possibility that their laughter is somehow coerced, a nervous attempt to placate the man eater on the bench.

Fielding has placed in the scene a curious phrase that should also trouble our reading. The story is Partridge's monologue, with the narrator-host entirely absent, but there is one moment when the consistency of the servant's voice seems to break down. Commenting on Page's wit, he remarks, "It is indeed charming Sport to hear Trials upon Life and Death." The phrase "charming Sport" can only be described as mordant sarcasm, with more than a hint of upper class diction as well; it is a tone hardly typical of Partridge's speech. His voice here seems, in fact, closer to that of the novel's narrator. The word "charming" occurs thirty times in the novel, and is almost always spoken by the narrator, and certainly no where else by Partridge.[19] The narrator, in fact, uses both "charm" and "sport" elsewhere not only ironically but specifically as intensifiers of sadism. We recall that Western was "charmed with the Power of punishing *Black George*, whom a single Transgression was sufficient to ruin" (148). And of another of the novel's sadists, Thwackum, a man whose "Meditations were full of Birch," and one who never misses an opportunity to beat Tom, the narrator describes his "Delight in the Sport" (133) of pedagogical flogging. Thwackum's sheer glee in his power to exercise the rod nicely adumbrates Page's inflexible severity, as we move from the petty tyrannies of the household to the grander stage of the Winchester Assizes.

For all the ways that Fielding has distanced himself and us from Partridge in this scene, heaping on him the disabling baggage of low class status and helpless superstition, the novelist nonetheless raises the possibility that it is Partridge who speaks for him here, for it is the servant alone who, witnessing the tawdry spectacle in Page's court, responds in a humane way. Twice he says: "I thought it hard." Partridge's comment has the further effect of indicting us and our laughter as readers. We, too, perhaps have found in Page's wit and Partridge's folly something like "charming sport." The laughter of both audiences—in the courtroom and among Fielding's readers—is a kind of denial of what is going on, a displacement of pity or terror or both into a response that must, Partridge reminds us, not be a laughter of delight, much less of Hobbes' "sudden glory," but of—what? Perhaps this what we must call the laughter of fear. Those in the courtroom are laughing from relief that Page's wit has found another target, but given that the audience would include others accused of equally capital crimes, that relief for some might be quite temporary indeed.

If our recognition of Partridge's humanity creates a moment of identification with him, we then must reread Frank's encounter with the ghost. The point of Partridge's story, we remember, is to warn against testifying at a capital trial. He is, in his story, presenting himself specifically as a witness against witnessing, a man with a "true" story about the need to hide the truth. But perhaps there are reasons specific to this trial why testimony is a bad idea, for if we look closely, we see that Fielding has at least raised the possibility that the thief is innocent. What *was* that "one very short Word" that the defense counsel wanted to speak? The tale begins with the comment that the farmer "lost" a horse and the accused man has, in turn and with perfect congruence, claimed to have "found" it, rather like Locke's example of the acorns discovered under the oak. As we saw with the case of Black George, the category of the lost and found is handled by eighteenth-century law as a matter of trover, not theft, and the legal consequences are minimal: one simply returns what was lost. Frank himself, the star witness, did not see the theft, was not even the owner of the horse; he only noticed someone in possession of an object which was presumably stolen. When Partridge comments, "the Fellow was hanged, as to be sure it could be no otherwise," are we to take his fatalism to reflect the indisputability of the evidence or the impossibility of countering the accumulated weight of "my Lord, and the Court, and the Jury, and the Counsellors, and the Witnesses"? Partridge himself knows the perils of a trial, having been convicted early in the novel of adultery by, as Allworthy calls it, "unanswerable, . . . manifest Evidence" (935); yet the apparently overwhelming evidence there was completely flawed.[20] Frank, deep in his cups and wandering in the dark, may literally have wrestled with a calf rather than a ghost, indeed killed the calf just as surely as his testimony killed the thief, but the outcome is the same as what he might expect if he really had encountered an angry ghost, a spirit on a mission returned from the other world—"he lay ill above a Fortnight."

Superstition here seems revealed, at least in part, as another name for guilt, not the guilt of a thief but the remorse of a guilty conscience for being, at best, a cog in a machine of judicial murder, at worst, the cause of an innocent man's death. The words Partridge uses to introduce his story come to mind: "If any Man was to be hanged upon my Evidence, I should never be able to lie alone afterwards, for Fear of seeing his Ghost." Partridge and Frank seem to merge as we read this scene, though it is Frank who testifies, and who suffers the consequences of that action. But if he originally was merely a friend who watched the trial, Partridge ultimately also becomes a witness, our witness, the one who tells Tom and tells us this "very short Story, . . . which is most certainly true." Frank's punishment, his confirmed expectation of ghostly revenge, is what Partridge told us at the outset he feared most: Frank "was never in the dark alone but he fancied he saw the Fellow's Spirit." Frank and Partridge inhabit the same spirit-filled world, and Frank's fear for his actions and Partridge's fear of the mere idea of testimony have come, by the end of the scene, to seem much the same thing. Both, we might say, are haunted men.

But the blending of Partridge and Frank is not the only distinction that turns blurry, for the nameless criminal and poor Frank also begin to lose their separate identities. Are they both criminals, however, or both victims? We remember that both Frank and the thief were "had up" before Page, both were the objects of his verbal intimidation. Frank's testimony appears less a victim's story than the confession of a criminal; Page extracts rather than invites his witness. In this light, the violence Frank suffers can be seen as the consequence of speaking words that cost a man his life—at least that is how he sees his beating, as the direct result of his testimony. He has been punished for an action that Partridge (and apparently now Frank, too) considers, if not illegal, then criminal from a moral point of view. Two acts of violence, we might say, follow from the same act of witnessing: the thief is hanged and Frank suffers a thrashing. The uncertain line of demarcation here, between witness and thief, the way each seems substitutable for the other, suggests that in this theatricalized court, those whom we expect to be the central players, the accuser and the accused, are almost irrelevant place-holders, "Fellows" who appear, disappear, and suffer their miserable fates while the engine of justice grinds indifferently on.

In the eighteenth-century courtroom, before criminal trials became fully "lawyerized" (to use John Langbein's word),[21] three roles that we might think of as distinct—the victim, the witness, and the prosecutor— were meant to blend together. From our historical distance, we might see a kind of narrative of justice implicit here: the victim, turning witness, becomes righteous prosecutor, and so finds the redress she or he deserves. It is a narrative predicated on the symmetrical separation of victim and criminal: victims prosecute, while criminals defend. But Partridge's tale upsets the comforts of this oppositional symmetry, exposing that the bond of pain that links these two actors in the drama of justice is more powerful than their assigned roles as antagonists. In a world where all the participants suffer—at the gallows or on the gibbet of insomnia—who can say, with clear authority, this man is the criminal, this the victim?

"Lud have mercy upon us and keep us all from dipping our Hands in Blood, I say"—such is Partridge's conclusion, and the episode at the very least invites us to see that moral as wise. He has seen something that he cannot "rest easy" about, and so must bear witness. Unlike all those others in Page's courtroom that day, he did not retreat into helpless laughter, or if he did, he now seems to regret it. His testimony to Tom and to us about the danger of acquiescing in the state's demand that a witness to a crime always give evidence is a cautionary tale, meant to warn individuals away from an action that has dire personal consequences in his mind, whatever the law says. Partridge is no self-conscious critic of the justice system, and as always, he is most interested in saving his own skin. This anecdote, however, threaded deliberately by Fielding with the matter of real people and possibly real events, has a resonance about the state of English justice larger than self-interest or hilarious anecdote. That resonance comes into sharper relief if we turn our attention to the trial's central figure, Judge Page.

Hanging On

If victim and criminal are bit players in this little drama, preserved from obscurity only by Partridge's saving witness, Sir Francis Page is the star, and the scene without a doubt belongs to him. The old man thoroughly dominates the trial, questioning the principals and running the show with utter and decisive confidence. A courtroom is inherently like a stage, and Page has the benefit of costume and setting, overseeing the action from a high and central bench, strikingly accoutered in vivid robes and a long wig. Yet such externals only frame his authority; he dominates by his intelligence and by the long habit of subordination that his courtroom audience brings when they appear before him. The intelligence, however, has been degraded into coarse wit. All Partridge can remember of Page is his thunder and his jokes: besides the sidesplitter about the halter, he made "twenty other Jests" (459). The word "witness" derives from "wit," but both are hollow concepts here. The witness, Frank, appears to be no more than a mere genuflection to the forms of evidence, and the jests of the comedian have replaced the wit of judgment. Page tells his jokes to relieve the tedium, a boredom induced by too many trials whose outcome he thinks he already knows. He has been playing this part too long. The Bishop of Salisbury passed on one apparently typical story to Edmund Malone (as he was gathering notes for his planned edition of Pope): it tells how the judge remarked of an accused man, "A very ill-looking Fellow; I have no doubt of his guilt."[22] The poor man, charged significantly with horse-theft, was in fact innocent and acquitted despite Page's assessment. The fellow in Partridge's story—on trial for his life and so probably equally ill-looking—is less fortunate. Page's sarcasm, his playing to the audience, his tolerance of the prosecutor's long-windedness and his refusal to allow the defense its short word all speak of a mind made up, and made up years before. His initial abuse of Frank can be read in various ways, but we can hardly escape the conclusion that the old judge believes that *everyone* who appears before him is guilty of something, and as such is deserving of some measure of his wrath.

The complement to Page's presumption of guilt is the sentence of death by hanging he so routinely passed, a habit which we know by now is far more complex than a simple reading of the law would allow. Partridge may say that the man's hanging could not have been otherwise, but that was not really the case. The fact is, according to Beattie's statistics, three quarters of those convicted of horse theft in the Eighteenth century did not hang.[23] In other words, the outcome certainly could have been otherwise, for it was precisely in nonviolent crimes such as this one that discretion came most into play. Page, however, ignores the opportunities in the system to be more nuanced and more merciful than the monolithic cruelty prescribed by a literal reading of the law. He was known as the hanging judge because, by all accounts, his resort to that sentence was so automatic. We should remember that when he makes his unforgettable sally—"thou didst not only find a Horse, but a Halter too, I promise thee"—he is not only pronouncing sentence of death in the guise of a joke, he is pronouncing that sentence in advance of a full hearing of the evidence and before the jury's deliberation. *The Dictionary of National Biography* recounts a story from late in his life; asked about his health by a colleague, Page, grim humor ever ready, said "My dear Sir, you see I keep hanging on, hanging on." Page's court thus comes to us as a dangerous compound of the fallible and the inevitable.

The prisoner here may be innocent, as Partridge was when he faced Allworthy on an adultery charge, yet the system's structure and the judge's temperament ordain a certain verdict. Whatever the truth of the "Fellow's" acquisition of the horse—outright theft or lucky find—once he arrived in Page's courtroom, he had indeed already found a halter.[24]

There is another historical layer to the scene, and a further irony. As we saw in chapter 3, the composition of *Tom Jones* and Fielding's rise to the magistrate's bench were parallel activities, and even in the absence of a chronology of the novel's composition, we can be sure that when he wrote the scene in Page's court, his own judicial ambitions must have been figuring largely in his mind. Eighteenth-century magistrates such as Fielding would become were not judges.[25] Like Justice Willoughby in Partridge's story, they heard evidence and bound over possible criminals and witnesses for trial, but Fielding never put the black cloth on his head and never personally condemned anyone to death. That was the job of trial judges like Page. It would, however, not be a distortion for us to understand the novelist who wrote this scene imagining himself in Page's position, for Fielding was already a part of the system he describes here and he was destined soon to assume an even more prominent role. We should also not forget that the Fielding who wrote *Tom Jones* was still a relatively young man (not quite 42 when the novel appeared), with good reason to think that his legal career, especially given his loyalty to his Whig patrons, might eventually culminate in a judgeship. Is he here, then, also engaged in some sort of examination of himself? Is there another self-portrait hidden here?

That question takes on more urgency when we recall that it was less than two years after *Tom Jones* appeared that Fielding published *An Enquiry into the Causes of the Late Increase of Robbers*. The novelist has earned an enviable place in English legal history as a reformer, particularly by his organization of the Bow Street Runners, but the changes that he advocates in the *Enquiry* are not really reforms in the justice system so much as recommendations for ways to perfect what already existed. He wanted, to put it succinctly, more people convicted of theft and more people hanged for that crime, and his reforms are suggestions for ways to accomplish those two ends. One of his most vehement points of discussion, in fact, concerns precisely the issue of victims of theft who refuse to testify because they are, as he puts it sarcastically, "Tenderhearted, and cannot take away the Life of a Man" (154)—someone, in other words, precisely like Partridge. Fielding notes that such tenderheartedness is one of "the very Virtues principally inculcated in our excellent Religion," but he makes that concession only to dismiss it: "the good-natured and tender-hearted Man," should, he says, "restrain the Impetuosity of his own Benevolence" (155).[26] He should restrain his mercy because, first of all, the law demands his testimony, and failure to comply amounts to treason: "his Country requires [the victim] to contribute all that in him lies to the Execution of those Laws; . . . he who prevents or stifles such the Prosecution, is no longer an innocent Man, but guilty of a high Offense against the public Good" (156). Moreover, because the law expects such service, those who refuse its responsibility are, in a real way, actually uncivilized: "Such tenderheartedness is indeed Barbarity" (156). Finally, the lives at stake are those of "Wolves" (156) and so not worth saving anyway. The comment merits full quotation:

> Here . . . is the Life of a Man concerned; but of what Man? Why, of one who being too lazy to get his Bread by Labour, . . . declares War against the Properties, and often against the Persons of his fellow Subjects; who deprives his Countrymen of the Pleasure of travelling with Safety . . . ; by whom the Innocent are put in Terror, affronted and alarmed with Threats and Execrations, endangered with loaded Pistols, beat with Bludgeons and hacked with Cutlasses, of which the Loss of Health, of Limbs, and often of Life, is the Consequence. . . . Let the good-natured Man. who hath any Understanding, place this Picture before his Eyes, and then see what Figure in it will be the Object of his Compassion. (157)

Fielding moves quickly here to stack the rhetorical deck, and the robber who at the beginning of the passage is merely too lazy to work for his bread is almost immediately thrust beyond the margins of society, as he becomes an armed and violent highwayman, indeed, an enemy of the state. The image he has conjured is a long way from that miserable figure in chains telling Page that he found a horse.

It is worth note that Fielding's target here is what he calls the tenderhearted, for there were reasons besides the milk of human kindness that might lead some to avoid testifying. Thanks to that criminal genius glanced at above, Jonathan Wild, testimony in the earlier eighteenth century had taken on a distinct air of corruption. Testimony was not necessarily what good citizens offered when they were robbed, rather it was a way that a gang leader like Wild kept his crew in line. This is the world famously popularized in *The Beggar's Opera*, a play that all by itself might be said to give testimony a bad name. To recall Wild's brilliant scheme, the devil's bargain his minions made was to turn over to him what they took; any skimming or hiding of their booty resulted in his testimony against them, testimony motivated not by public service but by the need to keep discipline among the troops. The fact that a grateful nation added a cash reward for those who testified in a successful prosecution only added an extra layer of easy profit to what was already a very lucrative scheme. "Impeachment," as it was called, occurred often enough that Wild could look like what he claimed to be, a "thief catcher." By the time the full extent of his sordid system became clear, however, in the 1720s, testimony against thieves had acquired an unsavory aroma. Hardly a patriotic act, it could look quite simply like another component of a criminal world in which prosecution and theft, far from occupying their apparently natural places in opposition, went slyly hand in glove together. Even setting Wild aside, testimony then as now was a common way that a thief might buy his freedom, by turning witness against an accomplice.

Clearly, Fielding's assault on reluctant witnesses uses the patriotic argument as a means morally and legally to rehabilitate testimony from its associations as another form of criminal activity. But it is important to keep in mind that he does not mention Wild here, nor he does allude in any way to the dark moment in the history of English law that Wild's regime represented.[27] His arguments are mounted not against those who say: since the system is corrupt, why bother? Fielding instead takes as his audience precisely the kind of person that Partridge represents. The servant is not opposed to testimony because a witness looks like a snitch; rather, as his account insistently reminds us, he is worried about "dipping [his] Hands in Blood," and the benevolence that Fielding warns against is not a compunction about transporting or branding a robber, but a qualm about killing such people.

Fielding, firmly aligning himself with the hard-hearted, thinks that hanging, and plenty of it, is the right thing to do, and immediately following his sermon against shy witnesses, we see him going on to attack the very existence of pardons for thieves, a practice as we have seen that was not only widespread but ancient in English law. He could, at one point, be thinking of Page, and with admiration: "To speak out fairly and honestly, tho' Mercy may appear more amiable in a Magistrate, Severity is a more wholesome virtue; nay, Severity to an Individual may, perhaps, be in the End the greatest Mercy . . . to the Public in general . . ." (164). Again: "a single Pardon granted *ex mera Gratia & Favore* [purely out of grace and favor], is a Link broken in the Chain of Justice, and takes away the Concatenation and Strength of the whole" (165). The perfect balance of the prose can obscure his point here: you stop theft by hanging thieves. All of them, the *Enquiry* seems to say, with a death rate for horse-theft presumably where the letter of the law would have it, at one hundred percent, however irrational that might seem: "No Man indeed of common Humanity or common Sense can think the Life of a Man and a few Shillings to be of an equal Consideration, or that the Law in punishing Theft with Death proceeds . . . with any View to Vengeance. The Terror of the Example is the only Thing proposed, and one Man is sacrificed to the Preservation of Thousands" (166).[28] Ultimately, the most striking thing about the *Enquiry into the Causes of the Late Increase of Robbers*, especially if we come to it from *Tom Jones*, is that it is not a call for reform at all, but a call for a quite remarkable literalism in the enforcement of the law of theft. Even the one reform he proposes that strikes a modern audience as humane—Fielding advocates eliminating the carnival passage to Tyburn, where London's public hangings took place—is a recommendation in the service of a more terrifying deterrence. He says it should be stopped, not because it is grotesque or cruel, but because it does not do the work of intimidating the populace that it was intended to do, and the last section of his pamphlet is devoted to the question of the best way to make hanging more frightening. Fielding's intention in the *Enquiry* is not change, but the perfect enforcement of the law as it was written.[29] As it happened, his proposals fell on stony ground and were not adopted, a refusal that was probably compounded of the perennial difficulty of altering legal practice in a systematic way, and the fact, more to the point here, that Fielding's suggestions were so at odds with the discretionary system then dominant.

It is revealing to insert Fielding and Page in the debate outlined earlier in this chapter concerning the meaning of the criminal justice system in the eighteenth century. Whether we think of the law, as the Warwick school does, as mystified ideology or as the product of broad social consensus or as an ad hoc construction born out of negotiation, Page's image of a man who refuses to play the part of justice tempered with mercy violates what seems to have been, however paradoxical or messy, prevailing legal practice. His reputation as a judge of unusual harshness suggests that he operated outside the norm, and his status as a kind of statistical outlier, in turn, helps clarify what the norm was. The expectation was that proportionality, however improvised, would govern practice even if it did not mark the statute law. But Page was a literalist, and if we had only the *Enquiry* to go on, we would have to see Fielding as a literalist, too. They seem as if, judicially speaking, they have a lot in common.

But what *did* Fielding think—I am tempted to say, *really* think—of Page? We know what Johnson and Pope thought, and a reader of

Tom Jones, as the "charming sport" comment indicates, can hardly escape the sense that Fielding, with these other writers, wants to criticize Page's reflexive harshness. Yet when we recall that he will, two years later, insist on just such severity in the *Enquiry*, that interpretation is immediately destabilized. We must face the strong probability that the Page we see in the novel is, quite consciously on Fielding's part, a version of at least part of the author himself. In this light, the judge's famed wit, so central to Fielding's construction of the scene, appears as a device by which he can emphasize their kinship: after all, both are entertainers.

There is a strong element of substitution that runs throughout this episode. Partridge's tale is a substitute for the one the Man of the Hill did not have to tell, the story of his trial for theft. The horse thief thus stands in for the Man, just as Frank, in suffering a beating he did not have to endure, substitutes himself for the hanged man in some kind of expiation. In a scene constructed as a double-plot, and replete as we have seen with other doubles of all kinds (Tom and the trial's audience, Partridge and Frank, the hanged man and the dead cow in the road, even Partridge and the narrator), the doublings and substitutions all point to one central stand-in: my Lord Justice Page, sitting in judgment, and sitting in for Fielding, comedian-jurists, yes, but hanging judges, both of them, all the same.[30]

Historians and biographers have always had trouble with Fielding's two lives, as novelist and magistrate. One approach is selectivity, on one side or the other. E. P. Thompson (who uses a quotation from *Joseph Andrews* as an epigraph to his study of the Black Act), can thus comment that "Men whose sensibility had been nourished by *Joseph Andrews* . . . found the Black Act less easy to stomach" (254), while another, Frank McLynn (as committed as Thompson to an anti-Whig stance) can call him "a notable propagandist for the Whig supremacy," and "the most able apologist for the Whig/Hanoverian regime."[31] Battestin, almost always anxious to defend his biographical subject as a human being, tries to extenuate the contradictions and at times the moral of his biography seems to be that a reformed rake like Fielding makes the best magistrate; he is able to find the *Enquiry* a progressive work—by "the lights of the time" (521). Paulson acknowledges the difficulties posed by a juxtaposition such as the one I have made here between *Tom Jones* and the *Enquiry*, and he attributes the difference to a profound disillusionment. Like Kurtz in the jungle, after a few years as magistrate, Fielding was ready to exterminate the brutes. Bertelsen's recent study of Fielding's work in the magistrate's office, with its thorough analysis of the actual crimes that his court dealt with, complicates the issue: "the everyday activity of Fielding's court was primarily concerned with idle and disorderly persons and small-time larcenists. . . . [R]ather than Battestin's 'horrid parade' it seems something more like a tragic-comical soap opera."[32]

One can, of course, grow weary of pettiness even faster than one tires of the truly horrid; probably, Fielding had his share of both. In either case, I imagine that he had lost patience with the discretionary system in which he toiled, and that the *Enquiry* reflects a kind of bitterness and cynicism about the intractability of the problems he faced. But I am not at all sure that the movement we see from 1749 to 1751, from the novel to the pamphlet, is best understood as a change in position brought about by circumstances. For if we return to the scene in the novel, we have to confront there the fact that he does not by any means unilaterally endorse Partridge's position, nor does he clearly imply that the outcome was wrong. Rather, the position Fielding adopts in the novel has already embraced Page as one face of himself, even as it stands far enough apart from him to see what is appalling about justice dispensed in his characteristic manner. What I believe to be true is that, in the novel, Fielding believes *both* that capital trials for theft are a kind of farcical theater of cruelty, *and* that crime should be handled harshly. Such a position is not necessarily a confused one; it may merely be honest to his best understanding of the complexities of criminal justice in his time. The history of criminal law reflects over and over a kind of desperation: societies believe that something ought to be done about crime, and so they do something, almost anything it seems, so that they do not look helpless, so that they can show that they are making some effort to control crime. And yet there is always dissatisfaction, a sense that what is being done is too arbitrary, that there must be a better way. The history of the criminal law is also and always a history of the attempt to reform the criminal law. Fielding the novelist seems to understand both the drive to solve the problem and the probable inadequacy of any solution proposed.

So, what are we finally to conclude about this little scene of a trial and a drunken tussle, tossed with Fielding's characteristic casual *sprezzatura* into the middle of *Tom Jones?* This episode can finally only be understood as another instance of Fielding's pervasive double-irony. The important point is not that Fielding proves himself, in a way that we can securely recognize, to be humane in the novel while he is not in the *Enquiry*, a nice guy one place and a hanging judge in the other. Rather, in *Tom Jones*, Fielding proves himself again in that characteristic double-ironic position, laughing and sympathizing at the same time at two opposed positions. Partridge, ever the straight man, is a humanitarian but he is also a fool; we admire his recognition that the trial is corrupt but we are not allowed to forget that he fervently believes in the reality of a ghost's revenge. Tom, our stand-in here as audience for the tale, has the good sense to see his friend's folly but is silent on the larger issues of justice and punishment; his laughter, like that in the courtroom, looks a lot like denial. Frank does the right thing when he testifies, yet his guilt is somehow not misplaced: he really *has* dipped his hands in blood. And that poor horse thief? He is a hapless victim, yet given the evidence, given the law, given the need to do something to stop theft when the options were limited, we cannot conclude that Fielding believes it was wrong that he had to hang: "it could be no otherwise." Page, in the end, is both a brutal monster and the author's own doppelganger; his comment about finding a halter is both completely inexcusable and really funny, and the difference between these two men may be less in the sentences they hand out than the kind of irony, including self-irony, that they deploy. Page seems stuck in one position, one role: *the* hanging judge. Fielding's knife-edge poise, of course, is easier for an artist than a judge, and irony—single, double, or infinite, however sharp as an instrument of self-knowledge or cultural critique—is not much use as a tool of public policy, such as the later Fielding found himself trying to formulate. But my point is this: Fielding embodies contradictions that he nonetheless also recognizes as such, a mental balance beyond the wildest dream of judicial disinterest, but one fundamental to this novelist's art.

Chapter 5
Gypsy Kings

Shelter from a Storm

In looking at theft in *Tom Jones*, we have thus far encountered considerable ambiguity, both in the nature of the crimes committed, and in the legal system whose job it was to both dispense justice and to hold such crime in check. Those ambiguities all come into even sharper focus when we examine another of the digressive interludes in the novel: Tom and Partridge's encounter with the gypsies. This brief, odd episode reinforces the same kinds of questions Fielding has already raised, with Black George and with the horse thief, questions that probe the nature of theft and its relationship to the meaning of property, as well as the limitations of the law. Moreover, the peculiarities of gypsy government bring us back again to matters of high politics, particularly the dynastic conflict of Stuarts and Hanoverians that has threaded this study throughout. To begin to think about what the gypsy episode might mean, we need to ask the same fundamental question we asked about the Man of the Hill, or any of the digressions in the novel: why are there gypsies here at all? As we see, we have again entered especially emblematic territory, and the episodes bear other comparisons as well. But first, I examine an old claim that the gypsies appear briefly here because they had made a cameo appearance in Fielding's own life.

Almost a century ago, in his biography of Fielding, Wilbur Cross speculated that the gypsy episode in *Tom Jones* was based on a real experience of the novelist's.[1] Part of his evidence was provided by a peculiar book—or rather, series of books—that purported to tell the life story of one Bampfylde-Moore Carew. Carew is now largely forgotten, but for a century, his was one of the most famous names in Britain. Indeed, such was his notoriety well into the nineteenth century that Thackeray could invoke him in *Vanity Fair* (along with Ulysses himself) as a figure who was the very epitome of restlessness.[2] The first version of Carew's life predates *Tom Jones*. *The Life and Adventures of Bampfylde-Moore Carew,*

The Noted Devonshire Stroler and Dog-Stealer had appeared in 1745, and recounts a picaresque life of petty crime whose contours are at least adequately suggested by the title. A twist in the tale was provided by the fact that Carew was of good birth (his father was a clergyman) and his life on the road began when he and some friends ran away from Tiverton School and joined a party of gypsies—a striking image of class mobility, but in a direction very different from the one imagined by George Seagrim.

Subsequent editions of Carew's story (and there were many) began to appear shortly after the publication of Fielding's novel in 1749, and they are marked by significant expansions and alterations, especially new passages relating to gypsies.[3] Such material was minimal in the original: Carew's encounter and brief stay with a gypsy party provided the transition out of his old life, as his hosts darken his skin with "a Liquor made from the green Shells of Walnuts"[4]—another instance, as with the Black Act, of blackened skin as an opportunity for identity transformation. Such deracinating fluid marked the beginning of his new path of roguery, but that path was not as a gypsy. Or was not until subsequent editions, which besides substantially expanding the gypsy material, also now included a new claim that Carew became their king, and which incorporated a number of references to Fielding. These additions are partially summarized in the long title of what is probably the third edition, from 1750: *An Apology for the life of Mr. Bampfylde-Moore Carew; commonly call'd the King of the beggars: being an impartial account of his life from leaving Tiverton School . . . and entering into a society of gypsies, to the present time: wherein the motives of his conduct will be explain'd, and the great number of characters and shapes he has appeared in through Great Britain, Ireland, and several other places of Europe be related: with his travels twice through a great part of America: a particular account of the original, government, languages, laws, and customs of the gypsies: their method of electing their king, &c.: and a parallel drawn after the manner of Plutarch, between Mr. Bampfylde-Moore Carew and Mr. Thomas Jones*. I say "partially" because Fielding-related materials continued to be added in editions after 1750, and came to include such material as a new "dedication"—no less than eighteen pages long—"To the Worshipful Henry Fielding, Esq.," as well as an unflattering and truncated summary of the novel in a new appendix: Blifil is left out entirely, and all the supposedly immoral incidents are highlighted.

These new editions were, it turns out, not the work of Carew at all (the first edition, while written in the third person, claimed that it was "related by Himself"), but of a canny opportunist, the London publisher Robert Goadby, who apparently saw in the popularity of *Tom Jones* a chance to repackage Carew's original text so as to capitalize on the new sensation. So, he or someone in his employ (his wife is sometimes suggested), simply went about transforming the original 1745 work. The new book amounts itself to a kind of novel, a counter *Tom Jones*, one which uses the framework of the old dog-stealer's story for a new work of fiction in parasitic relation to Fielding's. For my purposes here, what is most important about this new "novel" is its climax, where Carew not only becomes the king of the gypsies, but the very such king whom Tom meets in Book XII of the novel. Chapter 22 of *An Apology* recounts Tom's meeting with the gypsy king, but the scene is now told from the other point of view. In a sense, Goadby has picked up on that technique of Fielding's I have been so concerned with throughout this study: the meeting in a fictional space of characters who exist outside that space. But unlike the 1745 rebels or Judge Page or (as I turn to in chapter 6) David Garrick, here we have two fictions—Tom and a gyspy king named Bampfylde-Moore Carew—coming together in a kind of novel. Such a handshake across fictional borders might be only a curiosity in the history of marketing but for one, rather astonishing thing: Goadby's claim that the old rogue Carew had been elected the king of the gypsies somehow came to have a persistent factual status. It is, for instance, given pride of place in his entry in the *Dictionary of National Biography*.[5]

This mistaken belief appears to be the origin of Cross's claim that the episode has an historical basis. He insists that "It is almost certain that Fielding had met this man [i.e. Carew] who plied his trade vigorously at Bath and through the West." Cross's speculations are grounded in the canard about Carew's identity as gypsy king, and he goes on to imagine that Tom's visit to the gypsies' barn and his conversation with their king may have its origins in some similar adventure by Fielding as he made the rounds of the Western circuit: "Did Carew . . . on some occasion give Fielding shelter from a storm while travelling in the West?"[6] Cross's speculation may be fanciful, though the appearance of other real people in the novel does give him license, but it also raises a fundamental question, one that should frame any inquiry into the novelist's decision to include a night with the gypsies in his great feast of a narrative: what did Fielding know or think about gypsies? What about his readers? Whether he met Carew or spent a night in a barn with a gypsy band or not, Fielding had a picture in mind when he imagined Tom and Partridge's small adventure, and we cannot begin to understand the episode without an attempt to recapture what that image might have been. The context I try to create here draws upon the actual history of the gypsies in Britain, and uses the Carew material as an important source of information about the most common perceptions (and of course, and just as importantly, misperceptions) about gypsies that were abroad in mid-Georgian culture. What Goadby's elaborated version of the narrative of the "dog-stealer" gives us is a compendium of contemporary and popular lore about gypsies; as such, it helps clarify what Fielding's first readers might have thought when his novel suddenly presented them with a gypsy camp and a gypsy king.

We need at the outset to make a fundamental distinction between the actual history of a real people, the Romani, and the lore that has grown up around those groups called—generically, since there are substantial variations in language and culture among them—"gypsies." These threads have, as we will see, certain important points in common, but they are by no means the same. We also have to distinguish between what was known or thought about gypsies in the eighteenth century, and what we know today. There are also crucial differences between what we might call their legal status and their place in the imagination.[7]

The history of the Romani people begins in India, from which they began to migrate around the tenth century, arriving in Europe sometime after 1100. Their record—and it is not an easy one to reconstruct, both because of their dispersal and because their language was oral for most of their history—is largely tragic, and includes centuries of persecution, perhaps amounting to enslavement, in Eastern Europe and the murder of as many as half a million by the Nazis. Almost everywhere and always, the Romani seem to have met with profound distrust and discrimination, as well as constant legal harassment, and their story in the British Isles is much the same. They probably arrived in the fifteenth century, and by 1528, one estimate (of no certain value) put their number at 10,000.[8] Legal restrictions dogged them almost immediately, and two statutes passed in the reign of the first Elizabeth suggest how deeply the animus ran. The first of these in fact made it a capital crime simply to be a gypsy: they were commanded to leave the country within three months or face death; a second act made it capital to associate with gypsies for more than thirty days.[9] The latter act was, in fact, still on the books when Carew briefly joined his gypsy hosts, and was not repealed until late in the eighteenth century. The Romani in the British Isles were thus always a group targeted for expulsion, foreign matter that the host could not or should not tolerate. As such, they represented something very different from indigenous groups, like the Irish or the Scots, who were both branded as other but also subject to those strategies of exploitation that have recently been considered as part of a long British project of "internal colonization."[10]

Their trouble with the law—and Britain was of course in no way exceptional—was the fruit of their cultural distinctiveness and the kinds of fear such difference typically engendered but was also to a degree that is probably unreconstructable a self-fulfilling prophecy. However their itinerant life of "freedom" may have been romanticized (especially later, in the nineteenth century), the facts of trying to survive in hostile places were grim and the theft and fraud that came to be associated with them can be understood, not as some sort of automatic legacy of gypsy genes,[11] but as a survival strategy. Fielding himself, in his summary and analysis of the vagrancy laws in the *Enquiry* (laws that explicitly targeted the gypsies), understood quite well that the wandering poor are forced to steal in order to live. Speaking of the vagabonds of his time, he says, "Among the other Mischiefs attending this wretched Nuisance, the great Increase of Thieves must necessarily be one. The Wonder in fact is, that we have not a thousand more Robbers than we have" (144). Fielding's humane understanding of the moral dilemmas created by poverty is rather undercut by his proposed solution—"to hinder the Poor from wandering" (144), but that idea hardly originated with him. It had long been conventional wisdom that the best way to handle the vagrant poor was to send them back to the place where they came from, and make them (and their legal oversight) the responsibility of their home parish.

Such a solution was of course no solution at all for the Romani, who had no point of British origin to which they could return. Not to be itinerants would mean both that they had given up their identity as wanderers (their other name, we recall, is "travelers") and that they had found a place that would accept them, and in Britain in the eighteenth century, that place did not exist. Many of them were transported to the colonies and some were hanged, and it would be hard to say whether they were punished for stealing or for being gypsies, since their identity as gypsies in a sense forced them to steal. But the undeniable reality that many gypsies were thieves is still quite different from the assumption that they were all thieves by some sort of racial definition, and that image of a race of robbers clouds the more complex truth that they performed other kinds of labor, especially in metal-work as their long association with the trade of tinker would suggest.

So, a mid-eighteenth-century reader of *Tom Jones* would, when presented with the idea of "gypsy," think first of their marginal status, one reinforced repeatedly in the legal code, as a race of outlaws. What else would they know, or think they knew? First of all, and completely erroneously, they believed as we saw above that the gypsies were natives of Egypt and "gypsy" is of course a corruption of "Egyptian." Their actual origin in India was not established until later—though the initial discovery that their language had its roots in Sanskrit came as early as 1763.[12] Goadby's elaborated version of Carew's story provides a very illuminating picture of popular conceptions about gypsy governance. The title page of all the post-1750 editions promises an account of the gypsies' "Method of electing their King," and that "method" has important implications for Fielding's novel. The title, in fact, gives away the key word: "electing." An outsider like Carew could never rise to the position of gypsy monarch (even in Goadby's feverishly commercial imagination) unless there was a mechanism that would allow it, and that mechanism was election. That fact is crucial, and I return to it at length below.

If the legal status of gypsies in Fielding's time was miserable, they fared better as objects for imaginative depiction. While the height of romanticized gypsy life would await the nineteenth century, gypsies show up with some regularity in seventeenth-century drama and continue to appear throughout the eighteenth century. There are encounters with gypsies recounted in *The Spectator* (130), in *Pamela*, and, earlier in Fielding's career, in *Joseph Andrews*, where Joseph and Fanny have, as infants, both been stolen by gypsies. Such representations turn on a few stereotypes, endlessly reiterated: gypsy theft (including that romance staple, theft of children), gypsy craft (mostly to fraudulent ends), and especially gypsy fortune-telling, an activity that amounted to a kind of fraud. Fortune-telling is central to the gypsy material in both *Pamela* and *Joseph Andrews*, but as we will see, only tangential in *Tom Jones*. It is in the eighteenth century that they also begin to appear in various descriptions of what constitutes the "picturesque."[13] With these contexts in mind, let us turn now to Book XII, chapter xii: "*Relates that Mr. Jones continued his Journey contrary to the Advice of Partridge, with what happened on that Occasion.*"

A Company of Egyptians

That position in the novel is a charged one: Tom's travels are almost done, and only three chapters stand between him and his arrival in London. On his wandering path so far, Tom has faced a variety of experiences—sexual, criminal, financial, moral, and so forth—and those adventures all seemed to try to balance the entertaining and the instructive. His short visit to the gypsy camp, however, is unlike his other wayfaring encounters; it appears to fulfill a pedagogical imperative that it then denies, and its peculiarities of tone, structure, and significance require the closest attention. The episode is certainly exotic, perhaps the most exotic in the strict sense of that word in the novel, as Tom and Partridge, seeking a dry place on a wet night, stumble upon that quintessential ritual for the investigation of a foreign culture: "The People then assembled in this Barn were no other than a Company of *Egyptians*, or as they are vulgarly called *Gypsies*, and they were now celebrating the wedding of one of their Society" (666). This is, in fact, the first wedding *Tom Jones* has given us since the self-interested and blighted nuptials of Bridget Allworthy and Captain John Blifil at the novel's outset, and the mention of marriage here begins perhaps to herald that stampede to the altar that defines the narrative's conclusion, still six books away. But Fielding seems uninterested in exploiting the picturesque possibilities of a foreign wedding. The scene instead is constructed in explicitly pedagogical terms as, for the most part, a dialogue between Tom and the gypsy king. The king turns out to be an anthropologist's dream, full of candid detail about his people, and (in his role as judge) as ready with a lesson in judgment as the hero of any *bildungsroman* might wish to find.

But the narrator then takes away what he seems to give, for this digression ends on what is one of the oddest notes in the novel. Having described the gypsy culture in idealized terms, and having shown the remarkable sagacity of their monarch, the narrator proceeds to demolish the happy little world he has been at such pains to establish, closing the episode with a strong admonition, apparently directed at his readers, not to share in Tom's rapturous admiration for the society we have just observed.[14] The hero, it seems, has not only learned nothing, but has been outright seduced by an alluring vision of an impossible utopia, and the narrator, suddenly stern, must, in a kind of palinode to the chapter, warn us off following him into mystification—more gypsy enchantment, it seems. We naturally wonder why Fielding has bothered to construct a scene that he will then awkwardly have to disavow, and why our hero, so often on his journey (as in his earlier encounter with the Man of the Hill) ready to learn and truly perceptive, is suddenly so dangerously stupid— to the narrator, anyway. Indeed, if we are to believe the narrator, Tom appears to be much more naive here, at the very end of his travels, than he was at the outset. What might Fielding be up to?

One productive way to begin to explore this question is through the way that the novelist has structured this episode—or, more accurately, structured it in relation to the material that surrounds it. The odd conclusion to Tom's gypsy encounter is a reminder that his experience in their camp is much more definitively and elaborately framed than almost any of his road adventures; the encounter with the Man of the Hill, a much longer interlude, is also strikingly framed and the episodes bear other comparisons as well. Such elaborate framing around what is a very short episode has the effect of suggesting that what we are reading is something essentially emblematic. Manuel Schonhorn has analyzed the episode as ecphrastic, and I agree that the gypsies present us with a little picture, a world within a world, embedded in the narrative as a whole.[15] And as a picture, it is important for our understanding to see in detail how its frame is constructed, and how the scene works in relation to its surrounding elements. In brief, we have a long lead-up, in which Fielding builds an air of mock-suspense about the nature of the lights and commotion that Tom and Partridge—lost, drenched, and looking for shelter—have observed. The scene itself then follows, dominated by Tom's conversation with the king and a sudden accusation against Partridge for sexual misconduct. The aftermath consists of two speeches, a brief one by Tom praising the gypsies, and then the narrator's, condemning the kind of absolute monarchy that he claims that the gypsies represent. Two small exchanges immediately follow, both of which are significantly connected to this material: a conversation between Tom and his servant about the banknote of Sophia's which they have found, and an encounter with a novice highwayman.

As we saw in the Man of the Hill episode, superstition—that leitmotif that runs throughout the novel's road section—is an important part of this framework, and it appears both in the introduction to the scene, and—surprisingly—in the narrator's concluding remarks. The dominant voice that we hear as we approach the gypsies is Partridge's, and as always, what he talks about is his fear of ghosts and witches. Having spotted a light and hearing the audible noise of celebration, Partridge cries, "who could be merry-making at this Time of Night, and in such a Place, and such Weather? They can be nothing but Ghosts or Witches, or some Evil Spirits or other, that's certain" (664). Again, a digressive episode begins in the grip of Partridge's comically supernatural anxieties. But, unlike the Man of the Hill episode, Fielding here allows some mock suspense to build about the origin and nature of the sights and sounds that our travelers have discovered, as Tom and his servant engage in a prolonged dialogue about what lies ahead. Partridge rattles on: "what if we should meet with something worse than Witches, with Evil Spirits themselves?—Pray, Sir, be advised. . . . If you had read so many terrible Accounts as I have of these Matters, you would not be so Fool-hardy" (664–5). Tom, enlightened man that he is, presses forward, and finds a welcome in the barn. But from whom?

Fielding keeps curiosity alive through another page, and resumes the discussion he had begun in the important introduction to Book VIII, before Tom meets the Man of the Hill: "Had this History been writ in the Days of Superstition, I should have had too much Compassion for the Reader to have left him so long in Suspence [*sic*], whether *Beelzebub* or *Satan* was about actually to appear in Person, with all his Hellish Retinue; but as these Doctrines are at present very unfortunate, and have but few if any Believers, I have not been much aware of conveying any such Terrors" (665–6). He continues this reassurance that nothing supernatural is in the offing, but also delays any information about what will actually appear through three paragraphs, at length concluding with the revelation we saw above: "The People then assembled in this Barn were no other than a Company of *Egyptians*." The frame thus replicates the introduction to the Man of the Hill, emphasizing Partridge's fear and Tom's courage, and asserts again the narrator/historian's refusal to strain credulity by the use of the literally supernatural, but does all this in a notably dilated manner, giving extensive rein to Partridge's timorous reluctance, and insisting on the rational nature of the narrative at considerable length. The effect is to leave the novel's readers feeling that they have been led into something, deliberately and by stages—but into what? A world apart, of course, and in its tangible sense of separation, the gypsy universe again suggests that it should be taken or understood emblematically.

As noted above, Tom and Partridge have literally walked into a barn and a wedding feast, but it quickly becomes apparent that the scene's focus will be the gypsy king, and what follows resembles nothing so much as an abbreviated version of an episode in *Gulliver's Travels*; the Man of the Hill is also an interlude with a notably Swiftian feel. Our hero, like Gulliver, almost immediately gains the ear of the local monarch, who projects a *je ne sais qua* aura of power: "He was very little distinguished in Dress from his Subjects, nor had he any *Regalia* of Majesty to support his Dignity; and yet there seemed (as Mr. *Jones* said) to be somewhat in his Air which denoted Authority, and inspired the Beholders with an Idea of Awe and Respect" (667). Tom's immediate sense of the king's majesty is worth note here, in light of his final idealization of the king, and of the narrator's concluding comments on monarchy. What Tom learns from him about gypsy society suggests, as do Gulliver's encounters, that the barn's inhabitants seem to exist primarily in order to cast Britain in a bad light. The conversation is dominated by matters of history, politics, and the law, as the king characterizes his own ruling style, summarizes some salient points in gypsy political history, and then offers an overview of their criminal justice system. Immediately and with perfect timing for illustrative purposes, Partridge is hauled before the king and accused of attempted adultery; trial, judgment, and a surprising punishment then follow. All of these elements work together, it seems, to produce the picture of a small utopia, compassed by the walls of a barn, led by a shrewd and benevolent monarch.

The king, we hear, acts only "to do dem [that is, his people] Good" (668). His selfless concern, in turn, inspires their gratitude, and the resulting polity is a harmonious blend of mutual affection: " 'Dey love and honour me darefore, because me do love and take Care of dem' " (668). Such paternalistic perfection, we learn however, did not always obtain:

> About a tousand or two tousand Year ago, me cannot tell to a Year or two, as can neider write nor read, dere was a great what you call,—a Volution among de *Gypsy*; for dere was de Lord *Gypsy* in dose Days; and dese Lord did quarrel wid one anoder about de Place; but de King of de *Gypsy* did demolish dem all, and made all his Subject equal vid each oder; and since dat time, dey have agree very well: for dey no tink of being King. (668–9)

The king's illiteracy catches our attention here as an accurate depiction of gypsy reality, but so does the remarkable "Volution" his oral history recounts. Given the fact that gypsies were, in a sense, literally a people without history because of their illiteracy,[16] the fact that Fielding has given them one, however cursory, again suggests he is exploiting them for emblematic use, for the defining moment of gypsy history, of course, turns out to recall the recurring conflicts of English history between the crown and the aristocracy. In the gypsy world, it seems, the struggle was defined once and for all in favor of the monarch. The result is a social order without hierarchy of any kind, except for the presence of a king.

That role, it turns out, is a burden, primarily because it entails serving as the supreme arbiter in matters of crime and punishment; to be King of the Gypsies is mostly to be Judge: "For me assure you it be very troublesome ting to be King, and always to do Justice; me have often wished to be the private *Gypsy* when me have been forced to punish my dear Friend and Relation; for dough we never put to Death, our Punishments be ver severe. Dey make de *Gypsy* ashamed of demselves and dat be ver terrible Punishment" (669). Notable here is the absence of capital punishment, a striking difference from the British legal system where, as we have seen, death by hanging was the sanction for almost everything. The king himself sees the emphasis on shame, however, as the primary difference between British and gypsy justice: "The King then proceeded to express some Wonder that there was no such Punishment as Shame in other Governments," a point Tom disputes, insisting that "there were many Crimes for which Shame was inflicted by the *English* Laws, and that it was indeed one Consequence of all Punishment" (669). The king, however, immediately punctures Tom's complacency with a rejoinder that, again, reminds us of Swift: "Dat be ver strange . . . [f]or me know and hears a good deal of your People, dough me no live among dem, and me have often hear dat Sham is de Consequence and de Cause too of many your rewards. Are your Rewards and Punishments den de same Ting?" (669). His pidgin English renders his point a nicely layered one, and we can appreciate how both "sham" and shame can produce rewards in Fielding's Britain.

This high-minded discussion of theories of jurisprudence is then interrupted by "a sudden uproar": an inebriated Partridge is discovered in the arms of "a young female *Gypsy*" by her husband, who insists that the king render immediate justice on the malefactor. "*Partridge* was now hurried before the King; who heard the Accusation, and likewise the Culprit's Defense, which was indeed very trifling: For the poor Fellow was confounded by the plain Evidence which appeared against him, and had very little to say for himself" (670). The king then asks Tom, the pedagogical subject here, what he thinks should be done, and the pupil offers to pay off the angry husband: "putting his Hand into his Pocket, [he] offered the Fellow a Guinea." But this is the wrong answer. The king resumes his interrogation with a devastating question worthy of Sherlock himself, asking whether the husband had followed the couple from the beginning of their conversation until the moment it turned criminal. Learning thereby that the aggrieved spouse had in fact delayed his intervention, the judge proceeds to pass sentence, not on Partridge, but on the gypsy pair: "Me do order dat you have no Money given you, for you deserve Punishment not Reward; me do order derefore, dat you be de infamous *Gypsy*, and do wear Pair of Horns upon your Forehead for one Month, and dat your Wife be called de Whore, and pointed at all dat Time" (671). The *faux* cuckold must wear the cuckold's badge, and the *faux* whore must be treated as such; the punitive damages the king awards here represent the literalization of the crime as its own punishment—an imaginative judgment worthy of the *contrapasso* of Dante. Shame, most emphatically, has not been rewarded.

The final comments between Jones and the king are brief, and they summarize the gypsy monarch's central insight as a comparative ethnographer. He says, "me suppose you tink us all de Tieves," a supposition that Tom confirms, prompting the king's concluding apothegm: " 'Me vil tell you,' said the King, 'how the Difference is between you and us. My People rob your People, and your People rob one anoder' " (671). *Tom Jones* is a novel swollen with thefts of all kinds, and the king's last words on what we might call the endogamous nature of English thievery resonate with the narrative as a whole. Again, they seem like a judgment on Fielding's society in a quite Swiftian vein. The King of Brobdingnag is harsher when he calls the English the "most pernicious Race of little odious Vermin that Nature ever suffered to crawl upon the Surface of the Earth" (II, 6), but the sense that we are hearing a regal judgment difficult to dispute is as strong in *Tom Jones* as it is in Gulliver's second voyage.

The episode's curious conclusion then immediately follows. Tom "proceeded very gravely to sing forth the Happiness of those Subjects who live under such a Magistrate" (671), a small panegyric that prompts the narrator's concluding outburst. Partridge was almost seduced by a gypsy; poor Tom, yet once more it seems, has actually succumbed to charms that he should have resisted. The narrator's laborious demolition of the gypsy example runs for seven paragraphs, and approaches in length the entire conversation, including Partridge's trial, between Tom and the king. The argument here debates whether or not what the narrator calls "arbitrary Power" (671) or "absolute Monarchy" (672)—he uses the terms interchangeably—is the best form of government. He begins with the debater's oldest ploy, apparently conceding the opposition's central argument. Such a government *is* the best, he says, and notes that "Mankind have never been so happy" (671) as they were under the good emperors during Rome's Golden Age.

Their example, however, turns out to be in the service of the argument against absolutism; they represent an excellence that cannot be duplicated: "In reality, I know of but one solid Objection to absolute Monarchy. The only Defect in which excellent Constitution seems to be the Difficulty of finding any Man adequate to the Office of an absolute Monarch" (672). The narrator passes silently over the fascinating historical question he has just raised—if it is so difficult to find such men, how did the Romans get so lucky, and no less than five times in a row? Instead, he begins to pursue his prosecution of the idea more vigorously, noting that an absolute monarch deficient in the qualities necessary for a virtuous application of power would be, not merely incompetent or ineffective, but must instead be "attended with no less a Degree of Evil" (672). The next paragraph, the fifth, dispenses with all moderation and balance of tone, and deserves to be quoted at length for its sheer polemical verve:

> In short our own Religion furnishes us with adequate Ideas of the Blessing, as well as Curse which may attend absolute Power. The Pictures of Heaven and of Hell will place a very lively Image before our Eyes: For though the Prince of the latter can have no Power, but what he originally derives from the omnipotent Sovereign in the former; yet it plainly appears from Scripture, that absolute Power in his infernal Dominions is granted to their Diabolical Ruler. This is indeed the only absolute Power which can by Scripture be derived from Heaven. If therefore the several Tyrannies upon Earth can prove any Title to a divine Authority, it must be derived from this original Grant to the Prince of Darkness, and these subordinate Deputations must consequently come immediately from him whose Stamp they so expresly [sic] bear. (672)

The earlier concessions about the virtues of the Roman emperors of the Golden Age have vanished by this point, and the narrator concludes by insisting that not even "the least Degree of Prudence" would allow "an Alteration" in the English Constitution, and that it is better to submit to the occasional inconvenience "arising from the dispassionate Deafness of Laws, than to remedy them by applying to the passionate open Ears of a Tyrant" (673).

The last paragraph of these concluding remarks then returns explicitly to the gypsies, and the narrator insists that they are, rather like the Roman emperors, invalid as an "Example" that might be used to defend absolute monarchy; but the disqualification is not what we might expect, given the earlier direction of his argument: "we must remember the very material Respect in which they differ from all other People." That difference is not, as the king insisted, who robs whom. Rather, their secret is that "they have no false Honours among them; and that they look on Shame as the most grievous Punishment in the World" (673). One implication of this argument is that, if you have the right kind of legal system, then the problem of finding the perfect man to be king might just disappear, but again, the narrator is not interested in such speculation. This full-circle return to the gypsies presents us with an odd note on which to end his peroration, for it seems once more to idealize gypsy society at the expense of the English, and thus to undercut the whole thrust of the speech that has preceded it. To cite the beauty of ideal alternatives is not, rhetorically speaking, the best way to urge your own case, and yet the narrator, both with this conclusion and by his earlier mention of the Roman Golden Age, cannot seem to help reminding us of such paragons. It is as if he has not, in fact, quite made up his mind.

Who Robs Whom

I have summarized the scene in some detail so that, as we begin to tease out its implications, the peculiarities of the episode are clear. Those implications seem to fall into three categories: superstition, criminal justice, and politics. Those issues are distinct, in part because they align with the three components of the encounter: superstition dominates the lead-up to the discovery of the gypsies, criminal justice is the overriding concern of Tom's conversation with the king, and of course, monarchical politics is the subject of the conclusion. At the same time, these concerns blend together here, as they do throughout *Tom Jones*.

The episode, like the Man of the Hill, is firmly embedded in a context of superstition. Partridge's reiterated insistence that the barn holds a witches' coven, or worse, creates a lingering effect that (in a narrative maneuver that anticipates Radcliffian Gothic) does not quite dissipate when the rational truth is discovered. In Partridge's superstitious light, Tom's infatuation with the gypsy king looks like an enthrallment—his "Egyptian majesty" has cast a kind of spell on our hero. The line from the *Aeneid* that the narrator cites just as Tom enters the barn signals this effect: "*Dum stupet obtutuque; haeret defixus in uno*" [while in amazement he hangs rapt in one fixed gaze] (667). Aeneas is on holy ground, in the temple of Juno, and his "amazement" is provoked in part by the otherworldliness of the place in which he finds himself. But Virgil's hero is also looking at pictures, another reminder that we are about to see an emblematic scene. The narrator's Virgilian reference in this context is, of course, mock-heroic, but it is not only mock-heroic. The allusion helps create the sense that the gypsy camp really is enchanted—they are a race of fortune-tellers, after all—and that enchantment helps us better understand the discrepancy we see at the end of the scene between Tom's reaction to his encounter and the narrator's. There, the latter reacts to Tom in the same way that Tom typically reacts to Partridge, assuming the position of the enlightenment voice of reason who brushes away the cobwebs of superstition. Recall Tom's own outburst, discussed in chapter 1, when Partridge announces the Jacobite prophecy of the miller with three thumbs: "With what Stuff and Nonsense hast thou filled thy Head?" (440). The narrator debates the point more elaborately than Tom does with his servant, but the point is the same. The alignments, however, are more complicated: not only does Tom seem to occupy Partridge's typical place here, Partridge himself appears—if we think back to the "charming sport" comment, appears *again*—to be in an unexpected alliance with the narrator. The old Latin master, after all, was the one who warned Tom at the outset that the inhabitants of the barn might have supernatural connections, and—to take the narrator at his word—he was right. Our hero has been bewitched.

That surprising alliance of narrator and servant goes further. As we have seen, the most vehement of the narrator's arguments against absolutism is that it is a doctrine with ultimately diabolical origins: "If therefore the several Tyrannies upon Earth can prove any Title to a divine Authority, it must be derived from th[e] original Grant to the Prince of Darkness, and these subordinate Deputations must consequently come immediately from him whose Stamp they so expresly bear" (672). The reference here is again to that notion of "divine right" discussed in chapter 1; it is a crucial argument for theorists of absolute monarchy, and the narrator's point is that what apologists claim to be a right derived from God is instead descended from hell itself. His insistence that "arbitrary power" carries Satan's own tenebrous warrant is, to be sure, meant to be ironic, though it is notably heavy-handed irony, with no doubleness about; it is emphatically not what our genial and typically subtle host usually offers, and he sounds a lot more like the stern admoniser of the *Enquiry* than he does (I am tempted to say) like himself. The irony, in fact, is so leaden, we can not help but wonder if we are really meant to accept it uncritically. Partridge, after all was the one who was characterized at the outset of the journey as someone whose "Head [was] full of Nothing but Ghosts, Devils, Witches, and such like." In his introductory remarks to the scene, the narrator had dismissed as meretricious art those contemporary dramas which invoked demons: "To say Truth, the whole Furniture of the infernal Regions hath long been appropriated by the Managers of Playhouses . . ." (666). But this cozy Enlightenment comradery with his readers, at Partridge's expense of course, seems to have vanished scant pages later for it is these "infernal regions" that the narrator himself now invokes. While one might say that the irony shields him from the accusation that, like Partridge, he actually believes these matters, the convergence of a foolish voice in the scene's overture who insists that we are about to encounter "Evil Spirits themselves" and an apparently more urbane speaker in its epilogue who tells us that absolute monarchs, far from being little gods, are in fact a "Hellish Retinue" is a similarity worth pondering.

Tom's conversation with the benevolent gypsy despot seems to exist wholly apart from the supernatural concerns of the scene's introduction and conclusion and is instead dominated, once more, by matters of criminal justice. The king's work as judge begs comparison with the other judges we encounter in the novel, especially Allworthy and Page. As others have noted, Allworthy looks bad by comparison: both he and the gypsy get to judge Partridge on a fornication charge, but the magistrate of Paradise Hall fails to see that the evidence is flawed and that the witnesses are wholly unreliable, and he does the poor man a terrible injustice. Partridge ends up branded as guilty of a crime he did not commit, and Allworthy's judgment initiates a sequence of disasters which begin with the poor man's forced departure from the neighborhood and which culminate in his imprisonment for debt in Winchester jail. Page also makes a powerful point of contrast: if death by hanging was his habitual sanction, a choice that relieved him of the burdens of discretion, the gypsies' king must somehow find a way to do justice without benefit of capital punishment. Discretion is all he has; a kind of inversion of Page, he is defined precisely by his power to surprise.

He also serves as arbiter of justice in a society that is, apparently by self-definition, certainly by his self-admission, criminal. The king had hinted at this with a curious choice of phrase at the very beginning of his conversation with Tom: " 'Me doubt not, Sir, but you have often seen some of my People, who are what you call de Parties detache: For dey go about every where' " (668). "Parties detache" is a military term (French, like much eighteenth-century military terminology) for detachments, separated from central command, whose purpose was to forage.[17] The line between soldiers sent out to forage and a pack of thieves on a rampage was not always an easy distinction to maintain—another instance of the definitional ambiguities that surround theft—and the king's joke here seems to work both to euphemize gypsy robbery and to suggest that his community, apparently so foreign, may operate in ways not entirely strange to his young English interlocutor, who after all had fallen in with a company of soldiers only a few days earlier, a brave band who seemed notably reluctant to pay for their beer.

In entering the barn, Tom and Partridge have more or less literally walked into a den of thieves, and we see that traditional gypsy stereotype quickly confirmed in the plot by the conniving couple to entrap Partridge. Their design, while not precisely as blatant a theft as highway robbery, is extortion and so robbery nonetheless. As the king admits, "My People rob your People"—it's what they do, whether in detached parties or in an improvised scheme cooked up (under guise, of course, of an offer to tell his fortune) when opportunity in the form of a gullible and drunken Partridge walks into their midst. But the king makes that crucial addition to his self-indictment: "your people rob one anoder." He thus creates a kind of kinship between his people and the English, but he also points to an important difference. His distinction is, I think, a key moment, not only in this episode, but in the novel as a whole and its central concern with the question of theft. If we pull back from the immediate details of the textual moment, we can see that the gypsy chapter is surrounded by a particularly dense network of thefts of various kinds, some nakedly so, others more ambiguous. It is productive to use the king's distinction—the difference between what I call endogamous and exogamous stealing—in looking at these examples, for it is when we expand the scene's frame slightly to include material closely preceding and following that the whole episode, not just Tom's conversation with the king, reveals itself as urgently concerned with the question of theft.

Immediately before riding out into the rainy night on which he encounters the gypsies, Tom shares a bottle with that wonderfully slippery middleman in the plot, Lawyer Dowling; much of the talk concerns Blifil, whom Dowling rather likes, but whose unsavory character Tom discusses at length. The lawyer makes a telling slip, referring to Allworthy as "your Uncle" (657), and the whole conversation, centering as it does on matters of kinship and inheritance, read from the retrospective point of view of the novel's revelatory ending, make clear that Tom's half-brother has, by his misrepresentations and general skullduggery, plotted (successfully, at this point) to defraud him of his share of an inheritance from Allworthy. Thus, we have invoked, on the eve of the gypsy encounter, the plot that we might consider to be the central theft in the whole novel: Blifil's long and well-laid plans to get his hands on money meant for Tom. Later, upon leaving the gypsies, Tom and Partridge's first extended conversation is a discussion of the banknote belonging to Sophia that they found earlier and which we looked at in chapter 3: the servant, of course, is all for spending the money, particularly because their own funds are quite short, but Tom argues that such an action would be theft: " 'he who finds another's Property, and wilfully detains it from the known Owner, deserves *in Foro Conscientiae* [a court of conscience], to be hanged no less than if he had stolen it' " (676). All of this, of course, is a replay of the issues discussed with regard to Black George. As I pointed out, legally the issue is deeply ambiguous: by the law of trover, Sophia could recover her money, but since it has been found, not stolen, she could not prosecute as thieves those who have kept her money. What is important is that Tom considers it theft (just as Allworthy does when he learns of Black George's action), and also that the novel appears to be going out of its way to remind readers of the other primary acts of theft—or "theft"—that have marked the narrative.

Finally, in the very last encounter of the road section, and very shortly after departing from the gypsies, our travelers meet a lone man on horseback and begin a conversation in which "Robbery was the principal Topic" (678); their new companion then pulls a pistol and demands their money. Tom disarms and ultimately forgives the highwayman when he learns that he was driven to the desperate act (his first attempt at robbery) because he has "five hungry Children, and a Wife lying in of a sixth, in the utmost Want and Misery" (680). In the end, Tom gives the failed thief two of the three guineas he has left. The episode serves as a stark reminder that people, in this case an armed but incompetent robber in desperate financial circumstances, often steal out of need, and that the exchange of property in a charitable gift and the one that takes place in a robbery can functionally be the same thing.

The catalog I elaborate suggests the range of what it means, in the king's words, that the English "rob one anoder": fraudulent misrepresentation for financial gain (Blifil), strategic silence about a valuable object that has been found (what Black George does, what Partridge advises), and what in the end turns out to be something like armed begging, a way that the highwayman can dramatize his very real need. These crimes underline, moreover, the argument I made in chapter 3, that theft itself can be a most ambiguous business, an ambiguity created in part by the way these three "thefts" are also marked by a striking intimacy. Blifil's frauds are perpetrated against a man he knows to be his half-brother; Sophia's banknote (as were Tom's earlier) is not just an anonymous piece of currency that these travelers have happily found, but a possession that is specifically *hers*, contained in her recognizable little gilt pocket-book; and the highwayman, whom we will meet again in London, and whose name we discover is Enderson,[18] is yet another of those mirrors of Tom we find seeded throughout the text, a good man without money who has married ruinously for love. Tom, in other words, disarms and then makes a gift to someone who amounts to a version of what he might become if, penniless as he now is, he were to marry Sophia. Such are the varieties of theft that surround the gypsy episode, all of them exemplary of the king's perception that the English rob one another. The extortion plot against Partridge, by contrast, while miming intimacy in its sexual flavor, takes place between strangers, across lines of race and culture. Its exogamous sexuality figures the exogamous nature of the planned theft—"my People rob your People." The king's pronouncement seems not merely to be a joke, but a reliable guide that allows us accurately to taxonomize the thefts that we see.

Having disposed of Enderson, Tom and his friend proceed without further incident to London, but the road section concludes with one last comment on robbery. Tom's remark here is patriotic in a very strange way, but makes more sense in the context that the king has provided:

> *Jones* exprest a great Compassion for those Highwaymen who are, by unavoidable Distress, driven, as it were, to such illegal Courses as generally bring them to a shameful Death. "I mean," said he, "those only whose highest Guilt extends no farther than to Robbery, and who are never guilty of Cruelty nor Insult to any Person, which is a Circumstance that, I must say, to the Honour of our Country, distinguishes the Robbers of *England* from those of all other Nations; for Murder is, amongst those, almost inseparably incident to Robbery." (681)

What I call Tom's bewitchment seems here to be still in full force, and he remains very much under the spell of the gypsy king, however misguided in the narrator's opinion. Not only does he articulate a position diametrically opposed to the one Fielding will soon adopt in the *Enquiry*, by calling into question capital punishment for highway robbery (with the proper mitigating circumstances, of course), but he appears to have absorbed the implications of the monarch's last words, that the English people can be defined as a race by their habit of stealing from each other. Tom says, yes, we do rob one another, but in a *nice* way, without killing or cruelty. The intimacy of the crime, in the terms I use, militates against that kind of aggravated behavior—it's all in the family. Tom's comment, of course, is saturated with dramatic irony. Blifil, as the novel will soon take pains to demonstrate, would like nothing better than to see Tom, not merely destitute, but dead. Intimacy is, in fact, no guarantee against violence, but the king—still wiser than Tom—had not said anything about his host nation's capacity for violence.

Robbery, in *Tom Jones*, is not an action so much as a pervasive and inescapable moral texture for existence. If we step back far enough, the whole novel unfolds as a great feast, not (as the narrator promised in the book's opening chapter) of human nature, but of human theft. Or perhaps it is human nature to steal. We can recall that our hero is famously introduced in the novel as someone "certainly born to be hanged," a fate predicted by his early predilection for theft: "He had already been convicted of three Robberies, *viz.* of robbing an Orchard, of stealing a Duck out of a Farmer's Yard, and picking Master *Blifil's* Pocket of a Ball" (118).[19] At times in *Tom Jones*, it appears that there is nothing that anyone does that cannot be construed as a robbery in some way, and most of it, in the terms I am exploring here, is endogamous. Even the most overt and unambiguous acts of theft in the novel—the robbery committed by the Man of the Hill in Oxford, for instance, where "his Chum was certainly the Thief" (455), or the recollection of the real theft (and very un-English murder) committed by the notorious Fisher (discussed in Book VIII, 1), or even the horse thief, who makes the literally fatal error of riding his new possession to the local fair—are instances of stealing from close acquaintances or in close quarters, and the volume of such overt larceny is small compared to the kind of even more intimate robbery we look at: Blifil defrauding his brother, or Black George pocketing his benefactor's banknotes, or for that matter, Fitzpatrick's consumption of his wife's fortune, or the elder Blifil's grandiose designs on Allworthy's wealth. Almost everyone seeks to move property from someone else's hands into their own, and very little of it takes place at the end of a gun barrel. On the contrary, robbery seems to be what takes place between friends and family. To see human activity as dominated by the urge to steal emerges as a kind of epistemology, a way—albeit cynical, even bitter—to know the world. This is, at least in part, the wisdom of the gypsy king, and his vision of universal thievery provides *Tom Jones* with a kind of epigraph, and his privileged insight into the cosmos that Fielding has created suggests again that, whatever dread warnings the narrator has plastered on the walls of the gypsies' barn, we cannot ignore what the king has to say.

But the king is not merely a theorist of crime and punishment, a folksy Bentham or Beccaria, and his observation about who robs whom can be understood not only as an anthropological point about cultural difference, but as a way to distinguish two systems of criminal justice. As we have seen in chapters 3 and 4, the English system was obsessed with protecting property against theft, and the history of its criminal justice system well into the nineteenth century is a largely futile record of attempts to legislate away the problem of stealing. *Tom Jones* suggests instead that, in a world where most theft is endogamous, most robbery will inevitably go unpunished, as, in fact, most eighteenth-century theft of whatever variety did go unprosecuted. There ought to be a law for what Black George does, or for what Blifil attempts, or to eliminate fortune-hunters like Fitzpatrick or Captain Blifil, but there isn't, and can't be.[20] "Your people rob one anoder," looks like a description, not of crime, but of the network of social relations in England—this is how people behave, and the idea that theft is a crime which can be controlled by laws and punishment looks pretty hollow.

The world of the gypsies is an island inside the English island, a culture contained and yet apart, and because its business is theft, the punishment of theft—much less its prevention—is not the goal of its criminal justice system. We see, of course, this culture's response to only one crime, but the episode's emblematic quality suggests that the one trial that we do see is meant to be read as exemplary: this is how the gypsy system works. In one sense, the king as judge looks very English: discretion is at the center of his practice. But it is discretion used to a very different end: he neither condemns nor punishes the conniving couple for their attempt at extortion, that is, for their crime, but instead for the ways in which they have willfully shamed themselves, putting on a whorishness and a jealous outrage that are factitious. The English laws try to punish the act of acquisition, and the guilty are transported or hanged for having grabbed a watch or snatched a bundle of linen. The gypsy couple, by contrast, are sanctioned for what their acquisitiveness does to them. By playing unsavory roles in the service of their greed, they have become on an existential level the parts that they thought they were only feigning, and so the king insists that, at least for a time, they cannot shed those roles—that indeed, they will have to announce them.

Shame is powerful as a punishment because it is a tool of separation. The king's sentence makes the couple "de infamous *Gypsy*," and they will, for the length of their punishment, be "pointed at" (671) by the community. There were, as Tom's comment to the king suggests, analogues to this kind of juridicial shaming built into English law: formal institutions like the pillory or the custom of branding criminals for certain minor offenses, not to mention informal, extra-legal customs like the "rough music" that Molly Seagrim finds herself subjected to by her peers when she wears Sophia's cast-off gown to church. But, as we have seen, the king is skeptical about how seriously the English are willing to use shame as a punishment, a skepticism that the narrator evidently shares since he singles out the employment of shame by the gypsies as their signal difference from the English. What the gypsies understand, and what the English system fails to distinguish perhaps, is that the separation that is the engine of shame must paradoxically take place from a position that remains inside the community: the couple can be pointed at in a way that is painful precisely because they are still surrounded by those who make up their own tribe. Setting aside medieval holdovers like the pillory (which, while originally meant perhaps to function in much the same way as the finger pointing of the gypsies, actually usually involved crowd violence of a quite brutal kind[21]), the system of English punishments does not understand that separation in a literal sense from the community in fact reduces shame: held in Newgate to await trial, or sent off to the colonies to work off a sentence of transportation, the criminal is taken out of the community in which his offense might be viewed as shameful and placed in another circle, a circle of those exactly like him. This is the prison world that Fielding describes so vividly and horrifically in the opening chapters of *Amelia*, a world from which shame has been effectively banished.

In the light of this discussion, Tom's encounter with the highwayman Enderson is worth another look. A crime is certainly committed—a pistol is pulled and a threatening demand is made. If the affair were handled as the narrator, looking a lot like the Fielding of the *Enquiry*, had recommended a few pages earlier, with the criminal made subject to the "dispassionate Deafness of Laws," his fate would be clear: the gallows. But instead we have an outcome that mirrors what we saw in the gypsy camp: Enderson pours his story into the "passionate open Ears," not of a tyrant, but of Tom, and the result of that trial is an ad hoc full pardon and a gift of two guineas. Tom, like the gypsy king, has exercised discretion and improvised his justice, with the result that the would-be robber vows never to attempt another theft, a promise we find confirmed by later events. We have, by the side of the road and within a matter of moments, a crime, a trial, and—that great desideratum of later criminal justice—a rehabilitation. To underline the wisdom of Tom's course of action, we hear once more the contrastive voice of Partridge, here (completely contradicting his earlier qualms about capital punishment) demanding that the poor man be strung up: "it is very hard upon honest Men, that they can't travel about their Business without being in Danger of these Villains. And to be sure it would be better that all Rogues were hanged out of the Way, than that one honest Man should suffer" (681). Partridge asks for just the kind of consistent application of the laws that the narrator has just recommended. In his demand for laws which are deaf and so not susceptible to the kind of discretion that Tom has just allowed, he in fact anticipates just the arguments Fielding will make in the *Enquiry*.[22]

Enderson, however, gets neither Page nor Partridge nor the narrator nor Magistrate Fielding as his judge; he is not hanged, and when Tom encounters him in London some ten chapters later, he hails him as a hero, "When I do not love and honour the Man who dares venture every thing to preserve his Wife and Children from instant Destruction, may I have a Friend capable of disowning me in Adversity" (727). Tom, like the king, focuses not on the act of theft, but on what the motivation for theft says about the person's character. Enderson, the highwayman, is revealed as a man who has taken up arms in the defense of his family; no be-medaled soldier could have done more, and the feeling that wells up in such a breast should be not be shame but pride.

At the heart of the little tale of the reluctant highwayman, we discover a contrast between what the law would do and what Tom actually does, between the deafness of a dispassionate system, and the compassion of a man of feeling. As he meets Enderson's family, Tom cannot "forbear reflecting without Horror on the dreadful Consequences which must have attended them, had he listened rather to the Voice of strict Justice, than to that of Mercy when he was attacked on the high road" (728–9). In following the path of "Mercy," Tom aligns himself with the gypsy king, substituting his own judgment for what strict appearances would dictate; he learned something after all. We can recall here another peculiarity in the narrator's conclusion to this episode: his admonition appears to be directed at us, the readers, and not at his errant hero. Tom, in fact, seems to have gone native (it may not take the full thirty days that the anti-gypsy fraternization law specified), and he goes on both to ignore what the narrator has said and to exemplify precisely the kind of justice we have just seen in the barn. It is hard to imagine that we are not meant to applaud Tom for his wisdom and for his charity. What he learns from the monarch is not something impossibly utopian, but something he can and does put to immediate and beneficent use. We thus have a moment in the novel where the narrator appears to be alienated from the manifest direction of his own text. To state the question again, why would Fielding the novelist give us, in the gypsy king, an idealized example of justice at work, proceed to show how that model can shape a healing and human exchange between Tom and Enderson, but then insert between that example and its fulfillment a speech in the mouth of his narrator that says that it is all impossible?

Fielding calls into question what his narrator says here in another way as well, one that is especially self-reflexive and ironic. We recall that the gypsy king had announced his style of rule as both absolute and benevolent: "me never design any Ting but to do dem Good. . . . Dey love and honor me darefore, because me do love and take Care of dem" (668). The king's words here are a very close echo of the narrator's own politicized self-description, back in the introductory chapter to Book II:

> For as I am, in reality, the Founder of a new Province of Writing, so I am at Liberty to make what Laws I please therein. And these Laws, my Readers, whom I consider as my Subjects, are bound to believe in and

obey; with which they may readily and chearfully comply, I do hereby assure them that I shall principally regard their Ease and Advantage in all such Institutions: For I do not, like a *jure divino* Tyrant, imagine that they are my Slaves or my Commodity. I am, indeed, set over them for their own Good only, and was created for their Use, and not they for mine. Nor do I doubt, while I make their Interest the great Rule of my Writings, they will unanimously concur in supporting my Dignity, and in rendering me all the Honour I shall deserve or desire. (77–8)

The confusions engendered by the juxtaposition of these passages are both palpable and delicious. The narrator's rule over his readers, as promulgated in Book II, seems predicated on precisely the same principles as the gypsy king's dominance: absolute power in the service of the good of his people. Yet the narrator of Book XII, in flat contradiction to his earlier pronouncement, claims that such power as the king represents is an example of *jure divino* rule. The gypsy king, in other words, behaves in precisely the same manner as the narrator said he himself would, but the narrator then discredits the example that the king embodies as an impossible one, and bad politics to boot. Is he thus disavowing his own rule, revealing himself as a "Tyrant," as a tool of the devil, as another would-be "arbitrary" monarch not quite up to the level of wisdom and virtue that the job requires? Of course not—or not completely. The parallel of the king and the narrator is Fielding's sly way of reminding us, with a lovely deflation of his own pretensions (a deflation inherent in the hyperbole of the passage in Book II), that no autocrat thinks himself a devil, and absolute monarchs are probably always benevolent from their own point of view. But he also signals that his narrator may not be, at every moment, fully "adequate to the Office" he has assumed.

The Right to Choose Our Governors

The palinode with which the gypsy episode ends, when scrutinized in the light of the scene's full and complex framework, looks more and more imposed and irrelevant. Moreover, there are not only problems of tone whereby the narrator is contradicted by the spirit of the text, there is also a notable discrepancy in content, for the issues raised in his speech seem to be completely at odds with those that are central to the scene and its extended context. The concern throughout that material is theft, and the problem of what to do with thieves. But the narrator, in his seven paragraph rant, does not discuss crime and punishment at all; he talks instead about absolute monarchy. The narrator's speech, that is, seems to be about an issue that the context does not naturally suggest: why does he want to talk about "arbitrary power" when his novel seems to want to explore criminal justice?

One answer, again, is allegory. The narrator specifically says that the gypsies are an "Example" (673), the quotation from the *Aeneid* tacitly announces that the episode will be emblematic, and his conclusion is nothing if not an attempt to point the moral of the small tale just concluded, and that moral concerns, not criminal law, but politics. In an influential article on this episode, "Tom Jones and 'His *Egyptian* Majesty': Fielding's Parable of Government," Martin Battestin takes precisely this allegorical path. He has little to say about the actual life of gypsies in eighteenth-century Britain, but he does create a context for their place in the novel that suggests that the episode has a specifically allegorical role. There are two foundation stones for his argument: one, he claims that the misconception, common in Fielding's time, that the gypsies originated in Egypt meant that eighteenth-century histories of that ancient empire provide an especially rich context for understanding Fielding's portrayal, especially the way he describes their government and system of justice; and two, that their absolute monarch is meant to recall Stuart principles of *jure divino* kingship, and that therefore, they represent a "parable" of the exiled ruling family.[23] How useful is it to think of the gypsies' "parable of government" as an anti-Stuart polemic? Quite useful, as I hope to show. At the same time, I want to emphasize that political allegory is only one of the elements in play in this rich episode. The questions about theft that are raised here and that I have been exploring—what theft is, who robs whom, what do to about it— are at least as significant as the political questions about philosophies of governance.

I think Battestin is right to try to understand the gypsies as a specifically, even particularly, allegorical moment in the novel, but his attempt to stabilize their significance as unambiguously Stuart and Jacobite collapses under interpretive pressure. Why would Fielding create an ideal that he then immediately explodes? Why is it that Tom (and not say, the Jacobite fellow-traveler, Partridge), who earlier had an unquestioned loyalty to and an articulate understanding of, not only the Protestant succession, but its accompanying ideology of limited monarchy, fails so miserably to see that he has been presented, in miniature, with everything he rejects? The narrator's explanation of precisely why Tom is wrong to like what he has just seen seems prompted by a certain nervous realization that he has just propagandized for the wrong party. Having made that realization, why not cut the gypsies out of the novel—or at least rewrite the scene so the gypsy king seems less ideal? As a "parable," this episode—much like the Man of Hill—is quite ambiguous, especially in the Stuart and Jacobite terms that Battestin has invoked. Like the old man, the gypsies as an emblem have a surprising reversibility, and seem to point in two directions at the same time, as we can see by working through their possible significations.

Battestin is on target when he notes clear parallels between the narrator's "diatribe" (72) against absolute monarchy and a sermon on the same subject preached by Bishop Hoadly and published in 1708, *The Happiness of the present Establishment, and the Unhappiness of Absolute Monarchy*; the Stuarts' claim to the throne indeed rested on just those notions of *jure divino* kingship that the episode's conclusion is so anxious to refute. That connection—the gypsies represent absolutism and so do the Stuarts, therefore the former allegorize the latter—is the strongest foundation for Battestin's effort to find a stable point of significance for the "Egyptians." To fill out the historical context a bit more, as we saw in chapter 1, an insistence on absolute authority formed (along with his Catholicism) the chief offense of James II in the catalog of complaints that drove him from the throne, and the Stuarts' marriage to the doctrine was doubtless the reason Hoadly was so anxious to continue to attack it twenty years after the Glorious Revolution.

Other connections between the gypsies and the Stuarts could be made, even beyond the ones that Battestin cites. Their mutual condition as exiles is perhaps the most obvious. The gypsies, "Egyptians" as they were understood to be, like the Stuarts and their supporters, live in a foreign land, paying allegiance to their own monarch. Further, the way the episode is framed by Partridge's superstition, and the kind of enchantment that the gypsies exercise, reminds us of the issue we have explored throughout this study, the connection between the Stuarts and the supernatural. *Jure divino* kingship itself is part and parcel of this association with superstition. The narrator's elaborate joke about the derivation of "arbitrary power" from the Devil is his way of associating Stuart political philosophy with Stuart belief in mumbo-jumbo in general. A modern thinker, he implies, would no more buy the argument for divine right than he would accept the existence of witches. Absolutism is just another anachronistic superstition.

The gypsies' reliance upon theft as their chief livelihood, moreover, can be seen as a way to make fun of the Stuart aspirations to the throne; what the exiled family insist would be a restoration is actually robbery, and as we have seen, the narrator refers to the Jacobite army as "Banditti" (368) when he first mentions the Rebellion, in Book VII.

But it is here, with the episode's central issue of theft, that we begin to encounter problems of allegorical stability. For theft was also precisely the accusation thrown by the Jacobite loyalists at the supporters of the House of Hanover; the most powerful arguments in their arsenal spoke directly to the violation of property rights involved when a possession (in this case, the throne) passes without consent or compensation from one set of hands to another.[24] Fielding had reminded his readers of this very argument only a few pages before the gypsy episode: the night before the adventure in the barn, Partridge discusses dynastic politics with some other travelers, and the conversation seems placed deliberately to raise questions about the complexities to follow. An "Attorney's Clerk" (so, a figure of the law, if not a lawyer), who is a Jacobite, asserts, "if my Father dies seized of a Right, do you mind me, seized of a Right, I say; Doth not that Right descend to his Son? And doth not one Right descend as well as another?" (647). Theft, thus, is an issue that—allegorically speaking—cuts both ways, since it was part of the rhetoric of both Hanoverians and Jacobites. It is also a reminder, again, of the king's resonant epigram: even at the level of monarchy, the British people rob one another.

We can make other connections between the gypsies and the new dynasty as well: the king's comic pronunciation of the language serves as a reminder of another king, the initial Hanoverian monarch, George I, who ascended to the monarchy with no knowledge of his new kingdom's language. For that George, as for his Egyptian Majesty, the King's English, so to speak, is not so good. And the foreignness of the House of Hanover complicates the significance of the question of exile, for the gypsies' position in the English countryside is rather like that of the Germans who had now ruled Britain for thirty years. If their displaced condition marks them in some way as Stuart, their apparently happy acceptance of a position in a foreign land more closely resembles the House of Hanover. Like Britain's new ruling family, the gypsies are foreigners who have become comfortable in their new home, even if, like George I, they remain culturally distanced from it. If the Man of the Hill was the fanatic Protestant with the heart of a Stuart, so the gypsies, on closer inspection, are an absolute monarchy draped with some distinctly Hanoverian trappings.

One other issue complicates the attempt to make the gypsies a unilateral token of Stuart doctrine on monarchy, and here we return to the context provided by the Carew material. *How* did "his *Egyptian* Majesty" come to power? We know he is an absolute monarch, and we know that such a form of government began long before, when the great

"Volution" abolished the nobility and set one ruler over all. But how did this king gain the throne? On this key point of cultural knowledge, the novel is conspicuously silent. But perhaps it is silent because this was one fact about gypsies that Fielding's readers would think that they already knew. Whatever the actual methods by which Romani leadership was determined, and for that matter, regardless of the ancient Egyptian practice of absolute dynastic rule, the popular perception in eighteenth-century Britain, as we saw at the outset of this chapter and as all the Goadby elaborations of Carew's story reiterated for a wide audience, was that the gypsies *elected* their king. This is a point that Battestin completely neglects. The elective nature of the gypsy kingship was proverbial enough that, forty years later (perhaps with *The King of the Beggars* in mind), Burke, decrying the idea of elective kingship in the *Reflections on the Revolution in France*, will call such an idea "the delusive gypsey [sic] predictions of a 'right to choose our governors.' "[25] In other words, the average reader of *Tom Jones* in 1749, if presented with the concept, "gypsy king," would probably have as his immediate association, "elected." Goadby's description of this aspect of gypsy culture is worth quoting at length:

> There are perhaps no People so compleately happy as these are, or enjoy so great a Share of Liberty. The King is elective by the whole People, but none are allowed to stand as Candidates for that Honour, but such who have been long in their Society, and perfectly studied the Nature and Institution of it. . . . And they can have no Temptation to make Choice of any but the most Worthy, as their King has no Titles nor lucrative Employments to bestow, which might influence or corrupt their Judgement.
>
> The only Advantage the King enjoys, is, that he is constantly supplied with whatever is necessary for his Maintenance from the Contributions of his People; whilst he, in Return, directs all his Care to the defending and protecting his People from their Enemies; in contriving and planning whatever is most likely to promote their Welfare and Happiness, [and] in seeing a due Regard paid to their Laws . . . ; so that, perhaps, at this Time, it is amongst these People only that the *Office of a King* is the same as at its first Institution, viz. *a Father and a Protector of his People.*[26]

The model described here seems distinctly un-Egyptian, not only in its elective quality, but in its sense of the King as a protective father stripped of undue panoply, rather than (to mention another association that might attach to the pharaohs) a god to be worshiped.

Elected monarchs may have considerable, even absolute power, but they cannot rule *jure divino* for their "right" has come from the electors, not God. Election also problematizes the narrator's insistence that the flaw in absolute monarchy is the inadequacy of virtually everyone for the job. As we have seen, that argument was the very centerpiece of his argument against absolute power—as he puts it, the problem is "the Difficulty of finding any Man adequate to the Office of an absolute Monarch" (672). But the sequence abounds in examples of just such ability: besides the gypsy king, there are all those Roman emperors. The gypsies, it seems, have found a person "adequate to the Office" and elected him. Even Tom himself, perfectly Solomonic in his treatment of the highwayman, suggests that a good man can learn a lot about the right use of power from the proper teacher.

Burke helps us understand how the elective nature of gypsy kingship irretrievably complicates Battestin's arguments for a unitary significance for the gypsies. The great conservative invokes the "gypsey . . . right" in the context of his lengthy refutation of Richard Price's sermon, "Discourse on the Love of our Country," which had been preached in late 1789, and which of course served as the spring-board for Burke's subsequent *Reflections*. Price's discussion, like Hoadly's at the beginning of the century, was a meditation on the meaning and implications of the Glorious Revolution and the subsequent Revolution Settlement (though it is of course strongly colored by events taking place across the Channel). Price, as Burke makes clear, draws from the terms of the Settlement a threefold conclusion: that the British people have "acquired a right (1) 'To choose our own governors.' (2) 'To cashier them for misconduct.' (3) 'To frame a government for ourselves' " (99). Burke, of course, will have none of this, but it is instructive to see how, in his efforts to refute Price, he handles the deep contradiction at the heart of the events of 1688: James II may have been unwillingly removed from the throne, but Burke insists that the principle of hereditary succession was nonetheless and simultaneously confirmed. As he puts it, "Instead of a right to choose our own governors, they [the framers of the Settlement] declared that the *succession* in that line (the protestant line drawn from James the First) was absolutely necessary 'for the peace, quiet, and security of the realm' " (101). Immediately, however, he must concede—and here is where the gate is flung wide for the opposing arguments of Price and others—one uncomfortable fact: "Unquestionably there was at the Revolution, in the person of King William, a small and temporary deviation from the strict order of a regular hereditary succession" (101). But the invitation to William of Orange to take the monarchy, Burke quickly insists, represents a "special case," and therefore no principle can be drawn from it (101). Having made the one exception, however, who is to say that special cases cannot occur again? The fact is, in 1688 the British *did* choose their governor; they may not have thereby turned themselves into a band of gypsies, but they did forever flavor their form of monarchy with a connection to what Locke had called, in his great defense of 1688, the consent of the governed. Once more, the gypsies' monarch looks, as an emblem, distinctly Janus-like, with one face (his absolute authority) pointing to the Stuarts, but with the other (his election) looking in a distinctly Whiggish direction.

The notion of an elected king also resonates with the other ideal example that Fielding cites—the good Roman emperors. We noted above the prominence that they have been given in the narrator's speech: "Mankind have never been so happy, as when the greatest Part of the then known World was under the Dominion of a Single Master; and this State of their Felicity continued during the Reigns of five Successive Princes" (671–2). An asterisk follows, pointing to their names in a footnote at the bottom of the page. Fielding himself included only twenty-three footnotes in the novel, so the presence of the footnote here adds further emphasis by its very rarity: "*Nerva, Trajan, Adrian*, and the two *Antonini.*" Fielding's language here is very close to that which Gibbon (the novelist's great admirer) adopted to make much the same point twenty-five years later in the opening chapters of *The Decline and Fall of the Roman Empire*: "If a man were to fix the period in the history of the world, during which the condition of the human race was most happy and prosperous, he would, without hesitation, name that which elapsed from the death of Domitian to the accession of Commodus. The vast extent of the Roman empire was governed by absolute power, under the guidance of virtue and wisdom."[27] But these emperors were not merely excellent, and not only absolute in their power. This group of five wise men and splendid rulers all took the throne, not by direct succession through a family dynasty, but by adoption.

Adoption is a striking model: it concedes the power of dynastic succession by creating a sort of imitation of a father–son link, but it also and powerfully represents an act of selection, and thus puts us again, as with the gypsies, in a world where strict inheritance is not the governing principle. Adoption, and nonlinear succession, of course, also puts us in mind of *Tom Jones*'s own grand resolution, in which the prize property of Paradise Hall will pass to Tom, a very good man indeed, but most emphatically not Allworthy's direct heir. Their relation is, in fact, essentially adoptive; upon discovering the infant in his bed, Allworthy's resolution is "to take care of the Child, and to breed him up as his own" (44).

Later, when he believes he is dying and makes his death-bed bequests, he calls Tom "my Child" (244). While the end of the novel finally puts a genetic name on their bond, the very fact that their relation is that of uncle and nephew, and an illegitimate nephew at that, serves to remind us that their connection is not direct, and that Tom's inheritance has been in no way automatic. Tom Jones, the gypsy king, and the good Roman emperors are thus further linked: not only are they wise in the way they use power, they have also won their position by some form of selection.

The question of dynasty and inheritance, and the relation among the gypsies, and the novel, and the then literally warring factions in British politics all seem suddenly very complicated indeed, for what is at stake, it appears, is the emblematic significance of Tom Jones himself. On the one hand, his admiration of the gypsy king and his willingness to put into practice the edifying lessons in personal justice that he learns at the king's knee bespeak an alliance with a legal and political order not fully congruent, to say the least, with the best Whig doctrines. Those doctrines, which were the legacy of 1688, limited monarchical power and did so by subordinating the king to the constitution—that is, to the law. At the same time, and on the other hand, in learning from—and in a sense, imitating—the gypsy king or looking like one of the good emperors, Tom is not exactly revealing himself as a closeted Jacobite. Battestin's unilateralist account of the gypsies' significance as Stuart satire fails to account for much in their position, their behavior, and their political structure. While the Whigs (especially a very conservative one like Burke) could be made nervous by the elective implications of the dynastic interruption that occurred in 1688, the fact remains that the precedent of selection was now in place in the British constitution, and it is a precedent that seems to lurk in the allegorical shadows of this episode, as it does in the novel's glorious conclusion. The gypsy king's elective position, along with the adoptive model that worked so well in ensuring that Rome's happiest period would indeed be golden, both seem to adumbrate *Tom Jones*'s final resolution, in which inheritance becomes a victory of good nature (Tom) over the more rigid indications of apparent legal suitability (Blifil). The fact that Tom turns out to be Allworthy's nephew is really like the Roman practice of imperial adoption—it is an outcome that legitimizes an anomalous inheritance by creating and emphasizing an appearance of close kinship. But that very structure has a most uncertain relation to the realities of mid-Georgian politics. The gypsies, like the emperors, combine absolutism with elements of election/selection, a mixture that is consonant with the novel's resolution, but tantalizingly at odds with the alternatives available on the British political scene in the middle of the eighteenth century. This is the quality that I have elsewhere in this study called allegorical reversibility, for emblematically, the gypsies are both Whig and Jacobite.

Tom, to be sure, inherits an estate, not a kingdom. His travels and his travails are not the proving ground for a monarch, only for a country squire. But that may be Fielding's point: the allegory moves down class lines, rather than up, and Roman emperors and gypsy kings point to a young man who will be a gentleman, and not the other way round. The key issue, that is, may not be who should be Britain's monarch, but what kind of subjects he should have. Monarchy, it appears, is an "Office" no man is quite adequate for, not so much because of human nature but because of human history, which is always intruding, always in the way. The Stuarts are, at this point, neither quite forgotten nor quite gone, and the messiness of their departure is not yet fully cleaned up. The gypsies, a people without much history as Fielding has imagined them, do better than the British for this very reason perhaps. But Tom, an individual and not a nation, is less burdened by the past. He can be loyal to "the Cause of King *George*" (440) and at the same time learn something about the wise exercise of power from an absolute monarch, a nice bit of synthesis simply not available on a national scale. He will, we know, be a very good justice of the peace.

As I argue throughout, Fielding's sense of history is profoundly double. He wants to confound our polarizing tendencies, tendencies that lead us to see an emblem as aligned unambiguously with one political position or another. That does not mean here, no more than it did with Charles Stuart or the Man of the Hill or Black George, that Fielding is thereby searching for a compromise position or some happy synthesis of the available alternatives—Britain needs a monarch who is both absolute and elected, or whatever. Rather, he wants to expose polarities as a kind of intellectual trap. In the way that he has constructed the gypsy episode, indeed in the way he has written his novel, Fielding satirizes not absolute power but absolute positions, and that central target is given voice in the conclusion of this episode, through a beautiful irony, by the narrator himself. We might say that the narrator here is not Fielding, but "Fielding," the poor hack who had with what must have been depressing frequency to write what his Whig masters demanded, and the episode here, like the others we have been examining, seems constructed to allow him to make fun of the kinds of things that financial pressures made him say for his bread.

As always, the irony is a double one. The narrator's pompous, self-contradictory, comments are not contemptible, even if they are a bit hysterical, and riddled with contradiction. The gypsy king does an excellent piece of work as a judge, certainly the best we see by any judge in the entire novel, and he provides an example from which Tom can learn, but the barn is a fine and private place, and on a national scale, it probably is better to have a government of laws than one of men. The gypsy monarch has a shrewd take on British society, and it can really seem at times—either in the novel or from a magistrate's bench such as Fielding would shortly occupy—that the population is engaged in a kind of Hobbesian robbery of all by all. As the final word, however, that would certainly be too cynical for this novel. Fielding's irony will, by the time of *Amelia* a few short years away, cross the line that divides the genial from the bitter, but in *Tom Jones* he is still delighted by the fact that double-irony allows him a tantalizingly unspecified middle position, a place from which he can keep a delicious distance from polarized positions whose appeal he nonetheless can still cannily measure.

Chapter 6
Mirror Plots

Witness to History

Tom Jones' doggedly faithful companion, Partridge, has appeared in this study primarily as the voice of fearful superstition and inconsistent commentary on the criminal law, but if we look at the novel as a whole, we see him in a remarkable number of other roles: as schoolmaster and undistinguished but irrepressible Latinist; as brow-beaten husband and presumptive father of the novel's hero; as barber and surgeon; as a voluntary servant to a man, Tom, who is without money but whom he assumes to be rich; as a crypto-Jacobite more loyal to his personal safety than to the cause of the Stuarts; and (as he relates almost at the very end of the novel) a victim of ruinous litigation who "lay seven years in *Winchester Goal*" (938). He is often the butt of some joke, but he is also and surprisingly sympathetic at times. While he is a far more attractive character than his old schoolmate, Black George, he does display some of the same oddities in the way Fielding has constructed him that we discovered in the gamekeeper. He, too, is a site of association, for Jacobitism and for superstition, but also, as with George, for issues of class mobility, money, and criminal justice. Like George Seagrim, too, he turns out to be a character with a peculiarly intimate relation to his creator. That complexity emerged to some extent as we looked at his reaction to the trial for horse theft that was the subject of chapter 4, as it did in his comments on highway robbery in the last chapter. It is most prominent, however, in another small scene, where he again becomes the primary focus of our attention: his trip to Drury Lane, to watch Garrick play Hamlet.

His role in this scene is not identical to the one he played in Judge Page's court. The trial, as we saw, was an event in which he was not a material participant, and it occurred outside the plot and years before. He reports there on something he watched, and his narrative means to illustrate his conviction that it is always a bad idea to testify at capital trials. The circumstances of the *Hamlet* excursion are apparently quite different: this episode takes place in the time frame of the novel, and, at the playhouse, far from being a passive member of the audience, Partridge takes narrative (if not literal) center stage, and becomes in a sense an actor, not just an observer as he was in the earlier episode.

Yet the similarities between the scenes are striking. Both are strongly marked as digressions from the main action—they are almost independent short stories—and both are dominated by that trait that Fielding returns to throughout the novel, but never more strongly than in these two scenes, that is, Partridge's unshakeable belief in the reality of ghosts. Both scenes are comic, meant both to represent and provoke laughter, but their laughter is provided by occasions that seem, to put it mildly, ill-suited to comedy: a capital trial and what is, after all, the arch-tragedy of the English tradition, *Hamlet* itself. Each scene also seems centrally engaged with history, with the actualities of Fielding's own moment, and that actuality is marked by the presence in each of real men about whom Fielding and his audience knew a great deal: the trial judge Francis Page, and the preeminent Shakespearean actor of the age, David Garrick. The settings, too, the courtroom and the theater, are the two central venues of Fielding's adult life.[1]

The appearance again of the historically factual at these two moments underscores one crucial aspect of Partridge's role in both scenes, the fact that he is a kind of witness. "Witness" is a complex concept, covering matters legal, religious, and moral, among others.[2] Partridge is not a witness in the legal sense in either scene, and as we saw, when he is in court, he resists that role in explicit terms, becoming a kind of anti-witness. But both stories do center on an act of observation by the servant that seems to transcend what we associate with, say, the watchfulness of a mere audience, though he is part of an audience in both episodes. In part, it is his conviction that something important is happening—in Page's courtroom, in Garrick's theater—that sets him apart from those around him, audiences who appear to be content merely to be entertained, and so distracted from the matter of the real, the historical. In both cases, his observation leads him to attempt his own representations of what he sees, as narrative in the case of the trial, as a kind of literal re-creation in the case of the play. Those attempts to go beyond the mere observation of history to the making of it—"making" here in the sense that all historians are makers of the subjects they recount—prove remarkably suggestive for Fielding's own sense of history.

The Very Picture of the Man

Less than a month after Partridge tells the story of his experience in Page's private theater, he has a chance to see a real play, and one with a plot even grimmer than the story of the horse thief. If we follow those scholars who have mapped the plot of *Tom Jones* onto a calendar, then it is on a night very close to the winter solstice of 1745 that Tom, Partridge, Mrs. Miller, and her younger daughter attend a performance of *Hamlet*, with David Garrick playing the lead.[3] While we may think that the Prince of Denmark's tragedy is an appropriately gloomy entertainment for the darkest day of the year, Fielding's purpose in creating the scene seems on its surface to be surprisingly and unequivocally comic, an even larger festival of laughter than the horse thief's trial for his life. Tom's closest brushes with tragedy in his own life—wounding Fitzpatrick, the plot to see him to the gallows, his discovery that he has apparently slept with his own mother—lie just ahead, but Fielding gives this night to Tom's amusement. And very particular amusement it is: Tom wants to watch Partridge watch the play. In a novel that never hesitates to digress, this seems to be, much like the encounters with Page or the gypsies, a moment of especially pure digression—brief, freestanding, and utterly irrelevant to that long chain of complications and unravelings that constitutes Tom's tale.

As a few critics have hesitantly noted, however, *Hamlet* does share some of the same central issues that dominate *Tom Jones*, such as fathers and sons, and the problems of dueling and incest that follow so soon after what looks for a time like Tom's last night of fun.[4] But there is another connection here. *Hamlet*, of all plays, raises just the political issues on everyone's mind at that moment of crisis for Britain. On the same night that Fielding imagines Tom and his friends attending this play so fraught with issues of usurpation and tyranny, the young man who styled himself the Prince, not of Denmark, but of Wales was camped with his small army near the Scottish border, pressing his own father's claim for justice.

For the first readers of the final books of *Tom Jones*, in February 1749, memories of December 1745 would necessarily be fresh, and they would certainly have remembered the strong sense of panic that the capital felt. Charles Edward Stuart's army of Highlanders and Jacobites had, as noted above, reached its high-water mark near Derby earlier that same month and the period's tireless commentator on current events, Horace Walpole, had written a friend, "I . . . fear the rebels beyond my reason"—a common enough sentiment.[5] The rebels, of course, decided to retreat and, by December 20, had crossed the Esk back into Scotland. From a later perspective, the rebellion's manifold weaknesses are obvious and the disaster they met at Culloden the next April appears inevitable. But in the climate of fear and rumor that prevailed in London that December, such security was missing, and the air of national emergency was acute.[6]

But not in *Tom Jones*. Having introduced the grid of real time into his fiction, and having left his readers with no doubt about the timing of Tom's arrival in London, Fielding makes that striking decision we examined in chapter 1, a decision not to mention the rebellion or the capital's panic in the last six books of the novel, even though those realities were barely three years old. The events of the Forty-Five apparently disappear as suddenly as they were introduced in Book VII, when Tom made his short-lived decision to join Cumberland's army and fight the rebellion. Again, however, as in the gypsy episode, the absence of overt reference does not mean that Fielding is not thinking about history, and the *Hamlet* episode in fact provides the novelist with another occasion to consider the Stuarts and their last serious bid for power. Fielding has here again constructed one of his fascinating historical allegories, and we find that the events in the little world of Garrick's theater, both the play itself and the actions of those who watch it, allude irresistibly to that larger clash between the houses of Stuart and Hanover which was unfolding around and outside the novel's fictional space. Partridge, once more, is central to an understanding of this aspect of the scene. He is not quite what he first seems to be—the butt of the joke—for, as in the courtroom scene earlier, he acts as a witness to something important, and the mixed nature of our response to him complicates how we understand Fielding's position.

What, then, might it have been like to see Shakespeare's play of usurpation and revenge in December 1745? In 1601, Robert Devereaux, the Earl of Essex, had arranged for a number of productions of *Richard II* in London, hoping to inspire in the body politic treasonable thoughts, thus warming up the populace for his own attempt to unseat Elizabeth.[7] We can imagine Charles Edward Stuart no less eager to put *Hamlet* before the citizenry. Not only does it tell the story of a son struggling to do justice for a wronged father, the wrongs that Hamlet complains about—the criminal loss of the throne, the nation in the hands of tyrants—were precisely the issues at the heart of the Stuart claim for restoration. To be sure, no one ever accused William of Orange, much less the Hanoverian Georges, of murder; the Revolution of 1688 was termed "Glorious" in part because it was so bloodless. But terms like "usurpation" and "tyranny," not to mention "theft"—ideas, which Claudius represents with such unambiguous clarity—were central to Jacobite rhetoric, no matter that the Revolution was peaceful and that the new kings were more limited in their power. For the Stuart loyalists, James II and his heirs were the legitimate dynastic line, and the loss of their throne was an act of usurpation no less unholy for the lack of poison, the reign of the Georges no less tyrannical for the absence of Claudius's deadly schemes.[8]

Moreover, while *Hamlet* thus memorably prophesizes the Stuart sense of grievance, there are also more direct connections between the family and the play. We do not know precisely when the first production of the play took place, only that it took place sometime toward the end of Elizabeth's reign—a time when James VI of Scotland, the future James I and the man who would become the first Stuart king of Britain, was working hard to consolidate his claim to the throne while he waited for the old monarch to die. Unlike the later *Macbeth*, *Hamlet* was not written specifically to flatter James, but its plot does bear a notorious resemblance to the future king's early life, especially the so-called Darnley case. Like the Danish prince, the king was the son of a woman who married his own father's murderer; he, too, seems to have been pressured to seek the justice of revenge. Such striking parallels may tempt us to identify James's circumstances as a privileged source were it not so abundantly clear that Shakespeare drew on a wealth of sources.[9] What I emphasize, however is that *Hamlet* does carry a strong Stuart connection from the time of its first appearance, a connection only intensified by the family's later history: losing their throne not once, but twice (and with regicide thrown in 1649 for good measure), and seeking a restorative justice for a century after 1688.[10]

Through Partridge, the episode also points to the Stuarts in another way, one that is buried for a modern audience but would have been quite direct for the novel's first readers. On his arrival at the theater, as he regales his companions with all the wonders that he notices, Partridge makes one particularly detailed observation: "While the Fellow was lighting the upper Candles, he cry'd out to Mrs. *Miller*, 'Look, look, Madam, the very Picture of the Man in the End of the Common-Prayer Book, before the Gunpowder-Treason Service'" (852). The narrator occasionally refers to specific visual images in *Tom Jones*, as when he compares Bridget Allworthy to the female figure in Hogarth's *Morning* (66), but this is the only occasion in which a character makes such an allusion, and it is one unlikely to conjure up a picture for later readers. Yet for Partridge, this candlelighter's actions are the "very picture," the exact resemblance, of an image that Fielding's first readers (those who weren't Dissenters or Catholics, anyway) would have known well. Prayer books in the eighteenth century were frequently illustrated; the engravings for the most part were likenesses of saints and of biblical scenes and characters, but there is a curious feature particularly relevant here. Eighteenth-century prayer books ended with an illustrated parade of Stuarts.

If we look at a prayer book from Fielding's time, we see that the Gunpowder Treason Service is one of three rituals, all illustrated, all designed to commemorate the triumphs and disasters of Stuart rule: the miraculous preservation of James I through the thwarting of the Guy Fawkes plot, the martyrdom of Charles I, and the Restoration of Charles II. Moreover, the illustrations that accompany each service all focus on a Stuart monarch in a particularly heroic-looking pose: James I's moment of illumination when he penetrates the nature of the Catholic plot; Charles I standing bravely on the regicidal scaffold; and Charles II returning in triumph to take his rightful crown.[11] In other words, rather like *Hamlet*, the Prayer Book provides a set of images that young Charles Stuart might be very pleased to see invoked in December, 1745.

Partridge's reference, therefore, would undoubtedly have been known to most of Fielding's readers. But perhaps it struck them as an odd allusion as well, for the picture hardly seems to illustrate the work of theatrical candlelighting. It shows royalty and divinity, magic and mayhem in an image that is striking and very strange. Well into the next century, in 1823, Charles Lamb would say that it was one of the of "the earliest graphic representations which woke my childhood to wonder."[12] In Plate 1, we can see that there are no candles, and nobody is lighting anything. The all-seeing eye of God, not a stage-hand, provides the illumination, as it sends an image of Fawkes intent on his bloody work onto what appears to be a large circular mirror set on a pedestal. To the viewer's right, a Jacobean figure, certainly meant to be James I, looks into the mirror and recoils in horror, while indistinct figures on the other side flee in confusion.

The image may not picture a candlelighter, but the presence of the mirror here is extremely suggestive, for at this point in the novel, mirrors are everywhere, and the appearance of one at this moment in *Tom Jones* is remarkably rich with implication for the scene which is its immediate context. The mirror in the illustration can trace its origins to a long and complex history of the Gunpowder Plot's iconography and it is worth pausing for a moment over its details. It appears as a large orb, and sits atop a pedestal. Inside the circumference of the glass, we can discern

Plate 1: "Gunpowder Treason" (*The Book of Common Prayer*, 1745).

Fawkes walking with what appears to be a darkened lantern over a cobblestoned street toward a large Gothic building—presumably the House of Lords, the target of his terrorist scheme. At the right side of the illustration, standing immediately next to the orb, two men observe the image with obvious agitation. The figure in front holds a short sword and has brought up his hand to his heart. At the opposite side of the picture, and in a plane slightly behind the mirror and its observers, we can see four or five shadowy figures: some appear to be fleeing (their backs are to us) and one person is prostrate, as if dead or unconscious. Above the action, a large white circle appears in a cloudy sky; at its center is an eye, casting a bright beam of light that flows directly into the mirror and disappears into the building. The beam seems to represent a kind of divine projection, whereby God sends an image of Fawkes onto the mirror, revealing and thereby thwarting the plot.

Those images—Fawkes with a dark lantern approaching Parliament and the eye of God shining with the light of truth and so exposing the rebellion—are both conventional in Gunpowder Plot illustrations. The mirror is a less common device in seventeenth- and earlier eighteenth-century illustrations of the plot, but this version had appeared in standard editions of the Prayer Book by 1735 and so would have been widely known by the time that the novel was published. More important than the exact provenance of the mirror image is what its use calls to mind—that legendary moment of illumination in which King James, reading an intercepted letter from the plotters, has what was widely thought to be a supernatural moment of insight, when he suddenly understands the nature of the plot. The picture, that is, allegorizes an act of reading and interpretation.[13] The glass here represents the letter, and that connection of mirror and text is crucial for we are at this point in a particularly dense network of mirrors.

The illustration gives us action on three levels: inside the orb, Fawkes proceeds on his treasonous path; outside the orb, James and his companion (probably Cecil, his Minister) look into the mirror and react; and above, the eye of God discerns and reveals all. If we turn to Fielding's depiction of a night at the theater, we also find three planes of action. First, we see *Hamlet* the play, with its ghosts and madness, hypocrisy and grief, revenge and violence. Those images that the play gives us, like the picture of Fawkes inside his mirror, are bounded by the frame of the proscenium stage. Second, watching the drama unfold is another audience, one that includes Tom Jones, like Hamlet, caught up in a family drama centered on a brother's betrayal. Finally, outside the little world of the theater and its audience, appears that other young man, Charles Edward Stuart, camped to the north, pressing his own father's claim to a throne held, he thinks, by a usurper. These various reflections are further mirrored by the illustration Partridge alludes to, since it represents an earlier and similar moment in British history, when another conspiracy of rebellion threatened to remove the ruling family.

This summary does not come close to exhausting the mirrors we can find here. *Hamlet*, of course, is famously obsessed with the question of representation, and the Prince, in the very midst of the action, puts on a little play of his own, a mirror in which he means to catch the conscience of a guilty king. Garrick, the actor they have come to see, took to heart the Prince's demand that art hold the mirror up to life, and made himself famous by a style of acting that was, above all, mimetic. However, Tom and his companions do not directly watch Garrick or the play's action, but observe instead Partridge's spontaneous mimicry of the actor's performance—they watch, that is, not the play but its mirror.

We thus have mirrors within mirrors within mirrors: the play to itself in the Mousetrap, the play to the novel, both the play and the novel to history, one historical moment of threatened revolution to another, all wrapped around an image from another book, a picture whose dominant feature is a magical glass. It would be misleading, however, to think of any of these mirrors as simple reflections or perfect reproductions. Partridge may say that the candlelighter is the "very Picture of the Man" in the Prayer Book illustration, but here and always, "very Pictures" are never identical. Hamlet says he will have the players act "something like the murder of my father," and that phrase "something like" suggests the doubleness that is always a part of representation, that it is a duplication that is—and is not—the same as its origin. Thus, just as the Mousetrap mimes a version of the murder of old Hamlet, so Partridge burlesques Garrick; similarly, what in the play is direct fratricide becomes in the novel Blifil's sneaky plot to send Tom to the gallows. We can trace such near-mirrors here almost indefinitely: Hamlet's father lost his throne by poison, Bonnie Prince Charlie's grandfather fled his in a revolution. Even the historical doubling of 1745 with 1605 presents us with an unsteady glass: the Prayer Book and its dramatic illustration celebrate the preservation of a Stuart as monarch, while in 1745, it was a Stuart trying by rebellion to remove someone else.

The mirrors proliferate and what they suggest is both likeness and difference, both the way that plots and events are repeated and the way that they are never quite the same. Fielding the novelist, the architect of this hall of mirrors, sits outside, like the eye of God in the picture that he has planted in his work, projecting what we see by his creation of it, but reminding us always, if we are attentive, that all he gives us is only "something like" something else. That is a point about representation but it is also, I think, a point about how history is experienced and reported. In order to understand more completely how this mirror structure works, we must look more closely at one of these parallels with special historical significance, that between the version of the play that the novel has constructed and the 1745 revolt. Partridge, we see, is both mirror and witness, reflecting the play but also reporting on his—and Britain's—historical moment.

The Play's the Thing

The trip to the theater begins at that moment in the narrative when Tom has just received a letter from Sophia that makes no promises but which does offer him a glimmer of hope. His spirits thus cheered, Tom gathers his friends for a night at *Hamlet*, as we have seen, to observe Partridge, and not, surprisingly, to observe the greatest actor of his time. Tom, Fielding tells us, "expected to enjoy much Entertainment in the Criticisms of *Partridge*; from whom he expected the simple Dictates of Nature, unimproved indeed, but likewise unadulterated by Art" (852).[14] The situation may remind us of that *Spectator* essay in which we are invited to watch Sir Roger de Coverly attend the theater,[15] but Tom (after all, a country boy just arrived on what is, as far as we know, his first trip to London) is hardly a stand-in for the urbane Mr. Spectator, and his assumption of the role of the jaded sophisticate here is quite odd.

Partridge's allusion to Guy Fawkes occurs during the preliminaries, but the episode quickly arrives at its central thread: the servant's responses to the ghost of old Hamlet, or rather, his responses to Garrick's on-stage reactions to the ghost. At the moment that Hamlet recognizes the spirit of his father, Partridge "fell into so violent a Trembling, that his Knees knocked against each other." And while he insists he knows "it is but a Play," he cannot hide his terror and repeatedly shouts such instructions to Garrick (echoing the fervent pleas of Horatio and Marcellus for Hamlet not to follow the ghost) as "*No farther!*—No, you have gone far enough already." The emphasis throughout is on the way that Garrick's performance both inspires and licenses Partridge's most familiar emotion, fear. As the servant tells Tom, "you may call me a Coward if you will; but if that little Man there upon the Stage [Garrick] is not frightned, I never saw any Man frightned in my Life."

By the end of the episode, we are aware that the audience which Fielding has imagined in Drury Lane that night is one whose response is remarkably divided. First, there are those who watch the mirror of Garrick that Partridge provides. This group includes not only Tom and Mrs. Miller, but "all who sat within hearing, who were more attentive to what [Partridge] said, than to any Thing that passed on Stage." This audience watches something more like comedy than tragedy, for in Partridge's reactions they see, as noted above, what amounts to a burlesque version of the play—"the same Passions which succeeded each other in [Garrick], succeed[ed] likewise" in the servant. The other audience is Partridge himself, who is also interested in response, but the reactions he watches are those of Garrick. The great actor is able to arouse in the servant the tragic emotion of fear (though not, interestingly, pity), but he seems to offer no catharsis. "[Partridge] durst not go to Bed, all that Night, for fear of the Ghost, and for many Nights after, sweated two or three Hours before he went to sleep, with the same Apprehensions. . . ." (852–7). We can remember here the servant's reason for never offering testimony at a capital trial: "I should never be able to lie alone afterwards, for Fear of seeing his Ghost" (457).

The critics who have discussed this scene have often focused on it as a tribute by one man of the theater, Fielding, to Garrick, by universal testimony the greatest actor of the age, and a performer particularly identified with the role of Hamlet, and even more particularly associated with his reaction to the ghost. Joseph Roach, in his study of eighteenth-century acting, has called this moment "the most celebrated scene played by the greatest actor of his time, perhaps of all time."[16] Those who have seen the episode as flattery point to Garrick's "natural" style of acting as the source of Partridge's complete identification with the Prince's terror.[17] No believable terror in Garrick, no comic terror in Partridge. It is not obvious to me, however, that the great actor would have felt particularly flattered when he read this episode. Alas, poor Garrick—he cannot, at least in the pages of *Tom Jones*, command his audience. The only people in the playhouse that Fielding mentions—Tom, his friends, those in their vicinity—forget all about the star's performance and focus on the servant instead, very odd praise indeed. But Garrick's position as the ignored genius in the scene does emphasize the point that Fielding wants us to watch Partridge, and especially to observe Partridge's responses to particular moments in the play. He wants us to watch, not the action, but its mirror.

The way in which Fielding abbreviates his account of the performance is worth close attention. Only four or perhaps five moments from *Hamlet* are reported: there is the ghost's first appearance to Hamlet (and possibly his earlier encounter with Horatio and the watchmen as well), the performance of the play within the play, *The Murder of Gonzago* (best known, of course, as "The Mousetrap"), Hamlet's confrontation with Gertrude, and the grave digger's scene.[18] These four moments enable Fielding to exploit issues of theatricality and the supernatural, but they completely ignore *Hamlet's* violence. The deaths of Polonius, and Rosencranz and Guildenstern, and Ophelia, not to mention the corpse-strewn conclusion, are passed over without a word. The episode may center on Partridge's terror but the tragedy's abundant bloodshed plays no part in inspiring his fear.

We are back with Partridge's superstition again, and his apprehensions on this score, as they have been throughout the novel, are crucial. What we register first in this scene is that, despite repeated and unconvincing protests that he knows it's only a play, the great joke is that Partridge believes that the ghost of old Hamlet is real, and that a supernatural being has finally actually appeared before him. Partridge is not frightened by *Hamlet's* carnage, he's afraid of a ghost, a ghost he believes to be malevolent. He advises Garrick, "Ay, you may draw your Sword; what signifies a Sword against the power of the Devil?" (855).[19]

Partridge's superstition is crucial to this episode because of the questions about representation that his credulity provokes, questions whose significance are not only literary but political. For if the servant believes that the ghost is real, then what he has done is nothing less than to mistake a representation for a reality, a mirror image for the thing itself. But it would not be quite accurate to say that Partridge is incapable of recognizing a representation as a representation. Rather, he can recognize a representation only when it is distant enough from human experience to announce itself as a bald contrivance. After the performance, Partridge adopts, quite self-consciously now, the pose of the critic and very strangely announces that he didn't much care for Garrick's performance: " 'He the best Player!' cries *Partridge* with a Contemptuous Sneer, 'why I could act as well as he myself. I am sure if I had seen a Ghost, I should have looked in the very same Manner, and done just as he did. . . . [T]hough I was never at a Play in *London*, yet I have seen acting in the Country; and the King, for my Money; he speaks all his Words distinctly, half as loud again as the other.—Any Body may see he is an Actor' " (857). Instead of Garrick, Partridge prefers the actor (possibly "Honest Billy Mills")[20] who plays Claudius, a judgment belied by his own reactions during the performance, but one worth remembering, both for what it says about Partridge's uncertain understanding of mimesis as well as for its peculiar praise of "the King" as an all-too-obvious "Actor."

Partridge thus is comically credulous, uncertain about the distinction between illusion and reality, and incapable of distinguishing good acting from bad. And the effect of placing such a person in the middle of the audience is profoundly destabilizing. Against all odds, Partridge's burlesque turns a night at *Hamlet* into an evening of laughter. As Fielding tells us, there was "much Laughter in the Neighborhood of *Partridge*" as the servant "afforded great Mirth . . . to all who sat within Hearing." Partridge, like Fielding himself in his own career as a playwright, has turned tragedy into farce (we remember that Swift was observed to laugh on only a few occasions, one of which was at Fielding's *Tragedy of Tragedies*). What we have is a play within a play or perhaps a play beside a play, and Partridge's counter-*Hamlet* provides a very different experience for his audience than the one enjoyed by those outside the small circle around him, who indeed seem to prefer his performance to Garrick's—at least, his is the one they choose to watch. Tom's interest in his servant's reactions to the play has proven infectious.

That tableau—the observation of one audience member by another—resonates when the play is *Hamlet*, and Tom and his friends' visit to the theater is structured in close imitation of—that is, it mirrors—Shakespeare's Mousetrap scene. Hamlet performs a role there much like Partridge's in the novel, commenting on the action, playing the fool. Ophelia tells him, in words that Tom could speak to his companion, "You are as good as a chorus, my lord" (III, ii, 231). Moreover, the generic instability of Fielding's scene, setting up a comic chorus for a tragic action, duplicates a similar vertiginousness in Shakespeare, where the Mousetrap sequence mixes pantomime, the dialogue of *The Murder of Gonzago*, Hamlet's bawdy remarks, and Claudius's showstopping anger. In attending the play so that he can watch Partridge rather than Garrick, Tom here has reproduced Hamlet's covert plan, since Shakespeare's hero produces his play in order to watch how one member of its audience, Claudius, will respond. Partridge thus stands in for both Hamlet (as commentator) and Claudius (as object of attention).[21] But this only raises the question: if the scene at Garrick's theater is Fielding's own Mousetrap, who is he trying to trap and why?

Fielding's trap here is meant for his readers and the trap is the liability of any audience to see only one thing at work, and thus fail to register the irony. Partridge—like Claudius at the Mousetrap and as he was in Page's courtroom—is the only character in this episode who responds honestly either to Garrick's performance or to the tragedy unfolding before them. Tom and his friends, like the nervous spectators in Page's courtroom, have retreated here to the distance of humor, preferring laughter at the servant to tears for Garrick. Partridge, alone in this episode, knows what most audiences of *Hamlet* have known: something terrifying is happening on stage.

Earlier in the novel, Fielding briefly gives us another scene at *Hamlet*, one that is suggestive for the responses we see here. He cites the story of Henry Fisher, one of the century's most notorious criminals. Fisher had murdered and robbed his friend and benefactor, and, then "the Villain went two Days afterwards with some young Ladies to the Play of *Hamlet;* and with an unaltered Countenance heard one of the Ladies, who little suspected how near she was to the Person, cry out, Good God! if the Man that murdered Mr. *Derby* was now present!" (403). The callous response to Shakespeare, the refusal to look in the glass, thus marks a villain's heart. We should hardly condemn Tom and Mrs. Miller as the equals of the infamous Fisher, but we do not have to lump them with a killer to see that Fielding has coded a cold reaction to *Hamlet* as a troubling sign. Their reaction is not so much cold—their countenances, after all, are altered by laughter—as displaced, and not a little calculated. Tom goes to Drury Lane, not to experience something himself, but to see how his friend will react, and our response to those reactions is necessarily complex. Partridge's performance as an audience was supposed to be our entertainment, but our sophisticated superiority to his naivete is undercut when we, perhaps belatedly, recognize that his is the direct and honest reaction to what is a profoundly tragic action. We have been hoist by our own petard.

In the story he tells about Page to Tom and the Man of the Hill, Partridge's role was the typically retrospective one we expect of witness, as he offered his testimony about the trial after the fact. At Drury Lane, he is a witness of a very different sort. Here, his witness occurs simultaneously with the event that he is reporting. As such, he is both audience and actor, and his fun-house mirror version of Garrick means that he is actually performing in his role as spectator. Partridge's witnessing is theatricalized, and by eliminating the usual temporal gap between the acts of seeing and reporting, it implies the dramatic quality at the heart of all testimony.

Fielding has thus focused our attention—and the attention of the other characters in the novel—not directly on the play itself, but on the response of one person watching that play, and it is that fact that makes the connection between this episode in *Tom Jones* and the 1745 rebellion insistent. For the person whose response we watch is, as we have repeatedly been reminded, "a *Jacobite*, . . . [and] was persuaded . . . that the whole Nation were of the same Inclination in their Hearts" (441).

The Jacobite whom Fielding places in Garrick's theater at the very height of the Forty-Five has been contextualized in a very particular way: he believes in ghosts, cannot consistently distinguish representation from reality, prefers a bad actor to a good one, and turns high tragedy into comedy, at least for those watching him. At the same time, he is also apparently the only one in the playhouse with a heart. All these responses have a political significance, one neither simple nor straight forward.

As noted throughout this study, superstition was a hallmark of Stuart rule, and it is one of the strongest links between Partridge and the exiled rulers. That kinship in superstitious belief is one of the traits in his servant that makes Tom most impatient; we can recall his earlier outburst, "With what Stuff and Nonsense hast thou filled thy Head? . . . Monsters and Prodigies are the proper Arguments to support monstrous and absurd Doctrines. The Cause of King George is the Cause of Liberty and true Religion. In other words, it is the Cause of common Sense" (440). Writing in the same fraught year of 1745 about *Macbeth*, Samuel Johnson dryly noted that as "the ready way to gain K. *James's* Favour was to flatter his speculations[,] the System of *Demonologie* was immediately adopted by all who desired either to gain Preferment or not to lose it. Thus the Doctrine of Witchcraft was very powerfully inculcated. . . . Upon this general Infatuation *Shakespeare* might easily be allowed to found a Play."[22] That infatuation may have cooled for many, but not for Partridge.[23]

Partridge's credulous willingness to believe in the reality of ghosts and witches can thus be read as a small piece of anti-Jacobite satire. The same superstition that makes the servant believe in the ghost of old Hamlet also renders him susceptible to the supernatural charms of the Stuart family. Partridge's witness, in such a reading, becomes (as was Claudius's at the original Mousetrap) an act of self-incrimination, another announcement that he is both a Jacobite and a coward. But such a reading flattens the scene intolerably, and succeeds only by ignoring its contradictions and manifold ambivalences. This is an episode, like the one in Page's courtroom, whose sense of history will not stay confined in one interpretive box.

The ambivalence first appears in Partridge himself. The barber's reaction to Garrick's Hamlet yokes complete identification to a very peculiar scorn. By a kind of theatrical metempsychosis, Partridge completely takes on Hamlet's emotions, but he also claims that the part is not well-acted: "He, the best actor?" What does that odd mix suggest in the context of 1745? On the one hand, Hamlet is the character with whom we would expect a rabid Jacobite to identify since the Dane represents a type of Bonnie Prince Charlie, fighting for his father, struggling to remove a usurper from the throne. But Fielding frustrates this line of thought, even as he encourages it. For Partridge fears the ghost, and warns Hamlet to leave it alone as a dangerous devil. The order he shouts at Hamlet/Garrick, "*No farther!*—no, you have gone far enough already" is hardly what we expect a good Jacobite to shout at a stand-in for Charles Stuart—though someone seems to have said something very like it to the young prince when his army had reached Derby a few weeks earlier. Moreover, what are we to make of his peculiar taste in actors? Surely, a true Stuart loyalist would have to see in Claudius the image of Hanover, the wrong man on the throne. Yet Partridge prefers the tyrant (in the form of Billy Mills); his loyalty at the end is given not to Garrick as the young man battling for his father, but to the actor playing the usurper. And while we may say that Partridge prefers the actor and not the character that he plays, the fact remains that Fielding has already made it clear that the servant's grasp of that distinction is unsteady indeed. "The King for my money," he says. Is this another anti-Jacobite joke, with Partridge's nod of approval to Claudius meant to be a mirror of the choice of all those in 1688 and after who may have preferred James II and his progeny, but who never mustered the will for a counter-revolution?

Partridge's division here between Hamlet and Claudius, emotionally identified with one, publicly endorsing the other, is only deepened when we recall the way in which the scene at the playhouse in the novel duplicates so many of the circumstances of the Mousetrap in *Hamlet*. In both play and novel, a key member of a theatrical audience becomes, unwittingly but by someone's design, the central actor in the scene. In December 1745, there was abroad in the land an equally powerful interest in how people would respond. The audience in this case were the people of Britain, while the drama being played out for them in what Fielding elsewhere in the novel calls "the vast Theatre of Time" (325) was the event—comedy? tragedy? farce? it depended on your point of view, but for all sides the action was still generically uncertain—of the 1745 rebellion itself. For the success or failure of that attempted restoration depended finally not on Charles's skill or luck as a strategist, or on the courage of his soldiers, or on the size and spirit of the British army. The rebellion itself, I suggest, was a piece of theater, designed not so much or not only to take territory or win victories, but as a bold attempt to create a response in the people. Charles knew, as did his father (who would have taken the throne had the rebellion succeeded), as did the Pope and the King of France and all other interested parties, that the fate of the Forty-Five hung on what the British body politic did. Would they rise up? Would there be a spontaneous upswelling of love and loyalty such that the House of Hanover and their supporters would see that their claim was hollow and their hold on the throne as feeble as a child's? Or would the Young Pretender strut and fret, not on an empty stage or in an empty theater (for everyone was watching), but in a finally empty way, his heroically staged campaign in the end just an otiose diversion, a futile attempt that literally made nothing happen?

What Fielding seems to have recognized in the Mousetrap, as well as to have seen in his own nation's history, and what he then duplicates in *Tom Jones*, is a theatrical moment where the real drama is not on the stage but in the audience—in particular, in how an audience (or part of it) will respond. We recall, "all who sat within hearing . . . were more attentive to what [Partridge] said, than to any Thing that passed on Stage." Hamlet wanted Claudius to show his guilt; what do Fielding's readers look to view in Partridge? In the context of the Forty-Five, we could say that the servant here stands in for Britain, and while his responses (however contradictory) cannot stand as witness for the range of reaction to be found in a population of millions, he can testify for that part of Britain everyone at that moment was most interested in: those who might welcome a restored Stuart king. His responses thus take on a broader interest than they would have if they were only an instance, however clever, of partisan satire. Partridge in this scene, is not just a risible Jacobite; he is an illustration of the mind of a politically crucial segment of the British public, the segment Charles Stuart needed, the segment that ultimately failed him.[24]

Superstition like Partridge's, Fielding suggests, is at once the source of the Stuart's success and the deepest reason for their failure. The servant's willingness, even eagerness, to lend his all-too-open ears to any hint of the supernatural is a trait inseparable from his allegiance to the Stuarts. On a literal level, it is predictable that a character whose beliefs mark him as pre-Enlightenment would feel more metaphysically comfortable with a dynasty like the Stuarts, whose own ideology was so grounded in a world of values and beliefs then passing away.[25] On a symbolic level, the connection is even more striking. The novel's *Hamlet* episode finds a way to literalize that symbolic phenomenon we looked at in chapter 1, the Stuarts as a family of ghosts, absent from Britain for over a half-century, consigned to their exilic purgatory in the suburbs of the papacy, crying out like old Hamlet, "Remember me." But there's the rub. If Partridge believes in ghosts with all his heart, he is also afraid of them. Near the end of the road section of *Tom Jones*, Tom and Partridge hear a sound of drums and we are allowed for a moment to imagine that the two wandering young men, Charles Stuart and Tom Jones, might meet. Partridge's reaction is revealing: " 'Lord have Mercy upon us All; they are certainly a coming!' 'Who is coming?' cries *Jones*. . . . 'Who,' cries *Partridge*, 'Why, the Rebels; . . . would it not be the wiser Way to crawl into yonder Bushes till they are gone by?' " (635–6). And this moment of fear is reiterated in the scene at the theater, where Partridge, controlled by the terror that his superstition has inspired, warns Hamlet off following what is, after all, the ghost of a dead king, and cries: "*No farther!*" In the end, he rests complacently with his judgment and loyalty squarely on the side of "the King."

Partridge thoroughly believes in Garrick and the ghost, but when the play is over, he puts his "Money" on Claudius. That part of his being that makes him a Jacobite, his superstition, simultaneously renders him unfit for service in the Stuart cause—a double-bind, as Fielding describes it here, that forms a powerful theory about the failure of the Forty-Five and of Jacobitism generally. Johnson's comment, from almost thirty years later, is worth remembering here. Speaking of the dynastic loyalties of the British population, he said, "They would not . . . risk any thing to restore the exiled family. They would not give twenty shillings a piece to bring it about. But, if a mere vote could do it, there would be twenty to one; at least, there would be a very great majority of voices for it."[26] We might question, of course, the accuracy of Johnson's hypothetical exercise in a new round of elective kingship, but his analysis of the body politic is much the same as Fielding's portrait of Partridge—there may be support for the Stuarts, but it is fearful support, unwilling in the end to take any "risk." Those twenty shillings remained, like Partridge's money, with the King.

The drama of Partridge's response thus becomes a representation of the reaction of at least part of the British nation to the 1745 rebellion, but Fielding has something to say as well about the whole idea of a theatricalized monarchy. The conception of kings as players, as men who play a role (in part heavily scripted, in part improvised) on a public stage is as old as the office itself, but it seems to have taken on a particular urgency in England in the years of Tudor and Stuart rule. The reasons for that urgency are complex. In the last decade of Elizabeth's reign and in the earliest years of James I's monarchy, the English stage, of course, was at a pinnacle unmatched in its history, and so the more or less conscious conflation of statecraft with stagecraft by the monarch (and the parallel obsession of the playwrights with the institution of kingship) was perhaps inevitable. It is beyond the scope of this discussion to rehearse in any detail the work of the many scholars who have worked to illuminate, in all its subtlety, these connections.[27] But I think all observers of the British monarchy would agree that, while pomp and ceremony never disappear from the office, the succession to the throne by the House of Hanover meant a substantial lessening of the ways in which kings used what Orgel calls "the illusion of power." Some of this was no doubt practical (Georges I and II were born in Germany and any staging of their kingship demanded very careful direction indeed), some of it is the movement away from the old ideas of monarchy toward the more limited constitutional and bureaucratic conception that succeeded it—a movement suggested by Tom's comment that the "cause of King George" is the cause of "common Sense."

To think of Charles Edward Stuart's bold dash across England as a grand piece of theater, then, is not only to speak conventionally of "the theater of war" or the "theater of battle," it also calls up the way in which the Stuart dynasty's very conception of itself as a house of kings was bound up with a self-conscious understanding of monarchical power as a spectacle. And what Partridge represents, for all his cowardice, is something very like an ideal subject for this old order, an order that was not only Stuart, but magical and theatrical as well. Here we can return to a point that I emphasized earlier—it's not just that Partridge believes in ghosts, he also mistakes an illusion (an actor on a stage) for a reality. Despite his repeated protests that he knows it is all a sham, and despite *Hamlet's* insistent reminders of the artificiality of all representation, Partridge believes in the reality of the images before him. He may claim a sophisticate's knowledge of the theatricality of the performance—"Any Body," he says, may see that "the King" is "an Actor"—but our clearest sense of response from him is not his alienated understanding that Mills is "playing" Claudius, but his total absorption by Garrick's illusion. Seeing, for Partridge, is a quite literal kind of believing, and the artificial image before him is constantly transmuted into a real presence. "Lord have Mercy upon us, there it is."[28]

Partridge may not be a Roman Catholic, but he certainly does represent what Fielding considers to be the pusillanimous nature of the Jacobite partisans as well as their epistemological simplicity. But we cannot forget that the novelist emphasizes that Partridge's response to *Hamlet* is also in some fundamental way worth our respect, even our admiration. Just as Claudius knows that the dumb-show before him is no mere pantomime, Partridge—alone among those we see—recognizes that there is something occurring on Garrick's stage that he must respond to with the same intensity as he would if it were really happening—with the same intensity, we might say, that he responds to a capital trial. That may be naive, but it is not only naive, and it is at precisely this point of mixed judgment that what I called the political ambivalence of the episode begins to emerge. What does it mean that the character through whom Fielding explores and exposes the psychological and intellectual flaws of Jacobitism is also, in some fundamental ways, the most appealing person we see?

As I argue throughout, if the cause of King George was the cause of common sense and so "right," it does not necessarily follow that Fielding regarded that fact without irony. Through the complex drama of Partridge's response, and by the way in which he bears witness to what he sees, at once comically absurd and deeply human, Fielding can articulate his understanding of what Britain has gained in embracing the House of Hanover but he can also suggest what it has lost. On the one hand, Partridge, hopelessly and helplessly in thrall to the kind of theatricalized charisma that the Stuarts aspired to represent, is obviously a dupe, and so we tend to align ourselves with Tom and his friends as the agents of reason. Yet Fielding will not allow us to rest easy there. For in the depth and immediacy of his feeling, especially his awe in the face of mystery, Partridge manages to mock the very laughter he inspires. After all, Tom cannot bring himself to experience *Hamlet* directly; he literally turns his back to watch his friend instead. That refusal of mystery marks him, the pragmatic defender of his liberty and faith, as a thoroughly modern man, a citizen of a Britain both rational and unhaunted. But it marks in him as well a certain coolness, a cerebral detachment that signals what he—and by extension, Britain itself—has lost. Partridge's reduced and unintentionally comic version of *Hamlet* is not only the version Tom seems to prefer; it is all he can take. Perhaps the mysteries of *Hamlet* are so potent that only a Jacobite like Partridge could fully turn his gaze—could experience—that particular play in the last days of 1745, and even he has to retreat from the full implications of his emotional response, complacently putting his money on the King.

The generic unsteadiness of the scene in Garrick's theater leaves the readers of *Tom Jones* intellectually and emotionally uncertain of their ground. The Mousetrap may have been set for Partridge, but we are caught as well, as we watch our own response and find it difficult to pin down. Tom, the hero, is rational but he is also uncharacteristically and unattractively cold-blooded, laughing here as he laughed at the account of Frank and the calf in an utterly Hobbesian manner. He is laughing, we remember, at his loyal friend, whom he has placed in such a way as to demonstrate his own intellectual and social superiority. Partridge, typically and ludicrously credulous, nonetheless retains a dignity and humanity in the strength of his response. He is the one character in the scene who actually watches Garrick and responds to his legendary power of illusion. We shift uncertainly as we read the scene and in the end, we find ourselves unable wholeheartedly to embrace any of the players in it. That unsteadiness results, I believe, from Fielding's comprehension of both the pragmatic necessity of Hanoverian common sense and the attractions of the Stuart anachronism. The fact that such necessity and such attractions were irreconcilable in 1745 is certainly part of the meaning of this episode, but we cannot appreciate it fully unless we acknowledge the novelist's lucid awareness of the strength inherent in the appeal of both sides. Fielding had no need to make Partridge a Jacobite, or having made him a Jacobite, to create for this character points of sympathy and identification rooted precisely in his Stuart loyalties. Although the historical moment for the Stuarts was over by 1745, it appears that Fielding was able to see and sympathetically dramatize what remained potent in their appeal.

Before leaving the scene at Drury Lane, we need to return one more time to the scene's explicit gesture towards history, Partridge's reference to the Prayer Book and its illustration of the Gunpowder Plot. As we saw earlier, the mirror in that picture serves to frame the action with a reminder that versions of history are everywhere in this scene, and Partridge's act of witness here is the episode's central mirror, as his burlesque reflection of Garrick's Hamlet makes the Stuart cause visible in the glass of his own response. But I think Fielding uses Partridge in an even deeper way, and his actions represent not just an image of a certain political constituency, the Jacobites, but also a response to historical process itself. The key is the juxtaposition of the Gunpowder Plot with the 1745 Rebellion. Partridge's reference to the earlier crises allows Fielding to invoke, at the outset of his scene, the miracle of the Stuarts' preservation in 1605, precisely at the moment when the Stuarts have come to represent national peril. Fielding has thus found a very sly way to insist on the implacable contradictoriness of historical unfolding. A nation can despise and celebrate the same thing, and the magic mirror in the midst of this scene serves as an uncomfortable reminder that the search for historical continuity—the belief, say, that in moments of national peril, God will always save the British—is inevitably grounded in disquieting discontinuities. So, the same family preserved by God's providence in one crises must be excluded by that same divine aid when, a century or so later, they have revealed themselves as nothing more than papists and the allies of the devil. The historical typology that insists that past acts of divine help prefigure present and future such interventions requires a kind of blindness to the ironies of history, the way in this instance that Stuart heroes have turned into Stuart knaves. But then, mirrors often show precisely what we do not want to see, for their paradox is that they display not only persistence but, also and alas, change.

While Partridge is undoubtedly afraid, he is not afraid to look; what he sees, and what his companions all turn their backs on, is history itself. By invoking the Gunpowder Plot the moment that he enters the theater, Partridge announces himself as the voice of history in the scene; in watching the play, he further reveals that he is able to witness history. Tom, observing his servant and not Garrick, has chosen to ignore Hamlet, a character who is not only a hazy picture of himself, but who also anchors a play suffused with the stuff of British history for two hundred years: violence and treachery and regicide and a foreigner showing up at the end to collect an empty throne. If the magic glass in the picture has the power of prophecy, so, it turned out, did *Hamlet*.

Partridge, however, does watch, and his stubborn witness—uncontrollably reporting at every moment what he sees before him—reminds us that witnessing is another form of representation. The witness provides testimony which we hear as a substitute for direct experience, and as such, he is another instance of an attempt at duplication which can never be quite the same. Fielding highlights the way that the witness is always a substitute or a displacement by the way he has designed the episode to focus on Partridge's response rather than on the play itself. That response may be burlesque, but that does mean that we can therefore dismiss Partridge's report. As the whole scene has revealed, the problem is not in the way that he testifies but in representation itself, which in the end determines the nature of witnessing. Once we concede that displaced versions of history are all we can ever hope to have, we can begin perhaps to appreciate what Partridge has to offer. He may refuse to be a witness in the legal sense, fearing to dip his hands in blood, but both at Drury Lane and at the Salisbury Assizes, he proves himself willing to be a witness to history. That willingness is grounded in his conviction that, on both occasions, something important is happening, something he has to report, and it is that conviction that sets him apart from those who put a screen of laughter between themselves and history. Partridge, like the glass in King James' palace that exposed the secret of Guy Fawkes, is our mirror of history here, imperfect but with his eyes wide open.

Afterword: Sleepless Nights

Partridge has trouble sleeping. In the Page episode, the fear of sleeplessness haunts him. "I should never be able to lie alone afterwards," he tells us in the very first words of his monologue, "if any Person was to be hanged upon my Evidence." Frank, his friend and fellow witness, illustrates that such a fear is reasonable, "He was never in the dark alone, but he fancied his saw the Fellow's Spirit." As a result of the *Hamlet* excursion, Partridge is sentenced to his own spell of sleepless nights: "He durst not go to Bed all that Night, for Fear of the Ghost, and for many Nights after, sweated two or three Hours before he went to sleep." Partridge is afraid of the ghosts that he might see, but that fear is grounded in what he has actually seen. His insomnia may be another comic sign of his enslavement by superstition, but it is also a reminder of his watchfulness. Tom's servant sees things—an ambiguous phrase that nicely comprehends both his tendency to conjure spirits with his imagination alone, but also his unfiltered and horrified perceptions of what is really there.

In the way that he sees, Partridge goes well beyond anything that we might consider typical for a member of an audience, which is after all what he is in both in Page's courtroom and in Garrick's theater. In fact, as an audience member, he is a failure. An audience implies some design in its construction, and some intention for its response. But Partridge never gets the point. He is Garrick's worst nightmare, as he had been Page's, frightened of the wrong things, and for the wrong reasons. If Page could offer a rationale for his behavior, it would undoubtedly be Fielding's in the *Enquiry*: he is hanging the poor fellow purely as a deterrent, so that horses will not be stolen. The moral of any capital trial should be the same—don't do what the condemned man did. But that, of course, is not the moral Partridge draws: "Lud, keep us all from dipping our hands in Blood, I say," a conclusion that, as Fielding makes clear in the *Enquiry*, would render the entire criminal justice system ineffective. He is equally inept as an audience member at *Hamlet*, violating canons of respectful behavior, pronouncing lame critical judgments, failing to get the point that Hamlet must follow the ghost, must "go farther," or there would be no story at all. Page and Garrick intend to produce terror, and Partridge certainly complies. The problem is that his is not the terror they wanted to create. His response to what he sees is singular, out of control.

What he sees and comments on—the criminal justice system at work, the high drama of dynastic rivalry—are matters that were central in Fielding's life, and in the way that he responds, Partridge emerges as a kind of witness for the defense, standing up for or at least representing positions that Fielding elsewhere derides. He argues against capital testimony on precisely the grounds that the novelist-magistrate will later dismiss sarcastically, and his emotionally genuine response to *Hamlet* seems in some way dependent on his Jacobite sympathies. Our first impulse as readers is to say that Fielding has stacked the deck: the anti-Fielding, the spokesman for the other side is, as we have repeatedly seen, a fool of the worst stripe—credulous, cowardly, stubborn. Yet, as I hope these readings suggest, Partridge turns out to be a surprisingly effective counter-witness. Capital testimony serves a system that does not necessarily distinguish guilt from innocence in a just and equitable way; the Stuarts may represent an ethos that has been necessarily removed, but at what price in creating a more cool, a more calculated political order?

Partridge's relationship to his creator is made even more complex when we remember that the particular events for which he serves as our witness are matters that Fielding himself saw, perhaps many times. Whatever the historical status of the trial that Partridge recounts, Fielding must have heard a great deal about the legendary Page in his years riding the Western circuit and he certainly saw trials for horse theft. Garrick was his friend and theatrical collaborator, and the actor's legendary performance as Hamlet was a staple for many years at Drury Lane. If Partridge's responses are not Fielding's, he is nonetheless responding to occurrences in the novelist's own experience, and it is worth thinking about the possibility that this unlikely character might be another of those self-portraits, like Tom, Black George, or Page, with which Fielding has seeded his novel. We noted above the way Partridge's account of the trial at one point seems to shift its tonal register—when he refers to such proceedings as "charming sport"—and becomes at least closer to that of the novel's narrator. Such a moment, while virtually atomic in the scale of this vast narrative, does give us license to think further about Partridge and Fielding. The barber-schoolmaster, that is, may not only be a witness against Fielding, or against Fielding's publicly held opinions, he may also serve in some ways as a witness *for* his creator, and thus serve as another reminder of the novelist's capacity to be in at least two places at the same time.

Partridge's place in the novel is, of course, marked by a notable hiatus. He appears early and briefly, in the almost cameo role of Tom's purported father, and then again, much later and for the rest of the novel, as the hero's companion and servant. We learn about the interim—two decades—very late, in the sixth chapter of the novel's last book, and it is an account worth our attention. Fielding seems to encourage that attention since the story is rather glaringly out of place, being both detailed and quite irrelevant to matters at hand. At a time in the novel when the pace has turned very brisk, and every incident serves to push along the momentum of unfolding, Partridge's sad story is, once more, a digression, one that retards the action and which has no import for the grand denouement Fielding is preparing for our eager eyes. Unlike his other appearances, this tale is marked by neither superstition nor comedy, but again here, he is a witness, and this time, finally, he is a witness for and about himself.

His life since the day he found himself convicted of an adultery not his own fell, he tells Allworthy, into a number of parts: he remained some time in Somerset after his trial, but legal trouble rooted in debt forced him away, first to Salisbury, where he worked as servant to a lawyer, then to Lymington for three years in the service of another lawyer; here, he finally set up another school, which "was likely to do well" (937), but a legal action ruined him and he spent the next seven years in Winchester jail, presumably for debt; from there, he went to Ireland and had a school at Cork, then to Bristol for half a year, and finally to Gloucester, which needed a barber, and which is where he reunites with Tom. The common thread here is financial trouble , which provokes his geographical mobility (seven locations in twenty years), and variety of occupation: he is schoolmaster, servant, barber. Just on the cusp of that overwhelming shower of blessings that constitutes the novel's happy ending, we get a glimpse here of what must have been a typical kind of eighteenth-century life, a life dogged by status uncertainty (as he repeatedly crosses what appears to be a very fluid line between the minor gentility of a schoolmaster and the decidedly non-genteel life of a servant), and unremitting financial difficulties, difficulties exacerbated by persistent legal persecution.

The information value of this life history, in terms of resolving the plot, is nugatory. None of it is necessary to exculpate Partridge to Allworthy of the old charge of adultery, for Mrs. Waters is conveniently in the wings to take care of that. The story does have the effect of reminding us of the disastrous consequences of Allworthy's misjudgment in finding him guilty of a trumped-up charge, and so works as a powerful counterimage to Tom's concluding good fortune: this twenty-year catalog of struggle and suffering, not the inheritance of Paradise Hall, is what really happens when someone without friends or money is convicted in a show trial and forced to leave his home. But there is more going on here than the novelist's sense that he needs a small interpolated tale in a minor key to properly set off the bounties in his plot awaiting us just ahead. Fielding betrays a certain personal investment in this narrative, so banal and yet affecting, by the presence again (as with the gypsies) of one of his very rare footnotes. Almost all of the notes in the novel are strictly utilitarian, translations, and annotations, and only this note and one other fall into the category of what we might call the polemic. Fielding uses the note, goes out of his way to tell us, that the kind of persecution Partridge suffers is true. When the servant remarks, "now as I owed two or three small Debts, which began to be troublesome to me (particularly one which an Attorney brought up by Law-charges from 15 s. to near 30 l . . .)," Fielding feels forced to comment in a note: "This is a fact which I knew happen to a poor Clergyman in *Dorsetshire*, by the Villainy of an Attorney, who was not contented with the exorbitant Costs to which the poor Man was put by a single Action, brought afterwards another Action on the Judgment, as it is called. A Method frequently used to oppress the poor, and bring Money into the Pockets of Attornies, to the great Scandal of the Law, of the Nation, of Christianity, and even of Human Nature itself" (936 and note). This fact cannot be left, it seems, in the urbane hands of the narrator of this novel. We are looking ahead here to the world of *Amelia*, where Fielding will return to the subject of debt, and where the polemical current will be strong. But in *Tom Jones*, Partridge's tale, with its little added authorial commentary, seems anomalous, and especially so here at the end, where everything is coming up roses.

Debt, of course, was Fielding's besetting problem. It would be as impossible to connect the composition of Partridge's life story to any particular event in Fielding's life as it would be for any other episode in the novel. The fact that this story comes so late when it could have come so much earlier (Tom and Partridge's reunion back in Book VIII, for instance, would have been a logical place) does suggest, however, that Fielding may have felt compelled to include it at novel's end, not for reasons of plot or form, but because he had spent too much time with the bailiffs that week; there is an unmistakable testiness in his footnote which is easy to interpret in the light of his life. But if exigency intruded in this way, the fact of personal circumstance only reinforces the link of novelist and character; when he needs to vent some spleen about the sorry nexus of debt and the law, Partridge is the vehicle he chooses. The mirror he creates, again, hardly gives us a duplicate image: Partridge's struggle to survive and Fielding's inability to live within his means are not the same thing. And yet, they resonate. They are different points on the same spectrum. Partridge said, back at his reunion with Tom, "I was not born nor bred a Barber, I assure you. I have spent most of my Time among Gentlemen, and tho' I say it, I understand something of Gentility" (418); indeed, he will later insist, "I am no Man's Servant, I assure you; for tho' I have had Misfortunes in the World, I write Gentleman after my Name" (515). He thus speaks (*mutatis mutandis*) for his creator, who was not born a censored playwright nor a circuit-riding lawyer nor an overworked magistrate nor a hack for the Whigs, all of which of course he became, but a gentleman on a country estate, with the blood of lords in his veins.

In some sense worth close attention, then, without ever assuming a place as Fielding's spokesman, Partridge does function as his witness, as one character he has designated to tell us about a few of the things that he has seen, as a voice who can articulate some reactions to the stuff of his own experience, reactions that he cannot embrace but which, perhaps, he cannot fully disown. Partridge, the witness, always has a point. In a novel full of alternative trajectories—the Man of the Hill or Enderson as Tom, Mrs. Fitzpatrick as Sophia—Partridge traces a path with small but startling echoes of Fielding: going to trials, watching plays, speaking a bit of Latin, fighting with uneven success to keep a pack of ravenous creditors at bay. The implication of Partridge's witness, standing as it does both against and for Fielding, is that the novelist could imagine how he would have felt and what he might have believed if he had found himself in a place a little lower on the social scale. If Tom represents his fantasy of moneyed vindication, Partridge can be seen as the translation of his life into real nightmare, and the poor servant's insomnia is perhaps his own.

Notes

Introduction: Missing Pictures

1. The comment was made by Joseph Spence. The publication history of the novel is thoroughly discussed in the "General Introduction" to *The History of Tom Jones, A Foundling*, eds., Martin Battestin and Fredson Bowers (Wesleyan, CT: Wesleyan University Press, 1975), xlii–lxi. Further quotations from the novel are from this edition and are noted parenthetically in the text.
2. "Table Talk," July 5, 1834, in *The Complete Works*, ed., W. G. T. Shedd (New York: Harper, 1856), VI, 521.
3. *The History of Henry Fielding*, 3 vols (New York: Russell and Russell, 1963), III, 283–4.
4. For more on the dismissal of the Forty-Five as well as further discussion of its rehabilitation as a matter of consequence, see ch. 1, "Stuart Ghosts," especially the section "Revising History."
5. For instance, vol. 3 of Leon Radzinowicz's magisterial *A History of English Criminal Law and its Administration from 1750* (London: Stevens and Sons, 1948), "The Reform of the Police," has, as its first chapter, "Pioneers of Police Reform:Henry and John Fielding."
6. The tale is delicious but unverifiable, based as it is on an old tradition in a family (the Millers of Radway Grange, Warwickshire) that Fielding may have visited n the fall of 1748; see Martin Battestin, with Ruthe R. Battestin, *Henry Fielding, A Life* (London and New York: Routledge, 1989), 441. Further citations to Battestin's biography will be noted parenthetically in the text.
7. Walter Scott, *Waverley* (Oxford: Clarendon Press, 1981). See esp. the first chapter of the novel, "Introductory," where Scott makes a claim for the originality of a novel set so specifically "Sixty Years before this present 1st November 1805" (4).
8. Coleridge made this comment at the same time as he remarked on the novel's breezy day in May quality, cited above, note 3.
9. The first to compare the novel's structure to that of a Palladian design was Dorothy Van Ghent; see *The English Novel, Form and Function* (New York: Holt, Rinehart and Winston, 1953), 80: "We may think of *Tom Jones* as a complex architectural figure, a Palladian palace perhaps. . . . The structure is all out in the light of intelligibility; air circulates over and around and

through it." The point has been picked up and elaborated by Frederick Hilles and Martin Battestin. See Hilles' essay, "Art and Artifice in *Tom Jones*," in *Imagined Worlds: Essays on Some English Novels and Novelists in Honour of John Butt*, eds., Maynard Mack and Ian Gregor (London: Methuen, 1968), 91–110; and Battestin's chapter, "Fielding: The Argument of Design," in *The Providence of Wit: Aspects of Form in Augustan Literature and the Arts* (Oxford: Clarendon Press, 1974), esp. 149: "The same axioms that determined the form of Ralph Allen's 'stately House' at Prior Park or Lord Pembroke's bridge at Wilton have, in a sense, determined the form of *Tom Jones*."

10. William Empson, "*Tom Jones*," in *Using Biography* (Cambridge:Harvard University Press, 1984), 132. This is an edition of his uncollected essays, which Empson prepared shortly before his death. The essay on the novel had originally appeared in *The Kenyon Review* 20 (Spring 1958).

11. Empson also discusses this passage, though to different ends; see 134–5.

12. Martin Battestin, "Pictures of Fielding," *Eighteenth-Century Studies* 17 (Fall 1983), 1–13. Battestin here very usefully surveys the history of the various Fielding images and their provenance. He also argues that a chalk and pencil portrait in the collection of the British Museum, possibly by Sir Joshua Reynolds, is a picture of Fielding near the end of his life. Battestin later used it, in fact, as the illustration for the back cover of his 1989 biography of the writer, where the jacket copy labels it as "A drawing of Henry Fielding, c. 1753, attributed to Reynolds." I am not confident of that attribution. The man in the picture has an indisputably large nose, but I see little other evidence to make the connection securely. Fielding in 1753 was worn out and terribly ill, but this still looks to me to be a much older man than even a gouty, dying 46-year old. Despite Battestin's confidence, he acknowledges that "the experts whom I have consulted at the British Museum and the National Portrait Gallery have understandably declined to hazard an opinion as to the authenticity of the portrait" (3). Additionally, he argues that Fielding appears in Hogarth's famous *Characters and Caricaturas* (1743); see 9–13. This image, like the suppositious Reynolds portrait, as well as Hogarth's posthumous illustration, appears in profile. His identification seems to rest almost solely on the size of the nose and chin. One could also remark that profiles of men with big noses all have a family resemblance. More cautious is another biographer, Donald Thomas, whose life of Fielding came out shortly after Battestin's; among his 25 illustrations, there is no picture of his subject. See *Henry Fielding* (New York: St. Martin's Press, 1990).

13. James Joyce, *Ulysses* (New York: The Modern Library, 1934), 193.

Chapter 1   Stuart Ghosts

1. Frank McLynn, *Charles Edward Stuart: A Tragedy in Many Acts* (Oxford: Oxford University Press, 1991), 520. Not surprisingly, *Paradise Lost* was also high on the Pretender's list. He had also asked a correspondent for copies of both *Joseph Andrews* and *Tom Jones* in 1750. This fact is partially noted by Cross,

but he says nothing about Charles's response to the books. See Wilbur Cross, II, 36; for this reference in McLynn, see p. 519.
2. W. B. Coley, ed., *The True Patriot and Related Writings* (Middletown: Wesleyan University Press, 1987); and W. B. Coley, ed., *The Jacobite's Journal and Related Writings* (Middletown: Wesleyan University Press, 1974). See also Rupert C. Jarvis, *Collected Papers on the Jacobite Risings*, 2 vols (New York: Barnes and Noble, 1971), II, ch's 18–19, for a useful summary of this phase of Fielding's career as a journalist and pamphleteer.
3. See Martin C. Battestin, with Ruthe R. Battestin, *Henry Fielding, A Life* (New York and London: Routledge, 1989), 424–5; see also the General Introduction to *The Jacobite's Journal*, lv–lvi, lxi–lxviii.
4. In M. R. Zirker, ed., *An Enquiry into the Causes of the Late Increase of Robbers and Related Writings* (Middletown: Wesleyan University Press, 1987), 18.
5. See Hugh Amory, "The History of 'The Adventures of a Foundling': Revising *Tom Jones*," *Harvard Library Bulletin* 27 (1979), 277–303; Battestin, *A Life* and especially "Tom Jones and 'His Egyptian Majesty'," *PMLA* 82 (1967), 68–77; Homer O. Brown, "*Tom Jones*: The 'Bastard' of History," *boundary 2* 7 (1979), 201–33; Jill Campbell, "*Tom Jones*, Jacobitism, and Gender: History and Fiction at the Ghosting Hour," *Genre* 23 (1990), 161–90; Peter J. Carlton, "The Mitigated Truth: Tom Jones's Double Heroism," *Studies in the Novel* 19 (1987), 397–409, and "*Tom Jones* and the '45 Once Again," *Studies in the Novel* 20 (1988), 361–73; Thomas R. Cleary, *Henry Fielding, Political Writer* (Waterloo: Wilfred Laurier University Press, 1984), esp. ch. 6; Cross, II, 99f; Morris Golden, "Public Context and Imagining Self in *Tom Jones*," *Papers on Language and Literature* 20 (1984), 273–92; J. Paul Hunter, *Occasional Form: Henry Fielding and the Chains of Circumstance* (Baltimore: Johns Hopkins University Press, 1975), 184–6; Anthony Kearney, "Tom Jones and the Forty-five," *Ariel* 4 (1973), 68–78; Michael McKeon, *The Origins of the English Novel, 1600–1740* (Baltimore: Johns Hopkins University Press, 1987), esp. 418; Ronald Paulson, *Popular and Polite Art in the Age of Hogarth and Fielding* (Notre Dame: University of Notre Dame Press, 1979), ch. 6; and John Richetti, "The Old Order and the New Novel of the Mid-Eighteenth Century: Narrative Authority in Fielding and Smollett," *Eighteenth-Century Fiction* 2 (1990), 183–96. Few of these critics offer to complicate our sense of the ideological tensions at work in *Tom Jones* Exceptions include Campbell (who discusses the politics of gender almost exclusively but who concludes by speaking of the "voice" in the novel as one that is "from [history], and *of* it, in all its complexity, its contradictions"—188), Carlton (who is also interested in gender and domestic issues, and the way they may allegorize high political questions), Paulson (for more on his ideas, see below, pp. 10–11), and Richetti (who is sensitive to the political tensions in the novel, but who also emphasizes Fielding's strong alliances in *Tom Jones* to the Hanoverian–Whig establishment).
6. An ancient and complex controversy lurks behind my discussion here. That is the problem of when Fielding actually wrote *Tom Jones*. We have no hard evidence, and so contemporary references—in particular, the Forty-Five—have taken on a privileged status in trying to reconstruct the novel's composition.

Briefly, there are two schools of thought: one says that Fielding began writing his novel after the defeat of the rebels at Culloden; the second, championed by Battestin, theorizes that Fielding began writing before the rebellion, abandoned it to work on *The True Patriot*, and then resumed work later, once the Rebellion was safely quelled. Battestin's prime evidence is a famous discrepancy in the time scheme of the novel: Tom meets the soldiers in November, but his "parley" in the woods with Molly is said to have taken place on "a pleasant evening in the latter end of June" (255)—that encounter, the plot makes clear, transpired only about three weeks before Tom's banishment from Paradise Hall. For Battestin, the reference to June is a vestige of an original time scheme, one he abandoned when he decided to incorporate the Forty-Five into his novel. Battestin's theory has the virtue of offering an explanation for Fielding's silence about the Forty-Five in the first six books of the novel (a problem the other theory cannot really explain), but no one in either camp has a good explanation for why references to the rebellion cease once Tom reaches London, except to say that Fielding lost interest in the subject. For Battestin, see the General Introduction to the two-volume Wesleyan edition of *Tom Jones*, xxxv–xlii; for the other side, see Cleary, ch. 6, and esp. Amory, who surveys the various schools with great energy and intelligence.
7. McCrea finds a couple of allusions—on pp. 933 and 946 of the novel. See *Henry Fielding and the Politics of Mid-Eighteenth Century England* (Athens: University of Georgia Press, 1981), 236 n. 3.
8. See, esp., Frederick S. Dickson, "The Chronology of 'Tom Jones'," *The Library*, third series, 8 (1917), 218–24.
9. Ronald Paulson, *The Life of Henry Fielding* (Oxford: Blackwell, 2000), 230. Others who have argued for its importance include Amory and Kearney. A sophisticated argument for the irrelevance of the Forty-Five to the fundamental concerns of the novel and its view of history is made by Leo Braudy, *Narrative Form in History and Fiction* (Princeton: Princeton University Press, 1970), 176–7.
10. McKeon's point is, of course, embedded in a much larger argument about the competition between what he calls "progressive" and "conservative" ideologies. He identifies Fielding with the conservative viewpoint, which—while it rejects the merit-based ideas of the progressives—recognizes the failure of aristocratic ideology as well. McKeon's reading of Fielding has the virtue of recognizing, more than many, Fielding's resistance to a great deal of the change in the culture around him. But the dialectical subtlety of McKeon's argument may, in the end, overstate Fielding's ideological alliance with those who would move beyond the old aristocratic ideology. For a discussion of these terms, see McKeon, 159–75.
11. Also worth considering in this context is Homer O. Brown's discussion, cited above, one of the very few true poststructuralist readings of the novel ever attempted. Brown notes the parallel of Tom and Charles Stuart (and others besides) and asks the crucial question, "What does one do with these parallels?" (211). But his answer to that question is ultimately ahistorical, and he insists that the "vision of history suggested by *Tom Jones*"

is one of "events which give rise to a multiplicity of representations and misrepresentations in a constantly troping, deflected associative swerve" (228)—that is, by a process he calls "metonymic contagion" (211), events in the novel create their own parallels, promiscuously, endlessly, and without resolution.

12. McKeon is the important exception here, simply because he has made it possible as never before to think about romance in the eighteenth century in historical terms. He does not, however, treat the issue in *Tom Jones*.

13. J. Paul Hunter, *Before Novels: The Cultural Contexts of Eighteenth-Century English Fiction* (New York; Norton, 1990), 8. Hunter has Henry Knight Miller chiefly in mind here; for a more lengthy critique of the assumptions behind Miller's book, see Hunter's review in *PQ* 56 (1977), 520–4. For Miller, see *Henry Fielding's "Tom Jones" and the Romance Tradition* (Victoria: University of Victoria Press, 1976).

14. Pepys' transcription and other accounts of the escape are collected in William Matthews, ed., *Charles II's Escape from Worcester: A Collection of Narratives Assembled by Samuel Pepys* (Berkeley: University of California Press, 1966). For Charles Stuart's story, see McLynn, ch. 19, which he titles "The Prince in the Heather." For more on Charles II's story and its wide dissemination, see Harold Weber, "Representations of the King: Charles II and His Escape from Worcester," *SP* 85 (1988), esp. 492–3.

15. W. J. Bate and Albrecht Strauss, eds., *The Rambler*, vol. 1 (New Haven and London: Yale University Press, 1969), 19–25.

16. The argument runs throughout *Origins of the English Novel*, but see esp. 141–50, 212–14. Northrop Frye had earlier touched on the connection between aristocracy and romance, though without much development. See, especially, *The Secular Scripture: A Study of the Structure of Romance* (Cambridge: Harvard University Press, 1976), 57.

17. For more on this, see Brean Hammond, "Politics and Cultural Politics: The Case of Henry Fielding," *Eighteenth-Century Life* 16 (1992), 76–93.

18. For a useful compendium of all the relevant documents, see E. N. Williams, ed., *The Eighteenth Century Constitution, 1688–1815: Documents and Commentary* (Cambridge: Cambridge University Press, 1965).

19. In summarizing these events, I have relied on three accounts of the birth of the Old Pretender: George H. Jones, *Convergent Forces: Immediate Causes of the Revolution in 1688 in England* (Ames: Iowa State University Press, 1990), ch. 4; J. P. Kenyon, "The Birth of the Old Pretender," *History Today* 13 (1963), 418–26; and Rachel J. Weil, "The Politics of Legitimacy: Women and the Warming-Pan Scandal," in *The Revolution of 1688–1689: Changing Perspectives*, Lois G. Schwoerer, ed. (Cambridge: Cambridge University Press, 1992), 65–82. Bishop Burnet's account manages to suggest, with utter unself-consciousness, that the Queen was never pregnant, that she miscarried, and that her child died after birth. See *History of His Own Time* (Oxford: Oxford University Press, 1883), III, 244–57.

20. A comparison with the ending of *Joseph Andrews* is instructive here. The happy discovery of Joseph's identity is wholly a matter of paternity: Mr. Wilson is the one who discovers and confirms who the hero really is,

his son, and it is that conventional patrilineal relation that is crucial. See Martin C. Battestin, ed., *Joseph Andrews* (Middletown: Wesleyan University Press, 1967), IV, ch. xv.
21. *Political Essays*, Knud Haakonssen, ed. (Cambridge: Cambridge University Press, 1994), 219. While written in 1748, the essay was not published until 1752; see the introduction, xii. Fielding thus could not have read this essay, but I cite it as an example of how a reasoned analysis of the competing claims at the time the novel was written could acknowledge merit as well as liability on both sides.
22. Ironically, after the failure of the Forty-Five, Charles Stuart did temporarily convert, and in keeping with his romance persona, made a secret trip to London to do so, but by then, it was far too late in the game. See McLynn, 399.
23. A comment of Claude Rawson's is worth attending to here. While he says that "It will not do to infer too much from Tom's illegitimacy," he goes on to point out that this point in the plot was *not* inevitable and that "it was in some ways bold and unorthodox to make his hero a bastard and keep him so, and [he] could have re-manipulated his opening if he had wanted to avoid this." See *Henry Fielding and the Augustan Ideal Under Stress* (New Jersey and London: Humanities Press, 1991), 7. A more recent consideration of Tom's status, one that explicitly disagrees with my conclusions, can be found in Wolfram Schmidgen, "Illegitimacy and Social Observation: The Bastard in the Eighteenth-Century Novel," *ELH* 66 (2002), 133–62.
24. Paulson makes this point; see 202. Paulson's brief remarks on the issues I discuss are well worth consulting as another interpretation of Tom Jones and Charles Stuart; see esp. 202–7.
25. Carlton (in "Mitigated Truth") makes a cognate point, arguing that Tom combines two models of heroism—Cavalier and Christian—that correspond roughly with competing Stuart and Whig ideologies.
26. A particularly lucid and helpful discussion of this kind of allegory can be found in Stephen Barney's *Allegories of History, Allegories of Love* (Hampden, CT: Archon Books, 1979). He calls it "reification allegory": "Normally, . . . a reification allegory involves a person who meets reified fragments of himself and of the various orders of his world, in temporal sequence" (37). For a very different way of thinking of an allegorical element in Fielding, see Martin Battestin, "Fielding's Definition of Wisdom: Some Functions of Ambiguity and Emblem in *Tom Jones*," *ELH* 35 (1968), 188–217; reprinted in *The Providence of Wit: Aspects of Form in Augustan Literature and the Arts* (Oxford: Clarendon Press, 1974).
27. Cross discusses both names and ages, though he has little or nothing to say about their significance, and while he points out the Man of the Hill's age, he does not discuss its possible meaning nor the peculiarity of his name; see II, 195–7. The fact that Fielding does not bother to name the old man may be an instance of what the great Spenser critic, James Norhnberg, calls "the allegorical interpolant," that is, the sign that announces that the story has an allegorical level to be explored. See his *The Analogy of "The Faerie Queene"* (Princeton: Princeton University Press, 1976), ix.

28. Again, for a contrasting understanding, see Battestin, "Fielding's Definition of Wisdom." If his is not, in a strict sense, a theological reading, he certainly does want what he sees as the emblems in the novel to function in a fully moral way.
29. My phrase is, of course, meant to recall Keith Thomas, *Religion and the Decline of Magic* (New York: Scribner's, 1971).
30. Qtd. in David R. Coffin, *The English Garden: Meditation and Memorial* (Princeton: Princeton University Press, 1994), 95.
31. Transportation usually meant a time of indentured servitude in, first, the American colonies, and then later, Australia. It was considered a form of pardon for crimes that would otherwise call for hanging. For more on the system, and its relation to the structure of criminal justice in eighteenth-century England, see J. M. Beattie, *Crime and the Courts in England, 1660–1800* (Princeton: Princeton University Press, 1986), esp. ch. 9.
32. There is a textual matter worth note here. In the third edition of the novel, published in April, 1749, Fielding extensively revised the Man's discussion of the historical circumstances surrounding Monmouth's Rebellion. The effect of these revisions was greatly to emphasize James II's Catholicism, and Man of the Hill's horror at his supposed violations of the constitution. Fielding dropped this revision and restored the original wording in the fourth edition, published in the December of that same year. The revised passage is reprinted in Sheridan Baker's edition of the novel, *Tom Jones*, second edition (New York: Norton, 1995), 645–7. The Man of the Hill's, as well as Tom's, loyalty to the Protestant cause are equally clear in both passages, but Fielding's decision to tone down the vehemence of the Man of the Hill's comments can be seen, in the light of the reading I develop here, as a way to maintain the reversibility of his political significance.
33. See Battestin, *A Life*, " 'His Egyptian Majesty,' " and "Fielding's Changing Politics in *Joseph Andrews*," *Philogical Quarterly* 39 (1960), 39–55; Cleary; Morris Golden, "Fielding's Politics," in *Henry Fielding, Justice Observed*, ed., K. G. Simpson (Totawa, NJ: Barnes and Noble, 1985), 34–55; Bertrand A. Goldgar, *Walpole and the Wits: The Relation of Politics to Literature, 1722–1742* (Lincoln: University of Nebraska Press, 1976); Robert Hume, *Henry Fielding and the London Theater, 1728–1737* (Oxford: Clarendon Press, 1988); Thomas Lockwood, "Fielding and the Licensing Act," *Huntington Library Quarterly* 50 (1987); and McCrea.
34. For more on this, see Hammond, 76–7. See also, James Thompson, "Patterns of Property and Possession in Fielding's Fiction," *Eighteenth-Century Fiction* 3 (1990), 41 n. 43, where he speaks of "Fielding's Tory myth."
35. L. B. Namier, *The Structure of Politics at the Accession of George III*, 2 vols (London: MacMillan, 1929). In terms of expanded Namierism, I have in mind the studies of Owen and Plumb: John B. Owen, *The Rise of the Pelhams* (London: Methuen, 1957); J. H. Plumb, *The Growth of Political Stability in England, 1675–1725* (Harmondsworth: Penguin, 1969). Owen has been particularly influential for scholars of Fielding's politics, as well as

for those studying other literary figures of the time. See Howard Erskine-Hill, "The Political Character of Samuel Johnson," in *Samuel Johnson: New Critical Essays*, ed., Isobel Gundy (Totowa, NJ: Barnes and Noble, 1984), 107–8, for a discussion of how Owen shaped Donald Greene's *The Politics of Samuel Johnson*. See also Greene's characteristically vigorous rejoinder to Erskine-Hill in the introduction to the second edition of his study of Johnson's politics: *The Politics of Samuel Johnson*, second edition (Athens: University of Georgia Press, 1990).

36. Even a very long note would not be sufficient to summarize all the body work on eighteenth-century politics and history suggested by the phrase "revisionist history." For representatives of the various revisionist approaches, see the works by Linda Colley, *Britons: Forging the Nation, 1707–1837* (New Haven: Yale University Press, 1992), and esp. *In Defiance of Oligarchy: The Tory Party 1714–60* (Cambridge: Cambridge University Press, 1982); Eveline Cruickshanks, *Political Untouchables: The Tories and the '45* (New York: Holmes and Meier, 1979); and Paul Monod, *Jacobitism and the English People, 1688–1788* (Cambridge: Cambridge University Press, 1989); and also Cruickshanks, ed., *Ideology and Conspiracy: Aspects of Jacobitism, 1689–1759* (Edinburgh: John Donald, 1982), and Jeremy Black and Cruickshanks, eds., *The Jacobite Challenge* (Edinburgh; John Donald, 1988). Above all, see J. C. D. Clark, *English Society, 1688–1832: Ideology, Social Structure and Political Practice During the Ancien Regime* (Cambridge: Cambridge University Press, 1985), and *Revolution and Rebellion: State and Society in England in the Seventeenth and Eighteenth Centuries* (Cambridge: Cambridge University Press, 1986). Clark is certainly the most controversial of the revisionist historians (at least among those working in the period after 1688; there is another group of revisionists working on the earlier seventeenth century, particularly the English Revolution). Clark's *Revolution and Rebellion* is a historiographical essay, and examines the rise of revisionism among historians of both the seventeenth and eighteenth centuries; it also includes a very handy appendix ("The Recent Debate on Jacobitism After 1714") summarizing and listing much of the work in Jacobite history through about 1985. For a somewhat more recent summary and review, see Bruce P. Lenman, "Some Recent Jacobite Studies," *The Scottish Historical Review* 70 (1991), 66–74, and especially Jonathan Israel's "General Introduction" to his collection of essays, *The Anglo-Dutch Moment: Essays on the Glorious Revolution and its World Impact* (Cambridge: Cambridge University Press, 1991). As the title suggests, Israel's collection is focused more narrowly on 1688, but he makes clear how revisionist perspectives on that event open up a more complex view of the Jacobitism that followed. Colley is much the most cautious in this group, arguing for a viable Tory party in the years after Anne's death, but minimizing the importance of Jacobitism.

37. See especially, *English Society, 1699–1832*; the argument also appears in *Revolution and Rebellion*. Clark's work, and revisionist history generally, has still not been widely taken into account by literary scholars working in the eighteenth century. Howard Erskine-Hill is the most significant exception; in addition to the essay on Johnson cited above, see "Literature and the Jacobite Cause: Was There a Rhetoric of Jacobitism?" in *Ideology*

and Conspiracy, ed., Cruickshanks, 49–69. The Richetti essay cited above also uses Clark, though he puts him to work in support of what remains a Namierite thesis. For an extended and thoughtful consideration of Clark from the viewpoint of a literary critic working in the eighteenth-century, see G. S. Rousseau, "Revisionist Polemics: J. C. D. Clark and the Collapse of Modernity in the Age of Johnson," in *The Age of Johnson*, vol. 2, Paul Korshin, ed. (New York: AMS, 1989), 421–50. Clark's more recent *Samuel Johnson: Literature, Religion, and English Cultural Politics from the Restoration to Romanticism* (Cambridge: Cambridge University Press, 1994), which argues for a strong Jacobite sympathy in Johnson, has been received with some skepticism.

38. Besides Hammond (cited above), others who have recently made this point include Richetti ("The Old Order and the New Novel"), and Battestin, *A Life*, 514. Also important in this context is the James Thompson essay, "Patterns of Property and Possession," also cited above. Thompson's interest is money and property, rather than dynastic politics, but the case he makes for Fielding's fiscal conservatism is very suggestive for the discussion here. Finally, though *Tom Jones* is not his focus, see James Cruise, "Fielding, Authority, and the New Commercialism in *Joseph Andrews*," *ELH* 54 (1987), 253–76.

39. I should make clear here that the kind of conservatism we can recognize in Fielding as a result of the work of the revisionists is somewhat different than the "conservative ideology" to which McKeon connects Fielding. McKeon's conservatism is a dialectical reaction to progressive ideology (see note 11 above), but also represents a historical movement beyond an aristocratic ideology. From a revisionist perspective, there is the possibility of much more continuity between the traditional aristocratic viewpoint and Fielding than McKeon would allow. At the same time, what I call Fielding's "pragmatism" is very much like what McKeon calls in Fielding "the instrumentality of belief"—"an instrumental belief in institutions whose authority may be questionable" (392). My argument here is meant to suggest that such instrumentality, often expressed in his openly political writings and exemplified by the passage quoted above from the "Charge Delivered to the Grand Jury," may not be the governing perspective of a work like *Tom Jones*, and that his appropriation of Stuart materials implies a somewhat different ideological position than we could derive by examining his more pragmatic pronouncements alone.

40. Battestin is sensitive to the ways in which the political and financial pressures to which Fielding was subject make for a contradictory record. See *A Life*, 115–16. But the effect of his biography as a whole is to emphasize what he sees as the points of continuity and coherence in Fielding's development.

Chapter 2   Savage Matters

1. For a discussion of the similarities between Savage and Charles Edward Stuart (but not Tom Jones), see Lawrence K. Lipking, "The Jacobite Plot," *ELH* 64 (1997), 843–55.

2. James Boswell, *The Life of Johnson*, eds., G. B. Hill and rev. L. F. Powell, 6 vols (Oxford: Clarendon Press, 1934), II, 175. Further references are to this edition and are noted parenthetically in the text. While this chapter was in preparation, a parallel study appeared, attempting to sort out the Johnson–Fielding relationship; some of the same facts are stated and some of the same quotations are used, but the argument is very different. See Martin Battestin, "Dr. Johnson and the Case of Harry Fielding," in *Eighteenth-Century Genre and Culture: Serious Reflections on Occasional Forms*, eds., Dennis Todd and Cynthia Wall (Newark: University of Delaware Press, 2001), 96–113.
3. Marshall Waingrow, ed., *The Correspondence and Other Papers of James Boswell Relating to the Making of the "Life of Johnson"* (London: Heineman, 1969), 497, n. 10.
4. John Carroll, ed., *Selected Letters of Samuel Richardson* (Oxford: Clarendon, 1964), 197; further references to Richardson's correspondence are to this edition and, unless otherwise credited, are noted parenthetically in the text.
5. Representative here are both of Fielding's important recent biographers, Martin Battestin and Ronald Paulson. Battestin says, "Tom Jones *is* Fielding" (5), and Paulson argues that "For Fielding 'storytelling' ... is a covert means of dealing with [his] experiences" (xi).
6. Lawrence Stone, *The Road to Divorce, England 1530–1987* (Oxford: Oxford University Press, 1990), 317.
7. The standard life of Savage is Clarence Tracy, *The Artificial Bastard: A Biography of Richard Savage* (Cambridge: Harvard University Press, 1953).
8. Henry Fielding, *The Convent-Garden Journal and A Plan of the Universal Register Office*, ed., Bertrand Goldgar (Middletown: Wesleyan University Press, 1988), 283. Note one on that page refers to the subscription list for the *Miscellanies*. Goldgar also points out there that Fielding owned a copy of *Select Trials at the Old Bailey* (1742), which includes an account of Savage's trial.
9. For Savage's publishing history, see Clarence Tracy, ed., *The Poetical Works of Richard Savage* (Cambridge: Cambridge University Press, 1962).
10. For Fielding's movements that fall and his friendship with Ralph Allen, see Battestin *A Life*, 352–8. For Savage, see Tracy, *The Poetical Works*, 143f. In his recent essay, "Dr. Johnson and the Case of Harry Fielding," Battestin also notes (as he did not in the biography) that both men were in Bristol and speculates that they may have met. He and I arrived at this conclusion independently and apparently almost simultaneously. See the Postscript to this essay, "How Close Were Fielding and Savage?", 107–9. Neither here nor in the essay that precedes it does Battestin discuss the possibility that Savage or the biography of him by Johnson could have provided source material for *Tom Jones*.
11. George Sherburn, ed., *The Correspondence of Alexander Pope*, 4 vols (Oxford: Clarendon, 1956), IV, 417.
12. Tracy, *The Artificial Bastard*, 140–1. Johnson briefly refers to this romance and these poems in his *Life*; see 116.

13. For a detailed discussion of the Fielding–Richardson rivalry, both as a biographical fact and as a shaping force in the criticism of the eighteenth-century novel, see Allen Michie, *Richardson and Fielding: The Dynamics of a Critical Rivalry* (Lewisburg: Bucknell University Press, 1999).
14. For instance, see W. J. Bate and Albrecht Strauss, eds., *The Rambler*, vol. III of *The Yale Edition of the Works of Samuel Johnson* (New Haven and London: Yale University Press, 1969), p. 19 n.1 (where Johnson's friend, Arthur Murphy, is cited as a source for the identification; the editors, however, do not give a specific reference for the information); further references to the *Rambler* are to this edition and are noted parenthetically in the text. Also, Russell A. Hunt, "Johnson on Fielding and Richardson: A Problem in Literary Moralism," *The Humanities Association Review*, 27: 4 (Fall 1976). An especially good discussion of *Rambler* # 4 can be found in ch. 2 of Joseph Bartolomeo, *A New Species of Criticism: Eighteenth-Century Discourse on the Novel* (Newark: University of Delaware Press, 1994), esp. 77–85.
15. Here as elsewhere in this study, I am deeply indebted to Battestin's life of Fielding. For a summary of his genealogy, see 6–10; for Fielding's father, see esp. 15–23, and 30–9. Paulson's more recent and shorter biography is also good on Fielding and his father.
16. Quoted in Paulson, *The Life of Henry Fielding* (Oxford: Blackwell, 2000),13.
17. The authoritative account of Savage's life is Tracy's biography, cited above. I have also consulted Richard Holmes' more recent *Dr. Johnson and Mr. Savage* (New York: Pantheon, 1993). See especially his appendix, "Note on Savage's Birth and Identity," which provides a succinct summary of the various accounts of Savage's identity and a sensible assessment of their relative merits.
18. Richard Tracy, ed., *Life of Savage* (Oxford: Clarendon, 1971), 12. Further references are to this edition and are noted parenthetically in the text.
19. A recent study that discusses (among many other things) the financial realities of a writing career in eighteenth-century England is Catherine Gallagher, *Nobody's Story: The Vanishing Acts of Women Writers in the Marketplace, 1670–1820* (Berkeley and Los Angeles: University of California Press, 1994). Her focus is on women writers but she deals broadly with the problem of making of living by authorship, and also with the way that the economic struggles of writers could become part of what would now be called their public image.
20. Fielding was confined to the sponging house for two weeks in March 1741; see Battestin, *A Life* 295–6; for Edmund's final debts and death, see 297–301.
21. See Battestin, *A Life* 30–7.
22. See, above, pp. 189–90.
23. "The Strategies of Biography and Some Eighteenth-Century Examples,"*Literary Theory and Structure*, eds., in Frank Brady, John Palmer, and Martin Price (New Haven and London: Yale University Press, 1973), 254. See also, Paul Alkon, "The Intention and Reception of Johnson's *Life of Savage*," *Modern Philology* 72:2 (November, 1974). He says of an 1842

novelized version of Savage's life: "A bare outline of [its] plot sounds like the plan for a tragic *Tom Jones*" (149).
24. Holmes, "Appendix."
25. Tom's bastardy has been provocatively discussed by Homer O. Brown in "*Tom Jones*: The 'Bastard' of History," noted in ch. 1. Robert Folkenflick's omnibus discussion of studies of the eighteenth-century novel published in the 1990s includes some thoughtful comments on Brown's discussion of bastardy; see "The New Model Eighteenth-Century Novel," *Eighteenth-Century Fiction* 12:2–3 (January–April 2000), 459–78.
26. No biography of Page exists. A short account is available in the *Dictionary of National Biography*, 22 vols (London: Oxford University Press), vol. 15, 39–41.
27. Toni Bowers argues that "monstrous mothers" are common in the "low literature of Augustan England," but she also acknowledges that Johnson's portrait of Anne Brett, which she calls the "best known" example of the type, is exceptional even in this company—in part because the *Life* hardly qualifies as "low literature." See "Critical Complicities: *Savage* Mothers, Johnson's Mother, and the Containment of Maternal Difference," *The Age of Johnson* 5 (1992), 115–46. She elaborates some of the arguments made here (though without detailed reference to the *Life of Savage*) at greater length in *The Politics of Motherhood: British Writing and Culture, 1680–1760* (Cambridge: Cambridge University Press, 1996). For another reading of maternity in the *Life*, one that attempts (not terribly convincingly) to link Anne Brett's supposed monstrosity to issues of race and colonialism, see Felicity A. Nussbaum, " 'Savage' Mothers: Narratives of Maternity in the Mid-Eighteenth Century," *Cultural Critique* (Winter 1991–2), 123–49.
28. One should not make too much of the fact, but may be worth noting in this context: Fielding himself, strictly speaking, did not go by the name of his father, who spelled the last name, "Feilding." See Battestin, *A Life* 7–8.
29. Bowers, "Critical Complicities," 117.
30. Paulson's biography is particularly good on the role of the so-called "mixed character" in all of Fielding's fiction.
31. Anna Laetitia Barbauld, ed., *The Correspondence of Samuel Richardson*, 6 vols (New York: AMS Press, 1966), IV, 181.
32. G. B. Hill, ed., *Johnsonian Miscellanies*, 2 vols (Oxford: Constable, 1966), I, 297.
33. McKeon, *The Origins of the English Novel*, 417.
34. Bartolomeo's book, cited above, is excellent on the contradictions between Johnson's moral principles as stated in *Rambler* # 4, and critical pronouncements he makes elsewhere.
35. The translation of Horace (*Epistles*, I.2, 3–4) is by Francis. Johnson used both the Latin original and the English version as epigraphs.
36. Hunt, "Johnson on Fielding and Richardson," cited above. This point was also made, contemporaneously, more briefly, and without specific reference to *Rambler* # 4, by Leopold Damrosch, Jr. in *The Uses of Johnson's Criticism*

(Charlottesville: University Press of Virginia, 1976), 115–16. See also the similar brief discussion in Carey McIntosh, *The Choice of Life: Samuel Johnson and the World of Fiction* (New Haven and London: Yale University Press, 1973), 26. J. Paul Hunter gives a valuable overview and analysis of the role of didacticism generally in responses to the early English novels in his *Before Novels* (cited in ch. 1), 225–302. He refers briefly to Johnson's response to Fielding on 231.

37. The idea that, based on his own critical principles, Johnson really should have admired Fielding was advanced long ago by Robert Etheridge Moore, "Dr. Johnson on Fielding and Richardson," *PMLA* 66 (March 1951). His argument is marred, however, by the now-striking anachronism of its premises: "Johnson, like Fielding, is a man, and a man's man. . . . Richardson may be called, in all seriousness, one of our great women" (172).

38. Holmes, 15. The marginal comment is noted in Tracy's edition, 114, n. 83.

39. An especially good discussion of the ending of the *Life of Savage* appears in William Vesterman, "Johnson and the *Life of Savage*," *ELH* 36:4 (December 1969), esp. 659–60.

40. Tracy, *Life of Savage*, 140, n. 103.

41. "Novel," of course, was a term that Johnson used slightingly, to refer to insubstantial fictions; he would define it, a decade later in his *Dictionary*, as "A small tale, generally of love." The generic looseness of the category (which, of course, has never disappeared) does not alter my point: Johnson feared fictional reworkings of Savage's life.

42. A cluster of essays in *The Age of Johnson* 5 (1992) address issues relating to Johnson and sexuality. See Gay W. Brack, "Tetty and Samuel Johnson: The Romance and the Reality"; Annette Wheeler Cafarelli, "Johnson and Women: Demasculinizing Literary History"; Roy W. Menninger, MD, "Johnson's Psychic Turmoil and the Women in His Life"; and John B. Radner, "Boswell and Johnson's Sexual Rivalry."

43. G. B. Hill adds a short appendix discussing the provenance of this quotation, which cannot be certainly verified. See I, 538–9.

44. Research by Professor Laura Rosenthal, not yet published, suggests that fifty pounds was a common sum paid for the services of a gigolo; such a payment was sometimes called "stallion's wages."

45. My summary of the Johnsons' marriage is drawn primarily from the account offered by Walter Jackson Bate, *Samuel Johnson* (London and New York: Harcourt, Brace, Jovanovich, 1975). See esp. 143–63, 177–89, 261–5. See also Holmes, and Gay W. Brack's essay, cited above.

46. James Boswell, *The Applause of the Jury, 1782–1785*, Irma S. Lustig and Frederick A. Pottle, eds. (New York: McGraw-Hill, 1981), 111. The entire section, which Boswell labeled "Extraordinary Johnsoniana—*Tacenda*," is of interest as a frank discussion of Johnson's sexuality; the editors note that the passage is "much the most extensive and intriguing of the accredited Johnsoniana he passed over." That is, Boswell kept it secret ("tacenda") and did not include it in the *Life*. See 110–13.

47. For Fielding's libertinism, see Battestin, *A Life* 145–8.

48. For a different interpretation of Johnson's relation to the truth of Savage's story, one that argues for a crises of indeterminacy in identity that Johnson is trying to control, see Toni O'Shaughnessy, "Fiction as Truth: Personal Identity in Johnson's *Life of Savage*," SEL 30 (Summer 1990), 487–501.
49. The literature on the relations between the novel and history in the eighteenth century is extensive and growing. McKeon, cited above, remains unsurpassed as the deepest consideration of the emergence of the novel out of a heterogenous mass of narratives claiming some relation to the "truth." A cognate exploration, without McKeon's elaborate dialectical machinery, is Hunter, *Before Novels*, cited above. A more recent and narrowly focused study is Everett Zimmerman, *The Boundaries of Fiction: History and the Eighteenth-Century British Novel* (Ithaca: Cornell University Press, 1996). Also, John Richetti, *The English Novel in History, 1700–1780* (New York and London: Routledge, 1999).

Chapter 3 Black Acts

1. Throughout my discussion of theft in this and the next two chapters, I use the words "theft," "robbery," and "stealing" more or less interchangeably. The law, of course, makes important distinctions among these terms. But there is also a kind of unifying conception at the heart of all these crimes—the unwilling movement of property—and that is my concern. Here, I follow Fielding, who seems interested in keeping ambiguous categories that the law wants to make clear.
2. Fielding refers to the Black Act two other times in his work. See Martin C. Battestin, ed., *Joseph Andrews* (Middletown: Wesleyan University Press, 1967), 290; the reference there is indirect, alluding to the Act's prohibition against cutting down trees, and is not noted. See also W. B. Coley, ed., *The Jacobite's Journal* (Middletown: Wesleyan University Press, 1975), 128; here, Fielding ironically bemoans the fact that abuses in the book trade are not subject to the Act.

    Black George has received almost no critical attention; however, some critics have begun to focus our attention on the serving classes in Fielding's fiction. See John Richetti, "Representing an Under Class: Servants and Proletarians in Fielding and Smollett," in Laura Brown and Felicity Nussbaum, eds., *The New Eighteenth Century: Theory, Politics, English Literature* (New York and London: Routledge, 1987), 84–98; and Bruce Robbins, *The Servant's Hand: English Fiction from Below* (New York: Columbia University Press, 1986).

    For the definition of "trover," see Henry Campbell Black, *Black's Law Dictionary* (St. Paul: West Publishing, 1979), 1351.
3. My language here is meant to call to mind the work of Clifford Geertz, particularly the essays "Thick Description: Toward an Interpretive Theory of Culture" and "Deep Play: Notes on a Balinese Cockfight," both of which are reprinted in *The Interpretation of Cultures* (New York: Basic Books, 1973). I do not claim to be using Geertz's work as a precise model—a foolish enterprise since his work treats real people, not fictional characters.

However, I do owe him a more general debt, and I find quite useful his procedure of using an elaborated description as a way into interpretation.
4. My understanding of the activity of gamekeepers and poachers alike has been shaped by three studies: Douglas Hay, "Poaching and the Game Laws on Cannock Chase," in Douglas Hay, Peter Linebaugh, John Rule, E. P. Thompson, and Cal Winslow, eds., *Albion's Fatal Tree: Crime and Society in Eighteenth-Century England* (New York: Pantheon, 1975), 189–253; Frank McLynn, *Crime and Punishment in Eighteenth-Century England* (Oxford: Oxford University Press, 1991), esp. ch. 11, "Poaching," 202–18; and particularly P. B. Munshche, *Gentlemen and Poachers: The English Game Laws 1671–1831* (Cambridge: Cambridge University Press, 1981).
5. This particular *droit de seigneur* is well illustrated by the hunt Western enjoys immediately after losing track of Sophia at Upton. See 622–4. The possible limitation on this privilege—and of course it was serious—was a violation of the laws of trespass; see McLynn, *Crime and Punishment*, 202. The almost impossible contradictions of the game laws are well summarized by one legal commentator cited in Holdsworth: "It was theoretically doubtful whether from 1604–1832 anyone could lawfully shoot a pheasant, partridge, or hare whatever qualification he possessed" (544).
6. Munsche, *Gentlemen and Poachers*, 13.
7. See ibid., 12–14, and esp. 30–1, 42.
8. Interestingly, Pope's panegyric both to English liberty under Stuart rule and to the pleasures of the hunt does not mention the limitations of the 1671 law; nothing in the poem indicates the property qualification necessary before anyone could legally force those larks to leave their little lives in air. This may reflect Pope's sense that the liberty of the hunt increased under the Stuarts (since the law enfranchising the gentry passed under Charles II), but it ignores the fact the Stuarts in general were most zealous to preserve the old Norman claim to the monarch's ownership of all game; for the latter, see McLynn, *Crime and Punishment*, 203 and Munsche, *Gentlemen and Poachers*, 10–11.
9. McLynn, *Crime and Punishment*, 211; Munsche, *Gentlemen and Poachers*, 22.
10. McLynn, *Crime and Punishment*, 208.
11. Munsche, *Gentlemen and Poachers*, 44.
12. *The Water Babies, A Fairy Tale for a Land Baby*, Vol IX, *The Works* (London: MacMillan, 1885), 20.
13. Munsche, *Gentlemen and Poachers*, 31.
14. I should note that Western does not prosecute for a violation of the game law, only for a trespass, see 121. Battestin's note there misses the point that the two men have even broken the game laws. His discussion of whether or not Western's property has been officially designated as a game warren is irrelevant. Neither man is legally able to hunt, whether Western's land is a warren or not. Battestin does note the property qualification on 357–8 n. 3, but does not connect it to Tom or George.
15. For wages, see Munsche, *Gentlemen and Poachers*, 42; for fines, see Hay, "Poaching and the Game Laws," 189, McLynn, *Crime and Punishment*, 204, and Munsche, *Gentlemen and Poachers*, 21.

16. Empson, "Tom Jones," 139.
17. Battestin mentions that a man named Seagrim, who may have been a neighbor of Fielding's, welshed on a loan, forcing the novelist to sue him for debt, and he speculates that there may be a personal score being settled as Fielding appropriates the name of this debtor for his character. Certainly, if such a Seagrim was Fielding's neighbor or acquaintance (the evidence is not conclusive), it is possible to imagine the novelist reconceiving the betrayal of his own act of friendship into George's ungrateful pocketing of Tom's money. See *A Life*, 352.
18. To be precise, the monarch is named three times in the novel, on 368, 440, and 546, and always in dialogue, direct or indirect. Tom speaks the king's name once (440) and soldiers mention it on the other occasions.
19. E. G. Withycombe, *The Oxford Dictionary of Christian Names*, 2nd ed. (Oxford: Clarendon Press, 1950), 122–3; Withycombe asserts that the "name was rare until the advent of the House of Hanover in 1714" (122). He is seconded by another scholar of names: "scarcely a single George appears in our parish registers before 1700." See Charlotte M. Yonge, *History of Christian Names* (London: MacMillan, 1884; repr. Detroit: Gale, 1966), 115.

There is one more etymological point worth noting. "George" comes from a Greek root meaning "tiller of the soil." Black George is no farmer, but he is firmly rooted in the Somershetshire countryside that provides Fielding with the setting for the first third of the novel. Moreover, Fielding, good classical scholar that he was, may also have had in mind another word descended from that root, the poetic form known as georgic, made famous by Virgil, and the subject of a long essay by Addison earlier in the century. Insofar as "georgic" meant a poem about rural life, the opening volumes of *Tom Jones* themselves constitute a kind of georgic, with a character named George passing in and out of the action, as if to remind us, however mockingly, of the classical tradition. This pastoral connection is not, to be sure, entirely separable from the Hanoverian one. There was a tradition, especially popular among the Jacobites, and possibly connected to the etymology of the name, that the news of his succession to the British throne was brought to George I in a turnip patch. For the Hanover–turnip connection in Jacobite propaganda, see Paul Monod, *Jacobitism and the English People, 1688–1788* (Cambridge: Cambridge University Press, 1989), 57–8. Western probably has this tradition in mind when he complains that "the *Hannover* Rats have eat up all our Corn, and left us Nothing but Turnips" (321). Battestin's note there does not mention this as a popular form of Jacobite abuse.
20. I have not forgotten here the possibility that would immediately leap to a modern reader's mind—that George is named after the color of his skin. Black people were relatively common in eighteenth-century Britain, especially relative to their numbers on the continent. Still, despite the lack of any definitive statistics, all evidence points to a very small black population, and the novel gives us no reason to suppose George is black. Indeed, as I show below, it explains very clearly why he carries this

nickname. For the early history of blacks in Britain, see F. Shyllon, *Black People in Britain, 1555–1833* (Oxford: Oxford University Press, 1977). For representations of black people in eighteenth-century art, see David Dabydeen, *Hogarth's Blacks: Images of Blacks in Eighteenth-Century English Art* (Athens: University of Georgia Press, 1987).

21. The classic essay is Ian Watt, "The Naming of Characters in Defoe, Richardson, and Fielding," *RES* 25 (1949), 334–7. However, virtually all of Watt's discussion is devoted to the name of the hero of *Tom Jones*, and he says nothing about George.

22. According to the *OED*, the use of "black" to refer to someone who was black-haired goes back to the eleventh century.

23. Reginald Reynolds, *Beards: An Omnium Gatherum* (London: George Allen and Unwin, 1950), 242–3. I am also indebted to a conversation with John Dixon Hunt on this matter.

24. In search of a range of images of male faces of the era, I consulted *The Drawings of Thomas Rowlandson in the Paul Mellon Collection*, catalogue compiled by John Baskelt and Dudley Snelgrove (New York: Brandywine Press, 1978); drawings 66–101 are "Rustic Compositions" and no beards are to be seen (but drawing 114, "The Prize Fight of 1787," seems to show two men with beards, though the scene is so crowded with faces that I cannot be certain). Also, Joseph Burke and Colin Caldwell, *Hogarth: The Complete Engravings* (New York: Harry N. Abrams, n.d.); Hogarth represents a few beards. See "The Enraged Musician" (1741), which shows a scruffy-looking hautboy player with a barely detectable fringe around his chin; another musician, this time fully bearded, leads the procession in "Chairing the Members" (1758). The latter is part of an election series that also shows a bearded peddler in the picture titled "Canvassing for Votes." According to Ronald Paulson, these bearded characters are both Jewish, and are part of a complex commentary in the series on the so-called Jew Bill of 1753. See *Hogarth: His Life, Art, and Times* (New Haven and London: Yale University Press, 1971), II, 199–200.

I should add that among Hogarth's engravings not drawn from contemporary life, beards abound. The point about the beardlessness of eighteenth-century England is made very well by Hogarth's "Character and Caricaturas" of 1743. Three faces at the bottom of the page are renditions of figures from Raphael and are bearded; the host of faces (close to 100) above are all contemporary, they represent a range of classes and ages, and they are all clean-shaven.

25. Given the paucity of beards in eighteenth-century England, it is worth noting that George's is not the only beard in *Tom Jones*. Captain Blifil, who wins Bridget as a wife and produces young Blifil as a son, has, we learn, a face "totally overgrown by a black Beard, which ascended to his Eyes" (66). George's beard, as we will see, is multiply emblematic, and here we have an early association in the novel between a beard and ideas of social climbing and hypocrisy.

26. See, for instance and among many, James Thompson, "Patterns of Property and Possession in Fielding's Fiction," *Eighteenth-Century Fiction* 3 (1990), 40. Empson calls George "the thieving gamekeeper" (139).

27. For Lilliputian law in these matters, see *Gulliver's Travels*, I, ch. 6.
28. For Wild, see Gerald Howson, *Thief-Taker General* (New Brunswick: Transaction Books, 1970). An excellent brief discussion of Wild's career and methods can be found in Robert Hughes, *The Fatal Shore* (New York: Vintage, 1986), 613–4.
29. John Locke, *Two Treatises of Government*, Peter Laslett, ed. (Cambridge: Cambridge University Press, 1988), 287–8. For Fielding's library, see Hugh Amory, ed. *Sole Catalogues of Libraries of Eminent Persons*, vol. 7 (London: Mansell, 1975), 140–58.
30. James Thompson, "Patterns of Property and Possession" 33–4. Thompson's essay provides an excellent introduction to eighteenth-century money and its role in Fielding's fiction. He is not, however, much concerned with crime.
31. For a discussion of the literacy of servants, see Judith Frank, "Literacy, Desire, and the Novel: From *Shamela* to Joseph Andrews,"*Yale Journal of Criticism* 6 (1993), 157–74.
32. For a full discussion of the practice, see J. M. Beattie, *Crime and the Courts in England 1660–1800* (Princeton: Princeton University Press, 1986), 141–6, 167–81, and 451–8.
33. For the Black Act, see Leon Radzinowicz, *A History of English Criminal Law* (London: Stevens and Sons, 1948), I, 49–79; E. P. Thompson, *Whigs and Hunters, The Origin of the Black Act* (New York: Pantheon, 1975); Thompson reprints the Act as Appendix I of his book; see also, Pat Rogers, "The Waltham Blacks and the Black Act," *Historical Journal* 17 (1974), 465–86; Eveline Cruickshanks and Howard Erskine-Hill, "The Waltham Black Act and Jacobitism," *Journal of British Studies* 24 (1985), 358–65; and John Broad, "Whigs and Deer-Stealers in Other Guises: A Return to the Origins of the Black Act," *Past and Present* 119 (1988), 56–72.
34. Thompson, *Whigs and Hunters*, 271. Further references will be noted in parenthesis in the text.
35. The arithmetic is difficult: see Radzinowicz, *History*, 76–7 and Thompson, *Whigs and Hunters*, 23. Both think the theoretical total of new capitol offenses is on the order of 200 or more.
36. The literature on crime and capital punishment in eighteenth-century England has grown quite large and contentious in the last few decades. The best and most judicious survey of the question can be found in Beattie, chs 8–9 (the entire book, however, is relevant). Much more hostile accounts can be found in *Albion's Fatal Tree*, esp. Douglas Hay's essay, "Property, Authority, and the Criminal Law"; and in Peter Linebaugh, *The London Hanged: Crime and Civil Society in the Eighteenth Century* (Cambridge: Cambridge University Press, 1992). The assumptions about the criminal justice system that lie behind Hay's work (and that of all the Warwick school, including E. P. Thompson and Linebaugh) come under severe attack in John Langbein, "Albion's Fatal Flaws," *Past and Present* 98 (1983), 96–120. See also Linebaugh's rejoinder, "(Marxist) Social History and (Conservative) Legal History: A Reply to Professor Langbein," *NYU Law Review* 60 (1985), 212–42.

37. Sir Frederick Pollock and Frederic William Maitland, *The History of English Law* (Cambridge: Cambridge University Press, 1968), II, 452.
38. Respectively, these are the arguments of Rogers; of Cruickshanks, Erskine-Hill, and Broad; and of E. P. Thompson, all cited in note 32 above.
39. For more on a consensus of conservative values between Whigs and Tories alike, see J. C. D. Clark, *English Society 1688–1832*, noted in ch. 1.
40. Hay, "Poaching and the Game Laws," 212.
41. See ibid., 210–14, for more on this kind of confusion of rights and roles.
42. In this regard, it is also worthwhile to recall the way that Fielding splits George in two in Bk. VI, ch. xiii, where the gamekeeper argues with his conscience (which is to say, with himself) about whether to steal the money that Sophia has entrusted him to give Tom. See 319–20 for this example of a doubled George.
43. Discussions of the concept of character in *Tom Jones* must trace their lineage back to Ian Watt's oft-maligned discussion of the nonrepresentational quality of the characters in Fielding's fiction; see *The Rise of the Novel* (Berkeley and Los Angeles: University of California Press, 1957), chs 8–9. For Fielding's comments on character, see *Joseph Andrews*, 189.
44. I should acknowledge that Black George is not the most famous gamekeeper in the history of the English novel. Pride of place goes, of course, to Mellors, who is not only Lady Chatterly's lover, but Sir Clifford Chatterly's gamekeeper. Lawrence's portrait of Mellors is consistent with the point that I am making here, not only in the sense of the class exogamy at the heart of the love affair, but in the language with which Lawrence describes his gamekeeper. If we look at the scene where Connie and Mellors first meet, we see that Lawrence says that he made "a slight bow, like a gentleman," and, a bit later, Connie thinks, "He might almost be a gentleman." See D. H. Lawrence, *Lady Chatterly's Lover* (New York: Grove Press, 1957), 52. More recently, and to a far wider audience, a gamekeeper has appeared in the Harry Potter series. Hagrid, too, is marked by various kinds of category confusion: an instructor at the academy but not a full-fledged professor, half-human, half-giant, and so forth.
45. Compare here John Bender's account of how Fielding's practice as a magistrate resembled Wild's. See *Imagining the Penitentiary: Fiction and the Architecture of Mind in Eighteenth-Century England* (Chicago: University of Chicago Press, 1987), 159–60.

    But if Fielding the magistrate is pragmatically willing to appropriate some of Wild's methods, Fielding the conservative idealist recalls nostalgically a much earlier time in British history, a time (as he puts it in the *Enquiry*) where "a Traveller might have openly left a Sum of Money safely in the Fields and Highways, and have found it safe and untouched a Month afterwards." Black George's action seems definitively to establish that such a time is gone forever—not that it ever existed outside of legend. See M. R. Zirker, ed., *An Enquiry into the Causes of the Late Increase in Robbers* (Middletown: Wesleyan University Press, 1987), 133.
46. Sections I–III of the *Enquiry* specifically discuss the problem of luxury among the poor. For Fielding's ironic extenuation of the behavior of the

rich, see 83. The standard account of eighteenth-century thinking on luxury, see John Sekora, *Luxury: The Concept in Western Thought, Eden to Smollet* (Baltimore and London: Johns Hopkins University Press, 1977).

47. In his book on beards, Reynolds cites a sixteenth-century French attempt specifically to discourage beards among the lower classes: "the people were forbidden to wear long beards *qui . . . semblent cacher quelque dessein pernicieux contre le repos del'Etat*" (213).

48. Terry Castle does not mention Black George or his beard in her study of masquerade in Fielding, but her discussion is a valuable companion to my remarks here. See *Masquerade and Civilization: The Carnivalesque in Eighteenth-Century English Culture and Fiction* (Stanford: Stanford University Press, 1986). See esp. 92 (and the accompanying note on 356–7) where she briefly discusses the Black Act's prohibitions on disguise in light of eighteenth-century thinking about masquerade.

49. I would cite again the work noted in ch. 1 that has complicated our old sense of Fielding's politics and illuminated that which was socially conservative in his thinking. See Hammond, "Politics and Cultural Politics: The Case of Henry Fielding," Michael McKeon, *The Origins of the English Novel*; John Richetti,"The Old Order and the New Novel of the Mid-Eighteenth Century: Narrative Authority in Fielding and Smollet"; and the James Thompson essay, cited earlier.

Chapter 4   Hanging Judges

1. Fielding may be subtly linking his hero to this thief when, a few pages before the Man of the Hill appears, he has a rumor-mongerer report that Tom is "the Bastard of a Fellow who was hanged for Horse-stealing" (432).

2. The summary of criminal justice procedures and practices that follows is drawn from a number of sources. Besides Beattie (both *Crime and the Courts* and *Policing and Punishment*), Hay, Linebaugh, McLynn, and Radzinowicz, all cited earlier in ch. 3, I have also consulted Sir William Holdsworth, *A History of English Law, vol. 11* (London: Methuen, 1938), Peter King, *Crime, Justice, and Discretion in England, 1740–1820* (Oxford: Oxford University Press, 2000), as well as two important articles by John Langbein: "The Criminal Trial Before the Lawyers," *The University of Chicago Law Review* 45 (Winter 1978), 263–316, and "Shaping the Eighteenth-Century Criminal Trial: A View From the Ryder Sources," *The University of Chicago Law Review* 50 (Winter 1983), 1–136. Those articles have been consolidated, with new material, in his recent *The Origins of the Adversary Criminal Trial* (Oxford: Oxford University Press, 2003). Beattie's *Crime and the Courts* has been my primary guide; see especially ch. 7, "The Criminal Trial," but King's more recent book has also been important.

My sense of disagreement with John Bender may be evident here. His *Imagining the Penitentiary* has been influential, but I think his debt to Foucault has led him to underestimate the ways in which English habits in the eighteenth century are marked more by persistence than innovation where crime and punishment was concerned.

3. King, *Crime, Justice, and Discretion*, 355. He says elsewhere: "Although the formal criminal law and the legal handbooks sometimes appeared rigid and inflexible, in reality the administration of the eighteenth-century criminal justice system created several interconnected spheres of contested judicial space in each of which deeply discretionary choices were made" (1).
4. Beattie, *Policing and Punishment*, vi.
5. King, 17.
6. *Crime and the Courts*, 385.
7. King, 357.
8. Hay, "Property, Authority, and the Criminal Law," 23.
9. Ibid. 52, and 18. For more in this vein, see all the essays collected in *Albion's Fatal Tree*, as well as Peter Linebaugh's *The London Hanged*, noted in ch. 3. Linebaugh is less interested in the paradox—brutal law, often merciful practice—than he is in the identities of those who actually were sent to the gallows. One can read his powerful study and forget that most of those convicted of the kinds of property crimes he discusses were in fact not hanged but pardoned. Foucault's comment in this regard is also worth note. He is aware of the fact that England, compared to the rest of Europe, was quite slow to alter the fundamental shape of its criminal justice system, but he also has a conspiratorial reason for that tardiness: "Paradoxically, England was one of the countries most loath to see the disappearance of the public execution . . . no doubt, because she did not wish to diminish the rigor of her penal laws during the great social disturbances of 1780–1820" (14).
10. Langbein, "Albion's Fatal Flaws," 97. His attack also rests on the evidentiary point of falsifiability: Hay argues that the occasional aristocrat (like the notorious murderer Lord Ferrars) was executed in order to create the impression that the law represented impartial justice, thus concealing its real status as class protection. Langbein rejoins that Hay would argue the same point if Ferrars had walked away: a lord who was hanged or one who killed with impunity can both represent the power of the ruling class. Langbein's unstated but clear point is that the idea of ruling class conspiracy is the starting point for Hay, and that whatever evidence he finds he can put in the service of that argument. He calls this a "legitimation trick"; see 114–15.
11. *Crime and the Courts*, 622.
12. King, *Crime, Justice, and Discretion*, 373.
13. Some years ago, Hugh Amory made some very sensible remarks in this regard. He takes it as a mistake to think that "the Government was pursuing a policy" with regard to the criminal law: "eighteenth-century English legislation is notably particularistic. . . . moreover, Parliament was simply not constituted for the formulation of policies" (191). The criminal law, that is, grew in an ad hoc way, year by year, problem by problem, without regard to system or overall policy. See "Henry Fielding and the Criminal Legislation of 1751–2," *PQ* 50 (April 1971), 175–92.
14. "Fielding's 'Tom Jones': Its Geography," *Notes and Queries* 11 S. X. 26 September 1914. De Castro's note addresses the identity of Justice Willoughby, as well as the 1737 Summer Assizes. For more on Willoughby, see Battestin's note, *Tom Jones*, 458, n.1. For more on Page, again see his

entry in the *Dictionary of National Biography* XV, 39–41, noted in ch. 2. Pope's references occur in the *Imitations of Horace*, ed., John Butt (London: Methuen, 1939), Satire II, i, ll. 81–2, and *The Dunciad*, ed., James Sutherland (London: Methuen, 1943), book IV, 27–30. See also the discussion of Page in Thompson, *Whigs and Hunters*, 211–2.

15. See, for instance, the editions of Sheridan Baker, 296, n. 2, and John Bender (Oxford: Oxford University Press, 1997), 899 (note to 397). Donald Thomas also accepts the factuality of the trial in his 1990 biography of Fielding; see 144–5.

16. The episode runs only three pages and rather than cite the page numbers parenthetically each time I quote, I point readers here to the full passage in the Wesleyan edition: 457–60.

17. For the law about testimony, see *Crime and the Courts*, 21–2. Also, King, *Crime, Justice, and Discretion* 11.

18. The fact that Fielding mentions lawyers for both prosecution and defense is indicative that the trial for horse theft that we see in *Tom Jones* was at least beginning to be inflected by the emergent practice, even if Page acts in some ways much like an old-style judge. Beattie makes it clear that it would have been highly unusual for a prisoner to stand trial while in chains: only the most dangerous criminals were forced to do so; see *Crime and the Courts*, 339, n. 61.

19. The most common appearance of "charming" occurs in connection to Sophia, to whom it is attached by the narrator so frequently as almost to amount to an epithet. "The charming Sophia" appears in the novel seven times, including a final occurrence at the narrative's erotic climax: "that happy Hour which . . . surrendered the charming *Sophia* to the eager Arms of her enraptured *Jones*" (979). Derivatives of "charm" are used ironically elsewhere by the narrator, as when he speaks of Bridget's attraction to Captain Blifil: "such were the Charms of the Captain's Conversation, that she totally overlooked the Defects of his Person" (66). "Sport" appears only eleven times, all but two of which are by the narrator, and again generally in an ironic way. The two exceptions occur in the Man of the Hill episode, once by the gambler Watson (using it literally, of course, about gaming) and once by the Man, who accuses Tom of making up the Forty-Five as a cruel joke: "I see you have a mind to sport with my Ignorance" (478). A typical instance of the narrator's usage occurs in connection with Western's hunting: "As soon therefore as the Sport was ended by the Death of the little Animal that had occasioned it . . . " (624). I have used the on-line search engine at Bibiomania.com to make these word counts.

20. For an excellent discussion of evidence in *Tom Jones*, see Alexander Welsh, *Strong Representations: Narrative and Circumstantial Evidence in England* (Baltimore: The Johns Hopkins University Press, 1992), 48–76. Welsh does not discuss this scene.

21. *Crime and the Courts*, 8–10. Langbein, "The Criminal Trial Before the Lawyers," 263. See also ch. 1 of his *The Origins of the Adversary Criminal Trial*: "The Lawyer-Free Criminal Trial."

22. For Malone's story, see Butt's edition of the *Imitations of Horace*, 374.

23. In the years 1660–1800, the pardon rate for horse-theft was about 74%. See *Crime and the Courts*, 435.
24. Another point of eighteenth-century law needs elaboration here. In fact, at that time, there was no presumption of innocence; such a presumption emerged as a legal principle only in the nineteenth century, once the new-style trials centering on the contest of defense and prosecuting attorneys was fully established. As Beattie puts it, "if any assumption was made in court about the prisoner himself, it was not that he was innocent until the case against him was proved beyond a reasonable doubt, but that if he *were* innocent, he ought to be able to demonstrate it for the jury by the quality and character of his reply to the prosecutor's [the victim, we recall] evidence. That put emphasis on the prisoner's active role" (341). So, while Page may not have violated procedure as egregiously as it might first appear, he has certainly thwarted this prisoner's ability to defend himself.
25. Beattie covers this point very thoroughly; see *Crime and the Courts*, ch. 6, "Coming to Trial."
26. The quick dismissal of Christian morality here is reminiscent of the logic of the army officer with whom Tom discusses whether or not he should fight Northerton. Tom says, "But how terrible must it be . . . to any one who is really a Christian, to cherish Malice in his Breast, in opposition to the Command of him who hath expressly forbid it," whereupon Fielding, obviously in a satirical mode, has the military man answer, "Why I believe that there is such a Command . . . but a Man of Honour can't keep it" (383–4).
27. There is an indirect allusion later in the *Enquiry*, when Fielding mentions with praise Sir William Thompson (also spelled Thomson); he had been at judge at Wild's trial and had pronounced sentence of death on him. Thompson's name comes up as part of a discussion of the requirement that testimony be corroborated (Fielding is against that practice). See 163 and esp. Zirker's note there.
28. Fielding expresses this belief again three years later in the *Journal of a Voyage to Lisbon*, where, at the sad and premature end of his life, he approvingly cites the example of another judge who answered a prisoner's complaint about being hanged for stealing a horse: " 'You are not to be hanged, Sir,' answered my ever-honoured and beloved friend, 'for stealing a horse, but you are to be hanged that horses may not be stolen.' " *The Journal of a Voyage to Lisbon*, ed., Tom Keymer (Harmondsworth: Penguin, 1996), 16. Lance Bertelsen sees irony in this passage; see *Henry Fielding at Work: Magistrate, Businessman, Writer* (New York: Palgrave, 2000), 143.
29. A reader of Foucault's *Discipline and Punish* might miss the way that Fielding's writings on criminal justice represent a deeply conservative view. Foucault quotes at some length the *Enquiry's* analysis of the failure of public executions to deter as intended, and without a fuller knowledge of Fielding's position, it would be possible to see him (as Bender does) as thus in some way participating in the broad European shift toward the idea of the penitentiary. What Foucault does not mention is Fielding's continuing insistence on the importance of a very wide use of the capital sanction; he

just wants it done privately, in order to increase its terror. See *Discipline and Punish* (New York: Vintage, 1979), 60–1. Fielding's ideas on how to make hanging more frightening are in the *Enquiry*, 167–72 ("Of the Manner of Execution").

30. The idea of the comedian-jurist calls to mind Bertelsen's astute analysis of Fielding's magistracy, especially his discussion of the way the novelist mined the proceedings of his courtroom as material for the columns of his periodical, *The Covent-Garden Journal*, thereby more or less collapsing the distinction between crime and entertainment. The fact that such a distinction seems nonexistent in contemporary American culture should not distract us from the fact that Fielding's rather extreme version of this phenomenon was a matter of his own invention. Bertelsen's summary is worth attention: "[Fielding] records his court room activities, transcribes them into an entertainment column, and publishes them in a journal he writes and edits. . . . [H]is journalistic practice seems bizarrely analogous to a modern judge ordering his court clerk to video-tape the proceedings of a criminal trial, then personally editing them with voice-overs into a twice weekly television program. . . ." See *Henry Fielding at Work*, 28, and chs 1 and 2 generally.

31. The quotation from *Joseph Andrews* is: " 'Jesu!' said the Squire, 'would you commit two persons to bridewell for a twig?' 'Yes,' said the Lawyer, 'and with great lenity too; for if we had called it a young tree they would have been both hanged' " (290). For McLynn's comments, see *Crime and Punishment*, 243–4.

32. Battestin, *A Life*, 521: " . . . the *Enquiry* was acknowledged for what it was, by the lights of the time a masterly, authoritative attempt to diagnose and cure appalling social ills"; his "horrid parade" comment occurs on 459. Paulson, *The Life of Henry Fielding*, 284–5. Bertelsen, *Henry Fielding at Work*, 17; see also his introduction ("Fielding's Last Offices"), ch. 1 ("Judicial and Journalistic Representation in Bow Street"), and appendix 1 ("Fielding's Bow Street Clientele"). His invocation of the tragic-comic calls to mind the scene in Page's court as well.

A good example of the way Fielding's work as magistrate can be made into heroic narrative is Patrick Pringle's *Hue and Cry: The Story of Henry and John Fielding and Their Bow Street Runners* (New York: William Morrow, 1955). See esp. ch. 5, "Mr. Fielding's People," and ch. 6, "An Inquiry and a Plan." A more sober assessment is offered by Amory, who argues that the *Enquiry*, as an attempt to influence public policy, was essentially impotent.

Chapter 5 Gypsy Kings

1. Cross, *The History of Henry Fielding*, 2: 150–2.
2. Near the end of the novel, Thackeray speaks of his heroine Becky Sharp as being "as restless as Ulysses or Bamfylde Moore Carew": *Vanity Fair, A Novel Without a Hero*, ed., Peter Schillingsburg (New York: Garland, 1989), 585.

3. The editorial history of the various versions of the Carew story are difficult to summarize in a brief compass. The original version was published in Exeter, but almost all the numerous subsequent editions were published in London. Very helpful in sorting out the confusion is C. H. Wilkinson, *The King of the Beggars, Bamfylde-Moore Carew*, Oxford: Clarendon Press, 1931. This volume includes, besides its introduction, which usefully surveys the bibliographical tangles, both *The Life and Adventures* and the later *An Apology for the Life*. Unfortunately, for Fielding scholars, he removes from the latter all the *Tom Jones*-related interpolations since his interest is in Carew, not Fielding. I have also relied on the title-page summaries offered by the *English Short-Title Catalogue*. Little critical work has been done on the Carew material; one recent exception is John Barrell, "Afterword: Moving Stories, Still Lives," in *The Country and the City Revisited: England and the Politics of Culture, 1550–1850*, eds., Donna Landry, Gerald MacLean, and Joseph P. Ward (Cambridge: Cambridge University Press, 1999), 231–50. Barrell does not discuss Fielding.
4. Wilkinson, *The Life and Adventures*, 9.
5. As the *DNB* puts it, "He continued his course of vagabond roguery for some time, and when Clause Patch, a king, or chief of the gypsies died, Carew was elected his successor." The entry gives no source for its information other than the various iterations of the original book.

My summary here is indebted throughout to Wilkinson's account in his introduction, but I have also inspected various editions of the Carew text held by the British Library, especially those of 1745 and 1750. The *ESTC* has proven invaluable as well.
6. Cross, *The History*, 2: 150, 152.
7. The historical and ethnographic literature on the Romani people, both generally and those in Britain, is large, though there is little that focuses specifically on the eighteenth century. The account that follows is drawn from Jean-Paul Clebert, *The Gypsies*, trans. Charles Duff (New York: E. P. Dutton, 1963); Angus Fraser, *The Gypsies* (Oxford: Oxford University Press, 1993); Ian Hancock, *The Pariah Syndrome: An Account of Gypsy Slavery and Persecution* (Ann Arbor: Karoma Publishers, 1987); David Mayall, *Gypsy-Travellers in Nineteenth-Century Society* (Cambridge: Cambridge University Press, 1988); Judith Okley, *The Traveller-Gypsies* (Cambridge: Cambridge University Press, 1983); and Brian Vesey-Fitzgerald, *Gypsies of Britain, An Introduction to Their History* (London: Chapman and Hall, 1944). Incomparable in its range and depth is Katie Trumpener, "The Time of the Gypsies: A 'People without History' in the Narratives of the West," *Critical Inquiry* 18 (Summer 1992), 843–84. While ostensibly focused on the place of this people in the Western narrative imagination, her important essay also provides a rich historical consideration of the Romani generally. She explicitly addresses one difficult issue, that of nomenclature. "Gypsy" is an imposed name (one based, as we will see, on a mistaken piece of historical speculation), and Romani, as she puts it, is "a somewhat homogenizing collective term" for a category with considerable diversity (847n.). I follow her lead, in using "Romani" for the ethnic group,

and "gypsy" when referring to the various fictional incarnations of that group, particularly of course in *Tom Jones*.
8. Hancock, *The Pariah Syndrome*, 89; Vesey-Fitzgerald, *Gypsies of Britain*, 31.
9. Clebert, 80.
10. A great deal of work on this subject has been done in recent years. The field was, in a sense, defined and launched by Michael Hechter, *Internal Colonialism: The Celtic Fringe in British National Development* (Berkeley: University of California Press, 1975). A cluster of articles relating to this topic in *Eighteenth-Century Fiction* is introduced with a useful overview of the subject by Janet Sorensen: "Internal Colonialism and the British Novel," *ECF* 15 (2002), 53–8.
11. This was in fact argued; see Hancock, *The Pariah Syndrome*, 121.
12. Vesey-Fitzgerald, *Gypsies of Britain* 3.
13. For a good summary of the connection of gypsies to conventions of picturesque viewing, see Peter Garside, "Picturesque Figure and Landscape: Meg Merrilies and the Gypsies," in *The Politics of the Picturesque: Literature, Landscape, and Aesthetics Since 1770* eds., Stephen Copley and Peter Garside (Cambridge: Cambridge University Press, 1994), 145–74. For more on their place in the nineteenth-century imagination, see Anne F. Janowitz, " 'Wild Outcasts of Society': The Transit of the Gypsies in Romantic Period Poetry," in *The Country and the City Revisited*, 213–30. Also important in this regard is David Simpson's reading of Wordsworth's "The Gypsies," in *Wordsworth and the Historical Imagination* (New York: Methuen, 1987). See also Trumpener, "The Time of the Gypsies."
14. Tom's admiration, in fact, seems to mirror that of Carew when he and his friends first meet the gypsy party on running away from school: "in short, so great an Air of Mirth and Pleasure appeared in the Faces and Gestures of this tawny Society, (to which add the great Plenty in which they rioted) that our four Youngsters from that Time conceived a sudden Inclination to inlist into their Company" (Wilkinson, 9) *The Life and Adventures*, This passage is largely unchanged between this first (1745) edition to the latest I examined (1775).
15. Manuel Schonhorn, "Fielding's Ecphrastic Moment: Tom Jones and his Egyptian Majesty," *Studies in Philology* (1981), 305–23. Other discussions of the episode include Martin Battestin, "Tom Jones and 'His Egyptian Majesty': Fielding's Parable of Government," *PMLA* 82 (March, 1967); Robert Folkenflik, "Tom Jones, the Gypsies, and the Masquerade," *University of Toronto Quarterly* 44 (1975), 224–37; Henry Knight Miller, "The 'Digressive' Tales in Fielding's *Tom Jones* and the Perspective of Romance," *Philological Quarterly* 54 (1975), 258–74; and Judith Weissman, "The Man of the Hill and the Gypsies in *Tom Jones*: Satire, Utopia, and the Novel," *Ball State University* Forum 22 (1981), 60–9.
16. I borrow the resonant phrase "people without a history" from Trumpener.
17. Fielding may also be making a joke about cant languages: the gypsies were famous for their private argot (and a canting dictionary was one of the attractions of *The King of the Beggars* and the many subsequent editions of Carew's story). The king's use of a military term may be a way to remind us

that all groups have their peculiar language, though it is worth noting that Fielding specifically does not use the cant ascribed to the gypsies. This small piece of interpolated jargon may be, again, a way to emphasize the gypsies' emblematic quality: they stand for the idea of a group apart, and there are many such groups.

18. There is an editorial question about the name of this character that I should note here: the first edition inconsistently refers to him as "Enderson," "Anderson," and "Henderson." Sheridan Baker, in his Norton edition of the novel, argues strongly in an appendix that the correct choice is "Anderson," but I have followed Battestin and Bowers' use of "Enderson," since that is the text I have used. Baker's arguments are thoughtful, however, and worth consideration; see *Tom Jones* (New York: Norton, 1995), 647–9.
19. Lest we think that the theft of ducks is only comic, McLynn, in *Crime and Punishment in Eighteenth-Century England*, cites the case of a man who was transported for seven years for the theft of two ducks; see 287.
20. In 1753, four years after the publication of *Tom Jones*, Parliament did pass Lord Hardwicke's Marriage Act, which was intended to regulate a great many abuses: marriage by minors without parental consent, bigamy and other fraud, and so forth. But while it could make certain kinds of fortune-hunting less likely (by requiring consent, or by making the actual ceremony more difficult to perform because of limitations on venue or time or process), it obviously could not eliminate all fortune-hunting, as Fielding's depiction of the courtship of Bridget and Captain Blifil makes clear. See Lawrence Stone, *The Family, Sex, and Marriage in England, 1500–1800* (New York: Harper, 1979), 32–4, for one discussion of the 1753 Act.
21. See *Crime and the Courts*, 614–6.
22. We should recall that Enderson is not the only highway robber who escapes prosecution in *Tom Jones*, and that Tom's restraint here allies him with a character whose judgment we do not otherwise admire: "Mrs. *Western* . . . had even broken the Law in refusing to prosecute a High-way-man who had robbed her, not only of a Sum of Money, but of her Ear-rings; at the same Time d——ing her, and saying, 'such handsome B——s as you don't want Jewels to set them off. . . .'" (357). According to Radzinowicz, highway robbery was the form of theft most likely to result in hanging; see I, 637.
23. Battestin, 68–71. He does mention Carew, but only to dismiss the claim that Fielding met him; see 68–9. His historical context for gypsy governance is largely drawn from Charles Rollin's *The Ancient History of the Egyptians . . . and Grecians*, originally published in Paris and which appeared in a ten-volume English translation between 1738–40; Rollin's account draws largely upon the ancient historians Diodorus and Herodotus; see Battestin, 70–2.
24. See McLynn, *Crime and Punishment*, 58.
25. Edmund Burke, *Reflections on the Revolution in France*, ed., Conor Cruise O'Brien (Harmondsworth: Penguin, 1986), 101. Other references are to this edition and are noted parenthetically in the text.
26. For convenience I have quoted here from my own copy of *An Apology for the Life*, which is dated 1775. The material relating to gypsy governance and

society is identical here to that in the 1750 edition which I examined in the British Library.
27. *The History of the Decline and Fall of the Roman Empire*, 7 vols, ed., J. B. Bury (London: Methuen, 1909–14), I, 85–6.

Chapter 6   Mirror Plots

1. Paulson is good on the way Fielding's careers in the theater and the law shape his predominant metaphoric structures; see *The Life of Henry Fielding*, 132–3, and passim.
2. There is new theoretical interest in the idea of the witness, and there is a growing body of literature on the subject. For instance, see John Durham Peters, "Witnessing," in *Media, Culture, and Society* 23 (2001), 715–31; and Shosana Felman and Dori Laub, MD, *Testimony: Crises of Witnessing in Literature, Psychoanalysis, and History* (New York and London: Routledge, 1992).
3. For the chronology of *Tom Jones*, see Dickson, noted above, ch. 1, note 9. Also see Battestin and Bowers, *Tom Jones*, 853, n. 1.
4. See Irvin Ehrenpreis, *Fielding: Tom Jones* (London; Edward Arnold, 1964), 42–3; Maurice Johnson, *Fielding's Art of Fiction* (Philadelphia: University of Pennsylvania Press, 1961), 95–106; Berit R. Lindboe, " 'O *Shakespear*, Had I Thy Pen!': Fielding's Use of Shakespeare in *Tom Jones*," *Studies in the Novel* 14 (1982), 303–15; Manuel Schonhorn, "Heroic Allusion in *Tom Jones*: Hamlet and the Temptations of Jesus,"*Studies in the Novel* 6 (1974), 218–27. The most detailed attempt to read Fielding's novel alongside *Hamlet* is that of Douglas Brooks-Davies, in *Fielding, Dickens, Gosse, Iris Murdoch and Oedipal "Hamlet"* (New York: St. Martin's Press, 1989), 1–59.
5. *The Yale Edition of Horace Walpole's Correspondence*, ed., W. S. Lewis et al., 48 vols (New Haven: Yale University Press, 1937–83), vol. 19, 110.
6. On this point, it is worth listening to Fielding himself, writing about two weeks after the date he imagines Tom's visit to the theater: "the Rebels having been so long able to maintain themselves in Defiance of [Cumberland's] Army . . . ; their March into the Heart of the Kingdom . . . ; their Return with Impunity to join another large Body which have assembled themselves in *Scotland*; the immediate Apprehension of two great Invasions; and lastly the Menaces which the King of *France* hath thundered aloud . . . , seem all good Arguments for augmenting the present Army." *The True Patriot and Related Writings*, ed., W. B. Coley (Middletown: Wesleyan University Press, 1987), 180–1. These remarks appeared in the number dated January 7, 1746.
7. For the Essex rebellion, especially as it relates to *Hamlet*, see Karen S. Coddon, "Suche Strange Desygns": Madness, Subjectivity, and Treason in *Hamlet* and Elizabethan Culture," in *Case Studies in Contemporary Criticism: William Shakespeare, "Hamlet"*, Suzanne L. Wofford, ed., (Boston and New York: Bedford Books, 1994). For the detail about *Richard II*, see 385. Roland Mushat Frye also discusses this incident in *The Renaissance Hamlet: Issues and Responses in 1600* (Princeton: Princeton University Press, 1984), 265–6.

8. For a detailed discussion of the rhetoric of Jacobitism, see Monod, *Jacobitism and the English People, 1688–1788*. Also useful, though it focuses more narrowly on literary materials, is Howard Erskine-Hill, "Literature and the Jacobite Cause: Was There a Rhetoric of Jacobitism?" in *Ideology and Conspiracy: Aspects of Jacobitism, 1689–1759*, ed., Eveline Cruickshanks, (Edinburgh: John Donald, 1988), 49–69.
9. The argument was originally advanced by Lilian Winstanley, *"Hamlet" and the Scottish Succession* (Cambridge: Cambridge University Press, 1921), though it has enjoyed little favor in recent decades. Roland Frye looks through the parallels concisely and judiciously; see 29–37. The whole matter has been more recently revived by Stuart Kurland, "*Hamlet* and the Scottish Succession?" *SEL* 34 (1994): 279–300.
10. I should note here that the scholars who have worked on the question of the political appropriation of Shakespeare have been mostly silent on the question of *Hamlet*. For instance, Jonathan Bate, while detailed on the ways that other plays were rewritten or performed in such a way as to comment on political issues, says nothing about this play. See *Shakespearean Constitutions: Politics, Theater, Criticism 1730–1830* (Oxford: The Clarendon Press, 1989), esp. 62–3. See also Michael Dobson, *The Making of the National Poet: Shakespeare, Adaptation, and Authorship, 1660–1769* (Oxford: The Clarendon Press, 1992); Dobson comments on the ways that the attempt to make Shakespeare into the national poet intersect with the dynastic debate and how Shakespeare was sometimes cast metaphorically in the role of old Hamlet as a wrongfully displaced king; see 140.
11. I have examined as many illustrated Prayer Books as I could from the first half of the eighteenth century in the collections of the British Library and the National Library of Art in the Victoria and Albert Museum. A number of the British Library's Prayer Books were destroyed by bombing in World War II. Many of the copies that I looked at included illustrations for the three Stuart services; the specific edition described here is the one published by Thomas and Robert Baskett (the King's Printers) in 1745. It is difficult to establish the first year when this illustration was printed: holdings for the years between 1730 and 1745 are very spotty, with several destroyed copies listed, and a number of non-illustrated editions. Unfortunately, there appears to have been no study of Prayer Book illustration yet written.
12. "Guy Faux," originally published in the *London Magazine*, November, 1823.
13. A late seventeenth-century work on the Gunpowder Plot quotes James' own words to Parliament, describing this moment: "when the Letter was Shewed me by my Secretary, wherein a general obscure advertisement was given of some dangerous blow at this time, I did upon the instant interpret and apprehend some dark phrases therein, contrary to the ordinary Grammar construction of them (and in another sort than I am sure any Divine or Lawyer in any University would have taken them) to be meant by this horrible form of blowing us up all by Powder; and thereupon ordered, that search to be made, whereby the matter was discovered, and the man apprehended." See *The Gunpowder-Treason* (London: Thomas Newcomb and H. Hills, 1679), 7.

14. The episode at the theater is to be found on 852–7, and I do not cite page numbers for individual quotations in the summary that follows.
15. *Spectator* No. 335 (25 March 1712). I am indebted to Battestin's footnote in his and Bowers' edition of the novel for this connection, though I would disagree with his statement there that "the following scene was doubtless inspired" by Addison's essay. The *Spectator* may have given Fielding a hint, but his inspiration, as I hope to make clear, was more complex. See 852 n.1.
16. Joseph R. Roach, *The Player's Passion: Studies in the Science of Acting* (Newark: University of Delaware Press, 1985), 58–9. See his further comments on Garrick's Hamlet, 86–9. One of the hallmarks of his performance was the way he would freeze for an extended period upon first seeing the ghost, a posture probably not unlike the King's in the Prayer Book illustration, and yet one more mirror in the scene.
17. For the argument that Fielding created this episode to puff Garrick, see Battestin and Bowers, 853 n. 2. Also making this argument are Oliver Ferguson, "Partridge's Vile Encomium: Fielding and Honest Billy Mills," *PQ* 43 (1964), 73–8 (he speaks of the scene as "a striking tribute to Garrick's skill as an actor"—73), and Lindboe.
18. Curiously, the running account of Partridge's reactions seems to place the scene in Gertrude's closet *before* the Mousetrap. This may be Fielding's slip. Late in his career, Garrick produced a new acting script of *Hamlet* that radically altered the play as we normally know it by significantly abridging the last two acts. But this new version was not performed until 1772, and earlier in his career he used the standard acting script of the eighteenth century(a script whose abridgements mostly worked to minimize Hamlet's vacillation). For a good discussion of this standard script, of his later version, and of Garrick's performance as Hamlet generally, see John A. Mills, *Hamlet on Stage: The Great Tradition* (London and Westport: The Greenwood Press, 1985), 27–48. See also G. W. Stone, "Garrick's Long Lost Alteration of Hamlet," *PMLA* 49 (1934): 890–905.
19. Whether or not the ghost is some kind of demon has been one of the more frequently discussed topics in the criticism of the play in the last decades, and as with all aspects of *Hamlet*, the literature on this point is large. Anyone who wants to understand the argument that the ghost represents some sort of evil temptation, however, should probably still begin with Eleanor Prosser, *Hamlet and Revenge* (Palo Alto: Stanford University Press, 1967). Roland Mushat Frye has more recently surveyed the historical contexts and come to different conclusions; see 14–29.
20. This identification of Mills as Claudius was originally advanced by Ferguson.
21. The structure here calls to mind, though it is by no means the same thing, the so-called rehearsal-structure Fielding employed as a playwright, notably in *Pasquin*.
22. Johnson's comments were made in a pamphlet he published that year, *Observations of the Tragedy of Macbeth*, reprinted in *Shakespeare: The Critical Heritage, vol. 3, 1733–1752*, ed., Brian Vickers, (London: Routledge and Kegan Paul, 1975), 166.

23. For royal touching, see Keith Thomas, *Religion and the Decline of Magic* (New York: Scribner's, 1971), 192–206; for a discussion of the practice that emphasizes the eighteenth century, see J. C. D. Clark, *English Society, 1688–1832*, 160–7; for the doctrine of the king's two bodies and its relation to funeral effigies, see Ernst H. Kantorowicz, *The King's Two Bodies: A Study in Medieval Political Theology* (Princeton: Princeton University Press, 1957).
24. A later fiction about the Forty-Five illustrates the failure of the populace to rise up, Walter Scott's *Waverley*: "The mob stared and listened, heartless, stupefied, and dull, but gave few signs even of that boisterous spirit which induces them to shout on all occasions, for the mere exercise of their most sweet voices." *Waverley* (Harmondsworth: Penguin, 1972), 389–90.
25. Again, see Thomas. For the opposing view, one that insists that the old order persisted much longer than has been appreciated, see Clark.
26. *Boswell's Life of Johnson*, ed., Hill and Powell, III, 156. Johnson made his remark on 17 September 1777.
27. For brevity's sake, I cite here only three of the many who have been at work in this area: Stephen Orgel, *The Illusion of Power: Political Theater in the English Renaissance* (Berkeley: University of California Press, 1975); Jonathan Goldberg, *James I and the Politics of Literature: Jonson, Shakespeare, Donne, and Their Contemporaries* (Baltimore: Johns Hopkins University Press, 1983); and Stephen Greenblatt, *Shakespearean Negotiations: The Circulation of Social Energy in Renaissance England* (Berkeley: University of California Press, 1988).
28. Compare, on this point, an earlier passage in the novel, where Fielding explicitly addresses the issue of political theater; see 153.

Index

absolutism: and divine right, 139, 148–150; and gypsy government, 136–137, 150–156; Rome's Golden Age and, 136–138, 154–156; and selection, 152–156; Stuarts and, 149–151, 153–156
Act of Settlement (1701), 25, 29, 40, 84, 153
Aeneid (Virgil), 138, 149
allegory, use of, 32–33, 41, 43
Allen, Ralph, 49–50, 53
Allworthy, Bridget, pregnancy of, 28, 30
Allworthy, Squire: illegitimacy and, 28, 30; and inheritance, 56, 58; judgment of Partridge by, 183–184; and theft, 78, 81–83, 88, 95, 142, 144; Tom's banishment by, 39; virtue and, 26
Amelia (Fielding), 51, 107, 146, 157, 184
Anne, Queen, 25, 27, 29, 30
Aristotle, 35–36

"Bastard, The" (Savage), 47, 56
Battestin, Martin: and Fielding as crusading reformed rake, 45; and Fielding's illusiveness, 44, 45; and Fielding as magistrate, 100, 122, 123; on Fielding's anti-Stuart feelings, 18; and gypsy significance in novel, 149–150, 152, 153, 155
Battestin, Martin and Ruthe R.: and Fielding-Johnson relationship, 50–51, 62; and Fielding portraits, 188n12
Beattie J. M., 104, 106, 108, 117
Bedford, Duke of, 100
Beggar's Opera, The (Gay), 119
Bellaston, Lady, 59, 69, 71
Bentham, Jeremy, 107
Bertelsen, Lance, 122, 210n30
Bill of Rights (1689), 25
Black Act, 91–93, 96–97, 105
Black George: character of, 93–95, 205n42; Fielding as, 100–101; name of, 8–9, 83–86, 97–98, 202–203n20, 202nn17, 19; significance of, 8–9; and temptation, 88, 89, 100
Blifil, Captain, 56, 144
Blifil, Master: intimate fraud and, 141, 142, 143, 144; legitimacy and, 30–31, 56, 57, 58
"Bloodless" Revolution, *see* Glorious Revolution
Bonnie Prince Charlie, *see* Stuart, Charles Edward
Boswell, James, 51, 63–69, 71, 72, 73, *see also Life of Johnson, The*
Bowers, Toni, 60
Bow Street Runners, 118
Brady, Frank, 55
Brett, Anne (Countess Macclesfield), 48, 53, 55–59, 69, 73, 77
Bristol (Wales), 49–50
Brown, H. O., 41
Burke, Edmund, 152, 153–154, 155

Burnet, Bishop, 27, 46
Burney, Dr. Charles, 72

Carew, Bampfylde-Moore, 10, 125–128, 130, 151–152
Catholicism, *see* religion
Champion, The (Boswell), 47
character: development of, 94; purity of, 24, 61–66, 67–68
"Charge Delivered to the Grand Jury" (Fielding), 18, 43
Charles I, 164
Charles II, 22, 164
Clarissa (Richardson), 63
Clark, J. C. D., 43–44
class, *see* social status
Claudius (*Hamlet*), 163, 170–171, 173–177
Cleary, Thomas R., 45
Coleridge, Samuel Taylor, 1–2, 6
comedy: *Tom Jones* as masterpiece of, 1–2; tragic material as, 55, 71, 74
Common Prayer Book, 10, 163–168, 179–180
courtroom trials, as theater, 111, 112–116, 160, 171, 181, 210n30
Covent-Garden Journal, 49
criminal law, eighteenth-century: bond of criminals-victims in, 116; and death penalty, 105, 207n9,10; deterrence and, 107, 120–121, 181–182, 209n28, 209–210n29; discretion and, 104, 105, 106, 107; government formulation of, 207n13; judge's role in, 106; meanings of, 107–109; prisons and, 105, 106, 107; prosecutorial procedures in, 104, 105–106; social status and, 207n10; testimonial corruption in, 119–120; theft and, 104, 105, 207n9
Cross, Wilbur, 2, 20, 45, 125, 127

Culloden Moor, *see* Forty-Five, the
Cumberland, Duke of, 1, 6, 19

Daedulus, Stephen, 15
death, 33–34
de Castro, J. Paul, 110
Decline and Fall of the Roman Empire, The (Gibbon), 154
detachment, historical perspective and, 11–14
Devereaux, Robert, 162
Dictionary (Johnson), 50, 199n41
Dictionary of National Biography, The, 117, 127
"Discourse on the Love of our Country" (Price), 153
Dostoyevsky, Fyodor, 108
Dowling, Lawyer, 78, 90, 99, 141
"Drum," 4–5, 7
Dunciad (Pope), 110
dynastic politics: absolutism and, 136–139, 147–148, 150–151; as British theater, 176–177; divine right and, 35, 139, 148–150, 164–167; Jacobite Rebellion and, 5–6; legitimacy debate and, 25–30; and Roman rule, 136–138, 153–156; selection and, 152–153, 155–156

Elizabeth I, 175
Empson, William, 11, 13, 46
Enderson, 142, 146–147
Enquiry into the Causes of the Late Increase of Robbers, An (Fielding): and deterrence of theft, 143, 181, 209–210n29; and literalism of law enforcement, 118, 120–123, 146; and social mimesis, 96; and *Tom Jones*, 11–12; and vagrancy laws, 129
Eurydice Hiss'd (Fielding), 45
exile, 5, 7, 8, 37–39, 193n31

Faerie Queene, The (Spenser), 32
Fawkes, Guy, 164–166, 180
Fielding, Edmund, 52
Fielding, Henry: anniversaries of, 16; balanced perspective of, 2, 3, 11, 13; Charles Stuart as self-portrait of, 190–191n11; and criminal deterrence, 120–121, 209n28, 209–210n29; use of digression, 6, 7–11, 15; doubling of lives of, 122–124; financial pressures on, 3, 45–46, 184–85; as magistrate, 2–3; Partridge as mirror of, 182–183, 184–185; political ideology of, 42–46, 190n10, 195n39; political journalism of, 3, 11–12, 17–18; self-image of, 14–16, 188n12, *see also Enquiry into the Causes of the Late Increase of Robbers*
Fielding, Sir John, 14, 15
Fisher, Henry, 172
Fitzpatrick Mr., 144, 161
Forty-Five, the: historical significance of, 1, 2, 5–6, 7–8; as political theater, 174–177

game laws, 78–80, 90–92
Garrick, David, 10; acting style of, 216n16; audience reaction to, 181–182; criticism by Partridge of, 170, 173–174; as Hamlet, 168–174, 176, 177, 179; historic presence in novel, 160; illusion presented by, 167, 168, 169; Samuel Johnson and, 69
Gentlemen's Magazine, The, 50, 67
George I: foreignness of, 151; legitimacy of, 25, 31, 98–99; representation in *Hamlet* of, 163, 173–177
ghosts: characters functioning as, 33–35; gypsies and, 132–133;

Partridge and, 36, 160, 170, 181–182; Stuarts and, 7, 35, 37–38, 40–41, 163–168, 173, 179–180
Gibbon, Edward, 154
Glorious Revolution (1688), 1, 25, 29, 153, 162–163
Goadby, Robert, 127, 128, 130, 152
Gresham, Sir George, 84
Gulliver's Travels (Swift), 133, 136
Gunner, Lewis, 93
Gunpowder Plot (1603), 10, 163–166, 179–180, 215n13
gypsies (Romani): eighteenth century perceptions of, 127–130; framework of novel's episode, 131–133; government of, 134–135, 136–137, 150–156; history of, 128–130; language and, 130, 212–213n17; legal harassment of, 128–130; poverty of, 129–130; romanticized depiction of, 130; and shame, 134–135; and the supernatural, 132–133; and theft, 129–130, 136; as wanderers, 128–130
Gypsy King, *see* gypsies (Romani)

Hamlet, 10, 161, 162–163, 173–178
Hammond, Brean, 43
Hanover, House of, 1; *Hamlet* and, 162–163; legitimacy of rule and, 30–31, 98–99; shared conservative ideologies of, 44
Happiness of the present Establishment, and the Unhappiness of Absolute Monarchy, The (Hoadly), 150
Harlot's Progress, The (Hogarth), 85
Hay, Douglas, 92, 108, 207n10
Henry Fielding, A Life (M. Battestin and R. Battestin), 45, 50
historical revisionism, 42–44

History of the English Law Before the Time of Edward I (Pollock and Maitland), 90
History of His Own Time (Burnet), 27
Hoadly, Bishop, 150, 153
Hobbes, Thomas, 114, 157
Hogarth, William, 85
Holmes, Richard, 65, 68
Honour, Mrs., 69
Hue and Cry, 105, 110
Hume, David, 29, 30
Hunt, Russell, 64
Hunter, J. Paul, 22
hunting, as status privilege, 79

"Il Penseroso" (Milton), 38
"Incredulous Hatred," 36, 37, 42
inheritance: Richard Savage and, 8, 49, 53, 57; Roman emperors and, 154–155; Stuarts and, 25–31, 155; Tom and, 31, 61, 141, 155–156, 184
Irene (Johnson), 62
irony, Fielding's use of, 11–14

Jacobite Rebellion, *see* Forty-Five, the
Jacobite's Journal, The, 18, 21, 28, 30
James I, 35, 163, 164–166
James II: birth of son and, 26–30; Catholicism of, 36, 37; Glorious Revolution and, 163; removal from throne of, 1, 25, 29, 30, 31
Johnson, Samuel: and character purity, 24, 61–66, 67–68; friendship with Savage, 65–66; hatred for Fielding, 8, 47–48, 50–51; on Jacobites, 173, 176; literary authority of, 73–75; and literary genre, 54–55, 59, 199n41; sexual guilt and, 70–73
Jonathan Wild (Fielding), 86
Jones, Jenny, 29, 56, 59, 103

Joseph Andrews (Fielding), 21, 51, 94, 122, 130

Kent, Duke of, 93
King, Peter, 104, 106, 107, 108–109, 111
Kingsley, Charles, 80

Lamb, Charles, 164
Langbein, John, 108, 115, 207n10
legitimacy: and property, 77–78, 80, 92, 95; Richard Savage and, 47–48, 53–56, 59–61; and social status, 78, 80, 95, 97, 98, 100; Stuarts and, 25–30, 98, 163; of Tom, 31, 54–56, 59–61, 155
Life of Johnson, The (Boswell), 47–48, 63, 68–70, 72
Life of Savage, The (Johnson): authority of, 73–75; as biography, 55, 74–75; and character depiction, 63, 67, 69; depth of relationships in, 65; and illegitimacy, 59, 60–61; judgment and, 66–69; maternal abandonment in, 52–53, 58–60; publication of, 50; sexual repression in, 69; and *Tom Jones* publication comparison, 47, 54; uncritical depiction in, 73–74
literacy, class status and, 88–90
Lives of the Poets, The (Johnson), 73
Locke, John, 87, 114, 154

Macbeth, 163, 173
Macclesfield, Countess (Anne Brett), 48, 53, 55–59, 69, 73, 77
McKeon, Michael, 21, 22, 23, 24, 63, 190n10, 195n39
McLynn, Frank, 122
Malone, Edmund, 117

Man of the Hill, the: as allegorical model, 32–33; doubleness of, 39–40, 41–42, 43; exile and, 37–39; historic significance of, 8, 36–37, 41–42; name of, 32, 192n27; religion and, 39–40, 41–42, 193n32; Stuart ghosts and, 37, 40–41
"marvelous, the," 23, 36, 37, 41
Mary, Queen, 25
Mary of Modena and warming-pan story, 26, 27
maternal issues: in *Hamlet*, 161; Richard Savage and, 48, 52–53, 56–60, 73, 77; Tom and, 8, 27–29
Memoirs (More), 51
Mills, Billy, 169, 173, 176
Milton, John, 38
mirror images, 10–11, 163–167
Monmouth, Duke of, 30, 37, 39, 40
Montagu, Lady Mary Wortley, 52
More, Hannah, 51, 71

name issues: Black George, 8–9, 83–86, 97–98, 202–203n20, 202nn17,19; Man of the Hill, 32, 192n27; Richard Savage, 8, 48, 50; Tom Jones and, 29, 50, 60
Namier, Sir Lewis Bernstein, 42, 43, 44
National Portrait Gallery, 14–15
Nazis, 128
Nunn, Baptist, 93, 96

"Of the Protestant Succession" (Hume), 29
Oldfield, Mrs., 68–69
Overbury, Sir Thomas, 49, 68

Page, Francis: contemporary presence of, 160; courtroom dominance of, 111–112, 116–117; and criminal deterrence, 181–182; Fielding identification with, 45–46, 118, 121–122; as hanging judge, 117, 209n24; and judicial corruption, 9; and Richard Savage, 55, 58, 74; wit/sarcasm of, 111, 113, 114, 116–117
Pamela (Richardson), 130
Partridge, 10–11; and debt, 112, 140, 183–185; exiled status of, 38–39; as Fielding, 182–183, 184–185; as historical witness, 159–160, 163, 167, 179–180, 182; humanity of, 114; and mimesis, 170–171; as mirror of Hamlet, 167, 168–169, 171; and observer as performer, 172; and Stuart cause, 175–180; and superstition, 33–35, 36, 160, 170, 181–182; unfiltered response of, 171, 180, 181
Paulson, Ronald, 20, 21–22, 122
Peel, Sir Robert, 91
Peel Act (1829), 105
Pepys, Samuel, 22, 23
Pope, Alexander, 42, 50, 79, 110
Porter, Elizabeth, 71
Price, Richard, 153
property: labour-mixing theory of, 87–88; legal regulations and, 79, 81–83; qualification requirements of, 100–101
Protestantism, *see* religion
punishment: as criminal deterrent, 107, 120–121, 143, 181–182, 209n28, 209–210n29; shame and, 134–135; wickedness and, 12–13

Rake's Progress, The (Hogarth), 85
Ralph, James, 48

Rambler #4 (Johnson): and deviation from original portraits, 63, 67–68; as earliest feud document, 52, 61; and mixed character, 24, 65, 66; and "splendidly wicked men," 70, 71

Rambler #60 (Johnson), 64, 66

Reflections on the Revolution in France, The (Burke), 152, 153

Reform Bill (1832), 43

religion: and legitimacy of throne, 1, 25–27, 30; and Man of the Hill, 8, 39–41, 193n32

revisionism, 42–44

Revolution Settlement (1701), 25, 29, 40, 84, 153

Richard II, 162

Richardson, Samuel: and character development, 94; comparison to Fielding, 51, 63, 64, 65; Fielding criticized by, 15, 48, 54

Rivers, Earl, 47, 48, 53, 55, 57

Roach, Joseph, 168

romance: Fielding's use of, 21–26, 35–36, 44; Samuel Johnson and, 66–67

Romani, *see* gypsies

Rome, Golden Age of, 136–138, 153–156

Rowlandson, Thomas, 85

St. James's Palace, 26, 28

Salisbury, Bishop of, 117

Salisbury Assizes, 110, 112

Savage, Richard: in Bristol Jail, 49–50, 53; Fielding relationship with, 49–50, 51, 52, 53; financial instability of, 49–50, 53, 61, 68–69; and inheritance, 48–49, 52–53, 55–56, 58, 60–61; literary career of, 49, 50, 53; maternal abandonment and, 53, 56–60, 73, 77; mixed character of, 63, 66–72; murder by, 53, 57–58; name issues and, 8, 48, 50; and Samuel Johnson, 65–73; significance of, 8; varied depictions of, 73–74

Schonhorn, Manuel, 132

Seagrim, Molly, 145

shame, as punishment, 134–135

Shenstone, William, 38

social status: criminal law and, 88–90, 95–97, 207n10; of gypsies, 128–130; of Henry Fielding, 8, 78, 99; and literacy, 88–90; Partridge and, 113, 182–183; and Richard Savage, 8, 56; social mimesis and, 96–97; of Tom Jones, 27, 60–61; uncertainty of, 97, 183, 185

Sophia: lost property of, 141–142; resentment of, 12–13

Sophia of Hanover, 25

Spectator, The (Addison and Steele), 130, 167

Spenser, Edmund, 32

status, *see* social status

Stuart, Charles Edward: affection for *Tom Jones*, 17; appeal of, 31; exile of, 7, 8; and inheritance, 7; literary critics' analysis of, 20–23; plot placement of, 18–20; romance of, 21–26; significance of, 1; *Tom Jones* as "particular favorite" of, 17

Stuart, House of, 37–39; and absolute monarchy, 149–151, 153–156; and divine right, 35, 139, 148–150, 164–167; and *Hamlet*, 162–163; and legitimacy, 25–31; and religion, 1, 8, 25–27, 30; romance of, 7, 21–26, 36, 44; and superstition, 7, 35, 37–38, 40–41, 173, 179–180

Stuart, James Edward, birth of, 26–30
Swift, Jonathan, 21, 42, 133, 135, 136, 170

Talleyrand, 38
Theatrical Licensing Act (1737), 2, 45
theft: class status and, 88–90; criminal law and, 104, 105, 207n9; and gypsies, 129–130, 136; and intimacy, 144; law of trover and, 78, 86, 96, 114, 141; of property, 81–83; range of, 142
Thompson, E. P., 91–93, 96, 122
Thompson, James, 88
Thwackum, 113
Tom Jones: composition of, 6–11, 189–190n6; contemporary references in, 3–6; digression in, 6, 7–11, 15; and exile, 8; framing technique within, 7; historic legitimacy parallels in, 28–31; mixed characters and, 24; plot perfection in, 6–7; and posterity, 4–5; reversibility in, 8, 10; romance form in, 7, 21–26, 36, 44

Tories, 42–44
Tragedy of Tragedies (Fielding), 170
trover, law of, 78, 86, 96, 114, 141
True Patriot, The, 17, 18, 19
Two Treatises of Government (Locke), 87
Tyrconnell, Lord, 74

Virgil, 138

Walpole, Horace, 161
Walpole, Robert, 2, 61
"Wanderer, The" (Savage), 47
warming-pan baby, the, 26–30
Warwick School, 108, 121
Waters, Mrs., 59, 60, 71, 183
Western, Squire, 81–83
Whigs: and dynastic rule, 25–27, 30; Fielding and, 11–12, 42–45
Wild, Jonathan, 86–87, 95, 119–120
Wilkins, Deborah, 28
William of Orange, 25, 27, 29, 153, 162
Willoughby, Justice, 109, 110
"Windsor Forest" (Pope), 79